HOWL AT THE MOON

Happy Birthday

Melissa

HOWL AT THE MOON

POLLY BLANKENSHIP

GOODFELLOW PRESS

Goodfellow Press
8522 10th Ave. NW
Seattle, WA 98117

ISBN: 1-891761-07-2
Library of Congress: 2001 131729
Edited by Pamela R. Goodfellow
Jacket design by Rohani Design, Edmonds, WA
Jacket illustration by Doris Hayes
Book design by Brandon Massey
Author photo by Suzanne Wyman
Printed by Edwards Brothers, Inc. under the supervision of Tanya Eldred

This is a work of fiction. The events described are imaginary; the characters are fictitious and are not intended to represent actual living persons.

The text is set in 11 point Minion with 14 point leading.

To the good-hearted, friendly people of that sun-drenched
place called Texas.

Acknowledgments

There's a long line of people I want to thank profusely. My husband and children, who supported and humored me through the years, thank you with all my heart. My parents and kinfolk, scattered all over Texas, who encouraged me, helped with details and drove me down endless country roads, you have all been my sure foundation.

For all the things that turned out right with this book I owe a Texas-sized debt of gratitude to my teacher, editor, and friend Pamela Goodfellow. You pushed me to do my best, buffed out the baloney and didn't let me lose track of the heart in this story. To my fellow writers who listened and critiqued the countless scenes before this final version, your questions and laughter in all the right places were gracious gifts that kept me going. To Suzanne Wyman, a woman who knows her way around copy, merçi-buckets of times. And thanks to Devon, for letting me know when I had it wrong.

The bright sun reflected off the hood. Even with sunglasses on, it hurt her eyes. Devon glanced at the clock on the dash. They'd been on the road for four hours and it was only eleven in the morning. Jamie was playing quietly except for an occasional dino-growl. Three days of driving, much of it through snowstorms and heavy rain, combined with restless nights on hotel mattresses had tied her in knots. She wished she could straighten out her legs and stretch. It wouldn't be long now before she could.

At the crest of the ridge, the valley spread out before her. The wild hills, crooked ravines and brushy gullies ran down to the edges of the cleared bottomland. Green clusters of live oak trees and grazing cattle were scattered across the rolling pastures of golden grass. Like a simple-minded cousin, this valley was one of the best kept secrets of the Texas hill country. It was jealously guarded by steep bluffs of weathered limestone.

Devon glanced at the pale boulders atop Hart's Ridge. Every spring the high school seniors painted numbers, their initials, made some mark up there. Whatever they'd written last year had worn off already. Mother Nature was more powerful than paint or persistence. She'd used a bucket of brash rooster red. In those days, she had been confident the outside world would be grander and less confining and sure she wouldn't miss what she'd left behind. When she was eighteen, she knew everything.

The old highway curved. There it was, the sign she'd been waiting for, 'Blanco Springs, 2 miles.' Soon she'd be able to see the river. The thick, bushy cedar that shadowed the fence line along the Abbott's ranch zipped by. When the road curved again, a cluster of stone buildings came into view. The sight was accompanied by a little burst of energy and she gave the sedan more gas. As they rushed down another small rise, she waited for the roller-coaster tickle to coax a giggle from her son. He didn't make a sound. She stole a quick look at him. He was marching a plastic dinosaur on the console.

"We're coming into town, Jamie."

He raised his head to look out his window. "Where?"

"Straight ahead."

He strained at his seat belt to see over the dashboard. "Oh." The remark sank to the floor as he slumped down in his seat. "When will we be at Granny's house? I'm tired of sitting."

"Me too, kiddo. Hang on a little longer and we'll be there. You've got time to work on your smile." She made a face at him. He curled up one corner of his mouth. It was almost a smile. "You can run and play all afternoon while I unpack, I promise."

"Good." He let out a little huff before focusing his attention on his toys again.

The elm and pecan trees that grew along the flat river bottom leading into town were stripped of leaves. Maybe it was the bare branches or the fading sign, 'Welcome to Blanco Springs -- Home of Crystal Clear Water and Friendly Folks', that muted the glow memory ignited. She shook her head. The little town wouldn't look like much to a stranger. The old highway ran through the heart of the place with only a blinking red stoplight to slow the bleeding. It hurt to see it dying. It had been and always would be a part of her life. She hadn't realized that until she'd left.

She drove around the square at a crawl. The empty store windows stared out like orphans tugging at her heart. Bradley's Hardware had been vacant for years now but she could still smell the sweet aroma of Mr. Ben's pipe tobacco. She pictured him at the cash register, a bowl of bubble gum beside it on the counter. He was always ready with a rhyme and a piece of Double Bubble for every child who walked through the door. The Clothes Horse on the corner, her first taste of retailing, had closed much later, after she'd left home. The thin crackle of Mrs. Tenery's voice asking her 'where all she'd been that day' amid the screech of hangers as she rearranged clothes on a rack was as clear as if it had been yesterday. She'd given Devon a part-time job in high school and encouraged her to go to college.

She turned at the next corner and glanced around. She didn't recognize a single car or pickup parked in the square. The two men standing at the curb talking were strangers. No wait, one was George Bell, the cattle buyer. He turned his head to look as she drove by but turned away without a wave. He didn't recognize her. It had been ages since she'd been at a sale.

Some buildings were still occupied. Beasley's Grocery Mart was a necessity. There wasn't another place to buy milk and other essentials for twenty or thirty miles. Jake's Feed would be around as long as there were ranches. On the corner, Joanna's House of Beauty, where dye and hair spray would never go out of style, was a stubborn mainstay supplying a steady stream of gossip. The stone two story office front across the square was dark inside. With the steady decline of the town's fortunes only the letters on the plate glass window, saying Chamber of Commerce, were gold. There was a new shop on the next corner, Sassafras Gifts. Someone had dreams, foolish ones from a strictly business perspective.

Jamie growled. She glanced at him. He was racing a T-rex across his knees toward a prone brontosaurus. "Oh, help, ahhh!" Jamie cried out in a high-pitched voice for the poor beast.

She'd stopped at the intersection waiting for a truck to go by. "Want to drive by the school on our way out of town?"

He looked up with a frown. "Do we have to?" The whine in his voice grated.

"No, we don't." Her reply came out a little sharper than she'd intended. She didn't blame him for being irritable. They were both tired. She took off her sunglasses and rubbed her eyes. He was right. Getting home and out of the car sounded much better than dawdling.

She heard a honk behind her and checked the rearview mirror. Mabel Campbell, Mom's best friend, was behind her, waving. She waved back but Mabel was already out of her car and headed toward Devon's window. She shook her head. That woman didn't care if she stopped traffic, if there'd been some. But of course there wasn't. It was one of the saving graces of living in the middle of nowhere. No need for the latest traffic update to decide how to get home, hallelujah sister.

Mabel leaned over, all smiles and dangling earrings, and hugged her through the open window bringing the thick scent of gardenias with her.

"I saw those Minnesota plates and decided it had to be you two. Good to know you made it in one piece." She backed out of the window but kept her hands on the door. "Ellie's been fretting for days about you drivin' all by yourself through that winter weather."

Mom, the worrywart, true to form. Devon shook her head wishing she could convince her mother to relax. She could take care of herself. "I told her I'd take it easy if it started snowing, Mabel."

"Of course, honey, you have a good head on your shoulders, but you know how it is. Mothers worry."

"I know, Mabel."

She smiled looking past Devon. "Hi there, Jamie. Glad to hear you're going to stay in Texas long enough to get to know you."

Jamie gave her a weak smile before looking out the window in the other direction. Devon couldn't help but chuckle. He didn't have much experience with older women, especially talkative ones but he'd get plenty of practice around here.

"You look great, Mabel. How is Harry?"

"Right as rain but a little grumpy these days." She grinned. "His prostate is acting up." She looked down the street and back at Devon. "Well, guess I'd better let you go so you can get on home." She patted Devon's shoulder. "Glad to have you back. You too, Jamie, honey."

Devon checked the intersection as Mabel walked back to her car. It was still empty. She pulled out, anxious to see her mother and judge for herself if she was 'just fine' as she'd said over the phone. It'd been months since she'd seen her in the flesh. Six months since they'd buried her father. Adjusting to widowhood had to be rough. She'd help Mom in whatever way she could while she was home.

She zipped past the last house in town, anxious to get home. A quick glance in the rear view mirror gave her a fine view of flashing red lights. She groaned and peeked at the speedometer. Forty mph.

A short shriek of the siren brought Jamie's head up. She saw him from the corner of her eye as she slowed down and pulled over on the sandy shoulder. He got to his knees.

"Wow! Mom, there's a police car back there."

"I noticed. Sit down, Jamie." She took off her sunglasses and started searching for her wallet in her purse.

The county road that ran beside the field was dusty. The car stirred up a fine cloud as Devon drove. Anticipation was replacing her weariness with a tingle of excitement. She looked past the hay shed, between the brush along the fence and through the scattered trees to catch that first glimpse of the house. She was ten when they'd moved in. It had been like a second Christmas that year. She remembered how huge and luxurious it had seemed with its three bedrooms, two baths, central air-conditioning, a den with a fireplace made from rock they'd collected on the ranch and even a dishwasher. There it was, the house built with creamy Austin stone, a sturdy tile roof, and dark brown trim across the front porch. It stretched out across the plateau like a cat relaxing in the sun.

"The gate is just ahead, Jamie."

"Oh, boy!" Jamie was up on his knees in the seat looking out the windshield. He'd unbuckled his seatbelt but she didn't mind. The car was slowing down to a roll. As they turned in and passed through the open metal gate of the Comanche Creek Ranch, he yelled, "I see Granny."

Ellie waved as if she'd heard him. She was standing in the breezeway waiting for them to drive up the long driveway. As they came closer, Devon could see Mom had an apron tied around her waist. She'd probably been at the kitchen window fixing lunch while keeping an eye out for them.

As soon as the car stopped in front of the garage, she rushed forward and opened her arms. Jamie shoved the door open, bolted from the car and raced up to his grandmother. Devon was relieved to see him excited, happy to be here. She stepped out but lagged behind while they shared a rocking embrace.

"My goodness, Jamie, you are growing like a weed." Mom stepped back to look him over. "And you lost another tooth."

"It falled out this morning, Granny."

She laughed, sounding truly happy. Her hair looked whiter in the bright sun.

Her mother was getting older. Devon pushed the unwelcome thought aside with a quick smile. "We finally made it, Mama."

When they embraced, Devon closed her eyes. Her mother was wearing the perfume Pop had loved. It was as if he were still here. She hugged her mother tighter.

"It's good to have you home, Devon." After a squeeze and a gentle pat on the back, Mom relaxed her arms. Devon released her and straightened up.

Her mother looked thinner. Maybe it was eating alone. Devon was glad she'd come. "It's good to be home, Mama." She looked down at her son flashing that toothless grin. "Isn't it, Jamie?"

"Yes." He ran over to the new tire swing hanging from a pecan tree and climbed on.

"How was the drive through Dallas? The morning news said they had a storm coming."

She looked at her mother and smiled. They were going to worry about each other. "There was some rain but not bad."

"You must be worn out driving all that way alone."

"It was a long haul but we had a car full of dinosaurs for entertainment." She raised her arms and stretched to get the kinks out of her back.

"A policeman stopped us with his red lights, Granny." Jamie was sitting on top of the tire, hands clutching the rope, leaning back so far he was looking at them upside down. Devon lowered her arms to her sides wishing just once he could forget to mention an embarrassing moment.

"Really? Did you get a ticket?" Ellie's face had lost its smile.

"No." She sighed. "It was just Deputy Teague looking for lunch money. He saw my out-of-state plates."

"Well, they're cracking down on folks going too fast through town. Been too many wrecks lately. Somebody had to put their foot down."

She'd seen a total of four vehicles actually moving in town and they were in one of them. "I was going five miles over the limit, Mom. That's not exactly drag racing."

"No, it's not but we are having problems, so keep an eye out."

Blanco Springs' problems had to be minor ones compared to Los Angeles where drugs and gang wars created havoc every day. Minneapolis was safer. The cold kept mischief inside during the winter. Mom must be exaggerating. Everybody in Bravo County was too busy scratching out a living to get into much trouble.

Ellie smiled. "Goodness, come on inside. Bet you're both hungry."

Jamie hopped off the swing and gave it a twirl.

"I baked some chocolate chip cookies this morning, Jamie."

His face lit up. "I love chocolate chip."

"I know." Her mother chuckled. Jamie raced ahead as they walked into the kitchen together.

Devon had just opened the trunk to start unloading her car when Hank drove in and parked by the shed. He was the only full-time help around the ranch these days. She couldn't help but smile as he walked straight over in long, easy strides. He was a shy man, but had always been like an uncle to her. She hadn't hugged him since elementary school.

There was a hint of a smile on his face and the welcome in his eyes was warm and genuine. "Good to see you, Devon. Ellie's sure been lookin' forward to having you home."

"It's really good to see you, too." He was the most soft-spoken man she'd ever known and as strange as it might seem it bolstered her confidence in him.

He lifted his arm, long sleeves rolled up as always, and pointed at the tightly packed trunk. "Can I give you a hand?"

She reached out and touched his arm. "Before Mom comes out," she glanced toward the kitchen window and back, "I want to thank you, Hank, for everything. She would have been lost without your help."

"Oh, I don't know about that . . . but you're welcome." He patted her hand before dropping his arm to his side.

"Hi, Mr. Hank." Jamie had walked up from behind her somewhere. "Remember me?" He bumped against her hip and peered up at Hank, lips pressed together.

Hank leaned over, his hands on his knees so he was nose to nose with Jamie. "You bet I do, Jamie. I've been waitin' for you. I need another ranch hand to help me out around here."

"Really?" Jamie's eyebrows shot up and his eyes seemed to grow bigger.

"Yep, figured you could go with me to put out some cake for the cows directly." He straightened up and repositioned his Stetson to sit a little farther back on his head. "But I'm goin' to tote these suitcases in the house for your mama first." He turned toward the open trunk and started shifting luggage around to get to the handles.

Jamie was quickly beside him. "What kind of cake do cows like, Mr. Hank, chocolate?"

He stopped and looked down. "Since we'll be workin' together, you can call me Hank, son, just plain Hank."

Devon chuckled as she opened the back door of the car. She grabbed a plastic storage box full of toys and pushed the door shut with her hip. Poor man would be answering questions all afternoon.

"I'll show you where to put the suitcases, Hank."

Devon didn't know for certain, but she guessed it was about eight o'clock. She'd left her watch in the bathroom after Jamie's bath. They were rocking in the glider on the back deck enjoying their first night home and waiting for Ellie to get back. Jamie, in his pajamas, lay across her lap sound asleep. The hinges of the steel frame squeaked a little with every backward motion. She didn't mind, it blended in with the hoot of the owl near the barn. She combed her fingers through her son's clean hair that smelled shampoo sweet. He'd worn himself out following Hank around most of the afternoon and exploring the barn looking for a hideout, the kind of place only a child could invent. She looked down at his peaceful expression. At six, everything was new and exciting. Disappointments were quickly forgotten, dreams boundless.

She'd watched the sun disappear from its perch on Comanche Ridge remembering other nights like this. The jumbled rocks on top of Lookout Point, when lit by the last rays of gold, looked like a ruin commanding the eye to look up at it and sort through the past. Hunters and horse soldiers, both red and white, had stood up there scouting the surrounding hills for food or for enemies. Each night their spirits, hiding in the shadows of the live oak trees, rode their dark mounts with silent hooves searching for home.

That was one of her father's yarns and it had given her goose bumps when she was about Jamie's age. This country was filled with stories of heroes and cowards. It seemed the hills and valleys were shaped as much by imagination and the hot sun as by the steady erosion of wind and water.

The earth was wiser than men, Pop had always said. It could be harsh and unforgiving but not deceitful or cruel. Only humans held that distinction in her father's book and, after all that had happened to her, Devon realized she agreed with him. Her last boss had been an accomplished liar, so unprincipled that he'd found ways to corner her with propositions that had nothing to do with work. She'd never dealt with anyone so despicable. When she'd walked out of that office for the last time, she'd carried her pride with her and little else.

The stars, faint as a whisper at first, crowded the black sky until there wasn't a spot for one more. The sight provided a much needed reality check. The noise and constant hassle of the city confused things. Coming home to Texas, to see about Mom, had been a good idea. It would give her a chance to take a breath and reevaluate where she wanted to go while Jamie finished first grade. Besides, she wanted her son to have a taste of living in the wide-open spaces. Yes, it had been a good choice.

"Come on, kiddo, let's get you to bed. You're too sleepy to wait for Granny any longer." He mumbled a complaint as she sat him up and pulled him to his feet. He wrapped his arms around her and leaned against her hip. She led him in from the deck through the sliding glass door into the shadowy den, bathed in silence. She padded across the cool, uneven stone floor in her bare feet toward the soft glow from one small light.

Jamie tumbled into bed and curled up without a word. The smell of a hot iron clung to the smooth, white sheets as she lifted them to cover him. Remembering she had one more duty to perform, she slipped her hand under the pillow and found Jamie's neatly wrapped front tooth. She replaced it with the silver coin from her pocket.

She lingered by the open door watching the easy rise and fall of his chest in the faint light. He looked like his father. She took a deep breath feeling the familiar ache. Alan felt nothing for this beautiful child. She'd seen it in his cool, fleeting glance when she'd held their infant son for the first time. He'd said, from the very beginning, he didn't want children. She'd convinced herself he would change, love for his own flesh and blood would grow. Through the months of Jamie's little firsts: a smile, words, steps, Alan proved her wrong again and again. He blamed her, resented her affection for Jamie, and was unable to understand this child was a part of her, heart and soul. Their life together had crumbled.

He'd been honorable in one sense, setting aside a trust fund for his son's future. His idea of the responsibilities of fatherhood was defined by a precise mathematical formula, computed in terms of dollars and cents and fulfilled on a piece of paper he'd left behind. Jamie would carry the burden of never knowing his father, feel slighted as he grew older more than likely. Alan had no idea he'd lost something precious and for that she felt a great deal of sadness for him.

Their marriage had been a mismatch from the start, a mutual mistake. After the divorce, she realized she'd chosen to see what she wanted in Alan and had found excuses for the rest. It had been easier that way when they were both busy, working long hours. She leaned her head side to side to stretch the tense muscles across her shoulders. Maybe, someday she'd meet a man, who understood what love was all about. If not, she and Jamie would be okay.

She walked toward the dark kitchen massaging a sore spot at the base of her neck. The relief from the aspirins had been short-lived. She longed for a glass of wine but she was out of luck in this house. Too bad Mabel didn't live next door. She raised her chin as she rubbed and noticed the high cabinet over the refrigerator. Mom was a tea sipper but Pop wasn't. Switching on the light over the sink, she stretched on tiptoe and opened the cabinet door. Her father's bottle of bourbon was right where it had always been. Keeping it out of her sight had been his one concession to Mom's feelings about alcohol. She was surprised her mother had kept it around. Maybe she'd forgotten about it.

Devon was too tired to care right now. She just wanted to sleep. But until the tight pull of those muscles across her shoulders relaxed, she wouldn't. She grabbed a juice glass from the cupboard, poured herself two fingers worth of Pop's booze and added some water and an ice cube. After swirling the liquid a time or two, she ambled toward the oak dining table in front of the picture window. The six chairs huddled around it reminded her of busier days. The table full of noisy ranch hands gobbling down chicken and biscuits before getting back to work. Pop telling everyone what to do next. He liked being in charge and making all the decisions. He'd been an old-fashioned, hard work kind of man: stubborn, irritating, honest, and loveable, most of the time.

She looked at the ceiling and raised her glass in a toast. "Here's to you, Pop. I hope God's not a Baptist." Closing her eyes, she gulped. It singed her taste buds and burned all the way down her throat. She stared at the brown liquid left in the glass. It tasted awful. She set the glass down on the table.

Resting one hand on the back of her mother's chair, she remembered the other side of those days. Mom, on her feet all day long, cooking and cleaning up the kitchen with nothing to show for her effort at the end of the day. Woman's work was invisible to most men, certainly to her father, but not to her. Mom never complained. It was childish but growing up she had resented her mother's silence. That was a long time ago before she became a mother and found out a woman would do just about anything for the people she loved. Her mother was quiet but very strong on the inside. She could see that now.

Devon hoped she was a good mother. It was hard work, more than she'd ever guessed, a full-time job without a vacation. She looked at her image in the dark window. Her black hair blended into the shadows creating the illusion of a face floating in space.

"Not too bad for thirty-something." The little lines she'd noticed lately around the corners of her mouth deepened as she smiled. They were becoming a permanent part of her. Raising a child required a sense of humor and patience. She turned away from the window, thinking she had to work on that last part. Patience didn't come naturally.

It was eight-thirty. Her mother would be back anytime now from her mission of mercy. Good old Aunt Louise was being a pain as usual. She walked through the den and out to the deck again to lose herself in the ocean of black, peppered with silver. The temperature was cool but still pleasant, a wonderful change from the frigid Minnesota winter they had left behind.

Jamie had begged to finish first grade in Minneapolis. She'd felt guilty the whole trip for uprooting him again but she couldn't tolerate her boss. No one should have to dodge unwelcome advances. Taking a deep breath, she stretched and rolled her shoulders. She would give anything for a massage right now. That one gulp of firewater hadn't done a thing. Maybe another swallow or two would.

She retreated to the dimly lit kitchen looking for her glass. It was on the table. The ice had melted. She picked it up and added a splash more bourbon to her diluted drink. Tipping up her glass, she gulped down most of it and coughed. She noticed the radio on the counter in front of her and pushed the power button. The high-pitched twang of a steel guitar sliced through the quiet room. With a quick twist, she turned the volume down. She sat at the table, staring at her glass, half listening to the honky-tonk voices. Country music put life in perspective, happy one minute, sad the next.

Her eyes burned like fire. She leaned back resting her head on the top slat of the chair and let her eyelids drift down. The next couple of days she was going to take it easy, visit with Mom, do some fun things with Jamie before getting him squared away in school on Monday. Then and only then was she going to think about job hunting. A few days wouldn't matter. It would take a while. They'd live off the cash in the bank. The money from selling the California house was invested and provided an extra cushion.

She'd have time to help her mother deal with the ranch too. Pop had consistently ignored any advice she'd given him after she'd graduated and started working. Didn't like the idea of listening to a woman. She knew that, even though he'd never said it. It was the way he was raised. She'd tried not to take it personally. He'd never counted on dying before he was ready. She raised her head when she heard the hum of the Cadillac's engine in the garage and opened her eyes.

Ellie came in, dropping her keys on the counter with a clink. There was a sagging weariness in her shoulders that hadn't been there when she'd left. Even the wrinkles on her face seemed deeper.

"You look like your father sitting there drinking that stuff. I don't think you've been eating right. You're just skin and bones."

"According to the magazines, I'm fashionably trim, Mom."

"Oh, don't give me that baloney." Mom walked over and gave her an affectionate pat on the back while picking up the glass from the table.

"Looks like you've lost weight too."

"Maybe a pound or two." Mom turned away, heading back to the sink. "Jamie in bed?"

"Yeah. He fell asleep while we were rocking in the glider."

Her mother stretched to return the bottle of bourbon to its place of exile. When she opened the dishwasher to add Devon's glass, she began rearranging the load of dinner dishes.

It was a little like bumping a bruise watching her, more irritating than painful. Devon doubted she could ever please her mother even in the realm of kitchen cleanup. She glanced out the dark window. Two grown women living in one house was a recipe for disaster, just ask any man. She'd heard some comedian say that on late night television. It was her mother's house; let it go.

"How was Aunt Louise?" She arched her back and took a deep breath, pleased to feel a yawn sneaking up on her.

"Oh, she's doing fine. It's just a broken arm." There was a hint of resentment in her voice as dishes clattered. Devon turned to look at her and put her elbow on the table so she could rest her chin on her palm while she listened.

"I wish Gerald was a little more helpful around the house. That sister of mine has taken every ounce of usefulness right out of him." Ellie bent over, rummaged under the sink a minute before straightening up with a box of detergent in her hands. She set it down on the counter and looked directly at her.

"If he says one more time, these are our 'golden years' I'm going to strangle him."

Devon chuckled. Her mother frowned, shaking her head.

"Golden, my foot! Women around here have to die to get some rest." She filled the dispenser and shut the dishwasher. "Oh, I forgot to tell you, I promised a month ago to carry Aunt Jessie to the eye doctor tomorrow. He's in Kerrville. I hate to leave y'all all day when you just got here but there's nobody else to do it. You two want to come along?"

Just the idea of another day on the road was a lead weight dragging her to the bottom of a very muddy pond. "No. I'm sorry, Mom, but I can't face the thought, even though I love her dearly." Her ninety-year-old great aunt didn't need a squirming six-year-old at close quarters for a day either. "If we go anywhere it won't be more than a drive around the ranch. Jamie needs time to get all the wiggles out of him." Another yawn escaped.

"That's fine, I don't blame you. Weatherman said it's going to rain in buckets for a few days starting tomorrow evening."

Devon stood up and turned off the radio. "I've got to go to bed. I'm pooped!"

Ellie nodded, turning the dial to start the wash cycle. "Me too, been a long day." They turned off lights as they retired to the bedroom end of the house.

Her mother stopped in the hallway. "Sorry to be griping your first night home. That man just stirs me up, he's so useless." She sighed.

"That's okay, I know exactly how you feel."

Her mother smiled. "Guess you do. See you in the morning, honey. It's so good to have you home at last."

"It feels great to be here. 'Night, Mama." She went into the bedroom she had grown up in and stretched out across the chenille bedspread. She was too tired to brush her teeth. Maybe Pop's bourbon was finally kicking in. With her eyes closed, she listened to the wonderful quiet. There were no honking horns or sirens or noisy neighbors to wake her up in the middle of the night. They were home, nestled in safe and sound.

Τ he next morning, Jamie came bounding into her room. He bumped into the side of the bed. She kept her eyes closed, playing possum, hoping for a fifteen minute reprieve. Unfortunately, he didn't have a snooze button. The springs squeaked as he crawled onto the bed. She could feel his warm breath on her cheek as he lifted the hair off her face.

"Mama, it's time to get up." When she didn't react, he made the bed shake with a bounce. "Rise and shine."

Devon opened her eyes to see her son break out a big grin, revealing the newest space in the lineup of front teeth. "Morning, sweet pea."

He held up a shiny fifty cent piece. "Look what I got."

"So, the tooth fairy did find you last night. You'll have to put that in your piggy bank. Come here and give me a hug." As they snuggled, she glanced at the clock on the bedside table. "Jamie, it's only six thirty. You have all day to explore, you know."

"I'm hungry." It was all the explanation he needed for anything these days. There was a clatter of dishes from the kitchen. He raised his head and looked at her wide-eyed. "Granny's up." He squirmed out of her arms, hopped off the bed and ran out the door.

"You're always hungry, stinker." Devon yawned and gave up the bed. Pulling on her robe, she headed for the bathroom combing hair out of her face with her fingertips. "A nice hot cup of coffee . . . that's what I need."

After breakfast, Devon cleaned up the kitchen while her mother took a shower. Jamie came galloping by the sink wearing an old straw cowboy hat he'd found somewhere and the boots Ellie had bought him for Christmas.

"You can't ride the range in pajamas, cowboy. I think I'd better find some jeans for you to wear."

He rode his imaginary horse off into the den.

"Jamie, I'll put them on the bed, okay?" She shouted to be heard over the trotting. He answered with a boy-sized, "Yep".

She walked in trying to remember where she'd put his jeans. Her brother's old room was newly decorated with images of cowboys and galloping horses on the bedspread, curtains, and even the lampshade. Ellie had outdone herself trying to make Jamie feel welcome. When she'd first come in here yesterday, Devon had suffered guilt pangs that her mother had gone to so much trouble. But in the bright light of a new morning, she touched upon the obvious. They were all the family Mom had left to spoil.

Even though TJ's trophies and sports stuff had been put away this would always be his room. He'd had Pop's dark hair and Mom's hazel eyes. She looked at his favorite picture on the wall, taken his senior year. He was in full uniform, arm out fending off a tackle, Number 36, star running back, savior of the Wildcats. He'd been strong, fast on his feet, and always ready with a joke. His death had left its mark on all of them. She turned away and began to straighten the bed.

She yanked on the bedspread to pull it up off the floor. If her brother had become a football coach, like he wanted, settled down to live in some little west Texas town with a wife and a stairstep assortment of kids, she could have considered him a knucklehead frittering away his life worrying about damned football. She wished she could feel that kind of careless disappointment when she thought of him rather than the thin edge of guilt he'd left behind.

She slapped at the pillow and straightened the top sheet and light blanket before pulling the bedspread over them. She opened a drawer and took out a clean tee shirt. The jeans were in the bottom drawer. She laid out Jamie's clothes on the bedspread and looked around. With her son in here, his toys scattered around and dirty socks on the floor, surely it would feel differently after a while. It would become his room, a place with a future.

Devon walked into the bathroom and brushed her teeth before getting dressed. It felt good to be wearing scruffy jeans and not have to rush off somewhere. She slid open the closet door. Her old boots, scuffed, flat-heeled Ropers, were where she had left them. Carrying them back to the bed, she sat down and pulled them on.

There was a dry smudge of mud by one toe. Pop was still alive the last time she'd worn them. They'd taken Jamie fishing a year ago. Her dad had been so sweet and patient with him, showing him how to hold the pole and turn the reel, pointing at the bobber out in the water trying to get Jamie to understand that a fish would pull it down when it took the bait. It had been funny to watch them together but tears came to her eyes now. She sat up to blink them away and sniffed to keep her nose from running.

Her mother called down the hall. "Devon, I have to go. Takes me a while to help Jessie get ready."

She brushed a tear off her cheek and cleared her throat. "When will you be back?"

"Before suppertime." The voice came closer. "Need me to pick up anything?"

"No, Mom, we're fine." She stood up and walked to her door. "We're going to drive around the ranch in a little while."

Ellie was standing in the hall fussing with a necklace. "Can't see the blasted thing even with my glasses." Devon took over, straightened the chain and hooked the clasp. "What would you like for dinner? I'll cook."

"I've got a casserole in the refrigerator thawing out. You can put a salad together or whatever Jamie might like to eat. Bye, hun." She gave her a peck on the cheek and headed for the kitchen with her purse. Devon followed behind her.

As Ellie drove off stirring up dust down the long driveway to the road, Devon decided to pack a light lunch. They'd take a leisurely drive around the place, maybe stop by the spring for lunch and take it easy the rest of the day. When she finished putting everything in a small ice chest she searched for her little partner. He was out on the deck. For a few minutes, she joined him admiring the view of the ranch and the smell of dew moistened grass warmed by the sun.

"Well, Tex, are you ready to ride?"

"You bet!" Another Hankism right down to the drawl. The child was a sponge. He'd soak up a little of this life, almost like her childhood, while they were here.

"Good." She teasingly tapped his nose with her fingertip. "Going to wear that hat to keep the sun off your nose?" It was too big and sat lopsided on his head but he nodded. "Well then, let's hightail it out of here."

Jamie whooped with excitement and ran out the door. It was going to be a great day. She let out a 'Yee-ha' as she grabbed their lunch and jackets. The kitchen door gave a satisfying slam behind her. Jamie was waiting by the car.

"The road is too rough for the car, Jamie. We'll take Grandpa's truck."

The red '55 Ford was parked in the shed beside the tractor. When she opened the door, the soft brown leather seat still smelled of saddle soap. Jamie climbed in and bounced on the seat once with a smile. The sandy grit made a familiar scuffing sound as she got in and moved her feet to the pedals. The key was in the ignition. Mom used it to drive around the place now. Pop had put a new engine and transmission in it. With a twist of the key the engine hummed, ready to go. The gas gauge read three-quarters full so they were set. Hank waved as they drove past the barn, his dog Maggie barking a farewell.

She headed across the front pasture. The live oaks scattered here and there had wide branches that spread out to shade the animals during the heat of summer. Dulce, her old mare, and Ginger, Hank's horse, were grazing near the gate. When the truck stopped they came over to investigate. Jamie fed them the carrots she'd brought. She rubbed the blaze on Dulce's face.

"Hey, Sugarfoot, remember me?" It had been years since she'd competed or done any real riding on Dulce's back. The old gal wasn't up to racing anymore.

"I thought her name was Dulce?" Jamie was standing on the bottom rung of the metal gate.

"It is, but Dulce means sweet in Spanish and her stockings are white like sugar. It's just a nickname Granny gave her. Come on let's go."

Driving along the sandy west side road, she spotted the narrow trail of a snake. The warm sun had brought them out of their dens, the good ones and the poisonous ones too, no doubt. She'd have to teach Jamie to keep his eyes open and be especially careful in the brush. They bumped along the rocky stretch, past the big weeping willow, it's empty branches touching the crumbling rock foundation of the original homestead.

"That's where Grandpa grew up, isn't it, Mom?" He looked over at her, a pleased smile spreading across his face. "Granny has that picture of the way it used to look."

She smiled. "That's right." Now that he was older, he'd have memories of the ranch. She liked that. It'd become a part of him, too.

She drove across the drier range land. The cattle were gathered around the tank. There was a nice mix of colors in the crossbreeds, everything from red brown to cloudy white. Devon decided to stop and take a look. A curious young heifer came up to them as they got out. Jamie laughed as the flat, white nose nudged him and he gingerly patted it. Devon waved her hand as the animal stepped closer.

"Go on now." The creature ambled away.

They walked to the mound surrounding the water. "That's good. The tank has plenty of water in it. They've had a lot of rain this winter. I remember when we dug this one with a bulldozer."

"Can we fish?"

She put a hand on his shoulder. He remembered that last outing. "Not today. I didn't bring any poles." He frowned up at her. She laughed. "Hey, those catfish aren't going anywhere. Oh, look. There's a snapping turtle sunning himself on that branch in the water." He scanned the area she was pointing to. "If they bite you, it hurts like the dickens." The black shape plopped into the water and disappeared. "They're hard to sneak up on. Come on." They strolled among the cattle to get back to the truck.

"Mom, is it summer now?"

"No, it's still winter." It didn't seemed possible, at the moment it was so warm.

"It feels like summer." He leaned his head to one side and looked up at her. "How do you know it's not?"

"Because it's February, even in Texas. This time of year it can be nice one day and cold and stormy the next. Once we get into summer, you'll know it."

"Does Matthew still have snow?"

"I'm sure he does. We left Minnesota just three days ago, Jamie. It's cold there."

"Why?"

Devon took a deep breath and grabbed the door handle. It was going to be another day of a million questions. She needed to carry an encyclopedia in her hip pocket.

"Because Minneapolis is closer to the North Pole."

"That's why Santa always has snow."

Devon smiled at him. "Right. Let's go. We'll see if we can spot a deer." He perked up and hopped into the truck when she opened the door.

She drove along the spring fed creek, past the high rock wall carved by water ages before, to a grassy meadow where the larger trees grew. She stopped and searched for any movement among the branches. The deer around here were small and grayish brown, perfectly camouflaged. All she spotted was the shadowed form of a coyote loping out of sight. She drove along the creek that ran down its rocky path to the clear blue green pool formed in a depression of smooth white stone. They pulled up to the water's edge and got out. There were plenty of deer tracks all around. Jamie took off his boots and socks and she helped him roll up his pant legs. It was warm. His jeans would dry fast. She sat on a raised flat rock while he splashed in the shallow water and built boats from leaves. She leaned back, letting the sun warm her face, feeling relaxed, downright lazy. It took quite a while for Jamie to get bored. Lookout Point had a bird's eye view of half the county. A perfect place to eat lunch. She checked her watch. It was eleven thirty.

"Are you hungry, Jamie?"

"Uh-huh. Did you bring cookies?"

"Yes. Let's eat lunch up there today." She pointed out the spot. "It's the highest spot in the county. Come on. Get your socks and boots back on."

Once they were in the truck, Devon headed for the steep road that led up to the spine of the ridge. "Years ago the Kiowa and Comanche Indians would ride their horses up this ridge looking for game or watching for their enemies." Jamie patted his mouth and yelled, a first grader's idea of an Indian war cry, as they bounced up the rough road.

It took a while to get to the flat-topped crest but it was worth it. She parked and admired the view. The scattered hills and ridges, dotted with trees and thick patches of brush were interrupted by occasional off-white slashes of crusty limestone outcroppings with the endless blue Texas sky above. She felt closer to God up here. There was just enough of a light breeze to keep a red-tailed hawk floating lazily overhead.

She put down the tailgate and grabbed the ice chest. She set out the drinks, sandwiches, a cut up apple, and two cookies on paper towels. They sat on the tailgate letting their feet dangle while they munched. Devon pointed southeast.

"See Granny's house over there?"

He lifted his chin a bit. "It's little. We're taller than everything, Mama." He nibbled on his peanut butter sandwich.

"I used to think you could see the whole wide world from up here."

"But you can't, right?"

She smiled at him. "Right, just the best part of it. At least, that's what my dad always said." She had been up here with TJ many times. They'd listened to Pop tell stories about growing up in the tiny house below them, now a shaky relic, and explain what he wanted to do next to improve the ranch. He'd put his heart and soul into this spread. He'd worked hard and expected the same from everyone else. It felt strange knowing he'd never be back to finish.

"Mom, is heaven up in the sky?" She blinked away the tears in her eyes and turned toward him. "Matthew said so but I don't see anything." He was kicking his feet back and forth while his eyes searched the great blue beyond.

"It would be nice to think heaven is up there, following us around."

He nodded but his brow wrinkled.

She watched the cattle in the pasture below, unwilling to resort to a pat Sunday school answer however easy it might be. "I don't think heaven is a place you can see or touch, Jamie." She glanced at him wondering if she should be honest. She'd given up church long ago but she wouldn't take it away from him. It might give him comfort.

His puzzled expression didn't change as a question formed on his lips. "But . . . where's Grandpa?"

Devon stared at her boots struggling with the lump in her throat. She coughed and straightened up. He was waiting for an answer but she wasn't sure what to say.

"I can show you where he's buried in the cemetery, Jamie. But . . . I think his spirit is here." With a wave of her hand, she included all that stretched before them. "He loved this ranch and Granny and you and me more than anything in the world. Wherever we go, we take his love with us."

"Oh." The word escaped his lips in a whisper. He stood up in the bed of the truck scanning the horizon. Devon wanted to hug him tight to quiet that part of her that loved him above all else, but she didn't. Instead, she picked up the remains of lunch and left him to his thoughts.

As they bumped down the steep road, Devon remembered the Lizzie prints by the river. "Jamie, how would you like to see some dinosaur tracks?"

His eyes widened. "Really?"

"Yep, true blue footprints. This part of Texas used to be sandy beaches and the bottom of a shallow ocean."

"Just tracks, no teeth?" He looked disappointed.

"They're really big tracks." She laughed and headed north anyway, out the back gate.

The section of river bottom, protected as a state historic site, wasn't on their ranch but it was only a few miles away if she used the old shortcut. It had been a long time since she'd gone that way but it was faster. In some places the road was dry and rocky, a ground up crust of layers of limestone and sandstone, while in other places, deep sand, washed by rain and wind, filled smooth basins like a sandbox.

As they came to a flat, open area, she picked up speed. The truck squeaked as they rolled along. They were singing 'Hi-Ho' as Jamie called it, when an abrupt jolt bounced them off the seat. The steering wheel pulled hard to the right. She hit the brakes. The back end bucked as the rear tires rolled over whatever she'd hit. Once stopped, the cab had a decided list to the right. Her heart sank. She was looking at wall-to-wall scrub brush, rocks and dirt through the windshield. She rested her head on the wheel between her tight fists.

"Yahoo!" Jamie laughed. She glanced sideways. He was standing on the floorboard. "That was fun. What's wrong, Mama?" He was frowning, clearly puzzled.

"I have to take a look under the truck, Jamie. I hit something." She slapped at the seat with the palm of her hand silently cussing a blue streak. "You stay put."

She yanked the door handle and shoved the door open, hoping the damage wasn't as bad as she imagined. There was a deep rut behind them with a gaping washed-out hole. She saw it now that it was too late. Checking for any unfriendly critters first, she lay down on her stomach and crawled under the truck. The right front tire was as flat as a flitter, to use her mother's phrase. She didn't see anything bent or broken but that didn't mean much.

She backed out and sat up. Been awhile since she'd changed a tire. She dusted herself off and walked around to the back. There wasn't a spare in the bed where it should have been. She got on her knees and looked under the rear bumper hoping she was wrong. Nothing.

"Damn. I should have checked before we left." She stood up with her back to the truck. "Shit." She kicked at a rock. "Driving in this rough country like a city slicker tourist, for God's sake. You know better."

She looked around. They were stranded right in the middle of nowhere. She couldn't see anything except the ridges that flanked the wash on both sides, which meant, nobody could see them. Great, just great. Devon wasn't sure but guessed it was three or four miles to the house from here. She'd been stupid to leave the ranch on a lark. She put her hands on her hips, took a deep breath and counted to twenty. Try to look at the bright side. It was a nice afternoon with plenty of daylight left. Take a deep breath, Devon, now exhale. She walked back to the open door of the cab where Jamie was jiggling the steering wheel and making engine noises.

Seeing his six-year-old imagination at work, she had to smile. "Well partner, the tire is flat and I can't fix it out here. We're going to hike back to Granny's."

"Okey-dokey." He stopped bouncing on the seat, stood on the running board and jumped to the ground beside her.

She glanced around the cab after checking the glove compartment. There wasn't much worth carrying. She wished they had some water to take along. It wasn't hot but they'd get thirsty. Her grandfather's fancy livestock cane rested in the gun rack on the back window. Pop had used it when his trick knee acted up. She decided to take it in case they ran into something ornery like a snake getting a suntan. When she took it down, Jamie commandeered it even though the brass handle made it heavy. She rolled up the windows and put the keys in her pocket.

"Okay, cowboy. Let's go."

The road was little more than a sandy track following the ravine. Slabs of limestone had tumbled down in places from exposed layers at the top of the ridge. It was quiet and seemingly empty until a hawk screeched overhead. As wild and rough as this country was, she'd grown up loving it. At the moment, she couldn't remember why.

When a lizard scurried away in front of them, Jamie ran to catch it but quickly lost the race. He would run a while, then dawdle to poke at something he'd found with the tip of the cane. She tried to be patient as she cajoled and prodded him along. She glanced at her watch. They were out of sight of the truck but hadn't covered much ground in thirty minutes.

The grumbling of a bad muffler somewhere behind her, sounded like beautiful music. Devon turned around, her hopes raised that one of their neighbors could give them a ride. The dusty green truck, rattling over the rough road, slowly closed the distance between them. It was a letdown to see the Oklahoma plates. There would be no familiar face inside. She put her hand on Jamie's shoulder insisting he stay by her side as it rolled to a stop.

It was hard to see the driver. The reflection off the windshield made it impossible until he leaned his head out the window. He wasn't an old-timer. His dark blonde hair was too long. His red baseball cap cast a shadow across his face making it hard to tell more than that.

When he pushed up the stained bill of his hat, a breath escaped from her lips in response to his beautiful, pale blue eyes. They were a lustrous blue, the color of a tropical lagoon in a travel brochure. She couldn't help but stare. He was in his mid twenties she guessed and handsome. As a smug grin spread across his face, she gathered he knew it too.

"Howdy, honey. That yore rig back yonder with the busted tire?"

"Yes. I didn't have a spare." She flinched. She was no stranger's 'honey'.

He moved his head as he reached for a cigarette in the ashtray on the dash. There was a short red scar by his ear and a fading bruise above his temple. There were no tools or tack in the pickup bed.

An unsettling little flutter stirred inside her. What was he up to this far from town? "You work out here?"

"Uh-huh." The stranger glanced over his shoulder out the back window before he turned back. He took a long drag on his smoke, looking her over with a slow sweep of his eyes.

After months of putting up with her boss, she'd had her fill of being ogled. She wanted to send him packing but hesitated. There was an icy calculation in those eyes that troubled her.

Jamie bumped against her hip and frowned up at her. "Can we go now?" He let out an impatient little huff and jabbed at a rock with the cane.

A grin relaxed across the man's face as he slowly blew smoke toward her. The distinctive aroma of marijuana made her skin tingle as the hair on her arms stood up. He sat in his truck, holding that short joint between his fingertips, studying her. "You two all by your lonesome then?"

"No." She'd blurted it out before she'd thought it through. She was a lousy liar and now she was stuck with her answer. It was none of his business anyway. She looked down.

"Let's go, Jamie." She nudged him to start walking. The man was still parked, the engine idling. His easy grin had flattened out. He didn't believe her. She needed to come up with something.

"My husband is just up the road." She said it quietly, hoping Jamie wouldn't hear her fabrication. She should have known better. Jamie abruptly stopped and turned. A puzzled wrinkle spread across his brow. "But . . .."

"Hush, don't argue. Let's go." Unable to explain, she grabbed the cane from him with her left hand and clamped onto his hand with the other. She glanced at the stranger, forced a quick smile and started walking.

Her heart pounded in her chest when she heard the engine die and the squeak of the metal door behind her. She stopped and glanced back. He was a big man, at least six feet tall. His tee shirt stretched tight across broad, powerful shoulders. He dropped his cigarette and ground it to oblivion with his boot.

"Can't leave y'all out here." His voice was deeper, menacing. "I'll give you a ride." With a flick of his wrist, he threw his hat on the seat and ran his hands through his long hair.

She took a deep breath trying to calm down. Keeping Jamie behind her, she faced him. "Thanks but its not far. You've got work to do. We're fine." She squeezed Jamie's hand and turned away.

"Nobody else around to help, sugar." There was nothing sweet about the sarcasm in his voice.

She tugged on Jamie's hand hearing the brisk crunch of footsteps in the sand and glanced over her shoulder. He was coming straight at them, eyes focused on her, a scornful smile on his lips.

"You scared of me, honey?" He laughed as he caught up and snatched Jamie away from her. The bright sun blinded her as the stranger lifted her son above his head. "No point in walkin', boy."

She froze for a moment, shielding her eyes from the glare with a hand, realizing he was crazy enough to hurt Jamie. The confusion on Jamie's face, as he was swooped through the air, cut her apart before pulling her back together again. She rushed up beside him, thoughts racing like a brush fire warning her to choose her words carefully. "Please . . . be careful. He's only six. Please, he's afraid up there."

"That's better." The stranger set Jamie down in the bed of the truck.

"Look, I don't even know your name . . . .." She searched for a way to appease him.

"My friends call me, Buddy." There was nothing subtle about the smile on his face. The bastard was enjoying scaring her. He had her and he knew it.

She tightened her grip on the handle of the cane but caution banished the angry words on the tip of her tongue. "We'll ride in the back of the truck just to the top of the ridge."

He nodded. One corner of his mouth curled up. Perhaps her concession had mollified him. Jamie's face was pale, as he stole a quick glance at this creature that separated them.

"I'll get up there with you, honey." She headed for the tailgate but Buddy blocked her path. She wouldn't let him keep them apart another minute. "Get out of my way. He's too little to ride by himself."

His eyes were a glittering, cold blue. "No, he ain't." He didn't budge.

"Yes, he is." She raised her right arm, the one holding the cane, and shook the brass handle at him. "Now move!"

He grabbed her wrist and twisted. Stinging pain shot up her arm. The cane dropped to the ground and he kicked it away.

"I'm the boss, got that?" He yelled in her ear. "You think I'm stupid?" She leaned to one side almost crumbling to her knees and cried out as he increased the pressure. "No ring, no husband. Why're are you lyin' to me, bitch?"

"Let her go!" Jamie's little boy voice shrieked the command.

Buddy lifted his head and yelled back at twice the volume. "Shut up, you little shit."

"Stop it." Jamie swung a doubled up fist hitting him on the back.

Buddy pinned her against the truck with his body and grabbed her son's arm. Jamie's face was locked in a grimace, his eyes wide with fear.

"Sit or I'll beat the crap out of you!" He shook him and shoved him down on the metal floor.

She slipped out from under the crush of him but he was quick to realize she'd gotten loose. He hooked his arm around her neck and reeled her in until her back bumped into his chest. His arms tightened like a vise around her rib cage and he lifted her off the ground. She squirmed.

"Won't do you no good to fight, woman." His lips touched her ear. "If you behave, we can have us some fun. I might even show that boy of yours a thing or two about screwin' a woman before I'm through."

Every muscle stiffened. His palm muffled her scream. "What you fussing about? He's plenty old enough to find out his Ma's a slut. Be doin' him a favor." She twisted and kicked. He laughed until the back of her head connected with his jaw.

He grabbed one arm and slammed her into the fender. She slumped to the ground, breathless, trying to focus her eyes.

"Stupid bitch!" He stood above her wiping blood off his lip, then kicked her.

She curled up, sharp pain stabbing her ribs.

"That'll teach you."

Jamie cried out, "Mama." She looked up. He was leaning over the side of the pickup.

"Run, Jamie, hide." She wailed, praying he'd get the chance.

Buddy pounded his fist on the fender and Jamie backed away, out of sight. "You stay on your butt, boy or you'll be sorry."

He grabbed her by the shirt collar, lifted her off the ground and dragged her away. She wrapped an arm around his boot. He slapped her with the back of his hand before dropping her on the hard ground.

He was on his knees straddling her hips when she came to her senses and felt the touch of his hand on her skin. She swung at his face with her fists as he pulled at her blouse but he clamped one hand around her throat and squeezed. She gasped for air.

He leaned down, inches from her face. "I'm not ready to ride just yet, honey."

His eyes were wild. He'd kill her if she continued to resist. Jamie would be alone at his mercy. He'd leave when he was finished with her. She stopped struggling. All that mattered was getting home alive.

"That's better." He relaxed his fingers at her throat.

"I won't fight." The words sputtered out of her.

He grabbed her jaw, his fingers squeezing her cheeks. "I'll do anything I please, slut. You can't stop me." He laughed, straightened up and began unbuckling his belt.

She closed her eyes trying not to think or feel his hands. The truck was behind her somewhere. She prayed Jamie was hiding and couldn't see.

Buddy lurched sideways. Hearing Jamie's scream, she opened her eyes. He'd pounced on the man's back with both arms wrapped around his neck. He screamed, 'I hate you', over and over.

"God damn it!" Buddy coughed and pulled Jamie's hands away from his neck.

She clawed at his face trying to reach his eyes. He knocked her hands away and slapped the side of her head setting off a high-pitched ringing in her head.

The man reared up and bellowed. "You bit me, you little fucker." He reached over his shoulder, grabbed at Jamie, and yanked him off his back.

Her son flew off to one side and tumbled across the ground. Buddy's weight shifted as he crawled off her. She rolled away from him and got up, searching for some way to protect Jamie. The means lay at her feet.

"I'm gonna wring your damn neck, brat." Buddy fumbled to pull up his loose jeans. Jamie was on his hands and knees scrambling away.

With a white-hot energy coursing through her, she scooped up the cane, took a step to get closer and swung. Surprise stripped away the man's frown as he saw it coming. The brass knob slammed into his head. He fell with a thud. The hair above his ear was wet with blood. Trembling, she stared at the man on the ground, still and silent now.

She turned to look for Jamie. He was peering out from behind the rear wheel. She ran over. "You okay?" He nodded and crawled out. She made a quick head to toe survey before she hugged him. "Let's go. Get in the truck."

"I'll kill you." The deep, growling threat cut into her. Jamie stopped dead in his tracks. Buddy, propped up on one elbow, was holding a hand to his bloodied head.

A hawk screeched over head. Its shadow touched her face. She tightened her grip on the smooth hickory and raised the handle of the cane off the ground. "No, you won't. Go on, Jamie, get in." This desolate place could snare an injured man too.

She held her ground, facing Buddy but slowly stepping backward as her son climbed in the cab. She glanced away just long enough to reach in to start the engine. The ignition was empty, no keys. She leaned against the seat, weak suddenly, needing to catch her breath. The fight wasn't over.

"Ain't your day." Blood was smeared across his jaw and stained his white shirt as he dug in a front pocket. A twitch, that might have been a smile, flashed across his face. He pulled out a set of keys and jingled them. "Need these."

Straightening, she tightened her grip on the cane. "Throw them here."

He made a fist with the keys locked inside. "Fuck . . . you."

He was hurting but still dangerous. Scalp wounds bled a lot, even minor ones. She inched toward him, feeling the rapid beat of her heart all the way down her arms. He might be waiting for her to get close. She circled. He sat up. His head bobbed every so often as he tracked her. One eye was almost swollen shut, the skin turning blue.

"You'll need a doctor to stitch up that cut, Buddy. I'll get one for you."

He mumbled some curse and rolled forward to get on all fours. "Like hell you will."

She kept an eye on the hand with the keys and raised the cane shoulder height. She couldn't afford to underestimate him. He was too strong.

He put one foot under him, swayed, and steadied himself with his fists on the ground. He slowly rose, not straightening up completely before he lunged at her.

She swung, aiming for his head. The brass hammered in with a wet smack. His hands slapped at her legs as he dropped to the ground. She backed away, unable to take her eyes off him. He lay on his side, his head resting on one arm.

A gasp of air rushed out of her. Half of the cane lay in the sand. The rest was in her shaking hands. She opened her fingers and it fell to the ground.

His eyes were closed but the beast was alive, his chest moved up and down. The key ring was a few inches from his open hand. She snatched it up, stumbled to the pickup, climbed in and slammed the door. Her fingers trembled as she separated the keys and finally slid the right one into the ignition. As the engine rumbled to life she glanced at him. He hadn't gotten up yet. She stretched to reach the accelerator, pushed it to the floor and heard the wheels spin. A cloud of dust filled the air as the truck sped away.

The glare of the sun across the sand blurred everything to a dizzying sameness. Driving as fast as she dared, she concentrated on the two worn tracks in front of her, watching for ruts and wishing this were a city street instead of this godforsaken wasteland. The only thing important now was to get home.

Jamie was on his knees on the seat beside her, one arm rested across the back of her shoulders. He bumped against her side as the truck rocked. A stab of pain snatched a breath away. "Careful, Jamie."

He leaned forward to look at her face. "Are we okay, now?" His voice was thin, frail with uncertainty. His steady gaze focused on her eyes.

Her body trembled. It was impossible to control. "Yes." She blinked away tears and looked back at the road. "We're going to be fine."

He hugged her neck. She slipped her right arm around him, brushed her lips across his cheek and glanced up at the rear view mirror. They were well out-of sight of the bloody man. She swerved. The ashtray on the dash fell to the floor scattering ashes. She was sick to her stomach. She tried to swallow to fight the feeling but her throat was sore and desert dry. All she could do was squeeze her son tighter.

Jamie settled back beside her without saying anything more but he kept a hand on her shoulder. She winced with every jolt, hated every patch of scrub brush and useless rock that separated her from civilization. The truck swayed and bounced. Dust billowed in the open windows if she slowed down. She tightened her grip on the steering wheel and stared at the endless road.

The house appeared just ahead. She eased up on the gas pedal not remembering driving over the cattle guard or crossing the creek but she must have. She stopped in front of the garage and stared at the kitchen door. No one opened it or rushed out. No welcoming arms to end this terrible journey. She slumped forward bumping her forehead on the steering wheel as pain took her breath away.

"Mama?" Jamie grabbed her arm.

She sat back in the seat once again the focus of those trusting eyes. He was safe now, she'd managed that. She touched his dirty, tear-stained cheek. She needed to wash his face.

"We should get out." She pulled the door handle but had to push the door open with both arms she was so shaky. It squealed, metal on metal, when it moved. Her legs wobbled as she stepped down. She swayed, feeling lightheaded, and leaned against the back fender. Her stomach knotted and what was left of her lunch came up in two painful spasms. The bitter taste of bile mixed with the grit of sand between her teeth. She heard the crunch of Jamie's footsteps before she saw him racing away.

"Help, Hank, help."

"What's wrong?" Hank was running.

"Mama's hurt. Come see." Jamie cried out.

They were both rushing toward her. She straightened, turned away from the smell of vomit and wiped her mouth on her sleeve.

Hank stopped in front of her and stared, his eyes wide. "Good God Almighty, what happened? Are you all right?"

She glanced down, surprised to see splattered bloodstains on her blue blouse. It was torn and hanging out of her jeans. "Guess I'm a little banged up." She tried to tuck the front of her shirt in but it hurt too much.

"More than a little, Devon." He leaned down. "Did you have a wreck? Who's truck is this?"

She rubbed her throbbing temple. "We had a flat and had to walk."

Jamie stepped between them. "That's when the bad guy came and hit Mama."

"A man did this to you?" Hank interrupted, his voice booming out of him. "Why would . . . " Hank turned his face away from her. "son of a bitch." When he turned back, he was a different man with his eyes narrowed, jaws clenched, and fists ready. "Who was it?"

Devon shrank back from him. "I didn't know him." Her voice shook as the words came out. "He was tall, had long, blonde hair." She felt dizzy again, grabbed the steering wheel and leaned back against the truck seat. Jamie threw his arms around her and buried his face in her blouse. She rested a hand on his head.

"Better get you inside." Hank's voice was soft now. "Hold on to me, Devon." He held out his arm.

At a snail's pace, they walked through the garage. Jamie on one side and Hank on the other until they got to the door. Hank had Jamie hold it open while she climbed up the two steps into the kitchen. It was empty and cold inside. She headed for the sink, turned on the cold water and scooped up a handful to rinse her mouth. It was sweet and cool but she spit it out. Blood in the water. There were cuts in her mouth. They stung when she touched them with her tongue.

"Where's Ellie?" Hank was still standing beside her.

"She took Aunt Jessie to the doctor." She filled a small glass on the counter and washed another mouthful of water though her teeth.

"Where?"

She swallowed. "Kerrville, I think. I'm not sure." She sagged but Hank was there to hold her up. Every muscle in her body felt like rubber. He helped her sit down at the dining table. Jamie was looking at his elbow. It was bloody. Hank must have noticed it too and walked over to him.

"Are you all right, son?" He leaned down for a closer took. "Got a little scraped up but not too bad. We should rinse it with some water to get the sand off."

Jamie nodded his head and raised his arm. Hank turned on the faucet. "He threw me down 'cause I socked him as hard as I could."

"Good boy." He put his arm over her son's shoulder, held him against his hip, and gave him a couple gentle pats. It was the closest thing to a hug she'd ever seen Hank give. Tears filled her eyes. Through the blur, she looked down at the floor.

"Mama hit him too and bunches of blood came out."

"Good for her. Make it easier to find him. Pat it dry with this paper towel, Jamie."

"And then, when he was laying down in the dirt, we got away."

"Good thinkin'." He turned toward her. "If you have his truck and yours had a flat and no spare, Devon, he's stuck."

"I hurt him . . . to get away." She rubbed her hand across her wet cheek. It was sore.

"Good." Hank was angry, his jaw muscle tightening. "Now where did you leave the bastard?"

She had to think. "We were on the old road through Comanche Wash, past the Fletcher place."

Hank smiled. "He's stranded out in the middle of nowhere. I'm gonna call the sheriff before we head for the hospital." He picked up the phone and dialed. "Howdy, this Hank Walker over at Taylor Ranch."

Jamie opened the refrigerator door and took out the pitcher of lemonade. She watched him fill the glass on the counter, such a sweet, ordinary thing. He was a good boy but he had seen something no child should see and heard things no child should ever hear. She would never forget the sound of his scream. She leaned against the table. This room had been at the center of her childhood; a place where food defined the time, where arguments often started or ended, where the family gathered to mourn or celebrate, always a safe place. One more memory would be added now. One shared with her son.

"Listen Clarine, Ellie's daughter, Devon, and her boy just came in. They had a flat along Comanche Wash. Some S.O.B. came along and attacked them, beat the tar out of her. I'm carryin' them to the hospital but thought y'all should know right away." He looked over at her with a quick flick of his eyes. "I don't know, like I said her boy was with her. All I know is he was a stranger, tall with long hair. Don't know his name. Apparently, she managed to get a few licks in to bloody him. Should make him easy to spot. They got away in his truck so he's wanderin' around on foot. Think you could get somebody out there to round him up?"

She watched Jamie gulp down his lemonade and wondered how much he understood.

Hank nodded in her direction. "Right. That old road going north back of Fletcher's place before you get to County 235. Good. Thanks." He hung up the phone and took a step toward her.

"They're sending one of the deputies out there to get him, Devon. Said the Sheriff will have to talk to you but you need to see a doctor first." He patted the front pocket of his jeans. "Dang it. Left my keys out yonder. Jamie, run to the barn and get my jacket on the workbench while I help your mama walk out to my truck."

"Okay." Jamie ran out the door.

Hank looked her over in a quick pass and seemed embarrassed that she'd noticed. "They were askin' if he . . .." He couldn't quite look her in the eye.

"No." She couldn't say the word out loud either. "He tried but . . . no."

She looked down at her clothes. There were bloodstains all over, his blood. Her chest heaved as she gasped for air.

"Why did he do this to us?" She leaned forward, her aching head propped up by an elbow and a hand bracing her forehead, shielding her eyes from him. Tears pooled and rolled down her face. Her side ached with every breath. It hurt too much to cry.

Hank put his hand on her shoulder. "We'll get him, don't you worry. The doctor will fix you right up." He cleared his throat. "We better go. Takes a while to get there." He held out his hand to help her up. "Ready?"

She straightened and dried her face with her mother's apron which hung over the chair beside her. "Yes."

That was a lie. She wasn't at all ready to look into a stranger's face, or answer questions, or let someone touch her. But the constant gnaw of pain had grown stronger with every passing minute. If she didn't get help soon, she would get lost in it and she didn't want that. Jamie was counting on her.

Leaning toward Jamie, sitting in the middle of the bench seat, she held her arm against her side. It helped. His soft hair touched her cheek as she rested her head on the back of the seat. Hank was driving too fast. The truck rocked back and forth. She was getting sick to her stomach again. She raised her head and watched the horizon to fight it.

"Why was that man mean to us, Mama?"

She turned her head. Hank glanced in her direction, a bob of his Adam's apple his only comment. She looked into her son's earnest eyes. "I don't know." She was all out of reasons.

Usually it took quite awhile to get more than two words out of Hank but he kept up a steady monologue. "Now down that way, about quarter mile is a real nice fishin' hole. Have to take you over there one day."

"Okay." It was Jamie's halfhearted response.

Her head ached. She closed her eyes until she heard the two short honks of the horn. Hank waved and a cowboy on a cutting horse, working in a small herd waved back.

"That's Dusty Wells, quite a name for a dried-up old cowboy." He laughed.

They'd pulled onto the two lane state highway and gotten up to speed when Hank edged over onto the wide shoulder. "Slow down, dang it." He was frowning watching something in his rear view mirror. A dual-axle pickup hauling an open horse trailer carrying an Appaloosa flew past them. "New Mexico plates. Man drivin' like that won't get there in one piece. Horse will be a mess if he does." He shook his head and pulled back in to the right lane. "Some folks have no appreciation for good horseflesh."

"Yep." Jamie was stretching his neck to see over the dash.

She closed her eyes listening to Hank and the whine of the tires on the road.

"Look at that old Brahma bull out there stomping up a cloud of dust, Jamie. That ol' cuss must be worked up about somethin'. That's a ton of trouble on the hoof."

She didn't know if she'd fallen asleep for a while when she heard Hank's voice. "We'll be there soon, Devon."

She raised her head. They weren't close enough to see it yet. Hospitals made her nervous. They had ever since she'd broken her arm when she fell off Dulce. They would hurt her whether they meant to or not. Her side was so tender she dreaded it. All she wanted was to stop the roar of pain. But they'd ask what happened and she would have to describe it, to the doctors and the police. She winced at the thought that this horrible afternoon would become public knowledge to be gossiped about. It would become part of who she was to the people in town, making it harder to forget.

"They've worked on the clinic, Devon, since they finished the interstate through Buzzard Junction. Renamed the whole mess Tres Rios Medical Center. Don't know why they stuck that name on it."

He was talking out loud to himself it seemed, filling up the air. Maybe it felt too quiet to him.

"Mama." A warm breath touched her ear. "Will we have to get a shot?" Jamie's voice wavered.

She'd looked him over too quickly. "Does something hurt?"

He twisted his lips, like he always did when he was considering how honest an answer to give. "Maybe my arm hurts little." He rubbed it, close to the shoulder.

"We'll make sure it's okay. Don't worry." She pressed her lips to his forehead. She'd have a doctor check him from head to toe.

The truck pulled up to the emergency entrance. She unbuckled her seat belt and gingerly turned in the seat. Hank walked around to help. A wave of dizziness hit about the time she stood up. Hank kept her upright. Jamie was clinging to her. The double automatic doors opened releasing a flood of cool air tainted with the smell of ammonia.

Someone rolled a wheelchair over. "Have a seat, ma'am."

Hank helped her sit down. He answered a few questions and lied about being a relative saying he was her uncle. Yes, he said, she had insurance. No, he answered as she shook her head, she didn't have the numbers.

If she could stay very still it wasn't so bad. But she had to breathe and it was as close to agony as she could bear. She pressed her forearm against her side. It didn't help.

Jamie remained latched onto her hand and walked alongside her for the trip down a hallway as an orderly pushed the wheelchair through open double doors. A string of empty beds lined one wall. Jamie paled as he eyed the jungle of medical equipment.

A nurse walked in and told the young orderly to wait outside. She skimmed through the form Hank gave her, checked her watch and wrote something on the clipboard she held. She squatted down in front of Devon and studied her.

"My name is Connie. Looks like you've had some trouble." Her hair was black and very curly.

"I was working at the ranch and brought them in." Hank was standing beside her now. He lowered his voice. "Some S.O.B. attacked them when their truck broke down."

"We will need to notify the police."

"I already called the County Sheriff, ma'am."

"She was lucky to have you around." The nurse pulled over a stool and sat in front of her shining a penlight in her eyes. "We are required to file a report with the police. Do you know where you are, Devon?"

"At the hospital."

"Is there someone else we should call?"

Hank piped in. "She's stayin' with her mother right now. I'll get hold of her as soon as I can. She's out-of-town for the day."

Devon sagged a bit in the chair. What a shock this would be for her mother. She'd come home after a long day with Jessie to this terrible mess. Devon glanced at Jamie before looking back at the nurse who was now taking her pulse.

"I want a doctor to make sure my son is all right. He was knocked down and hurt his arm."

She wrote down something on their papers. "I have him down to be examined already. You're James?" The nurse gave him a pleasant smile. "How old are you?"

"Six and a half." He answered quietly without looking at her.

"You were both assaulted by the same person?" Devon nodded. She made a notation. "Did you know him?" Devon shook her head as the nurse wrapped a blood pressure cuff around her arm. "How are you feeling right now?"

The tight squeeze on her arm hurt. "I have a headache and my side hurts."

The nurse took the cuff off her arm. "We're a little short-handed today. Dr. Harris is on her way down to examine you, Devon. And Dr. Owen will be here in just a minute to see your son." The woman filled in some more blanks on the form. A man in a white jacket walked in.

"I hear there's a young man needing some attention." He squatted down at Jamie's eye level. "Hi, I'm Doctor Owen. Should I call you Jimmy or do you have another nickname?"

"His name is Jamie." Hank's voice seemed to come from nowhere. He placed his hand on her son's shoulder.

"Nice to meet you, Jamie. How are you feeling?"

"Okay."

"He may have hurt his shoulder." She wanted to say that before she felt any foggier.

The doctor gave her a nod like he understood how worried she was. "I'll give him a thorough look-over, ma'am. Don't worry." He stood up and held his hand out to Jamie. "While the nurse takes care of your mom in here, Jamie, let's go next door and I'll take a look at your arm."

His suggestion was met with stony silence. Jamie was close to tears.

"I think his Uncle Hank should go with him." She looked up at the man in the white coat. He had to allow it.

"That's me, Doc, Hank Walker." He stuck out his hand.

The doctor gave Hank's hand a quick shake. "I'd appreciate your company, Mr. Walker. We need to go through here." The doctor took several steps and motioned toward the hall.

Hank took Jamie's hand. "Come on, partner. They'll take good care of your mama. We'll stay right close."

She gave her son a light kiss on the cheek. The look in his eyes, full of apprehension, pleaded to stay but she had to send him away. "It's going to be okay. Go on. I'll be fine."

The new nurse raised the head of the narrow bed so she could sit up. She held the pillow against her sore ribs as the woman suggested. It helped.

"Don't worry, the neck brace is just a precaution." The gray-haired woman stopped talking and took her hand. "I know it's hard to describe something so terrible but your answers help us understand how you were injured." She smiled and gave her a consoling pat on the hand. "You haven't bathed or changed any of your clothes?"

"No."

"Good. Let me help you take those dirty clothes off." Devon groaned as she raised her arms to slip them out of the sleeves. "We can collect samples while you're here. It's evidence to identify him." She unfastened her jeans but had to rest it took so much effort. "If he raped you, Devon, or tried to, there will be traces of his DNA."

"He didn't get that far." She fought the urge to cry.

"You may remember more details later . . . ."

"I hit him." She increased the pressure of the pillow against her aching side. "As hard as I could." Her body shook as if it were crumbling. Choking on sorrow she gasped for air. Tears blurred the stark white surrounding her. An arm slipped around her back and she leaned into it as she cried, comforted by the steady pat on her shoulder.

"Good for you, honey," the voice whispered, "good for you."

She looked up blinking to clear her sight, unable to stop the tears rolling down her face. The nurse was sitting on the edge of the bed, waiting for the rest.

"He was going to rape me in front of my son." She covered her mouth to cut off a sob and lay back on the bed.

"Go ahead and cry. It's all right." The woman gave her a handful of tissues and pulled the white curtain around the bed.

Time didn't exist in the windowless room. Each minute was endless, like the painful throbbing in her head. The woman doctor asked again if he'd raped her. The word triggered memories of his rough hands on her skin. The parade of strangers, forgotten as quickly as they'd left, poked and prodded. She'd let them have a sample of her blood, take x-rays, scrape the dirt and bits of the man's skin from under her fingernails, and clean up the cut on her forehead. An injection had dulled the pain but not enough to stop feeling. The other doctor had told her Jamie was fine. Hank was watching over him. That was all that mattered.

The deputy wanted her to remember details and describe the stranger who had turned her life upside down. What did he say and when did he become aggressive? And what did she do? She described it as best she could, punctuated with tears.

As she stood in the silent room, chills raced across her bare skin. She closed her eyes and covered her breasts with folded arms. It seemed cruel to take pictures of her naked body. She wanted to be calm or even angry but she was too tired to feel anything but humiliation.

Devon sat in a wheel chair by the emergency entrance waiting for Hank and Jamie to bring the truck around. An orderly was standing beside her like a bodyguard. She looked up when she heard the automatic doors open with a swish. Sheriff Blanton walked in at a fast clip. Seemed like he'd always been around when there was trouble or bad news. She hadn't seen him since her father's funeral. She was locked in the same numbness now. His face was tense and the lines across his forehead furrowed deeper when he spotted her. He was holding the pieces of the cane wrapped in clear plastic. She dug her fingernails into her palms.

"You're finished with the doctor?" She nodded and looked at the small paper bag on her lap with the pills and instructions they'd given her to take home. He turned to the orderly as he grabbed the handles of her chair. "We need a little privacy." He looked around the waiting room and pushed her to an empty corner. He sat down on the vinyl couch. "We found your assailant. His name is John Colton."

The muscles in her throat tightened seeing Buck's grim expression. "What did he say?" The words were squeezed out as if she'd been hit again.

Buck hesitated, biting down on the toothpick in his mouth before taking it out. "It's complicated." He touched her balled up fist with a warm hand. "We found him right where you left him by the look of things. He's in a coma. They're transporting him to a hospital in Austin that handles head injuries. They don't know if he'll make it."

She stared at him, speechless, letting out a ragged breath. She turned her head and looked down at the seamless, gray linoleum floor. Her hair fell across her face hiding her from Buck's questioning eyes. For a moment, all she could hear was Colton's voice screaming at her. A wave of nausea brought her hand to her mouth.

"Devon, is this yours?"

She looked up. He held what was left of the cane in front of her. "It was Pop's. I hit him to get away. I told the deputy." Buck nodded. She put an elbow on the arm of the wheelchair, leaned to one side and rested her head in her hand. Buck moved closer and placed her other hand in his.

"Don't worry, Devon." He spoke softly, almost a whisper. "We'll work this all out." He glanced up briefly. "Hank's going to take you home."

Hank was standing nearby with Jamie. Her son's expression was as solemn and forlorn as an abandoned waif. It broke her heart. Their world had changed in the course of one afternoon. The orderly rolled her out the emergency doors. Buck helped her stand up while Hank opened the door of the truck.

"Let's go home." She held out her arm to Jamie.

When they drove up to the house, Ellie rushed outside. Hank helped Devon get out of the truck.

"Oh, dear Lord." Mama gently touched Devon's face. "How could anybody do this?"

"We're going to be okay." Devon didn't have the energy to move. Jamie was beside her.

"Are you all right, Jamie?" Ellie bent down. He nodded. She hugged him and gave him a kiss on the cheek. "Oh, poor baby."

"I had to leave Pop's truck out there."

Her mother straightened up keeping one hand on Jamie's shoulder. There were tears in her eyes. "That doesn't matter now."

Hank cleared his throat. "Ellie, I've got her medicine and instructions here for you." He handed her a small paper bag. "She has some cracked ribs and a mild concussion. Doctor told her to take it easy. Jamie's a little bruised up too but the doctor said he should be fine in a couple of days."

"Thank you so very much, Hank." She turned to Devon. "Let's get you in the house." Mom put her arm around her waist. They headed toward the kitchen door, Jamie in front and Hank on the other side of Devon. Once they were inside, she sat down at the table.

"I'm goin' on home, Ellie. Matty will be waitin' supper for me. If you need anything tonight, you just give me a holler." He started for the door.

Devon couldn't muster the energy to stand. "Hank." He stopped and turned toward her. "Thanks for all your help."

"Glad I could, Devon. You take it easy." A smile softened his lips. He waved as he opened the screen and walked out.

"I've warmed up that casserole. Are you hungry?"

Jamie was still standing beside Devon's chair. "Can I have a glass of milk, Granny?"

"Sure thing, honey. Would you like something too, Devon?"

"Just water so I can take a pill." Her side was really aching now. She was miserable sitting and longed to lie down.

Ellie grabbed the sack, read the doctor's note and found the pain medicine. "Says to take with food, Devon."

It hurt to chew and swallow, but she slowly ate half a banana and drank a glass of water to get the pill down. Jamie picked at the casserole and sipped his milk. She braced for more pain and stood.

"I need some help with my clothes, Mom."

"Okay, honey. Finish eating while I go with your Mama, Jamie." They shuffled to the hall bathroom.

"God, I look terrible." Devon leaned against the counter and stared in the bathroom mirror. She touched her swollen cheek and noticed the bruises on her arms and neck. "I didn't do anything to make him mad." She looked at her mother, not directly, but in the mirror. It sounded like an excuse coming from a child, hard to believe without any convincing detail but it was the best she could do, still bewildered by it all.

Ellie had tears in her eyes. "I know that." She held out her arms and Devon slipped between them. They were both sniffling. "It's going to be all right." Devon wobbled in her embrace.

"I hit him. With Dad's cane. He was going to hurt Jamie. Buck said he's in a coma."

"You did what you had to do. Right now, you need to rest."

"I want to take a shower to wash the smell of him off me." She unbuttoned her shirt and groaned trying to pull one arm out of a sleeve.

"Here, let me help you."

Behind the clouded glass door, she leaned against the wall of the shower letting the hot water slide down her and cried. Her mother stood waiting on the other side.

Ellie helped Devon lie down. Pulled the covers over her. Jamie lingered beside the bed, stroking the pillowcase. "Can I sleep with you tonight, Mama?"

"I'm too sore, Jamie. Let me give you a goodnight kiss." Devon touched his cheek with her lips as he leaned forward. She murmured something and closed her eyes.

"Please, Mama. I'll be careful." He nudged his mother's arm.

Ellie turned off the bedside lamp. He was whining. The child could see his mother needed rest. "Jamie, your mother's very sore. She can't have you bumping into her during the night." She looked down at Devon. Her eyes were still closed.

"Come on. She's asleep." Ellie gave him no choice. She grabbed his hand and pulled him out of the bedroom.

"But she needs me, Granny."

He yanked his hand free in the hallway. She glanced back at Devon's partially closed bedroom door. She wasn't going to argue with him. "Hush. You can help me take care of her tomorrow."

"But what if she has a bad dream and gets scared?"

Her grandson's wavering voice caught her unprepared. While his lower lip was resolutely sticking out, he was blinking to keep the tears in his eyes from flooding down.

"He said bad words and hit her and made her cry, Granny. We didn't do nothin', I promise."

Ashamed of herself for ignoring him, Ellie could have collapsed in tears. "Oh, honey." She got down on her knees and put her arms around his waist. "I'm sorry for being cross with you, Jamie. This has been an awful day for both of you." When his arms surrounded her neck, she hugged him tighter. Her heart ached for him.

After a moment or two, she leaned back and gently brushed the hair off his forehead. "I know you're worried about your mama. I am too, but she's going to be fine." She looked him in the eye. "Right now she needs to rest and take her medicine so she'll get better." She smiled hoping he would forgive her. "Now what about you? It's past time for your bath, isn't it?" He nodded. "We'll be careful not to get that bandage on your elbow wet." She stood up and took his hand. "After you get cleaned up, let's fix a nice cup of hot chocolate and have a talk. Maybe we'll read a story in my bed tonight. You can help me keep an ear out for your mama. How's that sound?" She gave his hand a gentle squeeze.

Jamie looked up and his face relaxed to a calm neutrality. "Can we put marshmallows in it?"

"You bet. Two or three if you'd like. I've got a whole bag full."

She was laughing. Her brother was chasing her across the pasture when he suddenly vanished. A room full of shadows and frozen quiet made her shiver. Her father held her hand. Tears stained his sallow cheeks. They stood before an open box with a shimmering white cloth on the lid. He was with the angels her mother's voice echoed.

"No." She screamed over and over shaking her head as she ran away. Her chest ached. Each breath thundered in her ears until a tumultuous rumbling overwhelmed it and shook the ground under her feet. She turned her head. Glowing headlights appeared in a billowing cloud of dust bearing down on her, moving too fast to escape.

Her body jerked. Devon opened her eyes in alarm. It took a second to realize she was in her bed at home as the sound of thunder died. The edges of the curtains were outlined by the dawn. To quiet the misery of her aching body, she concentrated on slowing her panicked breathing and relaxing the clutch of tight muscles mobilized to run from the nightmare she had conjured up. There wasn't a part of her that didn't hurt. It was time for more pills. She called out to her mother. It felt like an eternity before Ellie appeared by the bed. The agony was muted finally and she drifted off to sleep.

She could hear the wind rattling the trees and the rain beating against the window. Something warm and soft touched her chin. She opened her eyes to see Jamie's face a matter of inches in front of her. The side of his head was almost resting on her pillow. His brow wrinkled in concern as his fingertips touched her tender cheek.

"Does it hurt, Mama?" He was whispering.

The ache in her jaw made the answer simple. "Yes."

He straightened up enough to gently kiss her cheek. He settled back resting on his elbows. "Does that make it better?"

She smiled as best she could. "Much better." The expression on his face softened. She wanted to hold him but movement was pain. "How's my favorite boy?"

"Okay."

"Sleep all right?"

"I slept with Granny in her room. We made hot chocolate."

"Good." She could handle anything as long as he was okay.

Ellie walked in. She smiled at the two of them. "Well, there you are. You didn't wake your mother, did you?" Jamie shook his head but his expression said otherwise. She sat down on the edge of the bed. "How are you feeling this morning?"

"Sore."

"I gave her a kiss to make it all better."

"Well, that will help. The doctor's instructions said to give you plenty of fluids. And you need a little food to go with all that medicine. Maybe a little toast and hot tea?"

"Something softer, I've got cuts inside my mouth."

"All right, oatmeal should do. Jamie, come with me. You can help get your mama's breakfast."

"Okay." He straightened up and ran past her.

"Be back in a minute, Devon. You close your eyes and rest."

It rained steadily most of the day. Jamie was about to drive Ellie crazy. Every time she turned around, he had gone back into his mother's bedroom. She could understand his concern, but Devon needed to rest. It was hard enough to deal with the business of medications, ice packs, helping her to the bathroom and answering the phone every few minutes. Friends were concerned but she didn't have time to chat. She'd enlisted Hank's help in getting him out from underfoot once the rain stopped. He'd taken him out to check on an ailing heifer.

The overcast sky made everything look so bleak. She was peeling potatoes at the sink when she saw Buck drive up to the house in his sheriff's car. She hadn't expected him. She put the potatoes aside and rinsed her hands. The solemn look on his face when he walked into the kitchen didn't help matters.

He took off his hat and held it in his hands. "Howdy, Ellie. How's she doin'?"

"She's been sleeping most of the day. The pain pills pretty well knock her out. Figure sleep is the best medicine for her at this point."

"I suppose so. Think she'd be up for talking to me?"

"Not sure she'd make much sense. Can't it wait?"

"I can hold off until tomorrow, I reckon. Might work out better that way anyhow." He looked uncomfortable shifting his weight like his boots hurt his feet. "Mind if I have a seat?"

"Oh, of course not. Like a cup of coffee?"

"That'd be nice." He pulled out a chair, laid his hat on the table, and sat down. She took down two mugs.

"I got word this mornin' that Colton died at the hospital in Austin, Ellie."

The words snatched the breath right out of her lungs. She turned around to look at Buck. "What does that mean for Devon?"

"Homicides have to go before a grand jury."

She leaned her hip against the counter. Surely that wasn't the right word.

"Don't worry, Ellie. Her injuries make it pretty obvious she was protecting herself. No reason to think they'll rule anything other than self-defense." She got back to the business of pouring coffee. He was watching her as she carried the mugs over and sat down. "But we do need a formal statement from her for the record." He took a drink. "I've decided it would be best if I got a Texas Ranger to handle the investigation since I'm a friend of the family. No chance of anybody saying it wasn't done proper that way."

"Yes, I can see that." William would have agreed with Buck. He'd been a proud and honest man. She took a sip wishing he were in the chair beside her where he belonged. The house was too empty and quiet without him.

"Anyway, Bob Johnson, the Ranger I was talkin' about, will be putting all the evidence together. The autopsy will be done this evenin'. He'll need to talk to her tomorrow. Grand jury'll be meeting in a couple of weeks or so. The district attorney wants to have it all ready to go to them."

He was rattling information off so quickly that she was having a hard time following it all. "You said a grand jury? Will she have to testify?"

"More than likely, she won't. Her statement ought to provide all the information they need, but they can call her if there are any questions."

She stared out the window not really focusing on anything outside. "Maybe by tomorrow afternoon, she'll be feeling better. I'm not looking forward to having to tell her." She glanced at Buck, but couldn't tell how he felt from his expression. She didn't envy his line of work. "It's terrible what that man did to her, Buck. I guess you see it all the time. But the look in her eyes breaks my heart. I'm glad he's dead. Being a Christian woman, that's a horrible thing to admit. Hopefully God can forgive me for feeling that way, but I do."

Buck put his hand on hers and gave it a pat. "He was a very bad hombre, Ellie. Don't feel too guilty. Sort of fittin' that a woman killed him. No doubt, the good Lord was on her side. She was lucky to get away."

The sound of the spring stretching on the screen door was Ellie's first warning that Jamie was coming in. He ran into the kitchen but stopped short when he saw Buck.

The slam of the screen was like the crack of a whip and Ellie cringed. She turned in her chair to face him and shook her head. His boots and jeans were muddy.

"Jamie." He reminded her so much of TJ sometimes she couldn't be angry with him. Besides, all that unbridled energy and curiosity had to go somewhere.

"Sorry, Granny. I forgot." He stopped beside her chair.

"Hello, Jamie." Buck smiled.

"Hi." He was eyeing the revolver on Buck's belt. "Uncle Hank said you catch bad guys."

"Yep, every chance I get." Buck stood up and fished a toothpick out of his shirt pocket.

Jamie looked up at him. "Are you going to put that man in jail?"

Ellie braced waiting to see how Buck would handle the subject of the man's death. Buck bit down on the toothpick and looked at him for a minute before saying anything.

"Son, I can guarantee you he won't be hurting anybody else ever again."

Ellie leaned back in the chair and relaxed enough to take a breath.

"Good." Her grandson nodded his head, too young to ask the next question. "He was real mean." He was frowning as he looked down and tapped one leg of her chair with the toe of his boot.

Ellie ached watching him. He'd told her about trying to help Devon, being thrown off the man's back. He didn't understand that Colton was trying to rape his mother. Thankfully the brute didn't get far enough to make it clear. But he'd understood hate and cruelty. No child should ever see such ugliness.

"Mister Sheriff." He raised his chin to look up at Buck. "How many bad guys are there?"

Ellie put her arm around his waist. He'd been through so much in his short life. Buck stopped chewing on the toothpick sticking out between his lips.

"Well, I'll tell you what Jamie, I can't give you a number if that's what you're wantin' to hear." He put his hands on each side of the buckle of his wide belt. "There's more than I'd like but there's one thing I know. There are more good guys than bad guys, son. And I aim to keep it that way and so do all my deputies." He smiled at Jamie and patted his head. "Speakin' of which, I better get back to work." He picked his hat up and put it on.

"I'll be in touch, Ellie." He walked to the door. "Thanks for the coffee." He gave them a farewell nod and left them together.

Sunlight was pouring in through the curtains. Devon was hungry for a cup of coffee. She touched her face. It didn't feel quite as puffy. The ice packs had helped. Her mother and Jamie carried in a breakfast of scrambled eggs and biscuits, which tasted good even though she had to be careful how she chewed. Mom was quiet while Jamie chattered away. After the dishes were cleared, Ellie told Jamie she needed to discuss something in private and he reluctantly left the room to watch cartoons.

"Devon, I have to tell you something. I decided to wait until you'd had a good night's rest and some solid food in you." She sat down on the edge of the bed.

"What's wrong?" The words rushed out as she tensed up.

"Buck came by late yesterday afternoon." Ellie hesitated. "There's no good way to say this. The man, who hurt you, died in the hospital."

"Oh." That was all she could say, but she saw his cruel, angry face.

"The police need to have a statement from you about what happened. Buck called in a Texas Ranger to investigate. He's supposed to come over this afternoon sometime."

"I never should have gone out there." Devon looked out her window, at the bright sunshine. "He'll understand I was defending myself, won't he?" She turned back to her mother.

"One look at your face will convince him of that."

She stared at the wall above her dresser after her mother left the room. Her bruised arms were crossed over each other resting on her chest as if she were laid out ready for a funeral. It had been a fight she couldn't afford to lose. He'd given her no choice. She was feeling guilty because he was dead. Even with blood dripping down the side of his face, he'd threatened them.

He'd lunged at her. But the slow, unfocused look in his eyes she'd noticed troubled her. Maybe he'd simply stumbled getting to his feet. No, there had been nothing in his behavior to indicate he was willing to let them go. If the ranger asked, she would tell him she'd aimed for the wound on his head the second time no matter how it sounded. She tightened her fingers on her arms and closed her eyes hoping to calm the trembling core deep inside her before the ranger arrived.

Bob Johnson was a large man with broad shoulders and a shiny badge pinned to his shirt pocket. He leaned down and looked at her directly when he introduced himself and apologized for having to bother her while she was 'on the mend' but he was sure she'd like to have the 'matter settled.' He held a white Stetson in one hand and a tape recorder in the other. He put both of them down on the coffee table.

Devon took a quick breath to shake off the jitters. She was sitting on the couch, propped up with pillows, her legs neatly covered with a light blanket like an invalid. Her mother lingered in the background staying in the kitchen as she'd requested. With two fishing poles in the back of his pickup, Hank had taken Jamie for a ride around the place under the pretext of checking the water in the tanks.

The lawman plugged in the microphone and pushed a button. "Ms. Taylor, the statement you give today will become part of the legal record. A grand jury will review the state's evidence and make a determination in the death of Mr. Colton. You are entitled to have legal counsel present even though no charges have been brought against you. Since you do not have one present, I gather we may proceed."

"Yes."

"All right." He sat down in the leather chair beside the couch.

"Did you know, John Webster Colton?"

"No." She stared at the dark television screen.

"When was the first time you saw him?"

"We were walking, my son and I. My truck had a flat tire so we were heading home. He drove up to us and stopped." She clasped her hands in her lap to quiet the shaking.

"Did you ask him for a ride?"

"No, I didn't want to."

"Why not?"

She looked at him. He was making notes on a pad of paper. She cleared her throat. "I didn't think it was safe to get in his truck. He scared me. He was smoking pot." He stopped writing and glanced at her. There was an unspoken question in his eyes. "I don't smoke anything, Mr. Johnson, never have. We tried to walk away . . . but he got out and came after us." Her voice broke. She had to stop. Remembering it in detail brought back the taste of blood and the queasiness of fear. Her mother brought in a glass of water for her. It helped to moisten her throat.

"He enjoyed hurting me, Mr. Johnson." She looked at the man sitting across from her, the weight of what came next was bearing down her.

His brows deepened over his eyes, a kind smile on his lips. "I know this isn't easy, ma'am, but we have to have it all for the record."

She nodded and stared at the coloring book on the coffee table.

"You said he got out of his truck?"

"He grabbed Jamie and put him in the bed of his pickup. Then he came after me." She swallowed dreading the rest. "He threw me down and got on top of me. Said we were going to have a little fun . . .." She stopped and took a deep breath. "And . . . let . . . Jamie watch." She cleared her throat. "I was fighting him until he choked me. I couldn't breathe." Johnson nodded his head as he listened. "Jamie jumped on his back, trying to help me. He threw him off yelling he was going to kill him. He crawled off of me. I grabbed the cane and hit him."

"You struck him in the head?"

"Yes."

He wrote something. "How many times did you hit him with the cane?"

"Twice, the cane broke the second time. He was on the ground, unconscious. I thought I'd knocked him out."

"So you drove off in his pickup?"

"Yes."

"Was he alive when you left him?"

She looked him in the eye. "Yes, he was breathing."

Devon finished the last of her orange juice. She'd been home five days and had spent the last three in bed. She wasn't so shaky this morning. Maybe talking to the ranger had helped. It was all out on the table. The phone rang again. She could hear Ellie talking and the slam of the receiver.

When she walked by her bedroom door, Devon called out. "Who was that, Mom?"

Something had riled Ellie. Her cheeks were red. "News people! Act like I've got nothing better to do than answer the phone."

She must be the talk of the town. Devon decided she didn't care. Let them gossip.

"Asked me how we feel for heaven sakes! How do they think we feel . . . happy? Just makes me hoppin' mad. None of their damn business." Devon hadn't seen her mother mad enough to cuss since Alan walked out on her. For some reason, it struck her as funny. She smiled, her swollen cheek resisting it on one side. Ellie's tight lips gave way to a grin. "Didn't get to ask what Patsy said when she called a while ago."

"Said she'd just heard I'd been hurt. Her mother had called her. Wanted to know if I was okay, just like Tammy Jo and Loretta asked you yesterday." She shook her head. "I'm doing better but I'm not okay. I can't shake this feeling. It's hard to explain even to myself." She rubbed her forehead feeling a headache coming on.

Mama sat down on the edge of the bed. "When something awful happens, everybody feels mixed up. They don't know what to say to help."

"There isn't anything." She rested the back of her head on the headboard. "I'm tired of hurting all over."

"I bet you are." Mom stood up. "Rest. I'd better get back to the laundry."

"Where's Jamie?"

"He's out riding an old bike Hank brought over for him."

"Does he seem to be all right to you, Mom?"

"Yes, he's going to be fine, just like you will."

Devon used the assurance to bolster her own confidence. "I should get out of bed." She felt marooned in her bedroom. "When the pills take the edge off, I'd like to take a shower."

"I'll be back in ten minutes to give you a hand." Ellie left the bedroom.

She wasn't quite as stiff or sore as she'd been yesterday but bending in the middle or twisting her torso was out of the question. And she was weak. The walk from the bedroom to the shower took concentrated effort. Recuperating wasn't going to be as fast or painless as she wanted it to be.

After her shower, she shuffled down the hall with the speed and agility of the rust bound Tin Man. The only reason she didn't laugh at herself was it hurt. She caught a glimpse of Jamie playing fetch with Maggie through the living room window. It was a nice day, sunny but apparently cool. Jamie was wearing his jacket. The allure of sunshine, like a siren's song, had her inching her way down the front steps, in slippers and housecoat. She was quickly running out of steam but fresh air smelled good even in shallow breaths. Standing on the concrete walk that ran from the front door to the dusty driveway, she watched the drifting clouds waiting for Jamie to come running by. She looked past the end of the house wondering where he was.

The red of Pop's truck, parked in the shed, caught her eye. 'That your rig, honey?' It was Colton's voice. She covered her ears with her hands. His cruel laugh filled her head.

"No, stop." She turned too quickly, felt a sharp stab of pain in her side and grabbed the iron railing to keep from falling. No one had told her the truck was here. Concentrating on her feet, she watched the porch steps and reached for the door handle with a shaking hand. Once inside, she leaned against the door to close it and shut her eyes trying to calm her racing heart.

"What's wrong?" Her mother was rushing toward her. "You look positively bleached out." The fine lines between Mom's brows deepened.

So she looked like she felt. "I'm fine, really, just tired. I was on the porch getting some fresh air."

"You don't look fine. Did you fall?" She put her hand on Devon's shoulder. "You shouldn't go outside without some help. All those pain pills can make you woozy."

"I need to lie down for a while that's all." Ellie held her arm as they walked to the bedroom. "I noticed Pop's truck is back."

"Yes, Hank went out there yesterday, changed the tire and drove it home. He feels really bad about what happened to you."

Devon gingerly sat down on her bed. "Why?"

"He'd taken the flat tire off the truck and had it fixed the other day, before you came home. He left it in the shed meaning to replace the old spare but forgot about it. Figures that was one reason it blew. He's pretty unhappy with himself for not putting it in the pickup bed, at least. You'd have had it with you that way."

"Oh." She carefully leaned back bracing herself with her elbows. She couldn't wait for the day when it didn't hurt to lie down. "Tell him not to feel bad, Mom. I should have checked for a spare, especially before I drove off the place." She sighed with relief when she was totally flat.

"You rest. Be time for lunch soon." Ellie glanced over her shoulder as she left, clearly worried.

Devon closed her eyes, energy spent. If she were the sort to believe in fate, she'd have thought Hank's forgetting about the tire was proof that all the elements had come together to create her calamitous encounter with John Colton. If she did believe in it, she'd have to question the purpose it served. If she believed, she'd have a reason. If.

I t was day five A.C. She'd developed that abbreviation for After Colton, during the restless night to identify the collision of her life with John Colton's. The day his ended and hers changed forever. Devon thumbed through a magazine, trying to read. She sat up, pushed the pillows to cushion her back when she heard new voices. Clattering footsteps on the den floor warned her someone was coming so she pulled the covers up.

Aunt Louise marched in wearing green polyester slacks and a bright flowered blouse of red, orange, and blue that partially hid the cast on her arm. Her head was wrapped in a yellow terry cloth turban like an aging Carmen Miranda without the fruit or engaging smile.

"Good heavens, you look awful!" Her black penciled on eyebrows and cherry red lipstick looked more extreme than usual without the fluff of dyed hair to soften the contours of her narrow face as she peered at her.

Devon counted to ten. Her least favorite relative was blessed with the ability to piss her off in an instant. "I guess I do. Where's Gerry?" Devon knew he had to be around somewhere. He was like a lap dog.

"Oh, he'll be in here in a minute. He's getting a cup of coffee from Ellie. He wanted me to make sure you were decent first. You know how men are. We're on our way to the beauty shop. With this cast on my arm, I can't do a thing." She put on her glasses giving Devon a more thorough once-over. Her skinny eyebrows wrinkled over her narrowed eyes. "My goodness, you are black and blue everywhere." She pursed her lips. Her mouth shriveled like a red dried-up prune until she opened it. "What in the world did you do to make that man so angry?"

The question hit her like a punch in the stomach, and she gasped. She grabbed a handful of the sheet lying across her hips in a surge of anger and pressed her arm against her aching side.

"I didn't do anything." Her answer shot out. The bitter tone had no effect on her aunt's expression. Auntie was reading the label on the bottle of painkillers she'd picked up on the bedside table.

"Well, I can't imagine a man starting something without a good reason." Her self-righteous tone matched her cool sideways glance as she set the pills down.

"You don't have much imagination then, Louise."

Her aunt turned around at Ellie's sharp remark. Her uncle and her mother had walked into the bedroom.

"My goodness, you did get yourself in a heap of trouble." Her uncle's smile faded as a flicker of discomfort crossed his face.

"I told you she was hurt by that horrible man, Gerald." Mom frowned at him. "He was crazy."

Devon slid down the sheets to lie flat and moaned. She prayed her mother would get rid of them quickly. She didn't want to see or talk to Louise, ever.

Louise had turned toward her husband. "Gerry, we need to go. You know how Shirley is if I'm late for my appointment, she'll rush and make a mess of me for sure."

Devon glanced at the vain woman hoping Shirley would singe every hair off the old biddy's head.

"Yes, y'all better go. Devon needs to rest." Her mother's voice betrayed her displeasure.

"You take care of yourself, dear." Louise was walking out the door when she said it. Gerry followed her out in silence.

Mom stood in the doorway. "Be right back after I wring her neck."

Devon stared at the ceiling. Her aunt's question, her whole attitude, was a shock. A woman should understand. She hadn't encouraged him. She couldn't believe Louise thought she would. 'It won't do no good to fight.' She could hear him whispering. Tears filled her eyes and rolled down the side of her face.

"Don't cry, Devon." Ellie sat down on the bed. "I heard the tail end of what Louise said. Ignore her. She's a thoughtless, simpleminded old woman. She has no idea what you went through."

Devon blinked back the tears. "Will other people think I gave him some reason to attack us?" She looked at her mother's face trying to judge the truth.

Mom sighed, a gentle smile following it. "Of course not, honey. Anybody with sense knows better." She leaned over and kissed her forehead.

"It must have been in the paper by now." Her mother nodded. "What did it say?" Devon needed to know.

"There was one short paragraph yesterday, that was all. I was going to show it to you when you were feeling better. It said the two of you were assaulted by a suspected drug dealer when your truck broke down, that he'd died, and you'd been treated for minor injuries. That was it." She paused and handed her a tissue. "Now, dry those eyes and don't worry. Nobody else in town is as stupid as Louise."

After a week of taking it easy, Devon could prowl around the house without as much pain. Her arms and legs weren't so sore and stiff anymore and the bruises were fading. Only her midsection required special care. Bending over or lifting more than a feather was out of the question. A sneeze or a cough sent pain streaking from front to back.

It was a warm afternoon. She sat outside on the front porch watching Jamie play on the swing and ride that old bike up and down the driveway. Growing up, she'd run free and never considered being afraid of anything. She'd wanted to believe it was still that way, untouched by the harsh realities that plagued every metropolis. She'd never thought of the ranch as isolated, or worried about being easy prey to outsiders here. It had been foolish to be so blind.

As happy as he looked at the moment, she wished now she hadn't brought him home. The peaceful respite in the country for a few months she'd envisioned had gone terribly wrong. Things dark and forbidding had defiled it. She would never take safety for granted again. Before finding a new place to settle down, she had to think things through. Find a spot with a little wiggle room for her son and neighbors next door. Maybe she should consider working for a smaller company in a smaller city. Perhaps that would be a better fit.

That night, Jamie woke up and climbed into bed with her.

"What's wrong, honey?" He snuggled up beside her.

"There's monsters in my room."

"What kind?"

"Ugly, hairy ones."

"Oh. Think they'll come in here?"

"No, they're scared of you."

"Good, then I won't have to run them off tonight."

"In the morning?"

"If they're still there. I'm sleepy."

"Me too. Mom, can you play with me tomorrow?" He yawned.

"Sure, we'll find a game in the closet." She realized that wasn't what he needed. "Granny said there is a boy your age, named Tommy, just down the road. Maybe we should invite him over to play."

"Okay." His voice trailed off as he fell asleep. She put her hand on his chest and made a promise. She'd do her best to keep the monsters away by finding a safe place. A place with policemen and firemen close by, and street lights, and fenced-in backyards, and neighbors who kept an eye out for children walking home from school. She'd search until she found it.

It was Saturday, Ellie was humming and cooking. The whole house was filled with the satisfying aromas of fried chicken, biscuits, and black-eyed peas. Now that it didn't hurt to eat, Devon's mouth watered, anxious to taste everything. Sitting down with the feast on the table and the sunshine pouring in the window, she was determined to have a normal meal with cheerful, lighthearted conversation. Everything tasted wonderful so it turned out to be easy. Jamie ate both chicken legs and a big pile of mashed potatoes.

"Devon, when I called over to the school about getting Jamie enrolled they said you'd need his school records from Minneapolis. Hope you can find them."

"They're in my file box in the closet, Mom". Of course, she knew where they were.

Ellie got up and carried her plate and the bowl of black-eyed peas to the counter by the sink. "I can take him over there Monday morning if you aren't feeling up to it."

She looked over at her son. "No, we'll all go. I'll just put a bucket over my head to hide what's left of my shiner." She got a good belly laugh out of Jamie with that.

Her mother brought over the chocolate cake she'd made. "Did you know, Miss Thompson is still teaching first grade?"

"You're kidding." Devon's mind instantly fabricated a picture of a shriveled up, little old lady with a hearing aid. "She must be a thousand years old by now."

"Really?" Jamie's eyes opened wide with sudden interest. That set off a spasm of laughter in Devon.

"Oh, of course not, Jamie!" Ellie gave an exasperated chuckle and waggled her finger at her.

Devon clutched her side. "Oh, that hurts."

"Serves you right. She was all of twenty-three years old when you had her, Devon!"

"Really?" Devon was trying for the life of her to conjure up some image of Miss Thompson. "I guess I wasn't a great judge of age in first grade." She gave Jamie a quick wink that she immediately regretted because it pulled the tender, newly healed cut above her eye.

After lunch, Ellie and Jamie coaxed her out of the house with the promise of a surprise. Devon sat on a wooden bench by the corral as instructed. Jamie came out from behind the barn riding Dulce. He was beaming, ready to bust with joy. It warmed her to see that huge smile, the pride in his straight back in the saddle, his hands holding the reins just so. This is one of the reasons she'd come home, to let him breathe fresh air, learn to ride across the pasture on a horse, and see the wonder in the wild places as she had growing up. The sweet old mare carrying her son was a far cry from the spirited filly her father had given her for her twelfth birthday. She was glad it was Dulce giving him his first taste of horsemanship.

"Hank and I have been giving him pointers on riding." Mom sat down beside her to watch Jamie ride around in circles. "I need to go over to Jessie's and check on her. She's getting awfully feeble. Think she's called over here every day to ask about you. Why don't you come along, Devon? Do you good to get out."

Her mother thought fresh air was the cure for all that ailed you. While it was true that she was looking better, most of the visible bruises were a stylish yellow green, she was quite content to stay hidden from the world in her scruffy jeans and sweatshirt. She was uncomfortable with the thought of leaving the ranch. It seemed a childish admission for someone who'd driven and flown all over the United States by herself but she was, ridiculous or not.

"I don't have anything that goes with black and blue, Mom."

"We can stop and get Jamie an ice cream cone on the way back." Her mother added the famous last words. "We won't be long."

She was wavering, realizing she had to take Jamie to school in two days. And her great aunt had always been Devon's favorite relative.

"We can get an ice cream cone?" Jamie and his steed had come to a halt by the gate. Old Dulce had had enough of circles and Jamie's attention had been redirected by his sweet tooth.

The first trip out the front gate would be the hardest, she reasoned. She had to get used to it. "Okay, I'll go but with the understanding that we buy the ice cream and leave. I don't want to be on display at the Tastee Freeze and have to make small talk, Mom. You know everybody and his brother goes by the place." She wasn't ready for the stares she was sure she'd get or ready to answer the inevitable questions.

Ellie smiled. "Deal. Jamie let's take that saddle off and give Dulce some oats before we let her out in the pasture. "

About forty-five minutes later, they drove off in the Cadillac. Jamie had a small box of toys with him in the backseat for entertainment. He'd become something of a gypsy, keeping his favorite things close at hand. She didn't remember doing that. Of course, she hadn't been out of the state until she'd left for college, one suitcase in hand.

She concentrated on landmarks to avoid thinking of anything else. Finally, she could see the buildings of Blanco Springs up ahead. "When we came into town the other day, it was practically empty. I'm amazed anyone stays."

"It's a nice, sleepy little town." Her mother smiled.

She'd grown up hearing nothing but worry about dry wells and sick animals. Every decision tied to the price of beef. "Life isn't idyllic here, Mom." She could see the scarce number of items on the shelves in the feed store as they drove by. No one parked in front. They were one step ahead of financial disaster. "These businesses are struggling to scratch out a living. That new store doesn't have a chance."

"Doesn't cost so much to get by in this part of the country."

She looked at the dusty store windows all the way up the block. The day-to-day worry about how to pay for a roof over their heads had been too much for a lot of people.

"That depends on how you want to live, Mom. I'd need some choices, some opportunities to keep from going stir crazy. Haven't you ever wanted to live someplace else or do something different?" It was a question she'd asked before.

"I've traveled to visit you. I don't like big cities. They're too crowded. I'm comfortable here."

That was all the answer she got. It was easier to stay in familiar surroundings than adjust to something different. She'd moved enough to be familiar with the feeling of uncertainty that being a stranger caused, but it hadn't kept her from going. She didn't know if her mother was afraid of sticking her neck out or was simply easily satisfied. With Pop gone and the future of the ranch to decide one day, Ellie would have to do something. So would she. She didn't have a safe haven anymore, even here.

They drove two blocks, turned down a narrow dirt road and pulled into the driveway of Jessie's small, white frame house. Devon's great aunt had lived here for at least forty years. If this had been anywhere else, she'd have been in a rest home. Instead, Ellie and the neighbors kept an eye on her. Independence was valued and everyone was entitled to it. It was one thing Devon held dear too. A path of flat rocks led them to the front door. Her mother opened it and went in. Devon trailed behind with Jamie.

Mrs. Jessie Mae Lee, wearing a blue housedress, was sitting in her worn upholstered chair, positioned so she could watch the road. There were three flat pin curls in her thin bangs. She held up her arm as they walked in.

"Well, looky here who's comin' to see me."

"How are you feelin' this mornin', Ms. Jessie?" Ellie spoke louder than usual and bent over to kiss her cheek. "I brought Devon and her son, Jamie, to see you."

"Come closer and let me see you, gal." Jessie smiled broadly, displaying her own fine, white teeth and held out her hand.

Devon sat down on the edge of a chair next to her taking the cool, delicate fingers in her hand. Her skin was so transparent, the blood vessels running down the back of her hand stood out sharply.

"Hello, Aunt Jessie." Devon leaned toward her. This tiny, frail woman had raised four children by two husbands and lost them all. She had lived through her troubles with a legendary determination and had always served as an example when things in Devon's life had gone wrong. Now she was living out her last days with a smile.

"I hear you had a fella try to hurt you?" Jessie peered at Devon's face. "Looks like he got a few licks in."

Her body tensed. She was perched on the edge of the cushion bending forward in an uncomfortable position. "Yes, ma'am."

"Read in the paper, he won't be hurtin' anybody else." Jessie smiled and squeezed her hand. "Good. You stuck up for yourself. When a man gets mean, a woman's got to fight to protect her children. Yes, sir."

Devon relaxed. "It's good to see you again."

She patted Devon's hand, her eyes seeming to look far off. "Nothin' worse than losing a child, Lordy, nothin' worse. I know that all too well and so does your mother."

Ellie was standing on the other side of Jessie's chair. Devon glanced at her mother's face. There was the brief shadow of sadness in the droop of the eyelids shielding her hazel eyes. It pressed against Devon's heart as it passed. A short burst of canned laughter from the television drew her attention and she turned. Jamie was keeping his distance watching a game show on the little black and white television. Aunt Jessie hadn't spotted him. Devon stood up and took his hand.

"Jamie's here to see you too. You remember him." She pulled him closer until he was directly in front of the lady.

"Well, let's get a look at you." She leaned forward and took his hands in hers. "My, oh my. You're growing up so tall. How old are you now?"

"Six."

"Well, you are on your way to bein' a man then. Bet you'd like a cookie. Devon, go in yonder and help him get one." She pointed toward the kitchen and turned away from them. "Ellie, I need you to read somethin' for me." She reached for a stack of letters on a little table beside her chair.

She took Jamie in the kitchen. He didn't need a cookie but her aunt would be hurt if they didn't at least go through the motions. She looked around the kitchen noticing the few dirty dishes left in the sink and wiped the crumbs off the counter. Jamie captured the black cricket madly chirping by the screen door and released it on the back porch while Devon quickly washed the dishes and put them away. Jessie's small patch of grass needed to be mowed. With a sinking feeling, she hoped her mother wouldn't end up like this. Staying alone in the ranch house as it fell into disrepair, eventually becoming a ruin like her grandparent's house on the ranch. Devon shook her head at the idea.

"Come inside, Jamie." They walked into the parlor together. Mom was reading a letter out loud for Jessie. Once they were sure Aunt Jessie didn't need anything, they left the lady to her memories and the chatter of another game show that filled up her quiet little house.

Ellie promised she needed just a couple of things as they pulled into Beasley's Market. Shopping was a quick task in the small store with its creaking, wooden floor. The three or four customers and the cashier women she recognized but couldn't remember the names of now, stopped talking and watched her as she walked in. They were staring. The nice thing about a small town was everybody knew you. It was also the worse thing about a small town and one of the reasons she left. When the whispering started, she moved quickly down an aisle to hide behind the shelved goods while looking for Jamie's favorite cereal. She knew they were talking about her but there wasn't a thing she could do about it. Anything unusual added some spice to a lifetime spent in close quarters with the same people. While she understood their curiosity, the wounds were too fresh, the memories too uncomfortable to discuss with anyone. She was anxious to leave.

Suzy Atkins walked in. Devon saw her through a row of boxes and shook her head. Great. The ex-mayor's daughter, senior class president and all-round girl wonder was one of the last people she wanted to see looking like this. The Atkins women were the biggest blabbermouths within a hundred mile radius. The county would get a full description of her now.

Devon tried hiding behind the tall potato chip display. Unfortunately Suzy spotted her in record time and walked over to investigate, fulfilling her chosen role in the universe of being a pain in the butt. Devon took in the full scale, plumper version of the high school Suzy standing in front of her: a perky cotton dress, matching shoes and purse, and newly coiffed strawberry curls. Didn't look like she'd changed much. Still conniving and using men to get what she wanted more than likely, a chip off dear Aunt Louise.

"Oh, Devon, it is you!" She chewed up something in her mouth and swallowed. "I was so sorry to hear about that awful man hurting you! I just can't imagine! You were so brave! Goodness sakes, just look at you, poor thing!" As irritating as Suzy could be, she was trying to be kind, maybe.

Devon was stuck accepting her, perhaps, heartfelt sympathy. At least she wasn't like 'auntie dearest,' assuming she'd asked for trouble.

"We all prayed for you at church the other night. How are you and that little boy of yours ever going to make it all alone? Is that him by the candy?" Suzy glanced toward the checkout counter and so did she. Jamie was immobile in front of the three tiered candy rack.

Suzy's comment about handling life all alone rubbed her the wrong way, which wasn't hard for Suzy. More than likely she had hopes of discovering some tidbit to share at the beauty shop.

"We're fine." Devon added a little bite to her response thinking Suzy might get the hint to leave her the hell alone. Unfazed, the redhead smiled sweetly exhibiting perfect dimples joined by a host of freckles sprinkled liberally across her powdered nose and stood there waiting to be filled in. Change of tactics. "How are your kids, Suzy?"

She seemed pleased to have an opportunity to fill a new set of ears. Suzy took a big breath, displaying a strangely green tongue, and began an exuberant monologue.

"Oh, Arthur and Dottie Ruth are doing so well. I hate to brag but that son of mine is going to jump a grade next year. And oh, he wants to be preacher, can you believe it?"

Devon watched her mother's progress toward the cashier. Jamie had a handful of candy. Her mother must have forgotten how to say 'no'. That gave Devon a reasonable excuse to leave and subtract a few items at the checkout counter.

Closing the car door with a slam, Devon looked over at her mother. "Next time you go to town, don't ask me to go with you. I've been gawked at enough for a while."

Ellie chuckled. "You can handle a little curiosity, can't you? Besides, they don't mean any harm, you know that."

"I don't like being stared at. No telling what they are thinking."

"I've got to put in some gas before we go back. Be driving Jamie to school day after tomorrow."

"Right." Devon sighed. Another gauntlet to run on the road to a normal life. She'd make it, one cautious step at a time.

Jamie chimed in from the backseat. "Hey, what about the ice cream?"

They pulled in to the Handy Mart on the outskirts of town after a stop at the Tastee Freeze. Ellie filled the tank and went to pay for the gas. Devon and Jamie waited in the car. Mom left the windows down and radio on. Devon was listening to an ancient country anthem to wine and women on the radio.

"Hey, Jamie, how's the pitching arm?"She was startled by a man's voice.

Devon straightened up and looked back at a man walking up to the car. He was wearing jeans and a short sleeved shirt. Jamie was hanging out the rear window.

"Hi, got any more jokes?" He was smiling, as if he knew the man. That confused her.

The stranger laughed and pulled off his sunglasses. He was friendly, open. "Not on me." He seemed familiar, yet she couldn't place him. He may have noticed confusion on her face when he glanced at her.

"Hi. I'm Dr. Owen." He raised his eyebrows waiting for recognition. "I examined Jamie's arm in the hospital."

"Oh. Right." Devon could feel the blush warm her cheeks. Ellie walked up to him. "This is Dr. Owen, Mom. He took care of Jamie at the hospital."

Ellie was smiling now. "Nice to meet you, doctor. Are you new to the hospital?"

"Yes, ma'am. Started a few months ago. Well, I have to get some things and run. Almost time for my shift. Nice to meet you." He nodded politely to her mother. He looked back toward the car. "Take it easy, Jamie." He walked into the store.

"He is a handsome fella, don't you think?" Ellie looked over with too much sparkle in her eye as they drove off.

Devon shook her head. "I didn't notice. Considering my luck with men, I'm not in the market." Her mother had been talking about Devon meeting a nice man and getting married again ever since the divorce. She didn't want to start that up again.

"I haven't seen him before but I've heard about him." Ellie laughed. "He's the only unmarried doctor at the clinic. Every mother in the county with a single daughter over seventeen knows about him thanks to Joanne's House of Beauty. Poor man. They'll pester the tar out of him."

She laid clean clothes out on the top of the dresser for Jamie's first day of school. He walked in from the bathroom in his pajamas. "Teeth all brushed?"

"Uh-huh." He eyed the jeans and sat down on his bed. "Mom, do I have to go tomorrow?"

"Yes, you've missed two weeks not counting the Presidents' Day holiday." She glanced at him as she put down the socks trying not to read her own fears into his question. "Nervous about going to a new school?"

"I don't know anybody."

She sat down on the bed beside him. "You know Tommy. After tomorrow, you'll know everybody else." She kissed him, turned on the night-light and stood up.

"Mama, how can you tell bad guys from good guys?"

The question stopped all thought of walking out. She was at a loss for words, floundering, wishing there was a foolproof checklist to make them both feel better, safe.

"They say at school to be careful of strangers . . . but I only know Uncle Hank and Sheriff Buck here." He was moving his teddy bear's arms up and down as he talked in the dim light.

She sat down beside him. "It's not easy. We both know that." She put her hand on his arm. "I guess, you have to watch what someone does and see how it makes you feel to decide."

"Like when the man got out of his truck." He glanced at her.

She smiled, encouraged he understood. "Yes, just like that." His instincts were better than she'd imagined. He understood caution now. It was essential in facing this new world of theirs.

"The sheriff said there are more good people than bad."

"Well, he should know."

He put the bear down. "Will you go inside with me?"

She brushed her fingers through his hair. "I was planning on it. I want to see your room. I'll pick you up after school too."

"Good." He rolled on his side clutching his bear. "'Night, Mama."

"'Night, honey, sweet dreams." She kissed him again. She'd help him be brave tomorrow. TJ had done that for her. He'd taken her hand and walked with her to her room that very first day of school. It was what family was all about, after all.

The shabby motel curtains covered the window but the flash of the blinking neon sign outside came in around the edges. Joe shoved the lying bastard backward into the wall. His forearm pressed against the man's throat forcing the jaw up so he had to look him in the eye.

"Don't fuck with me, Delbert. Johnny told me you were helping him hide the stash."

A long strand of dark greasy hair hung down the side of Delbert's face. Sounds sputtered out of the man's open mouth. Joe relaxed the pressure so he could talk.

"I ain't lying, I swear. I weren't with him that day. Them cops was thick as ticks after . . . you know, but ain't easy findin' nothin' out there." He was sweating; his eyes blinking like a scared rabbit. "They'd be crowing if they had it."

He held up his knife, close to Delbert's face. The man flinched. He scraped it along the day's worth of dark stubble on the trembling chin of his brother's buddy.

"If it's gone, I'll string your guts on a barbed wire fence."

"It's gotta be there, Joe." Delbert's breath was cheap bourbon and cigarettes. "I'll show you where we been hidin' it."

Joe stepped back, his open knife still in his hand. He looked the scrawny worm up and down, deciding he didn't have the balls to lie or the brains to find a buyer. It was hard to believe Johnny had even talked to such a useless pile of shit. He should have known better than to think

Johnny had changed. The air conditioner in the window of the motel room was grinding out a moldy stench.

"You can trust me, Joe." The weakling rubbed his throat. "You'll see, I'm a good man to have around."

"You find the stash. I'll let you live." Joe folded the blade of his knife. The fool smiled showing his crooked, tobacco-stained teeth. He'd kill the idiot later so there wouldn't be any loose ends left.

Devon was content to stay on the ranch, a never-never land sheltered by routine chores to keep her busy and familiar faces to help her feel safe. She was physically stronger, her body healing. The nightmares ended but thoughts of Colton still crept in disturbing whatever progress she made to forget. Her briefcase and files were in her closet, out of sight. She was too distracted to search for employment. It took a confidence she didn't have at this point. She wasn't sure when she could leave. It just wasn't now. She lived one day at a time.

Every morning, she drove Jamie to the bus stop on the county road and waited with him. She couldn't leave him out there alone. She didn't ask if it would bother him. It didn't matter because it was simply impossible for her.

He liked school and quickly became pals with two classmates on his bus from nearby ranches. Sometimes, Tommy would ride his bike over to play, using a narrow path worn along the county road and across a pasture. Most days, Jamie entertained himself. He fed Dulce and rode bareback around the yard, shadowed Hank when he could, and played with the barn cats, Calico and Samson. She'd wanted Jamie to have a taste of the childhood she'd known, feel the joy she remembered racing across the pasture on Dulce's back with the wind on her face, and at times he did. But moments of darkness would creep into his dreams and wake him. They both needed to find peace somehow.

She started riding again. Hank had asked her to take Ginger out for a little exercise since he was too busy. There was no place as beautiful as the ranch in spring. The rolling hills were covered with green grass and bluebonnets as March edged into April. The blooms spread a thick, lustrous blanket across the pasture while the fiery heads of Indian paintbrush started poking up in places like exclamation points.

She rode Ginger to count the newborn calves, letting Dulce tag along for the exercise when Jamie wasn't with her. There were more than a hundred calves and pregnant heifers to locate. Jamie compared looking for calves to an Easter egg hunt. The newest ones were often nestled down in the grass, not far from their mothers, and each was distinctly decorated with colors ranging from a rusty red to a pecan shell brown with an array of white patches as brilliant and pure as fresh snow in the sun.

There wasn't a man-made sound to be heard most days. Nothing to spook the grazing cattle or the cooing gray doves on the fence or the deer bedded down under the trees by the creek. Nothing to spook her either but the lingering specter of a dead man just beyond the fences.

Devon parked the car. Ellie had been very quiet on the drive to the cemetery but Jamie's constant chatter had given her little reason or opportunity to say anything. As soon as she opened the car door, she missed the air conditioning. The weather front from the Gulf made the air thick enough to stir with a spoon. The clouds, like tufts of cotton candy stuck together, clung to the muggy blue sky unable to budge or shed a drop of rain. Jamie raced ahead of them, weaving between the headstones, toward the two oak trees.

Reading the familiar family names to herself as they passed, Devon walked beside her mother toward the northern edge of the cemetery. It was a beautiful place, peaceful. From this hill, she could see the winding path of the river and the lacy fringe of cypress growing along its banks.

"Which rock is Grandpa's, Granny?" He yelled his question from the shade ahead.

Ellie shook her head and chuckled. "Little boys are so rambunctious."

There wasn't anybody else around but she wished he'd stayed with her. He hadn't knocked over any flowers or disturbed anything but some folks didn't appreciate children running around in a graveyard. "Just wait there, Jamie, and we'll show you." He entertained himself trying to reach the lowest limb of the sprawling live oak as they walked toward him.

Resting under the shady edge of the branches, the graves were side by side. Jamie kneeled down and touched the chiseled letters in the pink llano granite reading the names and dates out loud.

"I still think of TJ as a boy. Hard to believe he would have been forty years old this month." Mom's voice was very soft. "I remember how he looked when he was born, and your father's smile."

Her comment sparked Devon's memory of crushing disappointment the day of Jamie's birth. Her joy muted by the cold expression on Alan's face. A tragedy expressed in silence. How she wished it had been different. When she looked down, the bright colors of the bouquet in her hand caught her eye.

They'd brought flowers for the graves. Ellie had the bouquet for Dad. She held one for TJ. She squatted down next to the faded plastic vase by his stone and focused on arranging the fresh flowers in the new vase.

"What does this say, Mom?" Jamie pointed to the words under her brother's name.She cleared her throat to read the phrase her mother had chosen.

"Taken too soon to meet his Lord."

"What does that mean?"

She looked at her endlessly curious son wondering how many chances he'd take as a young man. It was too frightening a thought to consider for long. "It means we weren't ready for him to die." She brushed away the dust on her pant legs, stood up and looked down at the river.

As hard as it was to lose Pop, there was some comfort in the knowledge that he'd lived a long, productive life. It had been different the bleak day they'd buried her big brother. In one reckless moment, his life was over and she'd had a small, secret part in it. He was a promise unfulfilled, the pastor had said, led astray by sin. Those words evoked a cold anger that day. She could feel the remnants of it, a hard, tight knot. Soaked in grief after the casket had been lowered, she'd left her brother behind and God too.

"But God's the boss, huh?" Jamie pulled on her arm to get her attention. "Does he like to watch the ranch too, like Grandpa?" His eyes, opened wide, watched her waiting for a reply.

"I hope so, Jamie." She put her hand on his shoulder wondering if TJ had found some kind of peace. He'd robbed the family of it.

"What are you saying about your grandpa?" Ellie had been so quiet Devon had almost forgotten she was close by. They both turned to face her.

With an enthusiastic bounce in each step, Jamie walked over to her. "Mama told me Grandpa isn't in the sky because he likes being a good ghost at the ranch where he can watch us do stuff."

Her jaw relaxed enough to let her smile. The puzzled scrunch of her mother's eyebrows, however, signaled some confusion. Devon had nothing to apologize for except forgetting how to speak Baptist. Heaven was open to interpretation since nobody ever came back to clarify things. Before she could explain, Ellie smiled.

"I hadn't quite thought of it that way, Jamie." Her mother touched his head, her fingertips smoothing down his hair. "But I imagine your grandfather did. He and your mother seemed to see things the same way." Ellie glanced in her direction briefly before surveying the view from the hilltop.

With a quick jab of irritation, Devon wanted to disagree with her. She rattled down a washboard of differences starting with women's rights. Only when it came to church, did they completely agree. But she looked away and said nothing. Her blouse was clinging to her skin. It was too warm and humid in the afternoon sun to argue.

"I guess we should go." Ellie sighed and looked down at the headstones. She picked up the old plastic vases. "Goodbye, sweethearts. I'll be back."

Jamie took off for the car. Rather than calling after him, she let him run and walked beside her mother across the field of stones.

They hadn't been home long when the phone rang. Devon picked up the desk phone on the second ring. "Hello."

"May I speak to Devon Taylor, please?"

"Speaking."

"Hi, Devon, it's Janet Blake, your headhunter extraordinaire. I'm glad I found you."

"Oh, hello, I didn't recognize your voice, Janet." She swallowed. The distasteful subject of her ex-boss would be coming up. The usual surge of indignation rushed through her veins when she thought of cleaning out her desk. She sat down.

"I just heard you left the job in Minneapolis. What happened?"

She'd never worked for or with any man like Leonard Jamison. He was a straight-faced liar determined to get her into bed. She hadn't encouraged him, far from it. It wasn't clear what he was up to for several months. He'd tried to use his position of power just like John Colton had used his fists. She'd handled the difficult situation in a professional manner but it had been terribly stressful. Her stomach still hadn't recovered from the experience.

"My boss and I had a difference of opinion on my duties after hours. I think you can fill in the blanks, Janet. When my complaints were ignored, I felt my only option was to quit."

"That can be a dicey situation. In a company that size, the smartest thing to do is leave sometimes. Don't imagine it was easy."

She sighed. "No, it wasn't." She leaned back in the chair relieved she could skip the details and put that chapter behind her. "I decided not to stay in the Twin Cities. Too cold up there."

Janet laughed. "That's why I moved to California twenty years ago."

"I called your office before I left, but was told you were sick."

"I had back surgery right after Christmas that forced me to lay low for a while. Had a stack of work piled to the ceiling when I got back to the office. I tried to call you the other day just to touch base on the new job. Surprised me when they said you'd left. Got this phone number from them. Do you have something else lined up or are you still in the market for a new opportunity?"

She searched for some shorthand for her situation. "I'm staying with my mother right now. I've had some family issues to deal with and an injury that has slowed me down."

"You're on the mend, though?"

She stared at the small print on the desk calendar. "Yes, but it's been a slow process."

"I can identify with that. When will you be able to go back to work?"

She rubbed her fingers back-and-forth across her forehead. "Not before June. I promised my son he could finish the school year here."

"Not a problem. I've got a couple of things in the early stages, most-ly West Coast. I can check with my Texas connections too if you'd like."

Devon smiled to herself. Janet was still a go-getter. "I would appre-ciate it, Janet. I haven't had a chance to look for anything yet." She didn't admit she'd been hiding. She could hear a beep in the background.

"My two o'clock is here, Devon. Got to run. I'll be in touch." The dial tone buzzed in her ear. Janet was off to the races with someone else.

She hung up the receiver and stared straight ahead not focusing on anything. Talking to Janet stirred up memories of the irritations she'd put up with in California: being jostled in packed elevators, sitting in an office in a glass covered skyscraper with windows that didn't open for a breath of fresh air, racing through a hectic day jittery from too much coffee, being stranded in daily traffic jams, going to sleep late, exhausted. She enjoyed working but not like that.

Ellie walked into the den with the trash sack in her hands. "Who was that?"

Devon took a deep breath. "Janet Blake, my old headhunter in Los Angeles. She wanted to know if I was in the market for a job."

"And?" Her mother stopped beside the desk.

"I told her I was recuperating from an injury. I didn't go into detail."

"Good. You aren't strong enough to work yet." Ellie nodded her head, picked up the can by the desk and emptied the wastepaper into the bag.

She glanced at the numbers on the phone thinking her mother wouldn't be pleased with the rest. "I asked her to keep me in mind if she had something promising after Jamie was finished with school."

Ellie straightened up still holding the empty can. Her face registered surprise with the lift of her eyebrows. "You want to move back to California?" She sounded disappointed emphasizing those last three words. She had a habit of asking a question when she didn't agree.

"Not really, but she might come up with a terrific job. I'd have to con-sider it." Devon didn't have much choice at this point.

"I wish you could live closer . . . but I suppose, you'll do what you have to do." With lips firm and straight, Ellie closed her mouth, picked up the trash and walked toward the kitchen. Devon had the feeling she'd wanted to comment but had thought better of it. It was a relief not to argue about it right now.

Her mother didn't know the chances of her accepting a job in Los Angeles again were microscopic. At least, they were today. Devon didn't know how she'd feel tomorrow, or next week, or next month. She wouldn't say 'no'. She couldn't say 'yes'. She hated how upside down she felt.

It had been one of those prickly PMS mornings when everything irritated her from the moment she'd crawled out of bed. She got Jamie off to school and the first load of clothes in the washer. Ellie rushed into the kitchen from outside muttering something under her breath. Devon didn't want to ask her what was wrong. She heard water running in the kitchen.

"Some critter scattered the hens and ate the eggs, must be one of those blasted coyotes. Not a single egg left." Ellie was talking to Devon but not looking toward the laundry room.

"Well, we have more than we can eat anyway." Devon walked past her mother standing at the sink and headed for the bedrooms to get the sheets off the bed.

"You sound like those people on television worrying more about protecting varmints than feeding humans." The bite in her mother's voice made it clear she didn't like the comment.

Devon stopped beside the dining table more than ready to snap back. "It isn't the end of world if you lose a batch of eggs."

"It's money down the drain and food we can't put on the table. Are you so citified that you've forgotten?" Ellie's hands were on her hips.

"I still remember where food comes from."

Ellie crossed her arms frowning at her. "Guess when you're sitting in an office twenty floors off the ground all day it's easy to forget someone else has to pay for the damage wild animals cause."

"That's where most of the jobs are." She huffed. "Everybody can't live out in the sticks. And most people wouldn't want to anyway."

"From where I'm standing, city life has done nothing but make you miserable."

They were heading for the same old argument. Devon held her arms out straight like a preacher begging for money. "Well, this is a long way from paradise, Mom."

"It's fine enough for most of us."

That familiar, what's wrong with you tone of voice pissed her off. "Well, you aren't me." She stared at her mother.

"No, I'm not. I'm proud of what your father and I built. It fed and clothed you and TJ."

Ah, her sainted brother. "TJ didn't want to be stuck out here either." She looked down and rested her fingertips on the dining table to avoid her mother's eyes.

"That's a lie." Ellie snapped back, good and angry now.

She raised her head wondering how different her mother's memories were of those days. "Then why did he and Pop go round and round about it, Mom? Think he wanted to worry about rain, or the price of beef, or be held hostage by the bank like everybody else around here?"

"He was here helping your dad when he died."

Devon stared at TJ's chair to the right of Pop's remembering their loud arguments. "He didn't want to be. Why do you think he was drunk?" She shot a look at her mother to see if the truth hit home.

Ellie stiffened. "Don't you ever say that!" She scowled at her. "You've turned your back on everything you used to love. We never should have let you go to California." Mom turned away from her, facing the sink. "All that money and those fancy things blinded you. No man around here wouldn't have walked out on you."

Liquid fire, skin deep, rushed through her, new armor protecting an old wound. She slammed her fist on the table. "I didn't marry Alan for his money and you know it."

Ellie's face was red. "Maybe not, but you liked spending it."

Devon threw up her hands, too exasperated for mere words. "We worked hard and had plenty to spend. What was wrong with that? I haven't touched a dime of his since the divorce." Her mother's expression was still hard and angry. Devon grabbed the back of the wooden chair in front of her. "Don't expect me to stay once school is out."

"I've never stood in your way." Her lips, pressed together tight, formed a straight, unyielding line.

No, Mom just judged everything she did. There was no satisfied feeling that she'd made her point, just a knot in her stomach. "Good." She pushed the chair back against the edge of the table with a bump.

With a dark look clouding her face, Ellie spun headed for the kitchen door. "I've got work to do."

"So do I." She shouted after her.

The screen door slammed and it was suddenly quiet.

Devon marched through the house and out the front door. She slowed down on the county road and finally stopped well past the mailbox. The shoulder was an unmanageable tangle of dry weeds. The mailman's truck wheel had worn a rut down to the rock. Staring at the narrow two-lane, she was stranded between feeling justifiably bitchy and lousy mean. The sharp words, hers and her mother's echoed in the emptiness. She walked back to the metal box and looked in. No mail, it was too early anyway. She slapped the door closed.

When she looked straight ahead, the sharp metal knots of the barbed wire strung on the crooked post oak fence reminded her of what they'd really argued about; this place and leaving. She'd been awake thinking about it most of the night after talking to Janet. She had to make a living to protect her future and Jamie's but this time using new rules. She'd get home at a reasonable hour and make time for her son. With his trust money for college, he'd have a good start in life. It was all he had of his father but at least he had that.

She paced a while, thinking. Every penny her mother had was in the ranch. No telling what she might get for it. Mom would come live with her eventually since TJ wasn't around. Be easier if it wasn't a million miles from here. She was responsible for all of them in one way or the other. She put both hands on the back of her neck, took a deep breath and exhaled. It was a long walk back to the house.

Devon stood beside the sink slicing a dill pickle on the cutting board. They had both apologized for the things they'd said. She wanted to forget the whole incident but there was a grain of truth in all of the angry words that nagged at her, playing over and over. Even so, she felt guilty for lashing out at Mom concerning TJ. That was a low blow and she wished she could take it back.

She scraped the chopped pickle into the bowl and started mixing the ingredients for tuna salad. When she raised her head looking for the pepper, a flash of white drew her attention to the window. A patrol car was driving through the gate. She stopped working on the tuna. No one from the sheriff's office had called. Whatever needed saying was important enough for someone to drive all the way out here. The vehicle pulled up to the front of the house. Buck was alone. She met him at the kitchen door drying off her hands as he opened the screen door.

He nodded. "Howdy, Devon." He stepped inside and took off his gray Stetson.

"Hello, Buck." He stood in front of her without his characteristic swagger or friendly chatter. This was a business call. The grand jury. The air was thick with worry and closing in around her. "Is something wrong?"

"No, honey. I've got good news." He smiled but there was a quiet reserve in it.

She crossed her arms in front of her to calm the rising uneasiness. There must be some hitch in the proceedings. "How about a cup of coffee or a glass of iced tea?"

"No thanks, I can't stay." He lingered beside the refrigerator. "Got the word this mornin' that the grand jury ruled in the death of John Colton. They agreed it was self-defense."

A sigh rushed out of her as every muscle in her body relaxed. She leaned against the counter and smiled. "What a relief."

"I told you not worry." He looked down at his hat and slid his fingers along the depression at the top. He wasn't smiling when he raised his head. The stiff set to his jaw and his uncharacteristic silence prompted caution like a whiff of smoke where there should be no fire. She swallowed before putting her suspicion into words.

"There's something else, isn't there?"

"Well, it's only a rumor at this point but . . . I've heard that Otis Young is makin' noises about a civil suit." He fixed his eyes on her. "He's a weasel of an attorney who'd do anything to make a dollar which is the main reason I'm tellin' you this. Supposedly, Colton's mother has hired him."

The mention of a mother took the starch out of her. She walked over to a chair and sat down. She hadn't thought about her attacker as an ordinary man with a family somewhere. She hadn't thought of someone crying for him or missing him or loving him. A terrible fear gripped her.

"Did he have children?" She stared at the floor, picturing a child's eyes full of tears.

"No. Wasn't married either." Buck's words were clipped.

She released the breath she'd been holding and fell silent, overwhelmed by the widening circle of suffering created by one reckless man. The peace she longed for might never come.

Buck cleared his throat. "Look, this is all hearsay right now, so don't start worrying just yet."

His warning was too late. She was knee deep in it. "His mother can do that? I mean, bring a civil suit?" She looked up at him.

Buck frowned and walked over to the table. "She can try. Boils down to wrongful death, loss of income . . . that kind of paper talk, big words which shouldn't amount to shit if you'll excuse the expression. When you consider he was a no-good, mean hell-raiser doin' drugs and no doubt sellin' the stuff, you did the world a favor."

"I didn't want him dead, Buck. There are a lot of mean, lousy people in this world but they don't deserve to die like that." She shook her head and looked down at the table trying to think logically through the fix she was in now. "Should I find a lawyer?"

He pulled out the chair next to hers and sat down. "Might not be a bad idea. I could recommend someone who'd love nothin' better than to tie into Otis."

She glanced at Buck. He was leaning forward with his hands on his knees. "Who?"

"His name is Ed Thurman. Just retired from the bench but he still has a practice. Only takes cases that interest him."

Devon couldn't trust herself to remember that name a minute from now. She stood up and walked over to the counter. She grabbed a pencil out of the old jelly jar beside the phone and the notepad on top of the telephone book. She wrote down the name in an unsteady scribble. "Where is his office?"

The chair screeched as Buck stood up. "In Jackson, right across from the county courthouse. Tell him I gave you his name and be sure to mention Otis Young. That'll make him lick his chops."

She looked up from her note. "Young is someone I'd better worry about, isn't he?"

"Well, he likes to think he can push people around. Knows the tricks of the trade to make someone jump through the hoops." He took a toothpick out of his breast pocket and put it in his mouth so that a third of it stuck out between his lips. "That's why you'll want somebody like Ed on your side. He'll cut Otis off at the knees if he tries to file a civil suit." He took a few steps toward the door.

Devon heard the truck pull into the breezeway and a door slam. Ellie walked into the kitchen giving her old friend an easy hug. "Hi, stranger. Surprised to see you out here. Everything all right?" She looked at Buck but followed his glance toward Devon. She raised a brow as if asking for some clue. Thankfully, Buck spoke first.

"Things are fine, Ellie. I was just on my way out. Came by to let Devon know the grand jury ruled justifiable homicide in her case." He glanced down at his watch before putting his hat on. "I'm afraid I've got to run. 'Bye." He tipped his hat, walked past Ellie and was out the door without another word.

Devon walked back to the sink. She poked at the tuna in the bowl with a spoon. The words 'civil suit' turned over and over in her mind.

"Well, that's good news. Why don't you look happy?" Ellie put her hand on Devon's shoulder.

Taking an uneasy breath, Devon turned her head to answer. "Buck said the man's mother has hired an attorney. She may file a civil suit against me." She dropped the spoon. It clinked against the bowl. "This is a nightmare that never ends."

Her mother was frowning, leaning against the counter with the weight of the news. "A civil suit? Good Lord."

She remembered Colton slamming her against the truck and screaming threats at Jamie. The memory flared into anger. "I should send his mother the hospital bill I got the other day. Why do I have to defend myself, damn it?" She spun around and paced in the middle of the kitchen. "I should sue her for raising such a cretin. Does she think I asked him to beat me up?"

"Of course not. Maybe she doesn't know the facts."

Devon stopped moving. Her mother was looking at her with those calm, benevolent eyes. She couldn't be defending that woman. Just the idea riled her. "It shouldn't be too hard to get the gory details."

"Don't scowl at me like that." Her mother's expression was lecture-quality stern. "You don't know what's going on in that woman's head. Buck said she may file suit, right? Once she understands what he did, she'll realize she is wrong to blame you." Ellie turned away from her. "I've seen plenty of women, who have no idea what their children are doing until it's too late."

The hurt in her mother's voice yanked her up short. Her comment about TJ earlier had rubbed salt in that wound. The spot reserved for regrets was heavier by one.

"I hope you're right, Mom." She pulled out a chair and sat down. "Buck said the lawyer may convince her I can pay a lot of money if she wins. Save us all a lot of trouble if I showed her my bank statement. Unless Jamie's trust could be considered . . .." Remembering an old nemesis eased her sudden surge of concern. "No, I'm sure Alan's mother made sure their attorneys set that up so it could never be considered mine." She shook her head and ran her fingers through her hair. "Buck recommended I talk to a retired judge named Thurman. Ever heard of him, Mom?"

"Name sounds familiar. I'm sure Buck wouldn't mention him unless he knows he's good."

"I wonder how much it would cost if I have to go to court?" All of her financial planning could go down the toilet. With her elbows on the table, she buried her face in her hands. "God, how I wish I could live that one day all over again."

She felt her mother's hand rest on her back. "It will work out. I know it will. Don't worry about money. I'll help if it comes down to that. I'm not about to let anyone punish you for protecting yourself and Jamie."

She sighed and straightened up. Ellie couldn't afford to do that but she appreciated the offer. "Thanks, Mom, but I'll handle it. I just won't let her win."

This had been one of those days where everything was going down hill. Even the tuna wasn't agreeing with her. Devon waited for the bus with mixed feelings trying to figure out why Jamie had gotten into trouble. She hadn't asked many questions because the principal, Mr. Dickerson, obviously didn't know the answers. She replayed the phone call in her head while she sat in the car.

"Your son started a fight in the lunch room today, Mrs. Taylor. No one was seriously hurt. He admitted striking the first blow but refused to tell me why he hit David, which disturbs me. The cafeteria monitor did not see what happened." The man had cleared his throat.

"Since he is a new student, I made it quite clear that fighting wasn't acceptable here. He sat in my office during recess and he will have to stay in tomorrow. School policy is two days without recess for fighting. Even at this young age, it is important to establish rules of good behavior. I hope we can count on your cooperation in providing clear direction at home that fighting will be punished."

She'd told him she'd talk to her son. There had been something in the way he sounded when he said he hoped she'd cooperate that had raised the hair on the back of her neck. She wondered if he said that to all parents or just the ones recently published in the newspaper for having killed someone. It had stopped her from thanking him for the call.

She was glad Jamie hadn't been hurt in the fight. She didn't want to see any more bruises, which was a ridiculous thought. A bumped head or scraped knee was an everyday event in a child's life. He would be upset she was sure. Trips to the principal's office were by design upsetting. So was staying inside all through recess. He shouldn't have started a fight in the first place. The thought flashed across her mind that the assault might have played some part in Jamie's aggressive behavior. That frightened and worried her. She countered the thought with the assurance that all little boys get in fights at some time or the other. TJ had. She would have liked to hear a man's perspective on how to handle this but Hank wasn't around. She'd have to play it by ear.

The yellow school bus came over the rise of the county road. She got out of the car and waited for it to pull up. Jamie stepped off looking at her briefly before lowering his head. He kept watching the ground as his feet scuffed along the road to the car. She felt sorry for him, knowing this was one more learning experience that had to be dealt with.

"Hi. Looks like you've had a rough day."

He glanced over the hood of the car at her, his eyes never settling directly on hers. "Uh-huh." He was leaning to one side as if the book bag hanging on his shoulder weighed more than he did.

"Mr. Dickerson called me this afternoon." He grimaced when she said the name. He looked miserable. She felt her resolve to be firm start to melt. "You want to tell me about it out here or in the car?"

He sighed, resigned to his fate, shuffled to the passenger door and opened it. After dropping his heavy load on the floor of the sedan, he sat down with a bounce.

She settled behind the steering wheel trying to decide where to start. A fly bumped across the inside of the windshield. "Did you get hurt?"

He cautiously glanced her way. "Nope."

"Did you hurt the boy you fought with?"

"Nope." He crossed his arms. "I just punched him in the stomach a couple of times."

She clamped her teeth together. He sounded like a bully. "Why did you hit him?" He hesitated a second. Either he picked up the change in her tone of voice or was busy thinking up a good excuse.

"Because he made me mad." The words grumbled out of him.

"You can't hit someone because they make you angry."

"You did." His lower lip jutted out defiantly but he continued to stare straight ahead.

His answer surprised her. She sat back trying to put herself in his shoes. He was old enough to make the distinction between the two circumstances. If not, she'd better clear it up. She turned in her seat.

"That was different. I was defending myself and protecting you."

"Me too." He frowned, looking directly at her, at last.

She studied his stormy expression trying to figure out what had happened. "He hit you first?"

"No." His answer snapped out.

She grabbed the steering wheel in frustration. This was getting her nowhere. "Jamie, I don't understand. What did he do?"

"He's a big fat liar." He looked over, chewing on his bottom lip, crocodile tears welling up in his eyes, which just about undid her. "David said you were going to jail 'cause you killed that bad man."

"Oh." She shrank back in her seat. He'd been defending her. She wished she could confront the parent with the pea sized brain and big mouth who'd given the other boy the idea. Jamie was watching her with those honest, blue eyes, a blink of uncertainty in them as if he'd blurted out some terrible secret. She leaned over the console and hugged him. "I'm not going to jail. I don't know why that boy said it but he's wrong."

"Are you sure?"

"Yes, I'm sure." She patted him on the back. This was no time to be technical. "It isn't against the law to protect yourself."

He rested his head on her shoulder. "Good." The word was a sigh.

"I need you to understand something, Jamie." She straightened up. "I'm not glad that man died." She concentrated on his trusting eyes. "He gave me no choice. We couldn't get away from him, you know that. I had to fight." She took his hand in hers. There was dirt under his fingernails. "People get hurt fighting, sometimes really bad like he did. That's why there are rules at school and why the principal makes someone stay inside during recess."

Jamie pulled his hand away and scratched at his cheek. "That bad guy breaked lots of rules."

"Yes, he did."

He screwed up his face. "He got all ugly with blood."

She forced herself to look through the windshield at the empty road ahead. "It was a terrible and sad day. I wish it had never happened."

"Sheriff Buck's supposed to make people do the rules."

She looked over at him. He was toying with the door lock. "Yes, that's his job. He doesn't want boys fighting at school either." She reached over and touched his arm. "Jamie, will you try something for me?"

"What?" He turned his head toward her.

"When somebody makes you mad, don't hit him." He frowned, opened his mouth to complain, but she raised her voice and kept talking. "Hitting isn't going to make things better, Jamie. It just makes someone want to hit you back. When they do, you hit harder. And then what happens? They hit harder too."

"But . . . .."

"When someone is being mean, the smartest thing you can do is to go play somewhere else. All I'm asking is that you give it a try the next time someone makes you mad."

"Okay." It was a half hearted response. "What if they hit me first?"

She looked him in the eye and tried to emphasize with her tone of voice how serious she was. "You'll have to decide if hitting back is the right thing to do. You don't have to use your fists to fight a lie."

She watched his face. He was trying to understand, the furrow of his young brow told her that. It was too much to ask in one troubling day. She put her fingers on the keys, all out of good ideas.

"Maybe you can ask Hank sometime how he decides what to do." She turned the key in the ignition. It was hard trying to help a boy grow up to be a man. "Let's go home."

"I have to admit that I'm not surprised Mr. Young took the woman's case, Ms. Taylor." Mr. Thurman had a deep voice well suited to legal oratory. She sat back in the desk chair. There was also something relaxed and friendly about him that she liked even on the phone. "If I were to advise you, I wouldn't recommend meeting her face-to-face. Things like that can get ugly. Bad enough in a court room. And I'd take his comment on the phone about Mrs. Colton possibly withdrawing the suit with a grain of salt. Doubt her son's drug habit is a surprise to her."

She rolled her pen between her fingers. "I'm still trying to understand how she can sue me. The grand jury didn't indict me. They agreed it was self-defense."

"Sheriff Blanton and I discussed the particulars after the grand jury adjourned." She heard something creak in the background, maybe his chair. "The practice of law can produce a quagmire of paperwork, Ms. Taylor. In a civil suit, the rules are different and they don't require the same level of proof to win a judgement. But even in civil court, your case is solid. You need to realize Mr. Young doesn't have much to lose as long as the woman's willing to pay him on the clock. I imagine he'd try filing for damages based on wrongful death."

"What does that mean?" She wrote the term down on her note pad.

"He'll try to claim that Mrs. Colton has suffered not only the stress of her son's death, but the loss of his love and affection."

With a hard scratch, she underlined the phrase. Using those terms in connection with John Colton was a travesty.

"Or she might claim loss of his financial support in her old age. I don't know how old a woman she is, or if Colton had been contributing to her income previously."

She drew dollar signs across the top of the paper. "Mr. Thurston, I'm not working. I have some money in savings, enough to keep us going for a while but that is it. My son has money in a trust fund set up by his father but it's not in my name."

"I doubt Mr. Young knows anything about your financial situation at this point. In my dealings with him, I've found he's an attorney more concerned with his bottom line than his client's. Unfortunately, the courts can attach future earnings in some instances."

She jumped to her feet. "That's not fair." She threw the pen down on the desk.

"It isn't likely to happen in this case. My point was, I can't tell you not to take this kind of suit seriously if he files. These things can hang on a long time, legal fees add up. I've seen some folks go through this rigmarole just to get even with the other side, knowing they'll never win. We don't know what this Colton woman expects from filing suit. I could speak to Young on your behalf and see what he really wants. If it looks like I can't talk some sense into them, we'll discuss fees."

She sat down, didn't say anything for a minute, just scribbled OTIS on the pad and circled it. Buck had made it clear Otis Young was less than ethical. He also seemed to have a lot of respect for Ed Thurman's ability to handle whatever Young might try. She'd be a fool to proceed without an attorney.

"That's more than fair. I'd appreciate it if you would talk to him for me. If we have to meet with him to settle this I will, anytime. However, I'll tell you right now, I won't pay her a nickel." She curled her fingers into a fist. "He forced me to fight and I did."

"I understand completely and couldn't agree with you more. I'll call him. Try to put the kibosh on the whole thing."

"I just want my life back to normal, Mr. Thurston."

"The circumstances and evidence in this case are solidly in your favor, Ms. Taylor. I'll be pointing that out to Mr. Young while I sully his enthusiasm."

"Thank you, Mr. Thurman."

"Call me, Ed, and you are most welcome. I'll let you know the outcome of our discussion."

From the minute she got up the next morning, Devon poured every ounce of energy into doing chores, anything to keep busy and distracted. Weeks of self-imposed exile on the ranch were wearing thin and the threat of a lawsuit didn't help. After lunch, she sat down on the bench in the barn to polish her saddle. When she reached for the wax, she noticed the light. The afternoon sun streamed in through the small gaps in the walls and roof. She was the sun's hostage. A fine web spun of sunbeams and tiny specks floating in the air surrounded her. When she was little, she'd played a game in here, hopping and dodging the shafts of light to keep from melting like the wicked witch in Oz. She was playing a grown up version of the game again. Imagining she was trapped by something as flimsy as a threat.

She put the wax down. There was no point in waiting to hear from Ed. She'd do what she could to prepare. After putting the saddle away, she walked to the house. She had files to review and income taxes to finish.

The next morning, she sat down at the desk in the den and poured over her financial records. By evening, she'd completed her tax forms and knew exactly how much she had to lose. If she had to go to court and lost, the money she'd invested, from the sale of the California house, would be fair game. Even if she won, she would probably have to use some of that money to pay legal fees. She sat back in the desk chair.

"Damn. Kiss your smooth transition to a new job goodbye."

"What?" Ellie was sitting on the couch watching a news program.

"Nothing, Mom. I'm finished filling out my taxes." She stood and picked up her heavy file box.

"Want me to mail them for you tomorrow?"

Tomorrow was beauty shop Thursday, Mom's day for a shampoo and set in town. Devon longed to get away, to see new trees, other houses, different faces.

"No, I'll go with you. I could use a change of scenery."

The next morning they parked on the square. It was warm and sunny. Ellie headed for Joanne's House of Beauty. Devon walked the two blocks to the post office. She ran into Mabel and Cliffy-Jean Campbell and exchanged small talk, which meant she listened most of the time. That was fine with her. It was oddly refreshing to talk to people with their own troubles. She stopped at Jake's Feed store to pick up a part Hank had ordered. It felt a little strange that she had to tell the clerk who she was. After putting the small box in the trunk of the Cadillac, she checked her watch. She had a good thirty minutes before her mother would be finished 'beautifying'.

She strolled down the wide sidewalk. Walking past the locked doors she'd gone in and out of for years, she realized she belonged to the past here. It made her feel all the more rootless.

She glanced across the square and noticed the sign identifying Tammy's bookkeeping business that shared the fine old stone building with Donald Ray's two concerns, Ray Real Estate and the Chamber of Commerce. There was a car parked in front of it. She didn't know if it was Tammy's but decided to stop in and see if her old friend was there. They'd been a part of a foursome that had stuck together from first grade through graduation. She'd talked to her on the phone briefly since she'd been home but hadn't seen her in several years.

She peeked in through the plate glass window but couldn't see anyone. A bell rang when she opened the wooden door. She walked over to Tammy's desk with its Barton Bookkeeping nameplate. It was neat as a pin, the framed pictures of her daughters stationed by the telephone. She looked down the hallway that led to the back.

"Hello."

The word bounced off the bare wood floors and high ceilings of the sparsely furnished old building. She glanced at Don's desk cluttered with stacks of paper. The rack for community brochures by the door held a few lonely pamphlets and the large county map on the wall had five or six red-flagged pushpins scattered across it.

"Be right there." She heard Tammy call out in her lilting soprano from somewhere in the back. With the clatter of shoes, Tammy appeared in the hallway and hurried toward her, all smiles.

"Hi, Devon." Still willowy, she was dressed in a long skirt and flowered blouse, the tortured tangle of curly red hair she'd fought in high school nicely tamed.

"It is so good to see you." They hugged each other tight. Tammy patted her on the back before letting her go. "You are a miracle, Devon."

Devon laughed not sure what to make of the comment. "It's great to see you, Tammy. I like your hair that way."

"Thank you." Tammy smiled and gently touched the poof of red. "It is still such a struggle to make it behave."

"I'm not interrupting anything, am I? Mom's at Joanne's, so I thought I'd drop by."

"Oh, heavens no. I'm glad to have some company. Have a client coming in after one o'clock to finish up his taxes but can't do anymore until he brings in his receipts."

"I just mailed mine in. It's always a relief to get that done." Devon turned and pointed toward the map on the wall. "Does Don have much of a real estate market to work with?"

"I don't think so. Every so often someone comes in looking for a small place to retire on. Tom Clark's had his spread for sale for quite a while, I know. Don did have a few developers nosing around last year but nothing came of it."

"That's too bad."

"Oh, I'm not so sure. We don't need a city full of people coming out here." She walked toward her desk and Devon followed. "Does Ellie want to sell the ranch?"

"No, at least not right away. I was just wondering how land values were holding up."

Tammy grabbed a wooden chair along the wall and pulled it toward her desk. "Here, have a seat. I'm so glad you came in. We used to see each other every day and now," she sighed, "now, we're scattered all over, busy with our families and jobs. It's a shame." Her voice trailed off.

Devon picked up the framed pictures on Tammy's desk. "Your girls are so pretty."

Tammy perked up. "They're growing up so fast. They're just as skinny as I was I'm afraid."

She smiled at her old friend. "They'll be fine. You filled out, so will they."

A shy grin gently curved her lips. "Yes, I did . . . finally." She touched her chin with her hand. "You look wonderful, Dev." A pink blush appeared on her fair skin. "You know," she hesitated, "I can't imagine handling your trouble so well."

She noticed Tammy couldn't call it what it was, assault and attempted rape. She didn't blame her. Everything about it was ugly. Maybe Tammy wasn't sure she could talk about it.

"I discovered I could only sit in a room and feel sorry for myself so long. It was getting me nowhere. Besides, I don't have a choice anymore than you would, Tammy. We have children depending on us."

That last line had come out sounding shaky. It was time to shut up. She had to get use to it. It wouldn't be the last time she'd be asked, even in an around about way.

"I guess you're right," Tammy shook her head and raised her shoulders as if warding off the thought, "but still, I can't imagine it."

She took a deep breath. "Neither could I, until it happened."

Anticipation was worse than the real thing. Devon gazed at her reflection in the mirror before putting on her makeup. Mr. Young had insisted on a meeting. He'd wanted Mrs. Colton present but Mr. Thurman had flatly refused. At this point, she just wanted to get it over with. Having to openly discuss such a personal, emotionally charged experience with strangers was going to be very difficult. The fact she knew she'd done nothing wrong put backbone in her resolve.

Ellie had fretted over the meeting. Devon told her she could drive herself to the county seat. It scared her but she wanted her mother to be at home for Jamie. Besides, the Simmons boys were cutting hay on the place. They were careful not to talk about it in front of Jamie. Devon didn't want his imagination to run amuck. Earlier this morning, she'd told him she was going to a meeting in another town and wouldn't be home after school. He'd hopped on the bus without looking back.

After blotting her lipstick, she stood back and looked in the mirror. She'd decided to wear her favorite lightweight suit, silk blouse, and comfortable heels. The ensemble worked, the image of a polished, professional woman stared back. She wanted Mr. Young to think she was not someone easily pushed around even if she was. Besides, she was counting on Ed to push back.

Buck had offered her a ride. He had a hearing in Jackson to attend. Devon had her suspicions that Ellie had asked him, but in truth, she was relieved to have company. It was a muggy morning. As she walked out to the patrol car, Devon reassured her mother everything would be fine. She smiled and waved, the whole nine yards, as they drove away.

It was eleven forty-five when they got to Jackson. Buck was hungry. Devon let him talk her into going to LuLu's Coffee Shop in the courthouse square even though the last thing on her mind was food. He convinced her she should eat something light, to keep down the butterflies, and whet her whistle with a glass of tea. Her throat was dry. She hadn't dealt with an attorney since the divorce. It had been an unpleasant experience and she wasn't looking forward to dealing with Otis who had such a bad reputation. Sitting in LuLu's would help pass the time if nothing else.

Buck opened the door and they walked in. There were booths along both walls and metal tables in the center. The little place was jam-packed. Buck took a quick look around, said "howdy" to men sitting at several full tables, and headed toward a booth in the back. She followed him. A waitress was passing with a tray of dirty dishes as they walked up. Devon was surprised to see Dr. Owen stand and shake Buck's hand.

"Mind if we join you, Mike? Lulu has a crowd today."

"Of course not, have a seat. I was lucky to get this spot." He smiled at her. "Hello, Ms. Taylor." He sat down.

She wasn't in the mood to make small talk with someone she barely knew but there wasn't any other place to sit.

"Hello, Doctor."

"Oh, you two know each other, good." Buck took off his hat and hung it on the rack at the end of booth. He stood waiting for her to scoot across the dark blue bench seat in a misguided sense of gallantry. She slipped in as gracefully as she could in a straight skirt and he sat down beside her.

"Have you ordered yet, Mike?" Buck reached over Devon and pulled out a menu wedged between the sugar bowl and the salt and pepper shakers. "I'm hungry enough to eat whatever they've got that's not movin'."

Dr. Owen laughed. "Nope, just sat down. I was suppose to testify in court this morning, about a brawl in the hospital, but now it looks like it will be mid afternoon before I can leave." He opened a menu.

"That's the way this business always is. I've got a hearing too. Your meeting will start on time, Devon. Otis keeps a close eye on the clock."

A waitress walked up and retrieved the pencil stuck in her hair-sprayed French twist. "Y'all know what you want yet?"

Devon skimmed the vinyl covered menu Buck had handed her. Nothing too inviting for someone with a sensitive stomach. Everything was fried or spicy.

"I'll have the steak and tea, darlin'." Buck smiled at the woman as if they were old friends.

"I'll have the chili. Tea will be fine for me too." Dr. Owen handed over his menu.

The only thing on the list she thought she could handle was soup and salad. "I'll have the soup and salad. What's the soup of the day?"

"Chicken noodle. You want a bowl or a cup of that?" The woman didn't bother to look at her.

"A cup will be fine. I'll have iced tea also."

"You got it. Be back in a minute with the drinks."

"Rangers are going to be hard to beat this year, Mike, you mark my words." Buck stopped talking while the waitress set down three sets of silverware, each wrapped up in a paper napkin.

"I always root for the Cubs. Win or lose, I don't care." The doctor grinned.

Buck laughed. "Well, at least they're good losers."

The three plastic glasses of tea arrived. They separated out the drinks among themselves. Buck grabbed the sugar and poured some in his glass.

The doctor looked at her. "What team do you root for Ms. Taylor?"

"I don't follow sports. Not enough hours in the day." She could have told him she thought all professional sports were a colossal waste of time and money but didn't. It was a personal grudge. She had no desire to delve into the effect it'd had on her brother.

Buck leaned in her direction. "You know Devon, Mike here has really done a lot in the short time he's been at the hospital. Thanks to him, we have a chopper to respond to emergencies all over the county."

Buck's praise brought a smile to the man's face but he shook his head. "Buck, you're stretching the truth. The clinic's administration had been working on it long before I got here."

Buck pointed his index finger at him. "True, but you just happened to know about a surplus helicopter the Army had settin' around. Sure hope you'll stay for a while."

Another waitress, younger and heftier than the first, dressed in jeans and a western shirt, walked up with a tray full of food.

Buck's plate-sized slab of chicken-fried steak was bounded by green beans on one side and a buttery mound of mashed potatoes covered with a pool of white gravy that streamed across the steak like lava. The waitress put a red plastic basket of rolls beside his iced tea. It smelled good but she couldn't imagine eating that much in one meal.

Her salad consisted of a wedge of brown-edged head lettuce, a dried out piece of carrot and two chunks of a tired tomato with pink dressing dribbled over it. She had the feeling that they didn't serve a lot of salads in LuLu's. The soup came from a can. At least the three packets of crackers were wrapped and had a chance of being crisp.

The doctor's dark brown chili looked thick. She could smell the spicy concoction from across the table. Several pinto beans poked through an orange puddle of grease that floated on the surface. Indigestion in a bowl. A slice of purple onion and a big square of cornbread rested on the plate. He obviously had a cast iron stomach.

"Devon's dad was my best friend, Mike. We grew up together, played football in high school, you name it." He buttered a roll and cut up some of his steak.

Buck loved to reminisce. He'd been on the team with her father and she'd heard them go on endlessly. She took a bite of salad knowing she could eat in peace.

"I was a guard and he was a runnin' back. He was somethin' to see. Yes, sir. Best damn running back we ever had, probably best one in the state." Buck smiled waggling a fork full of green beans at him. "He swore he had a bit of Comanche blood that let him run like the wind." He piled up a forkful of potatoes on top of piece of meat and put it in his mouth.

Devon stirred the dressing around in her bowl hoping it would help the taste of the sad lettuce. Her soup was lukewarm and too salty.

Buck nudged her with his arm. "Watched this little wisp of a gal grow up too." He had a mischievous grin on his face when she looked over at him. "She could ride when she was knee-high to a grasshopper. Dandy barrel racer too, did real good in competition until she quit. A lot like her daddy, too. Coal black hair and stubborn as a mule." He winked as he opened his mouth to take another bite.

She poked him with her elbow a little harder than she'd intended. "No, Buck, I picked up being muleheaded from you, remember?" She smiled. Buck slapped the table and laughed. He was a kind, good-hearted man even though he looked big and tough on the outside. He was clumsy around women and too loud sometimes but he was honest and dearer to her than just a friend of her father's.

She glanced across the table at Mike Owen. He'd been listening to Buck with pleasant attentiveness. He was a good looking man, really, short brown hair, green eyes, and a nice smile.

He noticed she was looking at him. "When I was examining Jamie's arm, he said you two had just moved here from Minnesota. Too cold for you up there?"

The doctor had a good memory. His question gave her an easy answer. "Right. When my car doors were frozen tight one sunny afternoon, I decided it was time to fly south for the winter." She'd just taken a bite of tomato and turned to look out the window while she chewed.

When she turned back, he was watching her. It made her feel uncomfortable in her own skin. She shifted her weight on the bench seat. After months of avoiding close encounters with her lecherous boss, she was sensitive to every look and every word from a man anywhere near her own age. Colton had added the element of terror. Even in a crowded restaurant, she couldn't control her discomfort, only do her best to hide it.

"What is it that you do?" He leaned back and stretched one arm across the back of his seat. He was making polite conversation. She could handle pleasant chitchat, needed the practice really. One day soon, she'd be working again and dealing with men.

She smiled and tried to relax. "I've spent most of my career in the swimwear industry, in marketing and sales."

"So you're working around here for a company?" He dropped his napkin in his empty bowl.

"No. I'm staying with my mother while Jamie finishes first grade. I planned on job hunting while he was in school," she looked down at her plate for a second, "but then, I was injured."

He nodded. There was something, a momentary sadness, in his face. Maybe he'd remembered how awful she'd looked that day in the emergency room. "I'm sure it's been very rough." Mike pressed his lips together and smiled. "Glad you and your son are doing okay."

"Yes, we are." It felt good to say it out loud. She hoped it was true.

"Ed Thurman will get Young off your back about this lawsuit, Devon and it'll be clear sailin' from then on."

Buck's comment interrupted her private thoughts. He'd said more than she wanted repeated out loud. He was impossible sometimes.

"There's Ed." Buck stood up and waved.

She raised her chin to see over the heads of the men in the next booth. A man with pure white, wavy hair walked up. Buck gave him a pat on the back. The last attorneys she'd been around had worn Brooks Brothers' suits and dress shirts with cuff links. This fellow was pleasantly rumpled. The sleeves of his white shirt were rolled up and his khaki slacks, held up with wide suspenders, were a little wrinkled. It was hard not to like a man wearing multicolored suspenders. He carried a large manila envelope in his hand and a khaki jacket folded over his arm.

"I'm Ed Thurman, Ms. Taylor. It's nice to meet you." He leaned over the table offering his hand. His handshake was firm, his smile was gentle.

"And this is Dr. Owen, Ed. He works at the clinic."

"A pleasure to meet you, sir."

Mike stretched across the table to shake the judge's hand. "Pleasure is mine, Mr. Thurman. If you'll all excuse me, I'm going to head back to the courthouse. You can take my seat." Mike slid out of the booth. He looked at her and smiled. "I hope your meeting goes well, Devon."

"Thanks, Mike. I hope so too." She'd managed to let down her guard a bit around him. That was progress. He walked over to the cashier.

Buck glanced at his watch. "I'd better make a phone call before I get tied up at the courthouse. I'll leave you with my friend the hangin' judge, Devon." He slapped the man on the back with a laugh and left them alone.

"Sorry we aren't meeting under more pleasant, strictly social circumstances, Ms. Taylor." The judge sat down.

"Call me Devon, please." He nodded as the waitress came over and gathered up the plates. He ordered dessert.

"Glad we bumped into each other before we go to Mr. Young's office. I reviewed the police reports and the grand jury findings. I think we can take the air out of this civil suit."

She breathed a bit easier. The waitress delivered his tea and apple pie.

He took a drink. "I'm afraid Mr. Young's tactics are often less than noble. I've been prowling around to find out what he's up to. He's previously handled the legal troubles of the late Mr. Colton so he's well aware of his nefarious past and how that will appear to a judge. I'd be willing to bet he's going along with this nuisance to pay the bills." He paused to cut off a bite of pie. "We'll head over to his office in a few minutes." He put the bite in his mouth, chewed for a minute and took a drink. "Let me add a word of caution." He cleared his throat. She tapped her heel on the floor. He had her full attention.

"I want you to put your armor on and let me do the talking. If Otis gets nasty, let me handle him." He stopped to take another drink. "Now where was I? Oh, all we're doing today is listening to see what he wants. Then I'll explain that like an El Paso snowball, he hasn't got a chance of being more than a puddle. Nothing is on the record and you don't have to say another word about this mess unless they end up filing."

She could feel her shoulders tensing up. "I understand. I don't have anything to hide."

He looked at her with the steady gaze of a man who'd heard those words proved wrong more than once. "I'm afraid it's not always that easy."

That comment threw her off balance. She leaned forward, her hands clasped together tightly. "What do you mean?"

"That the quagmire I mentioned the other day on the phone is still there. Delays and motions and maneuvering can be used as a weapon to frustrate and infuriate the innocent. Don't count on this to be resolved quickly or easily unless we are lucky."

"I'm not going to let this woman ruin my life because her son died and I didn't." The words rushed out with bitterness, an emotional knee-jerk reaction to his warning.

"Good." He nodded. "I'll do everything I can to end this sham and let you get on with living." He turned his attention to the pie on his plate.

His calm response settled over her. She leaned back. Most of the tables were empty now. She had to use her head this afternoon and keep cool.

"I think I'll go put on some war paint while you eat your pie."

He chuckled. "Good idea. I want him to see we mean business."

Their meeting was in an older two story building on the square. They climbed the stairs together, the retired judge still carrying his jacket over his arm. "Young's office is the last one on the right." He pointed down the long hall. "There's benches about midway. Meet you there in a second after I spruce up." He ducked into the men's room.

Phones were ringing. Devon checked her watch. They had ten minutes before their scheduled appointment. With nothing to do but wait, a major case of the jitters was back. It had been comforting to hear Ed say he didn't think she'd lose a civil suit but it was her life being battered around, not his.

Bright patches of sunlight lit up the oak floor as she walked down the hall. Tall windows let in the heat of the afternoon sun warming the wooden benches enough to smell the furniture polish. She sat for a minute, noticing the old-fashioned gold lettering on the door of the ladies' room before standing again. She couldn't hold still. Worry boiled around inside her. She crossed her arms to contain it, pacing a step or two before turning to look both ways down the corridor.

A man and a woman approached from the opposite stairwell. They were an odd pair, mismatched in size and not a word shared between them. The woman was older, tall and square, marching with heavy footsteps that echoed down the hallway as she swung her black handbag. The man, narrow shouldered and wiry, was younger, in his early forties she guessed. He searched for something in his jacket pockets as he walked. They were a puzzle to study while she waited for Ed.

They stopped in a square of sunlight across the hall. She was taller than Devon. He twitched with nervous energy while she stood like a monolith, her coarse, gray hair combed in a tight bun and an implacable bulldog set to her jaw. Without so much as lipstick to add color, her weathered brown face could have been carved out of wood.

The man glanced at Devon. He knew who she was. She was sure of it even though he'd quickly looked away. Her internal warning system went off, her muscles tensed in an unfocused distress. He whispered something to his companion.

Beneath sagging lids, eyes a familiar pale blue leveled a withering look her direction. Devon gasped in recognition, too stunned to move. The woman had to be John Colton's mother. The urge to run was overwhelming. She turned away, thoughts tangled in memories and started walking. She pushed open the closest door.

The biting smell of bleach filled the air as the door closed behind her. She was in the restroom. There were two stalls. One door was open. She rushed over to it. The toilet was torn apart on the floor. A sudden flush startled her and she glanced down at a pair of dark pumps in the adjacent stall. Devon retreated to a sink.

The metal door swung open and a young blonde walked out straightening her skirt. She hummed as she turned on the water in the other sink, the one closest to the door, to wash her hands. She smiled at Devon in the mirror as she pulled out a paper towel to dry her hands.

"Taking them forever to finish that toilet."

All she could do was nod. The woman fished out a tube of lipstick from her purse.

The door swung open and banged against the wall. She jumped. Mrs. Colton stalked in glaring at her. With the snap of a purse closing, the young woman turned to leave. She tried to follow the blonde out but her escape was blocked by the bulk of the woman walking straight toward her. She stopped an arm's length in front of Devon. The door closed on the rest of the world. All she could hear was the drip, drip of water and the rapid beat of her own heart.

"I know who you are."

The thin, scratchy voice surprised Devon. It wasn't as strong and menacing as the woman looked. That gave her courage.

"Well, I don't know you." Devon stepped back.

"Yes, you do, liar." Her voice rose in volume with a new bitterness as she moved closer. "You're the one that killed my boy." Her voice cracked, weakened. "Was all I ever had that was just mine. Now he's gone." The old woman pressed her lips together so that they were little more than a fracture in that stolid face.

Whether the woman meant to reveal any emotion or not, Devon recognized the sound of loss in the wavering delivery of the word 'gone' and the brief shadow of sadness in those eyes. She'd seen her mother do that and understood such grief. It touched her and she softened.

"All because of you." A cold, sharp edge was back in the thin voice. The corners of her hard mouth turned down as she critically surveyed her. "Pretty women always gave him trouble."

"Gave him trouble?" She bristled, staring at Mrs. Colton. Those icy blue eyes were glaring at her. She remembered the last time she'd seen that look. She was struggling under him, gasping for air while he choked her. She took a deep breath.

"You are so far from the truth . . .." Her voice shook at first but got stronger. "Don't blame me for what happened. All I am guilty of is protecting my son." There was no flicker of a response from the old woman. "Blame the drugs for making him crazy, if you want. Maybe that's why he beat me and threatened to kill my child. All I know is I didn't have any choice but to fight back." There was still no change in expression. It was useless. She broke eye contact. This woman didn't want to believe her.

Mrs. Colton raised her clenched fist. "Don't matter what you say or swear to, Jezebel. In the Bible, it's an eye for an eye."

Devon bumped into the sink backing away from the old woman. She was big but slow. When she pulled up that large, black handbag from the crook of her arm, it occurred to Devon she should worry about the contents. If Mrs. Colton had a gun in there . . . she'd better move fast.

The door flew open and two women rushed in.

The old woman scowled. "I've said my piece." She abruptly turned and marched out the door.

Devon steadied herself with a hand on the faucet. They were just girls, teenagers, who had hurried in. She leaned against the sink as her knees shook and stared at the small, white squares of the tile floor. Mrs. Colton was as crazy as her son. She glanced over at the girls. They were laughing and talking as one closed the door of the stall.

Devon straightened up and caught a glimpse of her face in the mirror. Her skin was pale, as if all the blood had drained out of her. Her cheek was cold to the touch. She wanted to get out of here. Cautiously, she opened the door. Mrs. Colton was nowhere in sight, but her unlikely white knight, Ed Thurman was. Dressed now, in a bow tie and jacket, he stood in the middle of the hallway looking at his watch. With a surge of relief, she rushed out to him.

His smile disappeared when he saw her. His white brows knotted as a frown deepened the wrinkles of his face. "You feelin' all right? You look a little peaked." He put a hand on her arm.

She noticed her shadow cast by the sunlight coming through the tall windows and glanced both ways down the hall to be certain that they were alone. "Mrs. Colton just cornered me in the bathroom. For a minute there, I thought she was going to pull a gun out of that suitcase-sized purse she was carrying." Her attempt at humor was shaky.

"That big, old woman who came storming out of there?" He stepped closer and lowered his voice. "Did she threaten you?"

She cleared her throat and studied at his face. "Is a reference to an eye for an eye a threat?"

He punched one fist into the other palm. "I'm going to ream Otis out for not keeping her away from you." He was fuming. "That twitchy little son of a bitch has just cut his own throat."

She reached out with a shaking hand. "Please, don't." She'd had her fill of threats, real or imagined.

"You'd better sit a minute." He led her to a bench and sat with her. With the warm sun on her back, she took a deep breath to settle down. "How about I go in to see Otis alone? I'm ready to tear into him and I'll do a better job in language not fit for your ears. Then we'll find our friend the sheriff and let him get you home." He was patting her arm like a school nurse when someone got hurt.

The last thing she wanted to do was sit in the hallway alone. She shook her head, feeling a growing indignation replace the jitters. "No, I want to see what he has to say. He pointed me out to her. And I'm not going to give either of them the satisfaction of thinking she's scared me off."

He rose and offered his arm. "Come on. We'll have at him together." She stood up still a bit wobbly. They walked arm in arm down the empty hallway to the office at the very end.

Ed opened the door with 'Otis R. Young, Attorney' painted on it. A thin young woman sat at a desk typing but stopped when he walked up to her. "Tell Otis, Ed Thurman is here." It wasn't a request.

The inner office door popped open. "Hello, Counselor. Come in, Ms. Taylor."

He looked much different than when he'd been walking beside his client moments ago. He moved with a relaxed ease toward them. He smiled, cool as ice, without a flicker of recognition on his face that he'd ever seen her before. That made her angry, taking the wobble out of her legs. With a broad sweep of his arm, he motioned toward two straight-back wooden chairs in front of his black steel desk. Buck was right on target about Otis. The man was a snake.

Thurman didn't move a muscle toward the proffered chairs. "Your client threatened Ms. Taylor in the restroom. Be advised, I will have a restraining order issued by this evening."

"Really? I had no idea. I just left the lady in the hallway after our lunch meeting."

He was lying through his teeth, the bastard.

"I apologize if she said anything rash, Ms. Taylor, she was distraught after our conversation. She's returning to Oklahoma this afternoon with her son's personal effects. I imagine she's already on her way out of town. Please come in and sit down."

Ed Thurman made a move toward the chairs and Devon followed his lead. The man smiled at her as she passed and she steeled herself for this charade. They sat down. There were several metal bookcases along the wall filled with heavy leather volumes. Not much more to decorate the square room but a diploma on the wall.

Young closed the door behind them and walked around to sit at his desk. "Let me apologize again. Unfortunately, I can't follow my clients into the ladies' room. She feels there was some prejudice against her son around here. We reviewed various reports relating to her son's death this morning. She saw the photographs taken at the morgue and that upset her. She wants me to pursue another angle for the suit." He looked at her. She glanced out the tall, narrow window to keep from saying something nasty before turning back to Ed.

"Such as, Otis?" Ed smiled as the younger attorney focused on him.

"Ms. Taylor's truck had a flat tire. Mr. Colton stopped and offered to help. Given that scenario, it is hard to understand how this ordinary situation led to a young man's death. I'm sure you can see why his mother might question what really went on out there."

If he were suggesting some kind of seduction on her part she wanted to laugh. It was ridiculous. She shifted in her seat itching to say something but kept her mouth shut as Ed had advised. She was silently rooting for Ed to let him have it.

"I believe Ms. Taylor's statement and the physical evidence made that clear, Mr. Young." He crossed his arms and leaned back in the chair.

She clasped her hands together to control her nervousness. Surely Ed could do better than that.

"Yes, to most folks it does, Ed." The two-faced bastard smiled. "Mrs. Colton, however, sees it quite differently. Ms. Taylor was taking the truck, her son's property, and her son tried to stop her which led to the fight in which he was clubbed to death."

The idea that she was the aggressor was bizarre. Having met the crazy woman, however, Devon could believe she might have come up with it. Hearing the attorney repeat it rattled her enough to make her heart beat faster. She waited impatiently to hear Ed's reply. He didn't seem the least bit surprised. In fact, he smiled and leaned forward a bit.

"Let me get this straight, Otis. That old woman wants you to ask a jury to believe that her son, all six-foot-two, two hundred pounds of him, was the victim of a truck jacking by an unarmed, hundred and twenty pound woman with a six-year-old boy in tow?" He chuckled but the smile quickly vanished. "You're harassing Ms. Taylor with this cockamamie threat of a suit, Mr. Young and I won't put up with it. She was lucky to get away from Mrs. Colton's monster. I will not allow you to minimize her suffering in this tragic encounter, in which she courageously endured the pain and indignity of being beaten to within an inch of her life while fend-

ing off his attempted sexual assault. And her small son was not only a wit-
ness to such brutality, he was attacked and threatened with death after
being pulled from his mother's arms. I will crucify you in court, Otis, pure
and simple."

Devon wanted to jump to her feet and cheer as Otis turned a rosy
shade of red and squirmed. She couldn't have said it half as well. Ed had
painted a truer picture of the viciousness she and Jamie had endured and
shoved it down Otis' lying throat. It was sanitized, of course, the visceral
response to terror left out but only she could describe that. She was thankful she didn't have to, especially in front of this despicable man.

"No, Ed, listen." Otis held up his hand to stop him. "I said Mrs.
Colton asked me to pursue that possibility today. I told her it was ill-
advised based on the evidence, but she is being difficult. I don't want you
both storming out of here. I am working on her to see the light."

The judge pointed his finger at the red-faced attorney. "Then explain
it better the second time to that old woman. I will not have this lady bothered anymore by your deluded client. If you want trouble, Otis, you will
have it, in spades. That is a promise, not a threat." He stood up and turned
toward her. "We are finished here, Ms. Taylor."

She was more than glad to get out of the sight of Otis Young. She
stood and walked to the door no longer feeling like a victim, but a fighter.
Ed had accomplished what they came to do. They'd won the first battle.
Maybe there wouldn't be any more. They didn't look back at the man seat-
ed at the desk or stop until they were outside standing on the sidewalk. It
was warm and muggy.

Finally free to talk, Devon couldn't contain her disgust for Otis.
"What a liar. He pointed me out to her in the hall. He knew she was going
in after me."

"I shouldn't have let you come to begin with. I figured he was up to
no good. I'll get a restraining order." He unclipped his bow tie and put it
in his coat pocket.

"Okay, if you think it's necessary but a piece of paper won't scare off
that woman. Hopefully, she is on her way to Oklahoma. What do you
think he'll do now?"

Ed took off his jacket and folded it over his arm. "Not much. This was
a fishing expedition to satisfy his crazy client and make Otis some easy

money. He'd have to file with Judge Franklin and convince him the case had merit. It hasn't got a prayer and he knows it." He smiled. "You find Buck over at the courthouse and go on home. If I hear more than a peep out of Otis, I'll let you know. He may string her along for a few weeks if he's got bills to pay."

"I hope you're right. Listen, thanks for your help. You did a great job of taking the air out of his balloon. I would have lost it. Oh, and your bill, do you have my mailing address?"

He smiled and leaned closer to confide something. "Actually, I consider it part of my civic duty to trip up Otis every so often." She could have kissed him. "Plus, you bought my pie, so you're paid up." With that, he turned and walked away.

D evon crossed the square at a brisk pace heading for the courthouse. She could have run a mile or two on pent up energy but
wearing heels and a straight skirt, that wasn't an option. She went in the
main entrance planning on waiting for Buck but saw him by the stairs
talking to several men. They were huddled in deep conversation. He nodded acknowledging her.

Ellie would be on pins and needles until she knew how the meeting
had gone. There was a row of telephones at the other end of the lobby. She
walked over. There was no one else around so she chose the one at the far
end. She dug out some change and dialed. Her mother answered on the
second ring.

"Hi, it's me."

"How did it go? Are they going to drop the lawsuit?"

The sense of triumph that had fueled her walk to the courthouse
faded and she leaned against the wooden frame surrounding the pay
phone. "I don't know. Ed thinks Young is just using the opportunity to
make a few bucks and won't seriously pursue it but there are no guaran-
tees. It may be a while before I know."

"Oh. I was hoping . . .." Her mother's voice trailed off.

"Me too." She stood up straight and glanced around at the heavy
wooden doors and polished granite floor. There was no point in men-
tioning her encounter with Mrs. Colton over the phone. "Buck was right
about Otis Young. He was a two-faced liar. I was glad Mr. Thurman was
there. He did a great job of handling Young. Told him he'd have a tough

fight on his hands with all the evidence in my favor." The operator came on the line. Her time was almost up. "I'm out of change, Mom. I'll give you the rest of the details at home."

"All right. When are you going to leave?"

"Buck is talking to some men right now but it won't be long, I'm sure. 'Bye." With that accomplished, she headed to the rest room and took her time getting back to the benches near the double doors to wait.

Buck walked up to her a few minutes later. "How'd it go?"

She stood up. "Not too bad. Ed rattled Otis's chain pretty hard after I ran into Mrs. Colton."

"By the look on your face, she wasn't interested in trading recipes. She give you a hard time?"

"It wasn't pleasant." She exhaled, feeling drained. The fight in her was gone. "She looks like Ma Barker's sister."

"So I've heard." He smiled as he crossed his arms over his chest. "I'm sure things will work out okay, Devon. Ed's a good man. Listen, my hearing is gonna hold me up a while. The judge called a halt to the proceeding while the attorneys haggle over evidence. This mess will probably drag on for another couple hours before I can head back. I ran into Mike in the hallway upstairs a little while ago. He offered to take you home so you wouldn't have to wait."

Something inside her curled up in a tight ball. "Oh, I don't think so." She avoided looking at him, the feeling of discomfort unsettling her. "I'm not sure how to say this." She glanced at his face. He frowned, looking puzzled. "But I don't really know him." She shrugged her shoulders. "I'm feeling a little . . . gun shy, I guess."

"Oh." With the slight nod of his head, it was clear he understood. He rocked forward and back in his boots. "I hadn't thought about that bein' a problem." He moved one hand up to his jaw and rubbed at the gray stubble starting to show. "Guess I should have. Sorry. Feel like you're one of my own kids sometimes." He looked at the floor and cleared his throat. "I've been in this business a long time and I'm usually right reading people. My gut tells me he is okay but . . .."

"I'm sure he is." She interrupted, touching his arm. "He seems very nice. It's me."

Their conversation was cut short as Mike Owen walked up to them. "Hey, Devon, everything go all right?"

"I think so." He was smiling at her. She felt guilty.

"Did Buck tell you I could give you ride home?"

"He did." She glanced at Buck before looking at Mike. This plague of reluctance to accept his offer was beyond her control. It felt foolish and sensible at the same time. "Do you live in Blanco Springs?"

"No, I'm closer to the hospital, been renting a little house at Junction. Driving a few more miles so you can get home isn't a big deal. My next shift isn't until tomorrow afternoon." He was waiting, calm and relaxed.

She was on the spot. "Well, I . . . .." She couldn't think about it all day. "Are you sure you don't mind?"

"Yes, I'm sure." He chuckled. "You'll just have to tell me how to get to your place."

He wasn't a complete stranger. They'd talked at lunch. He'd helped Jamie. She had to get over being afraid of a man without having a good reason. "Okay." She forced it out. "Thank you."

Buck smiled when she looked at him. "Well, it's settled then. You've had a tryin' day, Devon. Go home and take it easy." He put his hand on Mike's shoulder and gave it a pat. "I'll leave her in your care, Doc. I know you'll deliver her safe and sound." He clapped his hands together and rubbed them like he was ready for his next task. "Guess I'd better get back upstairs and see if the wheels of justice have started to turn yet. Drive safe now." With that, Buck left them standing there.

Mike took off his tie and unbuttoned his shirt's top button. "Man, I hate ties. Think that's why I went into medicine to avoid wearing a suit all day." He grinned. "My car is parked across the square. Ready to go?"

She put a smile on her face. "As ready as I'll ever be."

Stacks of marshmallow clouds filled the sky to the west as they cut across the courthouse lawn. A spring storm was brewing in the distance. The warm breeze that ruffled her hair brought with it the smell of rain. They passed the building where Otis Young had his office and Devon kept a cautious eye out for Mrs. Colton. The old woman troubled her in a way that couldn't be clearly labeled fear. It was closer to a threatening rumble, of something possible, but not certain, that was unnerving.

Mike unlocked the door to the passenger side of his blue Bronco and opened the door for her. She got in finding comfort in the thought of going home. He walked around to the other side and opened the door, laying his sports coat and tie on the back seat, before sitting down.

"I have to stop for gas before we go back." Mike turned the key in the ignition. "Been a nerve-racking day for you, hasn't it?"

She nodded not wanting to dwell on the details. They stopped at a station on the main road. While he filled the gas tank, she bought a couple of cold drinks. They headed southwest.

"Seems three-quarters of the population around here has two names like Billy Bob or Betty Sue." He grinned enjoying poking fun at the locals, as so many outsiders liked to do. He might have exaggerated the ratio but having lived other places she couldn't blame him for thinking it was comical. "How did you manage to escape with a one of a kind name like Devon?"

"It was my English grandmother's name." It was easy to talk about ancient history.

"What brought her to Texas?"

"She came out to the rough and tumble in the 1890's to teach the Queen's English to the cowboys. There used to be a small Presbyterian college in Riley. She met my grandfather at an ice-cream social and that was that." She decided to do a little poking around in Mike's sandbox. "How did you find your way to a little hospital in the middle of nowhere. You aren't a Texan but I can't place the accent."

"I'm not a Yankee." He looked at her with a good-natured shrug and held up his hand in mock defense. "That seems to be a capitol offense around here. I'm from Washington, part of the great Pacific Northwest, where trees grow tall and moss grows faster." He laughed. It was a warm, exuberant laugh that made it hard not to smile in response. "Ever been there? "

She could feel her smile sag as the image of Alan standing by towering trees with Mt. Rainier in the background flashed through her mind. "One visit, a long time ago. It was beautiful." She looked out her window.

"Oh, then you were there the day it didn't rain." He smiled at her as she turned to look at him. "To answer your first question, I got my clinic job here after a stint in the Army. I was discharged in November from Ft. Sam. I heard they needed someone to fill a vacancy in the ER. I was sort of treading water at the time, so I decided to come here to keep in practice." He talked with an easy friendliness as he drove. She leaned back and relaxed. He was pleasant and good company.

Mike turned on his headlights. It was getting darker as they drove the wide two lane road through this flatter ranch country. They were headed for a rainstorm that had turned the sky blue black. The clouds were churning into mountains as brilliant flashes touched the earth with spidery legs. It was beautiful. She liked the rain. In this country, it was the lifeblood of the land. Everybody prayed for it in the dusty summers. And it was a thing to marvel at when it rushed down normally dry, rocky creek beds in foaming torrents.

"That sky doesn't look good." Mike was leaning forward looking out the windshield. "The guy at the gas station said he'd heard it was going to be a real gullywasher tonight. Looks like it's coming in early."

The rain was a gentle sprinkle at first. The rhythm of the windshield wipers, like a metronome, increased as the front swept in. A gust of wind whistled over the car. As they drove through the increasingly hilly terrain, the rain began to pour down with a vengeance. Mike slowed a little but drove faster than she would have. It was hard for her to see the centerline in the glare of the headlights on the wet pavement. Devon squirmed in her seat and adjusted the shoulder harness.

"Look at this guy coming up behind us." Mike was frowning, his attention focused on the rearview mirror.

She turned to see a dark vehicle with two sets of lights racing toward them. The row of off-road lights, above the regular headlights, was a brighter white.

"Slow down, knucklehead." Mike hit the steering wheel with the palm of his hand.

The truck roared up behind them. The body was lifted like an off-road vehicle so the lights filled the rear window of the Bronco with a blinding glare.

"Pass me and get it over with." Mike steered the Bronco so the right tire was on the wide shoulder. The other vehicle pulled out but didn't pass. It stayed beside them. Devon's heart was pounding in her chest. Unable to utter a sound, she glanced at the road ahead dreading the sight of oncoming headlights.

Mike's voice was tense. "This guy's drunk. I'm going to stop."

The dark truck suddenly accelerated and slammed into the front fender of the Bronco. The force shoved her shoulder against the door and she could feel the tires break loose as they skidded across the slick pavement. Devon dug her nails into the armrests and braced herself. The Bronco plunged off the road, landed with a bone jarring thud, and bucked its way through a fence into a pitch-black field.

The headlights reflected off a patch of scrub brush in front of the hood. She looked at Mike. His hands were still on the steering wheel. She heard him take a deep breath.

"Shit, that wasn't fun." He glanced at her. "Are you all right?"

She moved her arms and legs to make sure everything still worked before she nodded. "Yeah, I think so." She felt a minor twinge in her side. "Could you tell who it was?"

"Not with all those damn lights. The truck was green." He turned his head to look back at the road. "The son of a bitch is gone, whoever it was." She noticed he was huffing and puffing as much as she was. At least he wasn't one of those macho guys who tried to hide being scared.

"Why would somebody run us off the road?" Her shaky voice was a match for her hands.

He turned to face her. "Some drunk, good old boy playing bumper tag probably. I've had a few patients come through the ER who tried it and lost control. There are a lot of strange cusses around here, if you don't mind my saying so."

She was surprised he wasn't hopping mad. They sat for a few minutes without saying a word, listening to the heavy rain pepper the roof. She was glad she wasn't stuck out here alone. They were okay. She repeated that to herself several times. Devon's heart calmed to a trot.

The storm was drifting south, a grumbling, roll of thunder accompanied a heaven-filling flash that illuminated the sloping, brushy field they were sitting in. There wasn't a house or electric light to be seen. Wide open spaces once again, just when you could use a little civilization.

"Guess the night isn't getting any younger. I'd better see if we can get out of here." He put the truck in reverse. They could hear the wheels spinning. He tried to rock the vehicle back and forth without much success. Mike stared out the windshield as the rain pounded and sighed. "Sure could use four-wheel drive right now. Can you look in the glove compartment for a flashlight?" She found it. He turned in his seat and reached for something behind him. He had a pair of rubber boots in his hands when he straightened around and smiled. "I've been in a Texas downpour before."

"Do you think we're just stuck?"

"Probably, looks sandy out there." He took off his shoes and put on the boots. He grabbed the flashlight, opened the door and quickly stepped out into the drenching rain, slamming the door behind him.

She couldn't see anything clearly through the blurry windows but followed the glow moving around the vehicle. It wasn't long before the door opened and he jumped in. He was soaked.

"Well, the good news is most of the truck looks fine and the water's warm." He ran his hand over his forehead.

She smiled, admiring his positive attitude. "And the bad news?"

"We're stuck. The front tire looks low but can't really tell if it's leaking or the way we're situated. Had that tire fixed a couple of months ago. It's going to take me awhile to dig us out and put on the spare if it's busted."

"What can I do to help?" There was a roll of thunder but it sounded far away.

He looked at her suit in a quick pass of his eyes. "Well, if you could get in the back seat and search through the stuff in the cargo area. If I have to change the tire, I'll need the pieces of board I've got back there to put under the jack. I'll get out my army surplus shovel to dig the tires out while you do that." After he had got out, he reappeared in the back window lowering the tailgate to get the shovel. He closed it again to keep the deluge from soaking everything inside.

She was glad she could do something to help. It would have been easier if she were wearing pants. She crawled over the console in a very unladylike fashion and leaned over the backseat looking through things. He was a packrat. She sorted through old magazines, newspapers, tennis shoes, ice chest, tackle box, fishing rod and a couple of baseball caps before she found the boards. When Mike came back, she knew the tire was flat without having to ask because he grabbed the tire iron. She handed him the two short boards she'd found.

"Thanks. Could you hand me the mini mag light out of the console?" She found it and handed it to him. He left the bigger flashlight inside. "I'll be back to grab the tire in a few minutes." She could hear him talking to himself. He needed help.

"What the hell. I won't melt." She took off her jacket, slipped out of her heels, and stripped off her panty hose, which she stuffed in her purse. She put on his old sneakers and got out using Mike's door. Her skirt and blouse were soaked in an instant. Slogging through wet sand and pouring rain in shoes too big wasn't easy. He was holding the small flashlight between his teeth and digging around the wheel with the shovel when she made it to the other side. "Looks like you could use a little help." He looked up, light shining out of his mouth. She leaned down and held out her hand. "Drop it, Fido." He got the picture and opened his mouth.

"Thanks. My jaw was getting tired. You're going to be drenched."

"Really? I didn't know that." She grinned at him. "Hope you don't mind me getting your tennis shoes wet. I didn't think my heels would work in the sand."

"You should stay inside. No point in both of us getting dirty."

"I thought you could use some better illumination." She pointed the beam from the heavy flashlight at the wheel.

"Thanks, that helps. I'm about ready to get this jack in place."

Together they managed to stabilize the jack with the boards. The tire was flat. The metallic clicking as Mike pumped the jack handle to get the weight off the ruined tire joined the music of the rain.

"How's Jamie doing?"

"Fine." It seemed an odd thing for him to ask but she realized they didn't have a lot in common to talk about.

"He's quite a little guy. Guess his father's pretty proud of him." Mike glanced up as he strained to loosen a lug nut, rain dripping off his chin.

She gripped the flashlight a bit tighter. It irked her when someone called Alan Jamie's father. "We haven't seen or heard from him since the divorce."

"Oh, I didn't mean to bring up a sore subject." He studied her face before handing her a lug nut to hold. "I can't imagine a man not wanting to keep in touch with his own son."

"Me either." She was glad he thought it was strange. "He didn't want children." She watched the raindrops strike the handful of heavy metal rings in her palm.

"Sounds like a real prince." Mike grunted with the effort as he pulled the tire off and pushed it toward the front bumper to get it out of the way. He walked to the back of the vehicle.

She looked up at the flashes of lightning illuminating the clouds in the distance. The thunder was little more than a low rumble. He rolled the new tire around. She wondered if he was ever married and had kids.

"How about you? Do you have kids?" She shook her head trying to keep the rain out of her eyes. He was lining up the lug bolts on the axle with the holes in the wheel.

"Nope, afraid not. Didn't have time to get married in medical school. Then there was the Army." He took the lug nuts out of her hand and began to put them on. "Got married when I was stationed back East but it didn't work out." He flipped one arm of the tire iron to spin the nuts on. "I'm getting a little old to start a family now." He leaned against the fender as he strained to tighten them. She didn't think he was more than forty, but without the first ingredient, a wife, he'd have to start at square one. He was smart to realize having children was a long-term commitment and better left to the young and energetic.

"Okay, let's get out of here." He lowered the frame with the jack. "I'll put the tools up, you get inside. Thanks for the help."

The rain was slowing down now that they were finished. She was wet to the bone and shivered. Her clothes stuck to her body. Water dripped down her face from her hair. She pushed it back, away from her eyes. She sloshed to her door, opened it, and poured out the water in Mike's tennis shoes before sitting down. Her bare feet left sand on the floor, his tennis shoes beside them oozing little puddles.

Mike finally slopped into his seat like a pile of wet towels. "Okay, let's get out of here." The truck slowly navigated the field. They rolled up the embankment and onto the highway. They both heaved a sigh of relief.

Watching the rain through the windshield, she knew they'd been lucky. The image of Mrs. Colton, angry and vengeful, came to mind. Her threat was just hours old. It was silly to assign any power to it, like a curse, but she wondered deep down if the woman had a hand in running them off the road. No, that was nuts. She was giving that old woman too much credit. Mike said he'd treated people who'd tried the same dumb stunt in the emergency room. The car heater was finally warming up her feet.

It was sad really. The old woman had chosen to ignore the truth, twisting the evidence to fit a different scenario. Maybe it helped her avoid feeling she'd failed him. Devon could understand that. When TJ died, everyone in the family wished they'd done something differently but they'd only had themselves to blame. Mrs. Colton could lay the blame at her feet. Hopefully, Ed was right and Young wouldn't have the nerve to file the suit. But remembering the woman's cold blue eyes, she wasn't sure it'd be that easy to change her mind. She shivered, hating being wet.

"You okay?"

She looked over at him. "Yes."

"Worrying about getting sued?"

"Something like that." Devon wanted it buried: the terrible memories, the legal finagling, all of it.

"Buck said the woman's attorney is a weasel."

She took a deep breath. "Pretty close." She stared out the window. "He said Mrs. Colton thinks I was stealing the truck from her son." The blatant distortion of the truth gnawed at her.

"That's nuts." He glanced in her direction. "You were defending yourself, plain and simple. Nobody can blame you for that."

"Oh, his mother can." The hard-edged bitterness in that woman's face was etched into her memory. "In that old woman's heart, he is still her little boy. She loved him and I killed him."

"You can't be feeling guilty?" He blurted it out.

She stiffened and turned toward him. "I understand how that feels. I don't think I'd be that blind but I might." She looked away realizing she'd shouted at him. "He was a cruel and vicious man but I'm not proud of the fact I killed him." She glanced at him. "I was just trying to get away."

"I didn't mean for that to come out the way it did." He watched the road ahead of them. "I think you were very brave to fight back under the circumstances. The coward liked hurting women. If you hadn't hit him as hard as you could, there's no telling what he would have done to both of you." Mike's voice grew louder and his words were harsh. "He would've killed someone eventually."

The conviction in his voice shook her, made something tremble inside her. "Why do you say that?"

"My second day at the clinic, I treated a young woman who didn't say 'no' and she was beaten to a pulp anyway. Buck told me John Colton was the one who did it. That girl was so terrified she wouldn't press charges. Buck had to let him go."

She covered her mouth. She wasn't the first. He'd slipped through the law and run into her. Thank god, she was the last.

Neither one of them said anything for a while. She didn't want to think. The water kicked up from the road by the tires splashed against the wheel wells as the engine hummed in the background. She rubbed her bare feet on the carpeting. The heater was drying out the sand from her feet and ankles.

She took a deep breath and leaned back in her seat feeling wrung out. "Wish I could blank out all my memories of that day."

"It's probably better to talk about it. Get it out of your system." In the glow of the lighted dash, she could see his faint smile. "Read that in one of those psychology books in medical school."

He was trying to be helpful but it wasn't that easy. Her clothes weren't plastered to her skin anymore, just a damp, wrinkled mess. Feeling generally uncomfortable, she looked over at him. He was sandier and wetter than she was.

"I feel as if I should apologize. You drove this route instead of the highway to take me home and look what happened."

"Are you kidding?" He glanced her way. "This is the most fun I've had since I've been here. If we weren't both soaked and covered in sand, I'd stop and buy you a good stiff drink but the bartender might wonder what we've been up to."

She smiled. "Two drowned rats leaving a wet, sandy trail across the carpet might get a lot of sympathy on a night like this, but this is a dry county, remember?"

He clicked on the interior light for a second to appraise her. He had a wide grin on his face. "Drowned rat? Never." She shook her head knowing she looked awful but appreciating his kindness. "If not a drink, how about dinner some time?"

She hesitated as a confusion of responses banged into each other. He'd taken being driven off the road in stride . . . managed the repairs without griping in this crummy weather . . . seemed to appreciate all she'd been through but . . . dinner sounded like a date. She wasn't ready for that.

"You don't owe me anything, Mike. You've already helped by giving me a ride home."

"At least let me treat you and Jamie to a hamburger or something."

She held up her hand. "No, you went out of your way to help me. We're even-steven."

"I just thought it might be fun. Not much to do around here."

She sighed. "Well, if you ever eat at the Tastee Freeze on the outskirts of town, we'll probably see you there."

"Good." He smiled. "Jamie and I will have some ice cream and if you want to sit with us, it'll be okay with me."

It was only six o'clock by the time they got to the ranch but it felt later. Devon was tired after such a stressful afternoon. Ellie must have seen the headlights because the outside lights came on. She and Jamie were standing on the front porch when the Bronco pulled up and stopped.

Devon opened the door and stepped down holding her jacket, heels, and purse in one hand. "Hi, sorry I'm late."

"I expected you over an hour ago." Ellie looked at Devon's wrinkled clothes and bare-feet and frowned. "What happened?"

"We had to change a tire in the middle of a thunderstorm. You remember Dr. Owen, don't you, Mom?" She turned toward the Bronco. The passenger door was still open so the interior light was on. Jamie was climbing in. "Jamie, get down from there."

"Hey, Jamie how are you?"

"Fine."

Ellie peered inside. "Hello, Dr. Owen. Would you like to come in for supper?"

"No, I think I'll head on home and clean up but thanks for the invitation, Mrs. Taylor."

Devon looked at him. "I appreciate the ride home, Mike."

"My pleasure." He paused, glancing at her son. "Hope things work out okay. Well, guess I better get going."

Devon pulled on her son's arm. "Come on now, Jamie."

"'Bye, 'what's up doc'" Her son giggled and jumped down.

"See you around, Jamie."

Devon shut the door and Mike drove off.

"Are you all right? I thought you were coming home with Buck."

She heaved a tired sigh and didn't look at her mother. "I was, but Buck's hearing was delayed. Mike was in the courthouse for some reason, so he offered to bring me home."

"That was nice of him."

"Yes, it was." She turned toward the front door wanting to drop the subject. "I feel so itchy, I'm going to shower and put on dry clothes."

After Jamie went to bed, Devon gave her mother the full blow by blow description of the incident with the truck and the appointment with the attorney, but skimped on the details about her encounter with Mrs. Colton. Ellie had enough to worry about. She went to bed that night thinking bad luck was following her. And those kinds of thoughts led her nowhere but round and round into a sleepless night.

"Jamie! It's time for dinner." Devon's eyes scanned the area around the barn and the tire swing. There was no sign of him. She stopped breathing for a second to listen. Nothing. "Jamie!" She cupped her hands around her mouth and yelled louder. She stood for a moment waiting for a reply but none came.

Devon walked back into the kitchen. Ellie was whipping the mashed potatoes. "Did he say anything when he went outside, Mom?"

"Just said he was going out to play."

"I'll go check the barn. Maybe he can't hear me." She let the screen door slam as she went out the kitchen door. When she was a kid, she could hear that sound a mile away. It was like the dinner bell. She kept an eye out for his red shirt as she walked toward the barn.

She stood just inside the open wooden doors, searching the shadows for any movement. The smell of leather and engine oil was strong in the warm air.

"Jamie." Calico emerged from the dark and mewed as she rubbed against Devon's leg. She ignored the cat. Standing still, she listened. Quiet as a tomb. Her eyes followed a beam of light that shone across the dirt floor, stopping on the shining metal scoop on top of a sack of oats. Maybe he was with Dulce. Breathing faster, she turned around and headed for the corral out back. The mare was rolling in the dirt but there was no trace of her little cowpoke. Devon looked toward the pasture, ears straining to detect any sound he might make. Would he have wandered that far from the house?

"Jamie!" Her voice betrayed the panic her imagination was building. She ran to the outer edge of the corral to get a better view of the open grazing land spread before her. Trees nestled in clumps along the distant creek. He wouldn't have gone that far.

"Where are you?" She was talking to herself now, afraid of the answer. Something had happened to him. Her insides seemed to collapse at the thought.

There was too much ground to cover by herself. Devon started to run back to the house when she saw Jamie standing in the wide doorway of the barn. The tight squeeze in her chest disappeared as a sigh of relief escaped her lips. She walked over to him.

"There you are."

"Is it time to eat?"

His matter-of-fact tone ruffled her feathers after the worry he'd caused her. "Did you hear me calling you?"

He smiled. "Uh-huh, I'm building a secret fort."

She was beginning to see red and it wasn't in his shirt. "Why didn't you answer me?"

"I was busy doing stuff." A little frown wrinkled his brow.

Apparently, he thought that was a reasonable answer. "James Robert, when you hear me calling, you had better answer, young man, or you'll be spending the rest of the day in your room." She poked the air in front of her with her index finger accentuating every 'you'. "Is that clear?"

His frown deepened and a grudging bottom lip jutted out but he finally nodded. She hadn't meant to yell at him like a harpy.

She put her hands on her hips. "You just about scared the stuffing out of me, do you know that? Go in the house and wash your hands."

Jamie headed toward the house at a trot. Devon turned her back on his retreat, walking toward the corral again, as unhappy with panicking as she was with her son's silence. She'd blown the whole thing out of proportion, let her imagination go wild. A coyote came out of a clump of cedar brush in the field with a limp cottontail dangling from his mouth. He stopped to eye her, before he loped out of sight with his prize. It seemed there was always something to take advantage of weakness, something faster or more cunning. She had reason to be vigilant but she needed to find some middle ground to keep from driving herself crazy.

Devon pulled off the road just past the mailbox. Being able to take Jamie to the bus stop each morning and wait with him until the bus rattled toward them, its brakes squealing as it stopped, was a luxury she had never been able to afford. She told herself she did it for the pleasure of this quiet intimacy with her only child and not her own paranoia. There had been no more accidents, no threats to worry about. After all, the old woman had decided against filing a suit. Ed Thurman had been quick to let her know and hadn't charged her a nickel. She would find a way to thank him.

Her legal worries were over and she should pull that file box out of the closet and decide where to start her job search. By the looks of things, the rain wasn't over yet. The wind was picking up again stirring the leaves on the branches of the scrappy burr oaks along the fence. A tornado had torn up a little town about a hundred miles to the north three days ago.

Jamie was inspecting the item he'd selected for show and tell. He shook the rattle Hank had cut from the tail of the snake he'd almost stepped on yesterday. "Mom, what makes the noise? Is there something inside?"

He always reminded her of how many mysteries and dangers there were to ask questions about. Hank had spent a good deal of time with him on the proper course of action around a snake.

"As I remember, each little section is hollow and makes that sound when they bump against each other."

Hank drove by in his blue truck and honked. Jamie leaned across Devon's lap to push on the horn twice to answer.

"Here comes the bus, Jamie. Put your show and tell in your lunch box so you won't lose it."

He did as he was told, carefully laying the Ziplock bag on top of his wrapped peanut butter sandwich. They stepped outside and waited for the bus to stop. She zipped up his light jacket before she gave him a kiss on the cheek. When the folding door opened, Jamie climbed on and waved as the bus pulled away.

Ellie was sitting at the table when Devon walked into the kitchen. There were dirty dishes in the sink and the frying pan was still on the stove. It wasn't like her to be lingering over her coffee this time of day. Something was wrong. Devon braced for bad news, grabbed her mug off the counter, filled it and sat down.

Ellie was idly sliding a fingertip along the edge of her cup.

Devon looked at her mother's face. "You feeling okay?"

Ellie took a quick breath and straightened up in her chair as if she'd been lost in thought. "Just thinking about your father. I keep expecting him to walk in that door asking me 'what's for supper' like nothing had happened. Sounds crazy doesn't it?" She sniffed and took a drink.

"No, it doesn't." Devon put her hand on her mother's shoulder. She couldn't say more. When her mother cried, it was gut wrenching to watch and next to impossible not to join her.

"We lived together for so long I knew what he was going to say before he said it. We'd sit out back in the evening talking about what needed doing next. I love this place but sometimes I don't quite know what to do without him." She glanced at Devon. "It's been nice to have you and Jamie here." She looked out the picture window toward the pasture. "I've been wanting some company."

Devon swallowed to ease the tightness in her throat and gave her mother a pat. "I'm glad we're here too, Mom." She was staring out the window too, watching the cattle grazing near the trees. It felt empty in the kitchen. Too many vacant chairs around the table.

"That tornado up north left a lot of families with just the clothes on their backs. The churches are collecting things for them. I decided last night to donate your dad's clothes. I think he would approve. Aren't doing anybody any good in the closet." Her voice trailed off. Ellie cleared her throat. "Would you help me pack them up this morning?"

Devon turned toward her mother and nodded her head. They both had tears in their eyes.

"I haven't disturbed anything in his closet. It was too hard. I wasn't ready for him to be gone, I guess." She raised her mug to her lips with both hands and took a sip.

Neither of them said anything for a moment. Devon couldn't finish her coffee. The inclination to eat or drink was gone. She silently steeled herself for the task to come wanting to make it easier for her mother.

"There are a few things I want to give you now for Jamie to help him remember his grandpa. That way, you'll have them wherever you end up."

Devon battled to get the words out. "He'll like that, Mom. He was talking about their fishing trip the other day."

Ellie dabbed at her eyes with her napkin. "I've got some boxes folded up and stored in the garage. Guess I'd better put up these dishes before we get started." The legs of her chair scraped across the floor as she pushed away from the table. She gathered her cup and plate.

"I'll help." Devon scooped up the remaining silverware and her coffee mug. They made short work of the kitchen, talking only when necessary, then went out the garage and carried the boxes to the bedroom.

"I think most of the clothes will fit in these." Mom sniffed but her voice sounded very calm. "I'll take them to the community center in Clear Springs this afternoon."

Devon opened her father's closet and flipped the light switch on. It struck her immediately why her mother couldn't do this. The things he'd worn were still a part of him. His gray, beaver Stetson on the top shelf was waiting for him. The lump in her throat made it impossible to swallow. She touched the silver buttons on his fanciest rodeo shirt and wiped away the tears in her eyes. Somehow in her head, she could hear his rousing 'hang on, cowboy' and hearty laugh. It was more than she could bear. In one quick sweeping stroke, she gathered an armful of long sleeved shirts ready for another day of work, hangers and all, folding them over before stuffing them into an open box. Better to do it quickly and in bundles. It was easier to deal with boxes.

"Devon, I thought you might want to keep some of your father's things in this box." She turned around. Ellie was standing by the dresser. "There's his knife, your grandfather's pocket watch, things special to him."

Devon walked over. She looked inside. The small leather wallet held together with broad overcast stitches around the edges caught her eye. Her fingers shook as she touched the crude hand-tooled 'D' on it. Third grade, that's when she'd made it for him. He'd kept it all these years. She picked it up and opened it. A scrawny, smiling eight year old in pigtails looked back at her. A piece of pink paper fell out. She unfolded it. 'I love you, Daddy' was written in red crayon surrounded by lop-sided hearts. Tears rolled down her cheeks. She looked up and wiped them away with her hand. The pictures on the wall were of her family, her mother and father in the center of them all.

"He carried that with him for months to show you how much he liked it." Ellie stood beside her now. "Finally, he put it away in here so he wouldn't lose it."

She turned and put her arms around her mother letting the tears roll down her face.

"He couldn't always get the words out he wanted to say, honey. All he knew to do was work hard." Mom consoled her with gentle pats.

"I know." Devon sniffed. "I need a tissue." She stopped hugging and walked into her mother's bathroom. The box was empty so she grabbed some toilet paper. She dried her eyes and blew her nose. After a deep breath, she walked back into the bedroom.

Ellie was filling a box with tee shirts and jeans. Devon began to neatly fold the hanging clothes and put them in the closest open box. She noticed silk pajamas on the bed that looked familiar. Alan had picked them out. She'd sent them years ago to Pop for Christmas. Obviously he'd never worn them. Come to think of it, she couldn't remember ever seeing him in pajamas. She looked down at her feet. What a nitwit she'd been. Having money for the first time in her life and encouraged by Alan's expensive tastes, she'd been foolish and extravagant, especially at first. Mom was right the other day. The proof lay folded on the bed.

The closet was almost empty when Devon realized the metal cabinet on the back wall was a locked gun safe. Her father had always been careful with his guns, but she was a little surprised he'd installed one.

"I wondered where Dad's rifles were. When did he put this in?"

"Last year. That little Clayton boy got killed playing with his daddy's pistol. Your father thought it would be safer to have a place to keep them out of sight whenever Jamie came to visit. I've locked them all up in there. I have no use for them."

"Are his handguns in there too?"

"Yes, and all the ammunition. I didn't want to take any chances."

Devon started carrying some of the boxes out to the garage. She remembered wishing the .22 had been in the truck's gun rack. If she'd had it on their walk, John Colton might have left them alone. On the other hand, it would have made things worse if he'd gotten hold of it. Before picking up the next load, she stopped by the bed.

"Would you mind if I plinked at cans sometime, Mom?"

"I guess not. Why do you want to." Ellie was taping a box closed.

"Just to see if I'm still Annie Oakley." She smiled remembering how her father had teased her with that title, so proud of the fact that she was a good shot. "Don't want to have to arm-wrestle a rabid skunk if I run into one while I'm out on the ranch."

Ellie smoothed the tape on the last box. She frowned. "I know what kind of skunk you're thinking about." She reached out to hold one of Devon's hands. "Can't say that I blame you but you're not going to run into anymore criminals roaming the county."

Devon squared her shoulders. She looked her mother straight in the face. "I just want to make sure I can hit something if I ever have to."

Elllie released Devon's hand but pointed at her. "I can't stop you, but be careful. I don't want any shot up children around here." She turned away. "Let's get these boxes out to the car."

Devon took advantage of her mother's absence after lunch. She drove to the isolated draw on the western edge of the ranch. It was rocky and drier here, farther from the river. The loose soil was only capable of supporting scrub brush and a few clumps of weeds or cactus. There were no cattle in this area.

The slopes of one decaying ridgeline sifted down like lion's paws hanging on for dear life, the sharp claws hidden under a blanket of rocky splinters. She parked the truck. Waves of heat rose from the rocky surface, well-cooked in the afternoon sun. It was close to eighty degree out here. She wouldn't stay long but the steep bank provided a safe backdrop for an errant shot.

She grabbed her bag of pop cans and pushed a few of them into the dirt to stand in a row. She walked back to the truck and took the larger revolver out of the box on the seat. It was heavy. The bullets slipped into each round chamber with a crisp click that inspired a certain confidence in the workmanship.

But this wasn't a piece of equipment, it was a weapon designed for protection. If she used it, it would be because someone dangerous was close . . . too close. She snapped the cylinder into place, walked about twenty paces from her lineup and focused on the first aluminum can.

She gripped the thick .357 handle and straightened her arm to point at the target. Her hand drifted down from the weight, but she lifted it back up. Looking down the barrel, she aimed and pulled the trigger. The loud boom ricocheted off the ridge as the weapon kicked, forcing her arm up. It felt like shooting a canon. She took her finger off the trigger and let her hand drop to her side. The can was gleaming in the sun, the smiling red logo smugly unblemished.

She shook her head. Damn, she'd forgotten a lot. 'You're shooting like a girl.' TJ had prodded her unmercifully with that phrase knowing it drove her crazy and made it harder to concentrate when they were practicing. She was thankful Hank wasn't around today. He'd have split open trying not to laugh at her.

She tried to remember her father's routine. She'd practiced it over and over. Silently coaching herself along she tried again. Use two hands, dummy. Look down the barrel, put the sight on the target and hold it steady. Now, take a deep breath letting it out nice and slow as you squeeze the trigger. Bam. This time she ruffled the sand near her target. She smiled. Your ass is mine, mister.

With a mock swagger, she grabbed a new target out of the bag. She tossed it toward a different spot wanting to try the old gunfighter game. Holding the revolver firmly with both hands she shot at it, not taking the time to line up the sights. The last two shots made the can dance. A man was a lot bigger. She lowered the heavy gun and carried it back to the pickup. She opened the cylinder and let the shells drop into her palm. The brass was warm as she wrapped her fingers around them. If she had to, she could use it. The thought calmed the part of her that remembered how much bigger and stronger Colton had been. It could be an equalizer but it was bulky and hard to handle. A gun could only help even the odds if she had time to get it out and if it was loaded. Couldn't carry a revolver this big around in a purse or a pocket. She'd try the lighter .22.

After several rounds, she hit the lined up cans and tossed cans every time with the smaller pistol, which bolstered her confidence. She carried it back to the truck, emptied the cylinder and left it on the seat. Someone looking for trouble might not be intimated by its size but it would slow a man down enough to allow time for escape. She walked over and surveyed the punctured aluminum strewn about.

"Nice shootin', ma'am." She tipped the brim of her cowboy hat playing her part in a game she and TJ had created. "Why thanks, Wyatt. Means a lot comin' from you." She picked up a root beer can full of holes and dropped it in the sack.

This wasn't the old West. People didn't walk around with six-guns strapped to their sides. She collected the ruined cans. And her mother was right. Having a loaded gun around was a danger to Jamie. The ammunition would have to be locked up. But an unloaded gun wasn't a weapon anymore. She wiped the sweat off her forehead. Okay, new rules. Don't be stupid enough to get stranded. Carry two spare tires and an extra drive belt. Watch your back. Take up karate.

After putting the revolver in its box, she looked at the rifle on the gun rack in the back window. She was more likely to run into a rabid skunk or coyote out here than come across another lunatic. A sick animal could be just as dangerous as a sick human like Colton. She set up her shooting gallery again and drove the truck farther from the targets. The small scope on the .22 rifle made it easier to be accurate. With it, she was deadly. Not a single can in the state of Texas was safe.

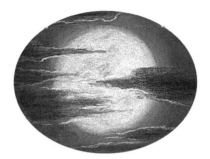

The next morning when she drove back to the house from taking Jamie to the bus, Hank's truck was parked by the corral. He must be checking on Dulce. She was worried about her old racing partner. She drove into the garage and got out. It was starting to sprinkle again. Hank was walking toward the house with Ellie. They stopped when they saw her and Mom waved for her to join them. She ran over.

Hank started talking before she could ask a question. "Old Dulce is still havin' problems, Devon. Come take a look." They headed for the corral. "I'd hoped that castor oil Doc suggested would do the trick by this mornin'." He stopped at the closed iron gate. "Bad sign the way she's been paddlin' around." He pointed to the dirt around the mare's legs that had been scooped away as if she were trying to run.

Dulce was on her side breathing in labored blasts, distress in every jerky movement. Devon grabbed the middle bar of the gate and hung on, gasping in sympathy for her gentle mare. She looked at her mother. Her expression was whitewash calm but her eyes glistened with sadness and it crept into her voice.

"I'll call Doc Jessup, Devon." Ellie turned and headed back to the house.

The old veterinarian, walking with a bit of a limp, carried his black bag to the shed. Devon hadn't seen him in years. His right arm was in a sling. He'd mentioned to Ellie that he was nursing an injured shoulder. She had the feeling he shouldn't be taking calls.

"Thanks for coming, Doc. Dulce's been down all morning. We brought her in from the pasture and Hank gave her the oil but nothing's gone through her. She looks terrible." An understatement at best. Her mother stayed inside the house unable to watch the mare suffer.

"They're real delicate creatures and can go sour fast. Sorry, my partner Pete couldn't come out here, Devon, but he was way out at Sandy Creek on a call. Take him too long to get back. I asked Frank to come and give me hand. He knows as much about horses as I do anyway."

The thought of seeing Frank's good-natured grin lifted her spirits. They'd pulled a prank or two on each other over the years but had always come out even. "Frank's around. Last I heard he was riding bulls."

"Oh, he quit that a way back. Just bought a place. He's ranchin' now days." He opened the gate of the pen and headed for the prostrate animal. "Well, let's see how she's doin'." He put down his bag and took off his hat, setting it on top of a post.

She leaned over to watch the vet examine Dulce, hoping he could do something for her. She straightened up when she heard a truck door slam and glanced at the person approaching. His wide brimmed cowboy hat was tipped down to fend off another rain shower but she knew it was Frank, even if she hadn't seen him in fifteen years. She recognized that long, slightly bow-legged stride. When he got under the shed roof, he took his hat off and slapped it against his thigh. "That you, Devon?"

She nodded, pleased he'd recognized her. "Hi, Frank. How are you?"

He walked over, put an arm around her shoulders and gave her an unexpected squeeze. "I'm fine. Good to see you. I didn't know you were home. You visiting or back to stay?"

He hadn't lost the playful gleam in his eyes or his infectious smile. She'd fallen all over herself in puppy love with him at the ripe old age of twelve but he never did seem to notice.

"I'll be around for a while."

"Good." He turned his head and shifted his attention to his father. "What do we have, Dad?" He walked over and squatted down beside Doc and Dulce's heaving body. Devon followed but stayed out of their way.

"Old gal is having a hard time. Fever. Gut sounds bad. Have a listen, Frank." Doc handed him the stethoscope.

"Isn't this the horse you did all your barrel racing with, Devon?" She nodded when Frank glanced over at her. He leaned closer to the mare and listened. He gave Dulce's head a gentle rub as he moved around to look in her mouth. The two men talked quietly. She backed away and leaned against the rough fence boards watching their solemn faces.

Doc Jessup stood up. He rubbed his chin and looked at her. "Wish I had good news, but I don't think she'll make it, Devon. We can try some antibiotics. I'd be lying if I told you I thought it would save her. Her gut is twisted. If she was mine, I'd put her down to end her suffering." He glanced at the mare before turning back to her. "It's up to you." Frank stood up and walked over to join them.

Yes, it was. Mom had told her to do whatever she thought best. Dulce was hers and always would be. "Would you give me a minute, Doc?"

"Sure thing." He retrieved his hat from the post and walked with Frank to their trucks parked at the gate.

The soft patter of rain on the metal roof sounded like tears. She got down on her knees by Dulce's head and combed her fingers through the red mane. Dulce's heavy panting reminded her of the times they'd galloped toward the last barrel. The rush of excitement as she'd leaned in the saddle, their bodies moving together as they cut around the steel drum, then spurring her four-legged partner to run faster, her breath matching her mount's as they raced for the finish. Now Devon's pounding heart and Dulce's panting had nothing to do with the thrill of competition.

Dulce lifted her head off the ground and squealed as if the pain were unbearable. The cry cut through Devon and brought tears to her eyes. She had to help her and there was little choice, even though the thought tightened around her heart. Dulce had done everything Devon had ever asked of her. She owed the mare.

She couldn't get a word of comfort out. Her throat ached from holding back the emotion churning inside. All she could do was rub the white blaze above the flaring nostrils. One more piece of the past would disappear from her life. One more connection to her childhood and the happy days with her father and TJ would become a memory.

"Goodbye, sweet girl." The farewell was a faint whisper. She stood and brushed a hand across her wet face before walking back to the two men standing by the barn.

She cleared her throat. "If you could take care of her . . .."

"You bet. We'll get the things we need."

She watched as Frank carried his father's medical bag and a bottle of blue liquid out to the shed. After that, she turned away and stared at the rolling pasture. New tears rolled down her cheeks. The warm air was filled with the smell of the rain and the gentle fragrance of the wildflowers.

She heard footsteps. Frank stood beside her. She looked toward Dulce. Doc was closing his black bag. The mare was finally at rest.

Frank put an arm around her shoulders. "She was a fine horse." He patted her. "You did the right thing, Dev."

She slipped her arm around his back. "I know." She sniffed and wiped the tears off her face. His smile was gentle. "I'm crying like a ten year old."

"You lost an old friend." He squeezed her arm. "I'd have cried if she were mine."

She kept her arm around him needing to be consoled a minute longer.

Frank and his father put away the instruments. Hank drove up and talked to all of them in quiet tones until Ellie invited everybody in for a cup of coffee. They sat around the kitchen table trying to make small talk. Mom put out a plateful of cookies before sitting down next to Devon.

Hank cleared his throat. "How's the new place workin' out, Frank?"

"Real well, Hank. Plenty of room for working horses and to raise a few head of beef. Pretty good hay barn." Frank grabbed another cookie, dipped it in his coffee and took a bite. "Great cookie, Ellie."

"Thank you, Frank." Mom smiled and stared out the window.

Devon was thinking about how to tell Jamie.

"Jamie is going to miss her." Ellie gave a little sigh. "He was out there every afternoon."

"I'll keep an eye out for a nice, gentle, saddle horse if you want me to, Devon." Frank smiled at her from across the table.

That was a crazy idea. "What would I do with one, Frank?"

He frowned. "You used to ride them."

Even after all these years, he knew how to ruffle her feathers. She stirred her spoon around in the cup before glancing at him. He didn't know anything about her anymore.

"That was a long time ago. I don't have a place to keep one and Mom has enough livestock to feed already."

"Just offered." He took a sip of coffee, watching her.

"Thanks." The word came out snappier than she'd intended.

"Well, time's a' wastin'. Come on, Frank." Doc stood up with a grin. "Better get you out of here before you get yourself in trouble."

With that, the two men stood. Frank gulped the last of his coffee and carried his cup and his dad's to the sink. "Good to see you again, Ellie. Thanks for the coffee."

Her mother walked to the door with them. "Come by anytime, Doc. You too, Frank."

Ellie smiled but Devon couldn't, not yet. Dulce was still out there.

Hank got to his feet about the time the other two men went out the door. "Guess I'd better bring the tractor around."

Devon sat at the table staring at her cup thinking about how she would explain it to Jamie. She didn't want to be out there to watch Hank haul Dulce off.

Ellie broke the silence. "The school bus will be here in a little while." She glanced at her. "Want me to tell him about her?"

"No, Mom. That's my job."

"What are you going to say?" She sat down beside her.

"Other than the fact she died?" Devon put one elbow on the table and rested her chin on her fist. "That's what I'm trying to figure out. If he'd been here, he would have seen how much she was suffering." She raised her chin and used her hand to rub the side of her neck. "Even if he had, I'm not sure he could've understood helping her die. What do you think?"

"I think I'd keep it simple. See what he wants to know."

"Yeah, you're right." Devon nodded her head. "I'll just keep my fingers crossed he isn't in one of those inquisitive moods this afternoon."

Devon sat in her car, waiting. The sun was drying off the puddles in the road. She'd decided the straightforward approach was probably best. Hank had moved Dulce to the brushy draw where her father had laid most of his animals to rest. He believed horses ought to rejoin the land where they'd roamed in life like nature intended. When the bus came into sight, she got out of her car. The bus doors slapped open and Jamie jumped down from the second step.

"Hi, Mom." He smiled wide enough to display his permanent teeth in their various stages like a bar graph.

"Hey. Did you finally get your turn at show and tell?"

"Yep but lots of kids seen rattlers. Did you know that?" They got in the car and Devon made a U-turn in the road. "We had a lady instead of Ms. Thompson today. She's got . . . bronco . . . sidis." He dug around in his book bag. "Look, I got a new reading book." He held it up.

"That's good. I'll look at it later, okay?" She pulled up to the garage and stopped. "Jamie, I need to tell you something." She turned off the engine. He was looking at her expectantly. "It's about Dulce."

"Is she still sick? Uncle Hank gave her some medicine yesterday."

"This morning she was feeling very bad. I called the veterinarian."

"Did he give her some new medicine?"

"No. She was too sick to get better. She died, Jamie." She watched his face trying to gauge what he was thinking.

He was frowning but didn't cry. "Did it hurt?"

Thank goodness, he hadn't been around to see her. She could answer that question honestly. "No, honey."

"I'm glad." He bowed his head. "She's a nice horse."

"Yes, she was."

"Ginger will be lonely." He looked up. "Can we go in now, Mom?"

"Sure." Maybe it hadn't sunk in. That was okay.

He pushed the door open, but stopped before getting out. "Hey, wait. Do we have to dig a big hole?"

"No. Hank has taken care of her." He jumped out of the car not asking for the details, flung open the kitchen door, and let it slam behind him. She sat alone for a minute longer.

Devon brushed her hair and put on lipstick. She'd changed. They all had. After Patsy had called this morning surprising her with the fact she was in town for the weekend, Devon had gone into her closet to find her senior yearbook. Through thick and thin, the four 'birds of a feather' had survived twelve years of school together. Ranging from tall to short, robust to slight, they must have looked like an unlikely quartet to everyone else, but their differences had complemented one another. Patsy, her best friend, had an easy smile, engaging charm and coasted through school content with passing grades. Tammy Jo was musical, a whiz with numbers and wanted little more than a part-time job and children. Loretta was the comic relief, funny to the bone, ground-in dirt practical and fearless about everything. And she had been the serious one, the tutor and moderator, harboring a wanderlust the others didn't share. Now for the first time since graduation, they were all in the same vicinity at the same time. Such a 'cosmic event' could not be disregarded, Patsy had bubbled. So they would meet again to reminisce and have some fun.

On her quest for the yearbook, she'd come across a shoebox full of pictures. One old snapshot deserved to see the light of day so she decided to take it with her. The four of them, clad in blue jeans, were lined up beside each other, arms draped over shoulders, laughing. The stands at the rodeo grounds were in the background. It seemed to her they were about thirteen. She couldn't place the occasion but she remembered the feeling that together they could do anything. She hoped the glue that had held them together for so long was still sticky after so many years.

Walking to the den, she ran through her checklist. Jamie was bathed, in pajamas, and the Disney video was in the VCR. All Mom had to do was pop the popcorn and tuck him in bed. She heard Patsy's signature honk and rushed to the kitchen. They met at the door.

Her sassy friend, still just a wisp of a woman with thick, black curls framing her face, gave her an affectionate hug before pulling away to give her the once over.

"Well, I'll tell you what . . . you look great. I was hoping you'd be fat and dumpy so I could feel skinny standin' next to you." She rolled her brown eyes and laughed.

Devon smiled and shook her head. "You are such a tease." She hadn't changed at all. "Your curves are still in all the right places I see."

"Thank you, ma'am. It's been, what, four years since I've seen you? Makes me glad the Travers bunch is having a reunion, so I could get Jeff to drive up here. Loretta called and said Tammy Jo was going to meet us at her place. I am ready to howl tonight."

Ellie walked in. "I thought I heard your voice, Patsy. How are you?"

"Oh, just fine, Mrs. T. My boys are growing like weeds. Between school and sports, it seems I spend all day in the car. I know my mama has shown you the pictures."

"Yes, you have a good-looking bunch of boys, Patsy. Jamie and I have our evening planned so y'all have a good time."

"I want Patsy to see him before we go." Devon grabbed Patsy's hand and led her to the den. Jamie was sitting on the couch watching TV.

"Hello, Jamie." Patsy put her hands on her hips. "Well, haven't you grown up to be the most handsome young man."

Jamie lowered his head and grinned as Patsy leaned down. Devon chuckled loving that sweet, shy look.

"Last time I saw you, you were just toddlin' around. I've got a couple of boys just about your age. Do you like to swim?"

Jamie looked up. His eyes wide with interest. "Yes, ma'am."

"Good. I'll talk your mama into letting you come over for a swim with my boys. I won't interrupt any more of your television show. We'll see you tomorrow."

Patsy stopped the car before pulling out on the county road. "I have to tell you something now that we're alone. I've been worried sick about you, Devon. You look fine, but how are you really?" There wasn't a trace of a dimple on her face.

She didn't want Patsy to lose her smile tonight. "I'm doing okay, so stop worrying." She reached over and patted her friend's hand.

The concerned look on Patsy's face didn't change as she pushed the gearshift lever into park. "How could you be? A criminal appears in the middle of nowhere? Almost kills you! You must have been petrified."

"I was." She wasn't going to lie. It would be ridiculous to pretend she wasn't.

Patsy's eyebrows rose in sympathy. "Oh, honey, it just isn't fair."

She was tired of that particular useless concept. "Life doesn't have to be fair." The remark sounded more bitter than funny. She sighed. "Look, Patsy, you're my friend. It's been hard, very hard but I'm healing, getting stronger."

With a firm set of her jaw, Patsy shook her head. "As awful as it might be to say, I'm glad that man is dead so he can't hurt anybody else."

"Me too." Devon clenched her teeth together. "It makes it easier to sleep at night."

"Do you have awful nightmares?" Patsy's eyes were watery.

Devon was determined to stop anymore tears from being shed. She'd cried enough for everyone. "Every once in awhile."

"Well, you're doing better than I would." Patsy reached over and touched her shoulder. "I admire your courage."

She turned in the seat to face Patsy. "I'm not any braver than you are. You'd have done the same thing."

"Oh, I don't think so." Patsy put her hands on the steering wheel and looked out the windshield. "I never told you about my little scare. It sounds childish, especially after all you've been through."

"What happened?" Devon tensed and leaned toward her friend.

"I was at the mall." Patsy looked at her. "This man smiled at me, and you know me, I smiled back. I didn't mean anything. When I walked out to my car, there he was, following me." She shuddered. Devon felt a tug of sympathy. Patsy was trying to shake off the fear the memory revived.

"I got in my car, locked the doors and took off like nobody's business. I could hardly drive I was shaking so. That's why I said I don't think I'd be as brave as you were. He followed me home. Drove right past the house when I pulled in. I didn't know what to do. Jeff called the police. They said the man didn't break any laws. I think sometimes, policemen don't really understand how that can scare you, like you're some kind of child without good sense. It's been three years now but I still worry about it sometimes." Patsy sighed. Devon watched her realizing it was hard to find something comforting to say. "Jeff checks all the doors and windows to make sure they are locked before we go to bed. Sounds kind of silly now."

"No, you had the right to be afraid. I would have been too." She touched Patsy's hand. "Glad you've got Jeff around."

"Yes, praise the Lord for that." Patsy shook her head and shifted into drive. "Let's not talk about this anymore." She gunned the motor, kicking up dust and turned onto the paved road.

Patsy drove too fast down the two lane road, threading their way among the rolling hills. "I really like those earrings, Devon. Bet you bought them up in Minneapolis, probably have everything under the sun in that king-sized mall." Patsy glanced over at her with an abbreviated smile. "I thought in your last letter, you were all settled in up there away from Alan and everything was fine. But Mama said Ellie told her you were moving back home."

"I have, but only temporarily." She could see two glowing spots off the side of the road ahead. "There's a deer on the shoulder, Patsy, slow down."

"I see it." She honked the horn and it ran. " Go on, pretty one."

Devon let out a breath. "I've been thinking of staying in Texas if I can find the right job."

"Hey, that would be great. Have you considered Houston? Jeff knows a lot of the bigwigs downtown. Maybe he can help you out."

"If I decide to look down there, I'll give you a call." Devon watched the fences and ranch houses as they drove. Loretta was the only one of their group spending her days working on a ranch and raising her family. Mom had seemed happy and busy when Devon was growing up. Loretta said she liked it too. Of course, her old friend had never lived anywhere else.

She wondered if she could live on a ranch again, day in and day out. While the quiet and slower pace was calming, now she noticed how isolated and vulnerable it could be.

"Would you ever consider moving back and living out here, Patsy?"

"Heavens, no. Drive me crazy to have to make a safari out of every trip to the grocery store. Why? Are you?"

"No, I can't afford to stay even if I wanted to, but Mama's lonely. I hate to leave her."

W hen they pulled into Loretta's place, every window in the house was lit up.

"All those boys of Loretta's must be having a party of their own." Patsy grinned. "I'm ready to have a little fun too." They both hopped out of the car as Loretta and Tammy Jo came out the back door. They collided about halfway between the car and the house.

Loretta extended one of her long arms and drew Devon into a hug. "Good to see you, stranger." Loretta had put on a little weight to fill out her large frame and she'd cut her long, black hair, but the smile was the same. "I think you've shrunk a little."

Devon laughed. Her sly friend was as dependable as a fly at the supper table. "Maybe you're just getting taller, Rett." Devon smiled waiting for the reaction.

"Good Lord, I hope not!" She put a hand over Devon's head and brought it back to her own ear comparing the differences in height. "Had me running scared there for a minute, peanut."

They piled into Patsy's car and drove through the countryside. While they gabbed and laughed, their years together were as crisp as yesterday. The embarrassing fixes they'd gotten themselves into had lost their sting and were just plain funny as they recalled them now.

They voted to ruin their diets with an order of onion rings and cherry cokes at the Tastee Freeze, for old time's sake, and parked in a slot at one end of the row of intercom stations. There were cars and trucks everywhere, some parked and some cruising. Patsy shouted out their order into the gray box. The garbled reply coming out of the static filled speaker was unintelligible so they hoped for the best. Unbuckling, Patsy and Devon turned sideways in the front seat so they could carry on a better conversation with Tammy and Loretta in the back. The radios of the vehicles parked around them were all set on the same country music station.

"Nothing changes around here." Tammy pursed her lips and followed one truck with her pointed finger as it circled the drive-in. "Boys driving around in their pickups while a bunch of girls sit in one of their daddy's cars giggling." Tammy shook her head, her hair glowing like a rusty halo from the headlights of circling vehicles.

"No point in changin' something that has entertained so many for so long, Tammy." Loretta winked at Devon. "Probably holds the birthrate at the high school down to fifty percent."

"Oh, Loretta!" Tammy playfully slapped at her arm.

Loretta's husky, slow drawl brought a smile to Devon's face. She could imagine the stares she'd get sounding like that in a hip southern California restaurant. They'd be too busy snickering to appreciate her on-target social commentary and great timing. They didn't deserve her.

"Hey, I almost forgot. I've got something to show you." Devon pulled the old photo out of her purse and held it up. The others leaned closer to get a good look.

"Oh my, we look like such babies. And my hair was a kinky mess."

Loretta turned on the dome light. "Stop whining Tammy, we're all a mess. Lord, this must be ancient. How old were we?"

"I'm guessing thirteen. What do you think, Patsy?"

"Let me look." Patsy studied the picture. "It was horse feathers day, don't y'all remember?"

They looked at each other and smiles started to spread across their faces. It was the day they'd taught big-mouthed Dickie Collins a lesson. They were laughing when the food arrived.

A girl, who didn't look a day over twelve except for an expansive chest, delivered the tray with two large baskets of golden fried onions and four sodas. Devon felt old suddenly and the rest in the car were silent. Several boys revved up their engines in a macho rumble as they went by and whistled to get the waitress' attention. The girl rewarded them with a coy smile. After she left, a sigh came from the back seat.

"Why couldn't I have had boobs like that?" They all turned to Tammy.

Loretta put her hand on Tammy's shoulder, accompanied by a solemn shake of her head. "Picture cantaloupes on a bean pole. You'd never have been able to stand up."

They chuckled and passed around the food after Patsy squirted a glob of ketchup in the middle of each basket. It felt familiar and comfortable sitting in that car; a kinship, solid and undiminished, shared without missing a beat.

"By the way." Patsy rolled her eyes in delight. "What's the latest in the saga of the Atkins sisters?"

"Oh, Lord, who cares?" Tammy let out a huff. "Just because Suzy thinks she's the center of the universe, do we have to talk about her?"

Suzy had been a burr under all their saddles. In every award program, every school election, her name came up like a bad case of heartburn. She ruined pranks and parties. They were only free of her at the rodeo. She was too ladylike to ride a horse, thank goodness.

Loretta smiled with a twinkle in her eyes. "That woman's hair gets redder than yours every time I run into her, Tammy. Looks like a match with a weight problem." She waited for the chuckles to end before answering Patsy question.

"Suzy's devoted herself to findin' a mate for little sister, Dee Dee now. Big job since Dee Dee's still dumb as a stump. Small wonder any man who's ever met her runs when he sees her comin'. I hear they've taken up popping breath mints to make sure they are always minty-fresh." Devon remembered seeing Suzy's green tongue and shook her head.

"According to my Aunt Florence . . ." Loretta's dramatic pause had Patsy shifting in her seat to lean closer, "Dee Dee waits for the singin' to start, then sashays into the church auditorium. All the single men are eyein' the door, ready to make a run for it as soon as the preacher quits. Dee Dee's all dimples sittin' cockeyed in the pew, battin' those eyelashes and not payin' the least bit of attention to the sermon." A sly grin crept across Loretta's face. "A few of those boys turned tail and became Baptists."

The car was filled with laughter.

Tammy nudged Loretta with her shoulder. "You are awful."

"It's the gospel truth."

"Don't sit too close to her, Tammy. No telling how accurate a bolt of lightning is." Patsy put one hand over her mouth to muffle a burp. She grimaced and held up an onion ring. "You know, these things don't taste quite as good as they use to."

They all had the same response. "Uh-huh."

Patsy dropped the offending crusty-fried vegetable and her napkin into what was left and put the blue plastic basket onto the tray attached to her window. "The moon is coming up. Let's go to the river."

"How about a cold beer?" Devon missed having one whenever she wanted. That was one price of living with her mother.

"Sounds good to me." Loretta chimed in.

"Maybe some bubbles will break up the grease. Here, take this." Tammy Jo handed Patsy their basket from the back seat.

The sky was a solid black holding up a brilliant sterling moon as Patsy drove down the old highway that meandered along the river. The windows were rolled down and the radio was turned up. Devon leaned back in the seat enjoying the feel of the wind blowing her hair.

Patsy pulled off on the sandy spot that dropped down to the water's edge and parked facing the river. The headlights shone on the flat ledges of cream-colored rock as the shallow water ran across them. When she clicked the lights off, the reflection of the moon shimmered on the surface like a silverplated reward for remembering this bend in the river.

They opened the doors and stood beside them. "I forgot how pretty this place is." Patsy quietly closed her door and the others followed suit. They walked to the water's edge, guided by the bright moonlight and the sound of water trickling over the rocks.

Devon stared at the shadowed trees on the other side of the river thinking about all the times they'd come out here and let the water lull them with its soft whispers while they shared their dreams. Once her eyes adjusted to the silver light, Devon looked from friend to friend. They had all changed but somehow they were the same, still able to care about each other. It was nice to know she wasn't as alone as she felt sometimes.

Patsy broke the silence. "Remember roaring around the countryside in that old pickup of yours, Retta? How did we manage to all fit in there?"

"We were skinnier, sugar lump." Loretta sighed and put one arm across Patsy's shoulder. "I almost feel guilty for sweet-talking old Harvey into buying us those six packs."

"No, you don't." The three replied in unison, laughing.

"It's so peaceful." Patsy's voice poured out into the stillness. "I'd forgotten how much I liked the little tree frogs singing." Patsy shook her head and sighed. "I'm sounding like a old lady. I'll get out the beer." She turned around to walk back to the car.

"No, you aren't." Devon called after her. "I know exactly what you mean. I felt the same way listening to the tide come in when I lived on the beach in California." She pictured the home she'd loved until the lonely end to her marriage.

"Tell us about Los Angeles, Devon." Tammy turned toward her and swooned like a teenager. "I've always wanted to go there."

"Okay." Devon folded her arms and thought about the place, a world away from here. "L.A. is a city full of beautiful people from somewhere else. Like they all ran away from home. Most of them working overtime to look young. If you're searching for love in a bikini, it's the place to be."

"Did you see any movie stars?" Tammy's eyes were open wide like an owl's, the whites reflecting the bright moonlight.

"No, most of them have moved to Montana, I think." Devon leaned sideways so her shoulder touched Tammy's in consolation.

"Oh." Tammy's voice slid in disappointment. "How about Minnesota? Is it really cold up there all the time, like a blue norther?"

"It is like a freezer in the winter, warm and sticky in the summer."

Patsy walked up from behind her handing out bottles. "So what happened to make you leave that new job?"

Devon shook her head and looked away. "Nothing." She was enjoying the fuzzy past and saw no point in rehashing that disaster. "I quit." She took a swig of beer.

"That doesn't sound like you." When Patsy got a whiff of something, she wouldn't give up until she'd heard all the details. It was her least admirable trait. "Come on, what's the real story? Tell us." The three friends drew closer to her.

She groaned. "Okay. Since you'll drive me crazy, I'll tell you, although there's nothing mysterious about it." She took a step to be free of the crowd and turned around. "My boss was a creep. A married one. He started with little compliments and worked up to propositioning me."

"I hope you told him which pile of crap he could stick his shovel in." Loretta blew across the lip of her bottle sounding two quick toots.

Devon took another gulp and shook her head at Loretta's gift for making barnyard references fit any occasion. "I didn't use that particular metaphor but the message was the same."

"How embarrassing. What did he say?" Tammy covered her mouth with her fingers.

Devon looked at Tammy amazed, no, to be honest, she was envious that Tammy could be so naive. "He thought I was playing hard to get." She took a deep breath and exhaled remembering the man's sleazy grin.

"Why is it, some men can't read 'no' even if it's printed across your forehead." Patsy jabbed her beer bottle in the air in disgust. "They should have fired him. Why did you quit?"

"After I complained, Leonard told his boss I was sending 'signals'. The boss believed him. Guess he had to since Leonard was his son-in-law." She squeezed the bottle in her hand before taking another big sip. "There was no place else I could go in the company so I resigned." She tasted again the bitterness of cleaning out her office while he watched.

"No woman should have to put up with that." Tammy Jo stepped forward, put an arm around Devon's shoulder and gave her a pat.

"Amen." Patsy and Loretta added as they surrounded her.

"Oh, good Lord! You just get home from dealin' with that creep and you have to fight off that . . . mean son of a bitch." Patsy slipped her arm around Devon's waist and squeezed. "Bless your heart."

Tonight, Devon didn't want sympathy. She just wanted to laugh.

Loretta cleared her throat. "Too bad you didn't get to kick your boss in the handle on the way out. That would have put a bend in his shovel."

Patsy giggled. "Amen, Sister Loretta."

Picturing Leonard Jamison's smug expression collapse in response to a blow from a well placed knee, Devon started to chuckle. "Actually, I'm considering becoming a nun." And that set them all off.

Patsy leaned her head back and let out a wild call and they all joined in. They sounded like a pack of coyotes, but it felt great. It released the frustration that had been eating away at her since she'd walked out of that office. Maybe they all needed to get something out of their systems because the howling continued for a while before ending in more laughter.

It was one in the morning when Devon got home but she was too stirred up to go to sleep right away. She went out on the deck and sat in the glider listening to the crickets. The moon was gliding west. Her life was drifting just like it. None of her friends' lives were perfect but they had roots. She wanted to belong somewhere again.

She hadn't been completely honest tonight. There had been more to her leaving than just her boss' behavior. Otherwise she would have stayed up north, beating the bushes for a better job rather than coming home.

But those last few months, she had simply gone through the motions. Chasing after more responsibility and better salaries had made her miserable and accomplished nothing of substance. She was past the point of trying to prove anything to Alan or anybody else. The only thing she was really proud of was Jamie and she couldn't escape the feeling she'd failed him. It had been nice to slow down and have time for him. Too many nights, she had come home late, given him a good-night hug and fallen asleep wrapped in guilt. She'd never do that again.

She pushed backward with one foot to start rocking and listened to the familiar squeak of the hinge that wouldn't stay oiled. She put her hands on the back of her head and leaned back. She'd set her sights on a decent job in the realm of a forty-hour work week and find a little house with a backyard, someplace closer to home so she could help her mother. She didn't want Mom to feel abandoned. There was no way she could live with that. Family was all she had. Distance had faded the memories her heart needed to survive the hard times. She rubbed her eyes, the fogginess of sleep clouding clear thought. So she listened to her body, stood up and went to bed.

Jamie loved the water. Devon thought he was part fish sometimes, the way he liked to swim under the surface and hunt for things on the bottom of a pool. When Patsy had mentioned swimming, she knew he wouldn't forget it the next day. She shouldn't have stayed up so late. Jamie was up early but she'd told him they would have to wait until later to call. Patsy called before she had a chance.

"Are you two going to come over?" Patsy's voice was maternal, questioning. "My boys are hopping mad about having to wait until I heard from you. Daddy had the thing full when we got here yesterday and they were shriveled up like prunes by bedtime."

"Jamie has been after me to call." Devon apologized. "I didn't know when you would be awake or what you might have planned today."

She quickly dispensed with excuses and packed up a few things while Jamie put on his swimming trunks. The afternoon was spent watching the boys happily splash and scream in the three foot, aboveground pool Grandpa Cline had set up for his grand kids. Jeff got in the pool for awhile and played with the boys, even Jamie. He was a nice man, an energetic father, and a good sport. He loved Patsy. It was obvious in the way he put his arms around her, talked to her and looked at her. She wished Alan could have been that way. Patsy was lucky to have him.

In the late afternoon, Devon told Jamie they had to go home. All the boys were drying off and getting dressed inside the house while she and Patsy talked outside.

"We have to leave in the morning. I'm so glad I got to see you." Patsy put her arms around her. "Hopefully you'll be here the next time we come, although it is such a long haul from Houston, I confess I do dread it. Jamie and Jason were getting along real nice, I thought." They waited by the front door for the boys.

"Patsy, can I ask you something?" Devon closed the space between them so she could speak softly. "If anything happened to me and Mama couldn't care for Jamie for some reason, would you take him and raise him for me?" She didn't want to stop until she'd blurted out everything. "You know how to handle boys. I realize you'd have to talk it over with Jeff. I haven't mentioned it to Mom either, but I guess, I'm asking if you'd at least consider it. There's plenty of money to get him through college. So your boys wouldn't suffer financially if he was with you."

Patsy frowned. "Are you sure Alan wouldn't want him?"

"I can't count on him. He didn't even want visitation rights. And I'd never have a moment's peace, even in the grave, if I thought his mother got her claws into Jamie. I know he'd be okay with you."

"Well, I'm honored you would ask me. But you can keep yourself out of trouble for twenty years or so, can't you?" Patsy forced a smile before hugging her tightly. Her voice cracked as she whispered in Devon's ear. "You can count on me."

Devon closed her eyes to hold back tears.

Patsy brushed her hand quickly over her cheek when the five boys came running out. "We have a big supper over at Jenk's house tonight."

They all walked out to Devon's car. She managed to cut Jamie out of the herd and get him in the back seat. Patsy leaned down to talk through the open window as Devon started her car. "Jeff will have us up at the crack of dawn to go back to Houston and I haven't even started to pack. You two come down and see us."

Devon reached out and took her hand. "Thanks, Patsy, we'll visit when things settle down." She put on her sunglasses and smiled. "I'll call you in a few days. Be careful driving home."

"We will, hon." Patsy straightened and clapped her hands together. "All right. Come on, boys. Time to make you presentable. Boys! Right now."

Devon backed out onto the narrow road and drove away. She could breathe easier thinking her son would be cared for should something happen to her. Ed Thurman could help her with the paperwork if Jeff would agree. She doubted Patsy would give up until she'd convinced him. Hopefully, it was one agreement they'd never have to fulfill.

Aunt Rose and Uncle Harold arrived Saturday afternoon to spend the night on the ranch. They'd driven down from the Panhandle for the annual family dinner at May Dell's Sunday afternoon. Rose was very close to Mom and had spent several weeks with her after Pop had died, something Devon would always be grateful for. Their eldest son, Lee, was in charge of the day-to-day operations of Harold's cotton business now, giving them the freedom to go whenever they wanted. Pop had the same dream of handing things over to TJ, but that died with her brother.

Sitting around the supper table that night, Rose entertained Jamie by telling him about his grandmother when they were both little girls. Jamie's eyes were wide as Rose described Ellie as a tough little scrapper who had played in the mud, climbed trees, and rode bareback like she was born on a horse.

"The worse paddlin' she ever got was for chewing some of Daddy's tobacco on a dare. I think she was about five because I was in second grade. You should have seen her face, Jamie, when our brother, Calvin, put that nasty stuff in her mouth." Rose pinched up her face and frowned. Jamie started giggling.

"He told her it'd taste better if she chewed." Devon laughed. Mom didn't but she had a smile on her face. "So she tried a couple of chomps but her face drew up like she'd been sucking a lemon and brown juice started dribbling down her chin." Rose chuckled and patted Mom's hand.

"Poor thing, she started to gag but Cal said she had to swallow it. He loved to play tricks on us younger ones. But poor little Ellie started crying and spit it out on his foot. Then she lit into him, cussin' a blue streak like she'd heard Pa do." Rose shook her head as everyone at the table laughed.

"Our mama had come out of the house about then and got an earful. Lauzy, Mama was as mad as mad could be. Ellie got spanked on the spot for talking like that, and Cal got one too for being so mean to his baby sister and getting into the tobacco. And I was scolded for not taking better care of her." Rose looked at Mom with an affectionate smile. "After that, your grandmother never believed a word Cal told her, Jamie, and I kept an eye on her."

After Jamie was asleep and Uncle Harold turned in for the night, the women stayed up, talking quietly in the den. Devon sat in the rocking chair. Ellie and Rose were sitting on the couch. She envied them. With TJ gone, she'd never have a lifelong closeness like theirs. The thought saddened her. Soon, they were all yawning. It was late, time to go to sleep.

Jamie was in the middle of the mattress with his arms and legs splayed out. She moved him to one side and slipped in between the sheets of the double bed. The nightlight cast shadows on the back wall.

Mom's big brother, Cal had been as rambunctious and devilish as her brother, TJ. Devon's childhood memories drifted back to a time when TJ still answered to Jimmy. Whether playing hide-and-seek in the old hayloft, bumping along on the lengthy bus rides to school, or racing back from the bus stop to be first at the kitchen door, he'd always been there.

When this had been his room, trophies and team pictures from Little League to high school were everywhere. He had two Dallas Cowboys pennants tacked up over his bed. He was going to play for them one day he'd bragged. TJ was a dreamer. He'd needed a crowd to cheer him on.

She'd thought he could do anything but in reality he was much better at sports than schoolwork. Even before he left for college on a football scholarship, she could see things might not work out as he'd planned. Athletes got hurt or someone better came along. She'd been a realist in that sense, like her father.

TJ had puffed himself up, looking every inch of twenty, when he stormed out the door that late summer afternoon. She shut her eyes tight not wanting to remember their last angry conversation. As the sole keeper of their childhood memories, she took a deep breath and thought back to happier times. They were children racing across the pasture, heading home. 'Last one in is a rotten egg.' He was laughing, teasing her to catch up, as she drifted off to sleep.

"Hey, Squirt, wake up."

"Don't call me that." Devon opened her eyes.

TJ was leaning against the frame of the open door wearing jeans and his favorite Dallas Cowboys shirt, the last one he'd ever worn.

She sat up, feeling cold. Something wasn't right.

"Where's all my stuff?" He wandered around his room. "Guess all this junk is his, huh?" He turned around and motioned toward Jamie, sleeping on the bed.

"Yes." She shivered.

He ambled toward the door, straightening his picture hanging on the wall before glancing in her direction. "Why are you mad at me?"

She didn't like his frown or the sharp disapproval in his voice. He didn't deserve an answer. She stared at him, waiting in hot desert air for the next breath.

He turned to face her, crossing his arms like she was on trial. "I'm the one hit that damn tree. I didn't do nothin' to you."

"You didn't do anything?" She shouted at him in disbelief. "Are you joking?" She jumped out of bed, fire blazing from his careless spark. "You went to that raunchy honky-tonk and got plastered, you moron. I'm more than mad, I could ring your stupid neck!" He chuckled, shaking his head as if she were a silly child. The fury of their last argument was alive again as she closed in on him. "You promised me you wouldn't get drunk.'" He laughed. She made a fist and hit his arm as hard as she could but he didn't so much as flinch.

"Big deal." He stuck his thumbs in his jean pockets, resting his shoulder against the doorframe. The cocky, football hero grin she'd despised was on his face. "I'd been there before."

She slapped him but there was no stinging sensation in her hand or sound and no change in his expression. "You idiot." She spun around, away from him. Thoughts she'd never spoken rushed out. "You put us through hell and that's the best you can do, big man . . . I hit the tree? Am I suppose to feel sorry for you or do you want a trophy for that?" She paced back and forth, aching to wound him and wipe the smile off his face. "You didn't have to listen to Buck tell us how you'd killed yourself and Travis," she was breathing hard, sweating, "but I did." She pounded a fist on her chest and held it over her heart. "I sat at the kitchen table, watching Mama cry and Pop's hands shake while he blamed himself. You missed that and the years of hurting. All you cared about was playing a stupid ball game and to hell with us! I wish I'd told Pop to go after you. God, how I wish I had!"

He wasn't slouching in the doorway anymore. He'd straightened up to his full height. "You were my kid sister . . . so I ignored you." He slapped his palm against the football he was holding. "Man's got to have pride or he's lost the game."

She wanted to cry. That was a crummy reason to die. She sat down on the edge of the bed, shaking. "Life isn't a game, TJ."

"Maybe it isn't for you." She heard the hurt in his voice and glanced up. He brushed his hand across his knee like he was dusting something off his jeans before looking at her. The grim set of his jaw made a smile impossible. "I did what I did because I wanted to." He swallowed and blinked before fixing his eyes on hers. "I didn't mean to hurt anybody."

Her heart thumped to life in her chest. "I know. That's what makes it so sad." The room was filled with his trophies and pictures again, things he'd cherished. "I was afraid you wouldn't love me if I told Pop, so I didn't. I lost you anyway." She ran her fingers through her hair to pull it away from her face. "I don't know why I'm yelling at you. It's too late."

When she looked over at him, he was turning the football in his hands. A faint smile touched his lips. "I had it comin'."

"Are you okay, TJ?" Tears were in her eyes.

He winked at her. "Sure." He was smiling as he turned away from her. "Enjoy life, Sis . . . for both of us."

"Wait, Jimmy. Don't go." He'd disappeared into the shadows beyond the door.

Her body jerked. She opened her eyes, touched her wet face with her fingertips. She was cold, shivering on the bed. The room was dark except for the dim glow of the nightlight. Jamie was soundly asleep beside her. She pulled the covers up to her shoulders and stared at the dark doorway almost expecting him to walk in.

The old anger had roared to life talking to him. She'd thought it was buried. It was all the talk of family tonight and staying in his room that had stirred it up. She closed her eyes. "TJ, forgive me for hating you." There was no reply of course. All she could hear was Jamie breathing slow and easy. She tried to match it and gradually felt her body relax as the tick of the clock on the bedside table faded away.

With Aunt Rose finishing her hair in the main bathroom and Mom in hers, getting ready for church, there wasn't much point in rushing through breakfast even though she'd promised her mother she and Jamie would go to church with her. Uncle Harold had finished reading the paper and started loading their bags in the car. Once they left, she could get dressed. They were going to their daughter Gracie's house this morning and meet everyone at May Dell's for a late lunch before heading down to his brother's place in Del Rio.

Devon peeked over the newspaper. Jamie had stopped looking at the funnies and sat poking at his cereal. "Mama, is my dad ever going to come back and play with me?" He looked up at her. The corners of his mouth were turned down.

He knew the answer. He'd asked before. She refrained from saying anything bad about Alan. It wouldn't help her son. "No, Jamie. He lives too far away." Giving him reason to think otherwise would be cruel but it still hurt to see him longing for something she couldn't give him.

"So I'll never have a dad like Jason has?" Jamie's voice was laced with disappointment as his spoon scraped the bottom of his bowl.

The sound of such dejection ached inside her and she didn't say any-thing for a minute. She hated leaving him without any hope of being like Patsy's boys or his friends at school. Besides, today was a new day, time for a new start. "If I got married again, you'd have a new dad." For the first time in a long time, there was a little bubble of hope she let rise inside at the thought.

"Oh." His expression was thoughtful. "Like who?"

"Like nobody yet." She leaned over and gave him a kiss. "Come on. I think the bathroom is free, so we can brush our teeth. Granny wants us to go to church with her this morning."

Sam Perkins had been in Blanco Springs one day and he already knew it inside out. After a couple of rounds at the honky-tonk twenty miles from here the night before, he knew who did what and when they did it. There were a lot of little towns like this, between here and the border, dying and filled with people too stupid to leave. Abandoned sheds, small caves, and empty back roads came in handy runnin' drugs. The only reason a man like him would be here, that's for sure.

He sat in his car across the street from the First Baptist Church watching them walk from the parking lot to the door. It made little sense to be doing this. He'd followed the boy and the Taylor women in from the ranch, keeping his distance so they wouldn't notice his gray sedan. Joe told him to take a couple of weeks to get the lay of the land and a good handle on the woman's routine. Shouldn't take him long in this one-horse town with ol' boys that didn't know when to shut up. Joe Colton was in Tulsa keeping his distance until the time was right.

Joe should have hired someone else to take the risk, but his crazy mother was set on Old Testament vengeance delivered by kin. The pull of blood was strong in that bunch. Joe promised his ma he'd handle it even though he knew Johnny had been skimming some off the top. As far as Sam was concerned, the cocky bastard got what he deserved. But Joe was his friend and he owed him. He didn't want to go back to prison anymore than Joe did, so he was being careful. Once Joe satisfied his ma, they could get back to business and make a bundle.

The Reverend Billy Clyde Stanford stood at the door shifting his weight from foot to foot. His boot camp crewcut was at odds with the nervous smile twitching at the corners of his mouth and the fine mist clinging to his upper lip. Her mother and Aunt Jessie stopped to shake the smooth white hand he offered. Devon scooted past them pulling Jamie along behind her.

This was his first church. He had just graduated from one of the local seminaries and was, undoubtedly, thrilled to have a job. She almost pitied him. The congregation was small, most of them older.

Devon waited by the double doors to the sanctuary for Ellie and Jessie to finish their welcome. Even though she would have been happy to sit in the last row, her mother headed for her pew, right-hand side and smack in the middle of the room. Aunt Jessie sat on the other side of her mother. Jamie wiggled beside Devon at the end of the hard bench delighted with the slipperiness of the wood. She draped her arm across the polished oak, her fingertips touching the soft cotton of Jamie's shirt to remind him to behave.

The sun lit up the stained glass window, the pride of the flourishing congregation when the church was built. It showered the floor with red, blue and gold. Billy Clyde marched up the center aisle to *Onward Christian Soldiers* and took a seat behind the pulpit. What the audience lacked in talent was almost made up for in enthusiasm and volume when the piano started to pound. The singing had always been her favorite part of the service especially when it was joyous, the harmonies old and simple like the lyrics. Jamie took full advantage of the opportunity to make noise and move around. He picked up the tune and although he got the words wrong he reveled in 'Bringing in the Sheets' anyway. She smiled through the whole song.

After a couple more rousing songs mixed in with the collection plate going around, Devon wasn't in the mood for an Old Testament hellfire and damnation sermon, but young Billy started in with the rumble of brimstone. She released a deep sigh of disappointment and wondered why he had chosen to launch his career with such a vengeance. He had managed to ruin the first day of her resolve to relax and enjoy life. Maybe he thought it was his job to make the flock feel they needed him to set them straight or a good tongue-lashing to put them a few steps closer to a pearly-gated Graceland, like the artist's conception on the bulletin.

She hated to see the faces around her change, the gazes lower and the mouths become grim. She wanted to stand up and challenge his self-righteous finger pointing at a group of strangers. But she would be the one chastised if she did and that kept her silent. Aunt Jessie watched him unfazed. And old Mr. Harris, sleeping peacefully with his mouth open in the pew across from them, didn't care at all. She shifted her body on the hard seat wishing she could leave.

Devon blotted out the harangue by looking past the fist slamming preacher. The large cross, high on the wall behind the pulpit, was empty. The straight, perfectly geometrical form created by two walnut boards was devoid of sentiment or emotion.

It was so unlike the one she had seen in an Italian cathedral. On it, a thin body hung on the edge of life. Arms stretched. A metal spike nailed them to rough wood. Hands with fingers curled in agony. She imagined it burned. The bloodied face glanced heavenward in that last moment of life. Every mortal's question on his lips, 'Why?' It brought suffering to life. Anyone looking at it felt an aching sorrow.

The preacher shouted something. She felt cold inside watching him shake his fist. Ranting about hell was noise, easy to ignore. Hell couldn't be described with words. She'd caught a glimpse of it in John Colton's face. It was much more terrifying than anything this young minister could conjure up.

She felt a gentle touch on her hand. An almost imperceptible nod of her mother's head sent her attention in the direction of her son and a scratching sound. He was scribbling with a stubby pencil in broad vigorous strokes on the church bulletin using a hymnal for a table. She covered his hand with hers. He looked up at her. Devon touched her pursed lips with a finger like her mother had done numerous times, years ago. He frowned. She raised her eyebrow and released his hand. He swung his feet back and forth with casual energy before returning to less enthusiastic scribbling.

She touched his curly hair. Up to now, she had been enough to guide him. One day he might need a firmer hand. TJ had tested Pop over and over. And Pop hadn't been enough. Maybe sometimes, there is never enough you can do. She bowed her head and prayed for real, hoping God would listen in here. *Please, let me be enough for Jamie. I couldn't bear losing him.* She straightened up as the piano started to play. They could finally leave.

After four stanzas, it looked like the preacher was going to have the congregation sing the invitational hymn until somebody gave up and came forward to be saved. Devon whispered a question. Ellie nodded and whispered in Jessie's ear. In unison, they all rose and tiptoed out. They had to hurry.

Devon opened the front door and helped Jessie into the Cadillac as Ellie got in to drive. Jamie was bouncing in the back seat. She shot him a stern look, which he ignored, while she helped Jessie with her seat belt. He knew better than to do that. Devon climbed in beside him and grabbed his arm.

"Jamie, sit down, right this minute and buckle up." He plopped down in the seat without a word but the scowl on his face said it all.

Jessie shook her head and pointed a thin finger toward the church. "I'll tell you what, Ellie. That boy's got a lot to learn about preachin'."

"I imagine you're right, Miss Jessie." Her mother's voice was modulated with an even calmness she reserved for the elderly lady.

As they drove out of the church parking lot, Ellie looked at Devon in the rear view mirror. She knew better than to ask. Devon looked at her mother's eyes reflected in the glass. "I think he needs a sense of humor."

"Me, too." Aunt Jessie chuckled.

Her mother smiled but didn't say a word.

Devon's relatives, on her mother's side, traditionally descended on May Dell's, home of the best fried chicken in the world, every spring around Easter if they could manage it. With family members spread out across Texas, it was hard to find a time when everyone could meet. It had been years since she'd been able to come.

On this bright Sunday, Devon stood with Ellie and Aunt Jessie enjoying the view before going inside. The others hadn't arrived yet. Jamie was playing on the swing set in front of May Dell's.

The restaurant sat on a small bluff overlooking the freeway. Hills like goose bumps rolled across an open, red-soiled plain while several mesas lined up in the distance. Scattered clumps of oak and mesquite were dressed up, waving their leaves. Brown-eyed Susans filled the median with their bright yellow heads. The colors were vibrant against the backdrop of the cloudless sky.

Her mother was silent, lost in thought as her gaze roamed the landscape. Devon realized Pop had been here with her last year. This would be hard for her, one more reminder. Their branch of the family tree was shrinking. First TJ, now Pop gone, whittled down to the three of them. Jamie was the hope for the future for both of them.

Jessie slipped her hand through Devon's arm and leaned against her. She straightened and put her hand over her great aunt's thin fingers with a gentle pat. Jessie closed her eyes and lifted her chin toward the sun, pleasure seeping out of her with a sigh. In her light pink dress and crown of pure white hair, the lady was a fragile blossom in an unforgiving world. Her affection for both women standing beside her was warm and sweet, like honey on a fresh biscuit, and she hung on to the feeling until several cars pulled up and the rush of greetings and hugs started.

The wonderful smells inside made her realize she was hungry. The long tables with white tablecloths were filled with heaping bowls of mashed potatoes, black-eyed peas, green beans, and platters of chicken and soft rolls rested at each end. After helping Jamie get his plate filled at the smaller children's table, she sat nearby with the adults.

Meal times with her kinfolk were social occasions. For a family of talkers, and she doubted there was any other kind of family in Texas, words were as much a part of the meal as the food. The platters of fried chicken and dinner rolls were passed around like the stories. All of Mom's sisters were here and her now infamous brother, Cal. Jamie had studied him with special interest when he was introduced to him. Cal, now in his seventies, had mellowed into a jolly old man.

CL, Aunt Margaret's husband, who had a gift for making any story funny, got things started. Down the long line of aunts and uncles, cousins and spouses words buzzed non-stop from all sides. She glanced from the silver hair and double chins to the deepening lines on her cousin Gracie's face. Time had gotten its licks in. Pop said that.

The food was wonderful, sinfully packed with calories. She enjoyed being in the middle of all of it again, a part of something so full of life, except for having to be in the same room with her Aunt Louise.

Aunt Jessie, sitting beside her, leaned to touch her shoulder. "This is mighty fine. Why does somebody else's cookin' always taste so good?" The pleasure of good food and noisy chatter spread across her face with a smile.

Devon grinned and turned to answer close to her ear. "Because you don't have to face the kitchen afterwards."

Jessie nodded her head. "Suppose you're right. Never did like doin' the dishes." She took a bite, chewing with her eyes closed to savor the taste.

Her cousin, Lucy, sitting across from her, was discussing college admission tests, recipes, and events at the Saturday Club, all at the same time with three different people. Devon had been able to do that before she'd left home. Now, it seemed she'd lost the knack for it and few of the names and places made the connections meaningful. She felt like a refugee struggling with translations at times.

Devon couldn't help but hear Aunt Louise talking every so often. She sat across the table and two chairs to the left from her. The woman didn't think before opening her big mouth. Whatever someone else had was better, more expensive, or prettier. Her children, Tom and Joanne, sitting at the other end, had learned to put up with her by moving as far away as they could and still be in Texas.

Somehow, her mother loved Louise anyway. She'd told Devon, one time, that Louise had been a sickly child. Her two older brothers, Leonard and Homer who had passed away several years ago, taunted and made fun of her as youngsters. Mom seemed to think that had made Louise nervous and cranky. Devon watched her, trying to be open-minded. Being told you are stupid and ugly growing up could twist anybody's psyche. Maybe that would explain why she was so obnoxious. She looked down the table at her mother's other sisters, Rose and Margaret. They were such good-hearted, generous women. It was a shame they didn't live nearby.

Her cousins, Gracie and Julianne, both mothers of teenagers, sat to her left. She listened as they aired their frustrations. "Kathy is such a pill these days. I could just shake her. Won't listen to a word I say."

Julianne countered. "Oh, I know how that feels. Just wait until she's eighteen. Tyler has got it into his head that he has to go to Baylor. Bill has tried to explain we can't afford to send him there with Justin graduating the next year. If he'd go closer to home, we could manage. He pitched a fit and stormed out of the house. Bill and I don't know how to get through to him."

"Comes a certain age, children aren't about to do anything you want them to do." Aunt Margaret had plunged in to the discussion. "You try to protect them the best way you know how but you can't stop them from running right into trouble. Some just have to learn the hard way."

Devon thought back to the turmoil she and TJ had created as teenagers. They had both been focused on what they wanted and resented interference or compromise. She remembered those restless times. They'd been too dumb to realize what was best. Her parents must have felt much the same way then, as her cousins did now. Worried, doing all they could, making mistakes out of love because the instinct to protect was automatic and subconscious. She understood that now. She regretted how blind she'd been. More than likely, she'd go through the same thing with Jamie no matter how hard she tried. Maybe that was the punishment for growing up.

By late afternoon, the food had disappeared from the table except for a bite of pecan pie left on a plate.

"Well, I'm full as a tick. Guess it's time to ante-up the bill." Gaston, cousin Betty's husband, stood up hiking his belt over his belly before reaching back to get his wallet. The rest of the men at the table followed suit. The tight cluster of hugging and kissing began to break up as families sorted themselves out, walked outside to their cars and said their good-byes.

Jamie and some of the other little ones had left the confines of the restaurant earlier to play on the swings. Calling him to come on, Devon walked to the Cadillac. After Aunt Jessie was all tucked in safe and sound, Devon looked around for her son. He was swinging.

"Jamie, time to go." She was tired and looking forward to getting out of her dress and heels. He let his feet drag through the dusty, worn patch in the lawn under the swing. She put her hands on her hips. "Jamie, come on, right now."

Listening to all the talk among her cousins dealing with their children had put her in no mood to be ignored. He sauntered over while waving goodbye to a boy about his age whom she didn't recognize.

"Jamie, we don't have all day. Scoot!" She opened the back door.

She heard Ellie's voice. "It's alright, Devon, we don't have to hurry."

When they got home, she put out playclothes for Jamie and changed into something more comfortable herself. She was dragging, tired after staying up late all weekend. Jamie was already playing outside. She decided to get some fresh air too. It would help her perk up and work off a bite or two of that pecan pie she couldn't pass up at May Dell's.

Ellie was reading the paper in the kitchen. Devon walked past her, heading for the door. "I'm going for a walk. Be back in a little while."

"Where're you walking to?"

Devon stopped. Her mother was looking up at her over her reading glasses. "Just down to the end of the pasture and back. I won't be long. I'll tell Jamie I'm leaving."

Devon headed down the road toward the pasture. The heels of her boots crunched as they bit into the scant soil, more rock than dirt, in the tire tracks. She stirred up a fine dust in the warm air. One by one, the cattle raised their heads and watched her pass. She lengthened her stride and swung her arms with enough gusto to get the blood flowing to her brain.

Taking in the broad sweep of hills and pasture around her, she walked toward the grove of oak trees. This was home. It was a part of her that couldn't be described without missing something or erased by living somewhere else. Feeling it tug at her, she'd come back. Devon knew her mother needed her with her father gone. Mom would be sixty-two this year, even though it seemed hard to believe. She was healthy, capable, but one day that would change. She'd seen it in the aging faces and awkward steps of her kinfolk today. The thought slowed down her footsteps.

A cottontail rabbit darted out in front of her. It startled her and her body jerked in response. She settled down with a deep breath and shake of her head. Pay attention, she chided herself, this is snake country.

If her father's sudden death hadn't been enough to remind her life could change or end in the snap of a finger, Colton had made it crystal clear. He'd also taught her to be afraid. It wasn't safe for a woman to live in this country alone. Too many things could go wrong. She'd have to figure out a way to help Mom leave the ranch one day and to do that she'd need to stick around for a while.

If she stayed right here, making a living would be tough if not impossible. Then there was the aggravation of putting up with the small minds of some folks in the community. The young bible-pounding minister had given her an earful of it this morning. Swallowing daily doses without saying something would be next to impossible. The sun-worshipping heathens in California had plenty of freedom to disagree. So did the hip, wool-bundled city dwellers of Minneapolis but around here it was different. She swatted at a tall clump of grass with her hand realizing she'd probably have a permanent case of heartburn.

She stopped in her tracks and chewed on the benefits of some middle ground. Austin and San Antonio were fairly close and big enough to provide some decent job choices. It would be easy to come home from those cities on weekends. Pleased with the idea, she patted her stomach.

"I think I can keep you off antacids." She turned around and headed back to the house. First step, a thorough search in Austin, a town she'd always liked, then move on to San Antonio, Dallas and Houston if she had to go that far. The rest of her walk was so filled with things to think about, Devon didn't notice where she was until Jamie called out to her.

Listening to the rain on the tile roof should have made it easy to sleep but it didn't. Devon stared at the ceiling. The far away rumble of thunder just stirred her restlessness. She flipped back the covers, sat up on the edge of the bed searching for her slippers with her feet. Once she'd found them, she scuffed her way down the hall of the silent house through the den to the glass door.

She slid it open and stood just under the eaves. Her silk nightgown fluttered against her legs. It was a velvet night. The air was warm and softened with mist while the sky absorbed any hint of light. She took a deep breath loving the sweet smell of rain. A breeze slipped through the trees with the muted rustle of a brush on a drum and the sound of trickling water became the faint trill of a piano.

She crossed her arms, embracing a memory, and wondered if Alan ever missed her. Thoughts of making love at the beach house while jazz joined the crash of the surf made her tremble as a breath rushed out of her and into the darkness. Nights like this would have been easier if sex had been a problem between them, but it hadn't. Her fingers tightened around her bare arms. More than likely, he had his choice of companions. She shook her head at her willingness to torment herself. This wasn't helping. She stepped back inside the house and closed the door.

Maybe a few minutes of innocuous late night talk would make her drowsy. She fumbled around in the dark bumping her knee on one corner of the coffee table while her hands searched for the remote. She was off balance and almost fell onto the couch. She found the damn control when she sat on it. She clicked her way through the channels seeing nothing of interest until a black and white image of a young Ingrid Bergman made her pause. Cary Grant walked into the picture. It was *Notorious*. She didn't need to hear the dialogue. Passion, clear and understated, was there on the screen, in the unquenchable necessity to touch and that endless kiss. Her lips tingled as she wished she could feel a kiss like that again.

Betrayal would be next for the lovers. She didn't want to see the hurt in the woman's eyes as she pleaded. It was too close to own her life, except they would work it all out in neat Hollywood style. Happy endings were reserved for the movies. She pushed a button and the light on the screen collapsed with a sizzle into a black hole.

There wasn't a sound inside or out except for the steady beat of her own heart and the rushing in and out of each breath. Her nightgown brushed her warm skin like a caress. The sensation awakened a memory on its own. Sinking back into the cushion, she covered her face with her hands to blot out yearning for his touch.

Another memory followed that yanked her back to reality. Alan had chosen the moment she was most vulnerable, shedding her clothes, to tell her. She'd crossed her arms to ward off the chill in the word divorce. Hearing the calm in his voice, she'd been too stunned to say much.

It hurt beyond words to realize he didn't need her. He'd simply gone through the motions of love and she'd filled in the devotion. The revelation had been numbing and she'd rocked Jamie for hours through that terrible night. The unhappy end of their life together was reduced to an image; a shattered vase and dying flowers strewn across a cold slate floor. A vase she'd thrown wanting something from him, even if it was anger.

But he'd seen their situation clearer than she had. It had taken her time to appreciate that point. He couldn't make her happy and had been honest enough to tell her. Alan was a charmer, bright, witty, at ease in every situation. She'd thought he was everything she wanted. Now, she knew better, knew how important honesty, commitment, and trust really were.

Pop had his flaws but he'd loved his family and worked hard to prove it. If she were making a chart showing the distribution of behavior in the human race, her ex-boss and John Colton were in the dangerous and deceitful end of the bell curve. In the middle somewhere was the man she needed: someone kind, dependable, a family man. She could wait.

She stood up and dropped the remote on the couch. Even if she couldn't sleep, she would go back to bed and rest. Tomorrow would be a busy day.

Devon dropped Ellie off at the beauty shop. After her shampoo and set, she was going to spend the rest of her day with Mabel, painting. Devon was alone and away from the ranch for the first time since the assault. The trip was a big challenge, a test of nerve. An hour's drive, even on well-traveled road, to the closest town with more than a hardware store took all the courage she could muster. Necessity had given her a reason to stick her neck out. She needed a few things for Jamie's birthday. He wanted a new bike, a bigger one, more like the one Hank had loaned them. The little one he'd learned on they'd sold before they left Minnesota. So she had to go pick up the one she'd order from the catalog. She'd promised to meet him at school on her way home.

It was well past lunch when she turned off the highway heading back to Blanco Springs. There was a new hamburger joint at the intersection so she pulled in. She was adding some mustard to her Wrangler burger when Mike walked up. It was nice to see a friendly face. They'd bumped into him at the Tastee Freeze a week ago.

"Mind if I join you?" He held his tray. He must have been sitting at another table because his hamburger was half eaten.

"Sure, sit down. This your day off?"

He smiled and settled into the chair facing her. "No, my shift starts in an hour." A frown spread across his face. "Oh, no. Suzy."

He bowed his head and put his elbow on the table trying to shield his face with his hand. Devon smiled. He must be a prime target like Mom had said. She had the advantage of other customers to hide behind but by leaning forward a bit, she could see Suzy ordering at the counter. She was dressed from head to foot in a yellow ensemble, twittering like a redheaded canary to the order taker. When she turned to survey the clientele, Devon quickly shifted back in her chair.

Suzy was carrying her drink over to their table, all smiles until she saw Devon. "Hello, Mike. I didn't know you knew Dr. Owen, Devon."

"He took care of Jamie in the emergency room, Suzy."

"Oh, of course." The woman hadn't taken her eyes off Mike. Suzy's eyes sparkled as her dimpled smile spread across her face. She popped something in her mouth and pulled a chair over from another table to sit down next to him. Devon looked out the window, lips tightly pressed together to kill the smile trying to sprout. Suzy was in full matchmaking for little sister, breath mint mode. "Mike, we are having a big BBQ on Saturday. Dee Dee wondered if you'd like to come."

Devon glanced at Mike. He held his napkin to his lips as he cleared his throat. He was stalling, she imagined. Devon looked down at her burger. She wasn't going to get mixed up in this.

"That sounds nice, Suzy, but I'm going to be busy clearing out paperwork." He wasn't a very creative liar. He took another bite of his hamburger. He didn't have a whole lot left. Devon smiled and looked up to see what Suzy's next move would be.

"Oh, couldn't you come for a little while, at least." Suzy's face became a picture of injured sainthood as she sighed disappointedly. "Dee Dee was looking forward to having you come."

Devon stirred her drink with her straw toying with the idea of telling a fairly innocent whopper to bail him out. If Dee Dee hadn't gotten any smarter, she felt sorry for anybody who had to put up with her for an entire evening. Mike chewed, a little longer than necessary.

"Several of the other doctors are coming, Mike, so you'd know lots of folks there."

Mike raised his cup and took a big gulp of his cola. At this point, Devon knew she was going to persist until he changed his answer. Smile and don't take 'no' for an answer. It was the way women like Suzy operated and Devon hated it. About time Suzy had a taste of her own medicine.

"I'm afraid I've already invited him to a party, Suzy." Devon looked over at Mike as she said it. He choked.

"Oh, I see." Suzy was pissed. She stood up. "I hadn't realized the doctor-patient relationship had gone that far." After a scathing appraisal of Devon from top to bottom, she turned and smiled sweetly at Mike. "Dee Dee will be sorry to hear you won't be coming."

She snatched her paper cup off the table and turned away. The counter boy holding up a basket of fries called out her name as she marched by but she didn't slow down except to yank open the door.

Mike exhaled with relief as the door closed. "Thanks." He turned to look at Devon. "Dee Dee is such a . . . challenge. I hope she's not your cousin or something."

Devon sighed. "No, but she was voted 'a fate worse than death' by the boys in school. Suzy can be pushy. You looked as if you could use some help, so I fibbed."

"I appreciate it. That woman is hard to shake." He grabbed a couple of french fries and ate them. "Every time I run into her she's nibbling on something."

"Suzy's addicted to breath mints." She picked up her hamburger.

"You're pulling my leg." He gave a sickly laugh and looked down at his food before raising his eyes to glance her way. "You know, I was going to ask you out to dinner. I just didn't get the chance."

"I wasn't fishing for an invitation. Just doing my part for the good of mankind, Doctor." She looked toward the door. "Can't imagine it'd be good for the gene pool if Dee Dee gets married." She'd barely touched her hamburger. She took a bite and chewed on the idea of going on a date.

He chuckled. "No, it wouldn't. You know, I hear there's a good restaurant out on Blue Lake." He rattled the ice in his cup.

She had been alone with him on that ride home but a date was different. He was a nice man but it was too soon. One thing at a time. Right now, she had to get used to going places alone.

"You don't want to go with me?" There was a hint of disappointment in his voice.

"I have a date." Which was stretching the truth a bit, but she wasn't chasing after him as if he were a prize bull. That was Suzy's job. The hamburger tasted good, so she took another bite.

Mike's eyes blinked in surprise. "A date? Oh." Apparently he hadn't considered the possibility that she might have something better to do. He stared down at his hand while rotating his glass on the table. "An old boyfriend or a new conquest?" He glanced up with a one-sided grin.

His curiosity pleased her. She swallowed and took a drink before answering. "Actually, a little of both." She fought to keep a straight face. "I've loved Jamie for years and his pal, Tommy, has definite possibilities."

The wrinkle of discomfort on his face evaporated. "Oh, I see. You like younger men."

"Absolutely. They're much easier to please. With a bag of popcorn and a pack of gummy bears, they're content for a couple of hours."

"So where are you going on your date?"

She picked up the napkin on her lap, dabbed at the corners of her mouth and dropped it by her burger. "You sure are nosy. Texas must be rubbing off on you."

"Well, I'm a scientist. We're all naturally curious. Like a french fry?"

She shook her head. "It's Jamie's birthday. We had a party planned for Saturday but chicken pox caused several of his friends to cancel. I talked him into delaying the party but he's hell bent on going to the movies. I'm taking the two healthy ones to a matinee."

"Maybe I could tag along. Wouldn't want to bump into Dee Dee on Saturday and blow my alibi."

"If you're considering going fifty miles to watch a long cartoon with two six year olds, good old Dee Dee has got you running scared." She wrapped up the paper holding the last of her hamburger.

"Not at all. I haven't seen an animated film in a long time. I appreciate the art work."

She leaned back in her chair. "Gosh, first medicine, now art. You're a regular Renaissance man." She smiled, enjoying teasing him.

He laughed. "That's right."

She lifted her brow. "Have you ever been in a theater full of children?" It would be interesting to see how many spilled drinks, sticky candy hands, and screaming toddlers he could endure.

"Not since I was one."

"Well, it's strictly casual wear, preferably something that doesn't stain. We're leaving midmorning to make it to the first showing." She paused, studying him. "I thought you had paperwork to take care of?"

"I have a couple of letters to get out. I can be ready anytime after nine or so."

She shook her head. "You're an uncontrollable fibber, Dr. Owen. I'm not sure you would be a good influence on my young men."

He grinned. "You're a great one to talk." He raised his hand and held up three fingers. "But no more, scout's honor. Let's go out to dinner when we get back."

"You're welcome to join us for the movie but dinner is out. Mom's planned something." That got her off the hook and it wasn't a lie.

She stopped by the post office on her way to school. The mailman had left a note in the box that a package had to be signed for. She'd stared at it when the clerk handed it to her. It was for Jamie and according to the embossed label, it was from Alan's mother. This was a first. She put the small box in the trunk, fighting the urge to trash it without taking it home. That was too rotten. She'd give it to him later, maybe in a year or two.

The school bell rang and children burst from every door racing toward the parking lot and the row of buses. She spotted Jamie and waved at him. Seeing him run toward the car busting with energy, another rush of guilt hit her. It was his seventh birthday. It wasn't fair to withhold a gift. He didn't have a father who cared about him but he did have grandparents. And they were making some kind of effort to communicate. Oh, but that woman. What was she up to now? She'd never sent anything before. Her fingers wrapped around the steering wheel and squeezed. She didn't trust Marian Montgomery as far as she could throw her.

She smiled when Jamie opened the car door and hopped in. "Ready to go to Mabel's and get Granny?"

Jamie was chattering about the day's events as she drove out of town. She was listening and nodding every so often.

"What's that?" Jamie pointed out his window.

She glanced in that direction. "The rodeo grounds." Dust was in the air. Several pickups with horse trailers, parked by the fence, blocked her view. Curiosity and fond memories made it hard to just drive by without a look. "Let's see what's going on. We've got time."

She turned off the road, drove across the field, and parked next to the wooden bleachers. They walked through the dry grass. Devon heard a horse whinny. They climbed the three steps to the first row of benches. At the far end of the arena, there were six saddled horses tied up by the gates. Young cowboys of various sizes were adjusting cinches and bridles, patting the noses of their mounts, and chattering with an excitement she remembered. The smell of dust filled the air, kicked up by the pawing horses. A couple of barrels were spaced for racing. She leaned against the metal rail watching the commotion with surprising fondness.

"What are they going to do?"

"Must be junior rodeo kids practicing." On their side of the arena, she noticed several stacked hay bales, each with a set of horns perched on one end. Someone with a sense of humor had made something like a rocking horse, draped a cowhide over the back and attached horns to the head. A mix of boys and girls, dressed in jeans, tee shirts and cowboy hats stood in the dusty arena. Several men stood among them. One tall man was talking while swinging a rope over his head.

"Look's like they're going to practice roping. That's why they've got the bales with the horns over there and I guess the rocking bull too."

"Why don't they use real cows like on TV?"

"When you're learning you need something that will hold still while you're getting the feel for throwing the rope."

"You know how to rope, Mom?"

By the tone of his voice, she gathered her stock had just risen a point or two. "Yes, but it wasn't my best event. I preferred barrel racing." She was proud of the fact she could ride and rope however useless the skill was now. He needed to realize girls could compete like any boy.

The man with the rope turned around. It was Frank. She felt a little rush of pleasure seeing his smile. He nodded in her direction before turning back to his audience.

"Do you know him, Mom?" He looked up at her.

"Yes. His name is Frank Jessup. I went to school with him. He was a professional rodeo cowboy for a while." She sat down on the first row of bleachers but Jamie stayed at the railing.

After a minute or two, Frank mounted a handsome buckskin horse and stopped not far from them. "Now, Monty, I want you and Jerry to practice comin' around and rope that mangy old rocking steer just like this." He took off on his horse and made quick work of putting his rope around the horns. Jamie glanced over his shoulder at her as he clapped.

Two of the bigger boys got on their horses and tried to duplicate his ride. It was clear that it wasn't as easy as Frank made it look. "Try it again, boys, you were close." He shouted his encouragement to the young men and walked toward the stacked bales with the small group of younger children. She glanced at Jamie. He was fascinated. If they lived around here, he would be ready for this in a year or two. He'd love it but . . ..

"Hiddy."

"Well, hello." The small voice surprised Devon. She turned to see a little girl, about four years old, standing beside her. She was dressed in blue jeans, red boots and a pink blouse with lace trim around the neckline. Her short dark hair framed a tan face and big brown eyes.

"My name's Annie. What's yours?" The child sat down beside her.

She smiled at the inquisitive little lady looking up at her. "My name's Devon." She raised her head and glanced around wondering where the child had come from and who was looking after her. There wasn't another soul to be seen in the bleachers other than Jamie. "That's my son, Jamie watching the roping." Her son turned and looked her way but the action in the arena was more interesting and he turned back to watch.

Annie leaned against Devon's shoulder and touched her arm with her hand. She had pink fingernail polish on. "I think you're bootiful."

The child's sweet smile inspired a genuine flood of affection. She would have loved having a little girl after Jamie. "Thank you, Annie. I think you're beautiful too." For some reason, she felt the little girl wanted something and waited to hear what it was. When the child didn't say anything more but kept staring at her, she decided to kick things off. "I like your nail polish. Did you do it all by yourself?"

"No, my sister helped."

"Is she. . .."

Jamie bumped against her knee. "Mom." He was eyeing the little girl critically. "Can we go now?"

"Annie!" The angry shout made all of them turn their heads toward the far end of the bleachers. A girl with a bouncing ponytail was heading their direction. She had a good head of steam up as she briskly swung her arms and stomped toward them, her boots clunking on the boards. Devon guessed she was about ten, just entering the gangly stage when arms and legs grow faster than the rest of the body. She stopped a couple of feet from them, one hand resting on her hip while the other pointed an accusing finger. "I told you to stay in the truck until I got back."

"I got hot." Annie shot back her reply with righteous indignation. Devon struggled to keep a straight face.

"I'm going to tell Daddy." Annie's sister pursed her lips. She glanced at Devon and her expression changed to one less angry and more guarded, wary of a stranger.

"You must be Annie's big sister." Devon liked the little wisp of a girl too much not to help her out. "She was just telling me that you were the one who did such a nice job of painting her nails."

"Her name is Beth." Annie whispered.

"It's nice to meet you, Beth. My name is Devon Taylor and this is my son, Jamie. We just stopped by for a minute to watch."

"I see you've met my girls." Frank stood at the edge of the arena looking up at them through the railing. He took off his hat and put it on the wooden walkway. "This your boy?"

"Hi, Frank." She smiled at his easy, straightforward approach. "Yes, this is Jamie."

"Howdy, Jamie." He stuck his hand up and Jamie leaned down to shake it. "You get a little older and I expect to see you out here swingin' a rope." He grinned.

Jamie turned toward her, his brows raised in excitement. "Can I, Mom?"

Devon wished he could but knew he couldn't. "Probably not, Jamie." His face reflected his disappointment. She'd explain later if he asked. "Annie and I have been having a talk, Frank. I'm afraid she forgot to tell Beth where she was going."

"Yeah, she can be a handful sometimes but Beth does a good job of keeping track of her for me." He winked at Beth and a lovely smile blossomed on the girl's face. She almost glowed.

"I'm not a handful, Daddy." Annie frowned putting her hands on her hips as she walked over to the rail. She squatted down in front of him.

He reached up and lifted her through the space between the two bars. He held her over his head. "Yes, you are, dumplin'. Two hands full." He laughed and spun her around. The child screamed with glee. He put both arms around her and touched her nose with his. "Now, you stay with Beth until I'm done, you hear? Then we'll get us an ice cream cone before we go home." They were very lucky children.

"Okay, Daddy." She put her arms around his neck and kissed him on the cheek. Frank lifted her up to the bleachers and put on his hat.

Devon glanced at her watch and stood up. "We need to go. It was nice to meet you, Annie and Beth. 'Bye, Frank."

"Hey. If y'all come by the Tastee Freeze in a while, stop and I'll treat you both to some ice cream. Can't beat an offer like that." He grinned with the sparkle in his eye that had once melted her smitten heart.

"We'll have to take you up on that offer another day, cowboy, so save your nickels." It was fun to tease him like they were kids again. As she stood to leave, Annie grabbed her hand.

"Can't you eat ice cream with us?" Her voice was pleading.

She leaned down and touched the child's soft hair. "No, Annie, we have to get home. But it was very nice to meet you."

"Come on, Mom." Jamie pulled on her arm.

She straightened up. "All right, Jamie, settle down." She wished he wouldn't be so jealous when she showed interest in another child. That was the problem with having just one. As they walked toward the car, she wondered if it was just as hard to spread affection equally between siblings. It probably was.

Devon took the new bike out of trunk when they got home. Once she'd adjusted the height of the seat, Jamie took off. She stood in front of the garage with Ellie watching him riding down the driveway.

"Mom, I have to tell you something. That package at the Post Office was for Jamie."

"Well, we figured as much since it's his birthday. Where is it?"

"Still in the car. It's from Alan's mother."

"Oh." Ellie sounded a little surprised. "Did he open it?"

"He hasn't seen it. I'm not sure I'm going to give it to him." Just thinking about Marian Trent Montgomery having any contact with her son made her nervous. "She's never sent him so much as a birthday card before. I'm wondering what she wants." The woman was furious Alan didn't ask for shared custody at least. Maybe the gift was an enticement, the first carrot to dangle in front of Jamie, so he'd want to visit her.

Mom frowned. "I know she wasn't very nice to you, Devon, but Jamie is her grandson, probably the only one she'll ever have. If she wants to send him a gift, you have to give it to him."

More than a little peeved at her situation, she exhaled letting the air rush out between her closed lips. "I guess you're right but I don't like it."

With the package on her mind, her appetite was gone. She'd fixed Jamie's favorite dinner: macaroni and cheese, green beans and applesauce. After the birthday candles were blown out and cake cut, Jamie opened her mother's gift; a red Texas Rangers baseball cap and jacket just like Tommy's.

"Thanks, Granny." He immediately put the hat and coat on and gave her a hug and a kiss.

With emotions still mixed, Devon handed him the other one. "This is a birthday present from your other grandmother."

"Do I know her?" He didn't wait for her answer and tore through the beautiful paper. "Wow! This is what I always wanted."

It was one of those hand-held computers to play games on. They'd been popular in Minneapolis and expensive. She'd told him he couldn't have one. She looked at her mother. Ellie raised her eyebrows and shrugged. Devon watched Jamie unpack the box and study the game discs. She reserved a smile until her happy son came over to show it to her.

"That's a nice gift. You'll have to take good care of it." She felt no pleasure seeing his smile this time. "We'll have to send your Grandmother Montgomery a thank you card."

Devon was late. She'd kept watch in her rear view mirror for ticket happy Charlie through town. The road to the clinic shot across rolling pastureland arrow straight. She drove a click or two under traditional Texas warp speed. There wasn't time to really appreciate the blue sky painted with scattered white clouds. The boys, busting with energy, were strapped in seatbelts but still managed to roughhouse in the back seat. When she turned into the hospital parking lot, she spotted Mike standing beside his Bronco. He smiled as she pulled up beside him. He opened the front passenger door and sat down in the bucket seat. He had a small gift-wrapped package in his hand.

"Sorry we're late. Had a hard time getting the boys rounded up."

"Just got out here a minute ago myself." He turned to look at the boys before buckling up. "Hi, Jamie. Who's your friend?"

"Hi, Dr. Mike. This is Tommy. Is that for me?"

"Nice to meet you, Tommy. And yes, it's for you. You can open it when we stop for lunch." He faced forward as she pulled out.

The boys couldn't hold still or stop pestering each other for more than thirty seconds even though the backseat was full of toys. There was a constant barrage of bumping and mini explosions from the imaginary war going on behind them. Mike looked back any number of times and grinned when he saw her watching him. He wasn't use to it like she was.

"Boys settle down." Devon checked the pretend mayhem going on behind her in the rear view mirror before glancing toward him. "Are they driving you crazy?"

"No, not all." He smiled but she wasn't convinced. Since he'd invited himself along, he'd just have to put up with two rambunctious boys all day. It would be interesting to see how he fared.

Wally's Burger Palace was a beehive teeming with noisy children. Devon ate her chicken sandwich while listening to corny, elementary school humor. Much to her surprise and the delight of the boys, Mike was a willing participant adding jokes of his own. He was good with kids. His gift which Jamie gleefully ripped open was a paperback book of more new jokes with cartoon illustrations.

Nibbling on the last of his junior hamburger, Jamie was studying Mike. Devon could see those little wheels in his brain were working on something. "Do you have kids, Dr. Mike?" There was a serious frown wrinkling his young face.

Mike raised his eyebrows in surprise. "No, Jamie, I don't. Why?"

Jamie smiled. "Oh, I just wondered. Matthew used to see his daddy on Saturdays when they got hamburgers and stuff."

He'd asked Mike several personal questions. It dawned on her that he was sizing Mike up as daddy material. Maybe she shouldn't have mentioned the possibility of having a new father someday. What the heck, Mike didn't seem to mind and Jamie was having fun. So was she. No point in taking any of this seriously.

Tommy stood and tugged on Jamie's arm. "Come on, Jamie, let's go outside and play." In a flash, they were racing through the door headed for the fenced in play area. Devon watched them through the window.

"Who's Matthew?"

She turned her head to look at Mike. "One of Jamie's friends in Minneapolis. When his parents were divorced, he was passed from the custody of one to the other at fine eating establishments like this. Guess that's why it occurred to him to ask you if you had kids. Pretty sad commentary on our times, isn't it?" Mike nodded. He was chewing the last of his hamburger.

She used the extra napkins to wipe the ketchup off the table. When she looked up, the boys were waving from the top of a slide. She waved back and watched them zoom down. She noticed Mike was watching them too. "Where did you find all those awful jokes?"

"I learned a long time ago they help my little patients relax in the emergency room. Thankfully, the jokes don't change much from year to year. The boys gave me one today that is a definite keeper."

"Which one?" Devon smiled, glad he'd come along.

"The elephant in the tree."

Devon chuckled and checked her watch. "I'd better start rounding them up. The movie starts in thirty minutes." Devon walked to the door and called the boys in.

The theater lobby was jam-packed. Devon guessed the ratio was one adult per four hyperactive children. The movie was an animated adventure with singing animals. With the continuous babble all around them and the occasional tired wail of a toddler, it was hard to hear the dialogue, but Jamie and Tommy didn't seem to mind.

When a cascade of candy rolled down the slanted floor like marbles, she had to stop them from getting down on the sticky cement. She looked over at Mike. He was chuckling.

Once the movie was over, the line to the women's restroom extended into the lobby. Both boys were holding themselves in need of relief. "You'll just have to wait, boys."

"But Mom, I need to go bad." Jamie crossed his legs.

"Come with me, guys. There isn't a line for the men's restroom." Mike looked at her, after the fact, to see if that was alright with her.

"Go ahead. Just don't run off and leave me." It was nice to have another adult to help out for a change. The boys liked him. They quickly disappeared into the other restroom with Mike. How she envied them. The line she was standing in hadn't moved.

By the time Devon joined them outside, the three men were discussing how to talk her into something. A traveling carnival was setup across the intersection from the little mall housing the theater and the boys had spotted it.

"Mom, can we ride the Ferris wheel? Please?"

"Jamie, we need to get back. I don't like being up that high, you know that."

He started to groan and complain which she hated. She looked away from him, not wanting to argue.

"How about if I take them? Haven't been on one in a long time. It'll be my treat. Is it okay with you, Mom?" He grinned at her.

The boys began to jump up and down. "Yes, yes, say yes."

Jamie's excited smile and the fact that she wouldn't have to go with him made her waver. "One ride, as long as I can stay on the ground and watch." She might as well let the boys have some fun since Mike had offered. Having a man along did add a different quality to an outing with boys. She didn't blame Jamie for wanting a father.

On the return trip, the boys were content in the backseat. A lot of men wouldn't have been such a good sport with boys they barely knew but he seemed to enjoy it. She liked him. He was easygoing and fun to be around.

"Dr. Mike."

Mike turned to look back. "Yes, Jamie."

"Do you know how to play baseball?"

Devon glanced up in the rear view mirror. Tommy was whispering in Jamie's ear.

"Sure do. Why?"

"My friends play t-ball but I can't 'cause I don't know how to catch with a mitt. Could you show me?"

Devon hadn't thought to teach him and he hadn't asked her. Maybe he didn't think she knew how.

"Sure. I could come over and give you a quick lesson." Mike glanced at her. "If that's okay with your Mom."

The pleading look on Jamie's face she knew too well. He was waiting for her answer before he started in with the 'please, Moms'. "That's nice of you, Mike, but Jamie doesn't realize what a busy schedule you have."

"When I'm off duty, there isn't a lot to do around here unless you go to Austin or San Antonio. I wore those towns out when I was stationed at Ft. Sam." He smiled. "It'll feel good to throw a baseball around again and help Jamie get the hang of it."

They drove into the parking lot with Jamie bouncing up and down on the seat. "When can you come over?"

She glanced over her shoulder. "Jamie, sit down and buckle up."

"I'll check my schedule, Jamie, then give your Mom a call."

Devon knew he was interested in more than baseball or avoiding Dee Dee. No grown man would have gone to so much trouble otherwise, unless she had completely misread the way he looked at her. It was flattering, but it made her uncomfortable. She had good reasons. John Colton was one of them.

Devon pulled up to Mike's vehicle. He got out but held onto the door and leaned down. "Good-bye, guys." They both shouted a loud 'bye'. "Thanks for letting me tag along, Devon. I enjoyed it."

"Good." There was an awkward silence. "Well, I'd better get Tommy home." She smiled.

"Yeah. I'll call you about the baseball thing."

She nodded. "Right."

He shut the door and knocked on the back window as he walked toward his vehicle. She drove out of the parking lot. Relax, she thought to herself, and don't make a federal case out of a man being nice. You need the practice.

"Devon, there's a phone call for you. Can you get it or do you want me to tell them to call back?"

"I'll get it, Mom." She bumped into Ellie in the hallway. "Who is it?"

"It's a woman. Something Baker, I think. Terrible connection, sounds like long distance."

Devon picked up the phone on the desk. "Hello."

"Hi, Devon, it's Janet Blake again. Can you hear me okay? I'm on the road near Malibu."

She closed her eyes and covered her other ear with her hand so she could concentrate on the voice coming through the receiver. "Hi Janet, what's up?"

"I got a call from CB Sims yesterday. He was looking for you."

"Me? Why?"

"Paul Jackson died about a week ago, heart attack. Keeled over in the middle of a meeting."

"Really, I can't believe it." She felt a pang of honest regret for one of the best managers in the business. She'd worked for him for four years in Los Angeles. She could picture Paul, all dressed in white, on the tennis court behind his house playing game after game, until he'd defeated all of his subordinates. He'd been a jerk about tennis but he was very good at his job. He'd taught her a lot and she'd admired him. "The company is really going to miss him."

"Right, and Sims needs to fill some vacancies as he reorganizes and wants people with a good track record in the industry. He said you were super at reading the tea leaves. That's why he wants to talk to you about coming back to the marketing department."

She ran her fingers through her hair pulling it away from her face. She couldn't ignore an opportunity to work at Selden-Kirshfield again. They were the biggest manufacturer of sportswear. "Sounds tempting." She massaged the back of her neck trying to decide what to say. "I've been working on a few leads here in Texas." That was a stretch. "Can I call you back tomorrow, Janet, after I've had time to think about it?"

"Sure, but don't take too long. I'll let CB know to keep your name in the hopper. If you're interested, he'll give you a call. You have my cell phone number?"

"No, let me get something to write with." She grabbed a pen and old envelope. "Okay, I'm ready." Her hand shook as she wrote Janet's name on the back.

When Devon hung up the phone, she stared at the numbers. It had been over three months since she quit her last job. Her professional life was in neutral. She wasn't sure she cared. If she never produced another marketing campaign, the world would keep spinning. Folding her arms across her chest, she walked into the living room and looked out the front window toward the road without seeing a thing.

Ever since the assault, it had been hard to concentrate. There was a niggling, ever present uneasiness in the back of her mind that slowed her down. Be careful, it whispered, watch out. As much as she could feel the tight clutch of it, she had to seriously consider working for CB. Her savings were limited. Time to get off her duff.

There wasn't much activity in town. Devon counted a grand total of four cars in the square as she wandered down the street to escape the fumes in the beauty shop. Her mother was just getting combed out so it'd be a good fifteen minutes before she'd be ready. She'd decided to visit Tammy, if she was working today.

She couldn't see anyone inside, but opened the wooden door. Tammy's desk was cleared off, no sign of number crunching. She might be in the back. "Hello, anybody here?"

Donald Ray's bald head appeared from a doorway to the back room. "Howdy, Devon. Come on in." He disappeared before she could ask about Tammy.

A breeze from the fan hanging down from the high ceiling ruffled some papers on his cluttered desk. Boots echoed on the hardwood floors as Don walked to the front of the office.

"I didn't mean to bother you, Don, I just stopped by to see if Tammy was working today."

"No, ma'am, she said she wouldn't be in today." His smile was broad and a bit too enthusiastic. He was a sweet man really, eager to please. He was wearing a tie with his white long sleeved shirt, which was a bit unusual even for a small-time politician on a warm day. "Glad you stopped by though. You're looking like you're doin' fine." He rocked forward on his toes then back on his heels. "You went to college and worked in California for a big company and everything, as I remember. You gonna stay closer to home now?"

"I don't know yet, Don. How's the real estate business?"

"Things are lookin' up." He rubbed his hands together like a used car salesman seeing a likely customer. "I mean, I've got a businessman from San Antone coming in," he glanced at his watch, "any minute now. He's real serious about investin' some big money. I haven't met him yet but well, it doesn't take much to see we could use some around here."

Devon had never seen him so nervous. He couldn't hold still anymore than a drop of water dancing across a hot skillet.

"His name is Lawrence Hall, maybe you've heard of him. From what I hear he owns half of Texas."

He'd roused her curiosity. "What does he want to invest in?"

He turned and with a broad upward stroke of his arm motioned toward the wall map. "Land, of course, not much else around. Wants to buy ranches, says he'll pay good money for them. Has a plan to build a fancy dude ranch kind of resort with a golf course, swimmin' pool, you name it, they'll have it." He stopped talking and looked out the window. A white Mercedes, an expensive, gold trimmed, four-door model, had parked directly in front of the door. "Oh Lord, there he is. Why don't you stay a minute and meet him."

She didn't have time to answer. Mr. Money was walking in. He was a regular Neiman-Marcus cowboy: tall, closely trimmed black hair, white Stetson, western cut crisp white shirt and black slacks, silver belt buckle and expensive black alligator boots. He was in his mid-thirties she guessed, younger than she'd expected. Maybe that's why he overdid the outfit. He took off his hat and held out his hand.

"Mr. Ray?"

"You bet." Don grabbed the proffered hand and pumped it. "Real nice to finally meet you, Mr. Hall."

"I'm Mr. Hall's assistant, Stephen Gregory." Don's face reddened but the assistant didn't miss a beat. "Mr. Hall is in his helicopter flying over some sites he is interested in. He asked that I drive you out to a central location to meet him." So Steve was a well-paid taxi driver.

"Oh, why sure, that'd be fine." Poor Don had broken out in a sweat. Must be a lot of money at stake.

"Is the lady coming with us?" He looked at her with the same bland mannequin expression he'd walked in with.

"Oh, pardon me, this is Devon Taylor, a friend and long time resident."

"Nice to meet you, Mr. Gregory. I was just leaving." She put on her cocktail party smile. "I understand Mr. Hall is considering building a resort in this area?"

"He is studying several possible sites." His smile had the polish of years of practice.

"Well, I'm off. I'm sure the tour will go well, Don." She smiled at her old high school classmate, who was now white as a sheet. She hoped he didn't have a coronary before the day was over.

Devon pulled in at the Tastee Freeze. It was a school day so the outside stalls for cars to park and call in their orders were empty. Ellie didn't want to eat in the car so they parked in one of the spaces at the front of the building. They went in and sat down. The cook and waitress were talking behind the counter. Some men in one booth by the window were eating. They ordered sandwiches and iced tea when the waitress came over. After giving their order to the cook, the young woman was right back with their drinks. Devon poured a little sugar in her glass and stirred.

"You're awfully quiet. Something wrong?" Ellie pulled out a couple of napkins from the metal holder on the table.

"No, I've just been thinking." Devon watched the ice in her glass float in circles.

"About what?"

"You, me, everything." She looked up at her mother. Her hair looked nice. Joann had put a rinse on it to darken the gray. "I'm worried about you living alone so far from town after I start working again. There's nobody around to help if something were to happen to you out there."

"Honey, I know that man scared you half to death, but I've lived in the country all my life without one second of trouble from anybody."

"I'll admit to being paranoid, Mom, but that's just part of what's bothering me." She took a deep breath prepared for the argument to come. "Have you thought any more about selling the ranch?"

"You know I considered it after the funeral." Ellie looked down. "But how can I sell it? Your father was born on that place in that old ruin of a house." She smoothed out the wrinkles in her napkin with her fingers. "It'd be like selling an arm or leg." The waitress walked up, set down their sandwiches and returned to the counter. "I heard a real estate man from Cross Creek, named Dunbar, talked the Gunderson's into selling their spread dirt cheap to a man wanting to raise some kind of African antelope." She shook her head while looking at Devon. "I'm not going to do that. Too much of your dad's sweat and mine went into our place."

Devon took a bite of her sandwich. Maybe this wasn't such a great time to bring up the subject. Ellie nibbled from her sandwich and drank her tea in silence.

"Doubt anybody would be willing to pay what it's worth, Devon. I wanted to keep it until I could hand it over to you and Jamie." Ellie paused, looking at her hands laid out flat on both sides of her plate. "Raising cattle is a hard life though." She lifted her head, her expression softened by a gentle smile. "I can understand if you don't want to live here, especially after what happened to you."

Devon moved her hand across the table to touch her mother's. "Pop would want you provided for first, Mom, and so do I. That's my main concern. All your assets are tied up in that place. If the county dries up, you won't be able to give it away. At your age, the sensible thing to do is switch over to more liquid assets that can appreciate in value without so many risks."

"Easier to talk about being sensible than doing it. I love that place as much as your father did. I'd be happy to die there like he did too." She looked out the front window. "Besides, I expect to make money this year."

Devon ran her fingers up and down her cool glass. She had the feeling they couldn't avoid the subject any longer and had to talk it through now. "What about next year?" She dried her moist fingertips on her crumpled napkin.

Ellie sighed and looked over at her. The lines on her face seemed deeper. "I understand what you're saying. We lost most of a herd to drought one year when you were little, and had to borrow money other years for one reason or another."

"There are lots of options, Mom. You can stay in the house and probably lease the rest to the Kimballs or somebody for a while. Or you may be able to sell the grazing land separately. It's too much for you to handle alone even with Hank's help."

"I've considered doing that. But every spot on it means something special to me. Be awfully hard to leave." Her mother's eyes were moist.

When Devon pictured strangers living in their house, people who didn't know what held a memory, it felt rock hard in the very center of her.

"I know this isn't easy, Mom. It's been my home too but you're more important than acres of land. I can study the real estate market around here and help you figure out what would be a fair price. It will take a while to find a buyer." She stopped talking when the men from the other booth walked by. They stopped at the counter, sweet-talking the waitress while they paid.

She hesitated before giving voice to the decision so recently arrived at. "I'll help you anyway I can, I promise. I've decided I'm not going to California. I'm going to call Janet back this afternoon and tell her."

Ellie's eyes widened reflecting her surprise. "Are you sure? I didn't think . . . .."

"I thought about it last night, Mom. I left it once and I don't want to go back there. We are going to stay in Texas. I'm going to send resumes to firms in Austin and San Antonio. I was thinking that once you sell the ranch, you could live with Jamie and me. We wouldn't be far away from here. You could come back and visit Mabel and everybody else whenever you wanted."

"That's sweet of you and I do appreciate the thought but I'm in no hurry to move and stare at concrete all day." Ellie sat looking at her folded hands on the table.

Devon's heart ached for her. "It was only a suggestion, Mom." She touched her hand. "Just think about it."

Devon heard a vehicle drive in. She walked around the house. Jamie had been talking of nothing else all morning but baseball practice. She waved as Mike stepped out of the Bronco.

"I think Jamie's in the barn." She headed that direction and Mike joined her. The powdery smell of dust and hay filled the air as they walked in through the wide doorway.

"Jamie, your baseball coach is here." She waited for her eyes to adjust to the shadows. All she could hear was squeaky whines and yipping. She walked over to the Border Collie lying in the straw surrounded by pudgy, little black and white bodies. "I don't know where he is. He's been so excited that you were coming over today. He's been playing with the puppies all morning. This is Hank's dog, Maggie. He's out of town for a couple days so we're keeping an eye on them." She squatted down and picked up a fat puppy. "They're a week old." She held it up.

"Looks like this little fella is getting plenty to eat." Mike leaned down and smoothed the short hair along the top of the sleeping pup's head with his fingertips.

She heard the soft thumping of footsteps behind them and put the pup down. Jamie came running toward them. Mike rocked sideways as her son crashed into him.

Devon stood up. "Jamie, be careful."

"Whoa, what kind of wild animal is this?" Mike ruffled Jamie's hair with his hand. "Hmmm, feels like a great Alaskan woolly bear."

Jamie laughed. "Hi, Dr. Mike. Can we play catch now?"

"Catch? What's a catch?"

"You know what it is."

"Well, lets see." He checked his watch. "Yes, I've got you on my schedule for this afternoon, Mr. Baseball. Your mom was just showing me the new puppies."

"Aren't they cute?" Jamie fell to his knees beside the noisy litter, his finger pointing out one particular pup. "This is the best one. He has a special mark on him, see?" Mike stretched to look over Jamie's shoulder. "Looks like Mickey Mouse. I'm going to call him Mickey."

"That sounds like a good name. Guess you're in charge of keeping track of these little guys?"

Her son's eyes sparkled. "Yeah, I'm big enough now."

Jamie got to his feet. "Granny said we are going to make ice cream for dessert. Have you ever had homemade, Dr. Mike? Supposed to be real good. Would you like some too?"

Devon lowered her head and shot Jamie a quick disapproving glance, which he didn't notice or ignored. He'd been told to always ask first.

"I've never tasted any, Jamie." Mike bent over with hands on his knees. "But it's up to your grandmother to invite guests."

"Oh, she will. I'll make sure." He ran out without further comment. She could hear him calling out, "Granny" followed by a door slam.

"Oops." Mike shook his head. "I didn't say that right somehow."

"That's okay." She stuck her hands in the back pockets of her jeans. A sad irony mellowed her cheerful mood. Mike could be a great dad and Alan didn't want to try. "You're very good with him." She wondered if he knew that.

He looked pleased and smiled. "It's easy. He's a nice kid."

She knew it wasn't that simple. "Thanks for helping him with the baseball stuff. For some reason, he doesn't want any help from me."

"For things like baseball, I think boys want a man for a coach."

She looked away. "I guess you're right." She started to walk out of the barn. "I'll go get him. We can't have spring training side tracked by ice cream."

Devon invited him for dinner, not just ice cream, when the catching and pitching was over. He ate like it all tasted good, which pleased her mother. Mike was relaxed, asked questions and respectfully listened to Jamie's comments. He didn't have an easy answer for everything, like trying to turn Suzy down the other day. It made her think that whatever came out of his mouth was honest, not manufactured for the audience as Alan used to do. He even helped carry the dirty dishes to the counter. The longer he was around, the easier it was to like him.

Mike was in the den talking to Ellie when she came in from getting Jamie in the tub. "Thanks for the great dinner, Mrs. Taylor. I felt like I was back home."

"You're very welcome, Doctor. Nice to have a chance to get better acquainted. You've been very generous to help my grandson."

"I've enjoyed it." He was looking at the framed landscapes on the wall. "These are beautiful. Who's the artist?"

Ellie smiled obviously pleased he liked them. "Thank you. I did them a couple of years ago. Those places are here on the ranch."

"Really? Devon didn't tell me you were an artist." He glanced at her with a familiarity that brought a rush of warmth to her cheeks. He looked back at her mother. "Have you sold many?"

"Just a few over the years."

"Well, they are great." He looked at his watch. "I've got to head for home. I'm on call in two hours." He took a couple of steps toward the front door. Leaning forward at the entrance to the hallway, he called out. "Great job catching today, Jamie. I've got to go. 'Bye."

Jamie shouted back a good-bye after a splashing sound. She walked out to the car with him, enjoying the little buzz set off by being around an attractive man.

"I have to work all weekend." He opened his car door. "How about going out for some Mexican food Thursday night? I know a great little place called Lupe's."

This time, it didn't rattle her. She wasn't too sure why but she felt comfortable around him now. "I haven't had any Mexican food since I've been home, not even a taco. That sounds good. Oh, but Founder's Day Celebration is this weekend. Mom and I have a lot to do before Saturday."

"We could make it an early evening. How about six?"

"Okay."

He got in his Bronco and drove off. She turned around and headed for the front door. That little tingle of excitement was back. She smiled. "I have a date. How about that." She imagined TJ hooting at her about now, by the front door, as he did before her first date. In a way, it was her first date. It was time to blot out the memories of John Colton and start enjoying life again.

Ellie hoped the evening would go well for Devon. No telling how long it had been since she'd gone out on a date. Mike showed up five minutes early so she was talking to him in the den when her daughter walked in. Devon was wearing a long, multicolored skirt and a periwinkle blue knit blouse with a scooped neckline that showed off her lovely shoulders. Her hair was pushed up off her neck for a change. She favored her father's side of the family with that black hair and strong chin. The doctor seemed to approve, judging by the look on his face. Devon looked happy too and that was a wonderful sight to see.

Jamie scooted in close behind Devon with a big smile on his face. He bumped into Mike's leg and they wrestled a bit. This was the way it should have been for her daughter. Devon deserved a nice man to love and Jamie certainly needed a father. Mike wanted a family too. That was obvious. She sighed as they closed the front door and left.

Lupe's Cantina was on a straight stretch of state highway a few miles south of the hospital. The brightly lit restaurant with a big parking area sat in the midst of ten trailer houses and a run down, one pump gas station. Dos XX, in neon, blinked in the windows. The restaurant was essentially one large room filled with metal tables and chairs, a brown linoleum floor, and brightly colored paper decorations. Latin melodies were floating across the room from an old tape player as Devon and Mike walked in.

A small man with coal-black hair streaked with gray greeted Mike warmly as they entered. "Dr. Owen, it is good to see you." His English was laced with a thick Mexican accent. "Jorge is very good, stronger every day." He bowed slightly to Devon. "Welcome to Lupe's, *Señorita*."

"Let me introduce Mr. Gonzales, Devon. He is the owner of Lupe's."

"*Con mucho gusto.*" She held out her hand and smiled. It was nice to feel relaxed. Life was smoothing out finally.

Mr. Gonzales smiled and bowed his head slightly as he took her hand. "*El gusto es mio.*" He showed them to a table and handed them menus. "Lupe come soon to take your order."

After he left, she looked at Mike. "Who is Jorge?"

"His son. I patched him up when he was injured a few weeks ago." Mike picked up his menu.

"I didn't realize I was having dinner with a famous doctor." She peeked at him over the top of her menu.

He studied her, a serious wrinkle to his brow. "Actually, Dr. Schweitzer and I do get royal treatment for providing brilliant medical care." He raised an eyebrow and grinned. "It's just one of the many benefits of dining with a health professional."

They were laughing when a pleasantly round woman, order pad in hand, walked up to Mike. "Good evening, Dr. Owen. It is good to see you."

"Hi, Mrs. Gonzales. It's great to see you. This lady makes some of the best tamales in Texas, Devon."

The woman, with lovely brown eyes looked at Devon before a shy smile crept across her lips. "Oh, Doctor, you tease too much. What may we serve you tonight?"

They ordered the special, which had a little of everything: tamales, enchiladas, chili con queso, and quesadillas. Devon looked around at the nearby decorations. Some of the items were gaudy *piñatas* while others were fascinating old kitchen utensils and artwork obviously from Mexico. Only two tables were occupied so the restaurant was quiet, the music muted.

Lupe came back with two beers and salsa and chips. "We have a special celebration tonight. You will enjoy it."

"I'm afraid we can't stay late, Mrs. Gonzales."

"Then you must come back again." Lupe smiled and left their table.

Devon dipped a chip in the dark red salsa. "Must be gratifying to see your patients and their families out in the community well and able to work again."

"Unfortunately, my patients aren't all pillars of the community. When the waiting area is full, they aren't all happy when they see me either." He laughed. "Most of the time though, you're right. It's great." He took a drink of beer.

A bad day at the office for her was a smudge on a graph. She couldn't imagine dealing with the suffering he saw every day. She hadn't considered having to help anyone brought in either. One day he might care for the woman John Colton beat up, and the next be asked to patch up John Colton with a fractured skull. How awful to ask that of anyone.

More customers came in, most smiling and laughing, filling four big tables. There was a festive feel to the place now. She picked up a Spanish word she knew every so often. Devon wished she'd asked Lupe what the celebration was all about when she'd mentioned it earlier.

A young man delivered the hot plates filled with food. He pointed at Mike's beer glass. "*Una otra cerveza, señor?*"

"No, iced tea please. How about you, Devon?"

"Tea will be fine for me, too." The smell of the food made her mouth water.

It was spicy, tangled with stringy goat cheese, and tasted wonderful.

"What is it like to be in marketing?" He took a bite of enchilada.

She stopped peeling the husk from her tamale just long enough to look up at him. "I used to handle all the trade shows for a big sportswear manufacturer. It was fun and I traveled a lot. I was good at it, too, but enticing customers to buy new beachwear doesn't do much to make the world a better place, except perhaps to boost the gross national product." She cut into the golden tamale with her fork.

"Nothing wrong with that. It keeps people employed so they can pay their doctor." His generous smile made her laugh. "Would you like it better if you switched to something else?"

"Hmmm. These days I'd rather invent indestructible clothes for children." She took a bite. "Lupe does make good tamales."

After a few minutes of munching, Mike stopped eating and looked over at her. "You know, I don't understand something."

"What?" She took another bite.

"We've known each other, what, two or three months? I've been trying to figure out what kind of guy walks away from a woman like you and a great kid like Jamie?"

She was embarrassed by his flattery and looked down at her plate. "Men leave women all the time. It's a sign of our screwed up times, haven't you heard?" She glanced over at him.

"I know you said he didn't want children but that's a lame excuse in my book." Mike scooped refried beans with a tortilla chip. "He must have been a jerk."

"No, Alan is successful and very bright, just not husband material." He was too busy chewing to comment. She poked at a bite of enchilada with her fork. "I couldn't see the forest for the trees."

She put her fork down on the table. Admitting she'd been stupid from the start was getting easier. Maybe that was some kind of progress.

He sat back in his chair. "What didn't you see?"

She pressed her napkin to her lips and returned it to her lap before looking him in the eye. "That he said all the right things but didn't know how to love someone, not even himself, poor thing. It took me a long time to figure that out." She sighed, letting one corner of her mouth curve upward at the irony of it. "I was his revenge."

"Revenge? You? Come on." He wrinkled his brow.

It was nice that he doubted her. "You didn't see his mother when he introduced me. She was livid he'd eloped with a country girl. Alan hates her, you see. They were like icebergs in separate oceans when they were in a room. It might have helped if I'd grown up with a couple of oil wells in the backyard, but I doubt it. Having a son, her grandson, was the only thing I ever did that pleased her." She took a sip of tea and put down the glass. "When we split up, she wanted Jamie. 'To raise him properly' was the way she put it. But Alan gave me full custody. We were both weapons. It was the one, almost noble thing he ever did, keeping Jamie away from her ... and maybe he realized it would have killed me to lose my son. That is as close to love as he could get." She moved her fingers over the cool surface of her tea glass and wondered if Alan would have described it that way.

"Sounds like he broke your heart."

"That's a bit of an overstatement." Alan had but she didn't care to admit it.

"No, it's not. It hurts like hell." She raised her head surprised at his comment. "I'm divorced too, remember?" His smile was gone.

She could've kicked herself for being so self-absorbed. He'd been so kind to her. She hadn't considered that he could be just as wounded from his divorce. Prejudice from her own experience had kept her from seeing it or even asking. She wanted to know his story. "What was her name?"

"Leslie." He was focused on her eyes. "We were married for two and a half years."

"You didn't want the divorce?"

"No. I didn't think there was a real problem. She'd had a rough mis-carriage and after that, things just fell apart." He pushed his plate to one side and glanced around the restaurant before looking back at her. "She wasn't cut out to be a military doctor's wife. That's what she said. Didn't like having to move or be alone so much. I worked long hours, weekends and nights, and there wasn't much I could do about that."

Devon could understand how that could strain a relationship. It had hurt hers. In the beginning they'd both traveled, spent less and less time together. Alan was gone most of the time after Jamie was born.

He shook his glass to rattle the ice around before taking a drink. "She married a guy who comes home on time every night for dinner."

"Life is never as simple as it's supposed to be." She glanced out the window when the flash of headlights caught her eye. Several more cars were turning in.

A boisterous group of customers walked in. The cantina was sud-denly humming with Spanish chatter and ripples of laughter. The music seemed louder.

"Looks like the place is going to fill up." He checked his watch. "Guess we should get a move on."

The beer and glasses of iced tea had caught up with her. She leaned over the table so she wouldn't have to shout. "Think I'd better make a trip to the ladies' room before the drive home."

Mike stood when she did. "I'll meet you by the cash register."

When she walked out of the ladies' room, the entrance was full of newcomers. The air was thick with the smell of cigarettes and beer. She began to thread her way through the crowd. A young couple, thoroughly involved with each other, blocked her path. The man stood behind the woman, his arms wrapped around her, squeezing her body close to his. He was smiling, his lips touching her ear as he said something. His hand moved up to touch her breast. Devon looked away feeling her own chest shrink back in reflex. A warm breath ruffled the hair by her ear and sent a chill down her back. She shook her head and lifted her shoulder to fend off the voice she was afraid to hear.

A sudden blare of trumpets made her jump in alarm. Voices rose as music started to play and the great sea of bodies, pushing and brushing against her, started to move. The room was hot, suffocating. Her heart was drumming in her ears. She tried to dig her way through the crowd with her arms.

Something snagged her elbow and she tugged to get free. Mike's face appeared in front of her. He was frowning. "What's wrong?"

"Let me go." He released his hold on her. Feeling dizzy, she focused on the door and pushed her way out. Standing in the center of the parking lot, surrounded by cars and trucks, she was disoriented. It was cool out here.

"Take it easy, Devon." Mike stood beside her. The colored lights from the cantina touched the side of his face.

She nodded her head and took several deep breaths. Music from the restaurant filled up the night air.

"Better now?" His voice was calm, quiet.

"Yes." She exhaled feeling steadier.

"Kind of tight in there."

"Yes." It was embarrassing to have him watching her. She didn't understand what had just happened but it was intense and unpleasant. It frightened her.

"Ready to go home?"

"Yes."

By the time she buckled her seat belt only a nervous twitch scampered around under her skin. They rode in silence on the dark and empty road with the windows open. The air rushing in whistled and teased the loose hair around her face. Just seeing that couple had made her run like a scared rabbit. She looked ahead at the white line caught in the head-lights.

"Didn't know they had so much business in that little joint."

"The food was good." It was the only reasonable thought she could put together.

"Glad you liked it. One of the doctors recommended it when I start-ed at the hospital. I've eaten in there several times and always enjoyed it." He touched her hand. "Feeling okay?"

"Yes." She forced a smile.

"Want to tell me what happened in there?"

She searched for a plausible explanation. "A little claustrophobia, I guess, with all those people crowding."

"You looked scared to death."

"No." She didn't want to go into it. "I'm fine."

They rode in silence. She considered telling him about it, but decid-ed against it. He'd think she was nuts.

"My roommate in college had a couple of flashbacks after being mugged. Ted said all the feelings just came out of the blue as if it were hap-pening again."

He was guessing something like that had happened to her. "What did he do?"

"He talked to a counselor on campus. He remembered hearing a laugh in the dark before they jumped him. Anything close to that trig-gered the flashes apparently. So he worked on getting used to those kinds of things. After a while, he was okay."

"They stopped?"

"I think so." He smiled. "He took karate lessons too so he could beat the crap out of anybody who tried it again."

By the time they were back to the ranch, the jitters were gone. She was feeling fine, but a little desperate to stay that way. The news that flashbacks weren't uncommon wasn't reassuring. She wanted to avoid another one. It was probably some little thing that'd start it. She'd call that phone num-ber they'd given her at the hospital and see if they could clue her in on how to manage it.

He pulled into the driveway and stopped by the front door. He walked around and opened her door.

She stepped down. "Thanks for dinner, Mike. I had a good time."

"You're welcome. I enjoyed it, too." He touched her arm and leaned down to kiss her.

She wanted to feel safe and comfortable with a man again. The aroma of his aftershave was earthy, inviting. She liked the gentle touch of his lips and the faint scratch of his chin on her skin. It was a simple, getting to know you kiss, quickly over.

"I'm glad we went out." He smiled down at her. "I've got to go."

"Good night."

He walked around to the driver's side and opened the door. "Hey, I forgot." They looked at each other through the open passenger side window. "There's a hospital party Sunday night at Dick Evans' house. He's a radiologist. It's casual, kind of a patio barbecue thing. Can't remember when it starts. Would you like to go with me?"

"I don't know. It's going to be a pretty busy weekend."

"Don't say no yet." He smiled. "I'll call you tomorrow with the details."

It was impossible to dislike him. She returned his smile. "Okay."

The Friday night performance at the grade school was the kickoff event for the Founder's Day weekend. The little gymnasium was filling up. The folding chairs rattled as parents and other proud relatives shuffled them around. Devon stood with Ellie by the double doors. She'd forgotten the attendance at these grade school programs was about two bodies shy of a jam-packed high school football game. The only seats left were in the last three rows.

"Let's sit on the inside aisle, Devon, so I can get a picture." Ellie headed for the last row.

She spotted a head of bright red hair across the makeshift auditorium. Suzy Atkins-Rogers was standing up facing the audience talking to a man in a suit. She was laughing and gesturing toward the crowd, definitely in her element.

Devon sat down next to her mother and paged through the little program. Mercifully, Jamie's first grade class would start things off. She could relax once he'd recited his verse about Jim Bowie.

"Hi." Annie Jessup bumped against Devon's knee. She was all in pink again, from the barrette in her hair to her dress, fingernails and right down to her socks.

She couldn't help but smile at the delicate little girl. "Hello, Annie. Did you come to see your sister?"

"Uh-huh. Can I sit here with you?" She put her hand on top of Devon's.

She looked around before answering. The girl seemed to have a knack for taking off on her own. She spotted Doc Jessup standing by the door with a frown on his face. He was probably looking for Annie. She waved to get his attention and pointed down at the child beside her when she caught his eye. "You should sit with your family, sweetheart. I see your grandpa. I'm sure your mama and daddy will want you with them."

Annie tilted her head to one side, a wrinkle disturbing her young brow. "Don't you know my mama's in Heaven?"

Devon's smile withered with the joyless thought that a mother's kiss would never touch that sweet face. "Oh, no I didn't. I'm sorry." The words, so inadequate, rushed out of her. Now she understood why the little girl seemed to cling to her, perhaps to every woman she came in contact with.

"That's okay. Heaven is a nice place. Daddy says she can see me all the time and blows me a kiss every night. If you close your eyes real tight you can feel it." The child kissed her own hand and blew it toward the high ceiling. Devon had to swallow hard to force down the lump in her throat.

As Doc walked down the row of chairs toward them, he wagged his finger at the child. "Annie, I told you to stick with me, dang it." His lips were puckered up as if he'd taken a bite of a crabapple.

The little girl took his hand and sent a lost puppy look in his direction. "I forgot, Paw paw. Can we sit here, please?" She patted the chair next to Devon.

The man was no match for her. He looked around the room as the edges on his frown disappeared. "Not much choice left, I reckon. Mind if we sit here, ladies?" He smiled at Ellie. "Noreen was going to come with me but she's still fightin' a cold."

Her mother returned his smile. "Please do, John. I meant to ask you the other day how you hurt your arm."

Annie sat next to Devon. He sat beside his granddaughter and leaned forward in his chair to explain. "Had an old Brahma bull shove me into the side of a stall, Ellie. Bruised my shoulder and cracked the shoulder blade. Gonna leave the bulls to my partner from now on."

The first graders began to file in quieting the more boisterous conversations in the audience. Devon felt a rush of nerves as she watched Jamie shuffle in. The entire class of fifteen seemed to find it impossible to stand still as they waited for the teacher to introduce their presentation. The six year olds teetered, scratched and waved while reciting a poem about the Alamo written by the teacher.

Every child had two lines and some of them struggled mightily with a word or two. She silently mouthed the words as Jamie said his part out loud and smiled when he remembered the word strife that rhymed with knife. The little group sang a song and marched out of the auditorium to applause and chuckles.

She wished they could leave as she eyed the long line-up of classes waiting to perform but there were refreshments afterwards and she'd promised Jamie they would stay. She skimmed through the names of the children listed in each class. She only recognized a couple. Fourth grade. Beth Jessup and Dottie Ruth Rogers, Suzy's daughter.

As the fourth graders came on, she couldn't help but recognize Dottie Ruth. She was the only redhead in the group and looked like a reprint of her mother. History seemed destined to repeat itself. Dottie stood in the front row and skillfully handled a lion's share of the performance.

Beth was standing on the risers in the middle of her gangly classmates but she didn't bother to sing or even open her mouth at the right moments. Devon watched her wondering if she was unhappy or bored. It was hard to tell. She couldn't help but feel sorry for her. The trials and tribulations of puberty were just around the corner and Beth wouldn't have a mother to ease the trip.

As Beth's class marched out, Devon noticed Annie had fallen asleep in her grandfather's lap. She watched the fifth and sixth graders thinking how big they looked compared to Jamie's class. Imagining what he would look like at twelve, she wondered if she would know how to help him deal with a grown-up body.

The principal ended the ceremonies inviting everyone to enjoy the punch and cookies. The children rushed in from the side door to join their families. Devon stood up so Jamie could spot her in the noisy crowd. She glanced down at Doc Jessup, holding Annie in his lap. "What happened to Frank tonight?"

He looked up at her. "He had a horse get loose and tangle with barbed wire. Made Beth unhappy that he couldn't come but he had to take care of it. Hard when a man's got to be mother and father."

"I know." She nodded her head. They were such cute kids but a handful for Frank to manage alone. "What happened to his wife?"

Sadness darkened Doc's face and drew the corners of his mouth down. "She was killed in a car wreck when they lived in Ft. Worth. Such a shame to lose her like that. Annie was just a baby."

Jamie rushed up and wrapped his arms around her waist. "Did you see me, Mom?"

She touched his cheek thankful she was here for him. "I could hear every word. You did great."

Flush with excitement, he turned to Ellie. "Did you see me, Granny?"

"You bet I did." Ellie's face beamed with pride. "I took a picture of you saying your piece. Stand next to your mother and I'll take another one of the two of you together."

As Devon put her arm over his shoulder to draw him closer, Jamie clasped her hand between his, letting it rest on his chest. She smiled for the camera as he leaned against her hip. The thought crossed her mind to cherish the moment as the flash went off.

Jamie raised his chin to look up at her. "Let's get some cookies now, okay Mom?"

"Sure. You lead the way." Jamie scampered off toward the long tables of refreshments.

She glanced at Doc. He was standing up. A sleepy Annie sitting up on the chair beside him. "Goodnight, Dr. Jessup." She leaned down to talk to the little girl in pink rubbing her eyes. "Goodbye, Annie." There was always something about a sleepy child that gave her the urge to cuddle them. She wanted to hug her as an expression of her sympathy, too, but she didn't. It wasn't fair to encourage a little one. She couldn't resist touching Annie's dark hair, however, to gently brush it away from her eyes and smile before turning away. Annie would be fine. She had a good father and fine grandparents to look after her.

The Founder's Day celebration was still a big event in the life of this little town. It wasn't the Super Bowl but it took the whole community to put it together. Everybody was pitching in to get the picnic grounds ready for the onslaught of visiting friends and relatives as well as the few tourists who roamed through here in the spring. Ellie had left early to help set up and arrange the dessert tables.

After the rush of cooking and packaging the day before, Devon's task on this May morning was simple. Bring the ice chest and jug of iced tea and pick up Aunt Jessie. On the way, Devon had to make one detour. Aunt Jessie wanted to drive out to the old cemetery well north of town where most of her family was laid to rest.

Devon knew where it was but she'd never stopped and walked through it. It was filled with the families of pioneers, the folks of faded photographs, dressed in stiff collars and long gowns.

She opened the gate in the plain chain-link fence of the small Hawkin's Prairie graveyard to let Jessie Mae in. The ground was hard and powder dry, even though there had been a good rain two days ago. Many of the headstones, the names and dates eaten away by sand laden winds, sat off-kilter as if they drifted in a dusty sea, with an occasional sprig of grass poking up to ruffle the surface. Only one tree provided a bit of shade. Devon stood under it with Aunt Jessie while the lady got her bearings. Jamie was close by, walking along a row of worn markers, his boots scuffling in the gritty dirt as he explored, the only sound she heard.

"When I was younger, I used to think God took the ones worth havin' to Heaven and made the rest of us stay without them as punishment." There was sadness in her aunt's voice, a sigh of resignation. "But I've decided that's too mean, even for God."

She raised her hand. "My son, Franklin, is over there, I believe." They walked side by side toward several headstones set apart by white, flat rocks. "Don't know if I ever told you about him." Jessie glanced at her and Devon shook her head in answer. "He was killed this very day in nineteen hundred and thirty-five for no good reason at all." Her eyes were fixed in the distance as they stood over him. "I was about your age then. I remember it like yesterday. Everything I said, and should have said." She shook her head slowly. "You see, I sent him off that day." Jessie clasped her hands, her fingers worked fitfully as she talked. "It was my fault . . . that he was there when that fella come along in the car."

Grief crept into Jessie's voice, Devon didn't want to hear the rest. She looked down at the fine cracks of the dry earth at her feet, feeling her skin grow hot and her blood pump faster.

"I cried for two days straight when they brought him home, so broken. I never wanted to die so bad. But the damage had been done to my poor, sweet boy."

With tears welling up in her eyes, Devon looked up at the dear lady's face shaded by her straw hat. A faint smile softened Jessie's mouth.

"I had my husband, George, and little Faye, to tend to in those days. Figured if I ever got the chance, I just might send that man who killed my boy to Hell myself, that's how crazy mad I was." She peered at Devon. "Guess you might have some idea how that feels."

Her stomach tightened. "Yes, ma'am, I'm afraid I do."

"Don't be afraid of those feelings, child, God gave them to you for a purpose." She grabbed hold of Devon's arm. "When you had to fight, the Lord gave you the strength, like David when he slew Goliath. Now you can move on, like I did. When I heard that man died, it was a big relief not to have to hate him anymore. That's when my heart started to mend. Has yours started to mending, Devon?"

She looked at Jessie whose spirit was so much stronger than her appearance. "Yes, ma'am, it has."

She heard Jamie laughing and turned to see what he was doing. He was at the corner of the cemetery fence, scrambling around carrying one of his boots in his hand. He bent over and grabbed something.

"Think I'd better go see what is going on, Aunt Jessie." She walked over. It didn't take long to see that the ground was alive with tiny frogs hopping madly in every direction. Jamie was putting the ones he'd caught in his boot.

"Bunches of baby frogs, Mom." He looked at her just long enough to state the obvious.

There was a large tangle of green on the other side of the metal fence where the ground sloped down. They'd hatched in a little over grown pond and were trying out their new legs. "They're cute, Jamie, but you have to let them go."

He stopped and frowned at her. "Why? I want to keep them."

"We have frogs at home. These need to eat bugs around here."

"Can't I keep one or two? Let them live with our frogs?"

"We don't have anything to keep them in until we get home tonight. They'll hop right out of that boot. You can play with one while we're here." She turned around and walked back to Jessie. He hobbled beside her, carrying one boot in the crook of his arm.

Jessie leaned forward as he opened his cupped hands to show her his prize. She smiled and gently stroked his hair. "That's a mighty fine frog you caught, son. You are quite a little rascal, you surely are." She straightened, her eyes looking back at her son's headstone. "Always listen to your mama when she tells you to be careful, boy, for you hold her heart in your hands."

Jamie didn't comment or even raise his head. But tears filled Devon's eyes and she turned away.

As they drove to the park, there were at least five tiny frogs hopping around in the car. But after listening to Jessie, smuggled frogs weren't worth an argument. Once they got out though, it was Jamie's responsibility to collect the little hoppers and put them in a safe spot in the grass.

In the shade of the pecan trees, the crowd was growing. The pavilion was set up for the Founder's Day festivities. Latecomers walked up with folding chairs as an industrious group of women, arranged a serving table laden with covered cakes and pies while the men wrestled with ice chests full of soda and sun tea. Devon could just see the top of Stubby Pritchard's baldhead behind the smoking barbecue grills made from steel barrels. When he lifted one of the black lids, the mouth-watering smells of meat slathered with sauce billowed out filling the warm breeze. Devon's empty stomach grumbled. It was a little after twelve. She hoped it wouldn't be long until the mayor gave his speech and they could all eat.

After ten minutes of droll conversation with Bernice Clemens, Devon managed to excuse herself and headed toward the food. She'd settle for a potato chip or a carrot stick at this point.

"Hey, Devon." A familiar voice that she couldn't quite place rose above the murmur of the crowd.

She turned to see Molly Duncan churning toward her. She was a swirling weather front, all by herself, in a soft, long dress of bright jungle colors and the usual jangle of tribal jewelry rattling the calm. Energy exploded out of her and left fall out, usually a smile on the faces she passed. Molly was simply one of those people impossible to ignore.

"My favorite, little digging partner. How in the hell are you?" An exuberant smile spread across her face as she opened her arms and pulled Devon to her ample bosom.

"Ms. Duncan." Devon's smile was smothered in curly gray hair as Molly gave her a rambunctious hug.

She pushed Devon away to look her over. "You still aren't big as a minute. What happened to calling me, Molly?" She had to be in her sixties by now. Her tan face was sporting more wrinkles but the green eyes still had the same bright enthusiasm gleaming in them.

Devon laughed, soaking up some of the woman's cheerfulness. "I'm great. How are you?"

"Busy, busy. Are you here for a visit or have you come to your senses and decided to stay in Texas?"

"I'm sort of in-between jobs, right now, but I'm thinking of sticking around. Are you still out digging for treasure?" Devon couldn't resist the joke. Every rancher Molly had asked for permission to dig thought she was looking for something of monetary value.

"Oh, I found a big prehistoric site, honey. Now all I need is time and money." She laughed.

"Last I heard you got a degree in business and were living in California mixed up in crass commercialism. You have no idea how that disappointed me. I'd planned on making you my assistant."

"You know how Pop was about being practical."

"As I remember, he said there was no use in a person digging in the dirt if it wasn't to plant something or find water. Your daddy was a fine man and a good rancher, but he didn't have a lick of imagination." Molly squeezed Devon's shoulder. "I could use someone with imagination and a mind for business to help me drum up benefactors. Do you have a new job all lined up or could I get you to give me a hand? The money is bad, but working with me would make it all worthwhile." She grinned with a teasing easiness that made it seem only days since they had worked on their hands and knees sifting through rock chips.

"Sounds tempting, Molly, but I do have other responsibilities these days. Come on, I'll introduce you to my son."

"A son. Wonderful! Bet he likes to dig." Molly waved her arms as she talked nonstop on the way to find Jamie.

The afternoon was filled with food, a political speech or two and plenty of gossip. Loretta and Tammy set up their lawn chairs in the shade close to the swings. It was a good central location to keep an eye on the wild packs of kids crisscrossing the park. Devon settled in with them a while. The news that Dee Dee Atkins had unexpectedly eloped with the Dr. Pepper deliveryman scattered through the crowd. The single men in town had shouted a collective 'Hallelujah' when the announcement first became public. According to Loretta, that included the ones who had never prayed a day in their lives. Suzy's job as matchmaker was over at last. It was nice to be old news finally and not worth a whisper.

She had thrown away the last of the paper plates and napkins from lunch. A man whose black hair was frosted gray at the temples walked up to her and held out his hand. "Devon Taylor, right?"

She extended her hand. "Yes."

He shook it with exuberance. "My name's Fred Clark, I'm with Travis Junior College. Molly Duncan steered me over here. Said you would be around for a while and might be interested in a job I've been trying to fill."

"Really." She wondered what in the world Molly had said.

"You're in marketing, right? I've just been given the task of attracting new students and to put us on the map, so to speak. I could really use someone with a fresh perspective and some experience at drumming up business. Would you be interested?"

He finally took a breath so she could get a word in. "It was nice of Ms. Duncan to recommend me, Mr. Clark. I'm flattered that you would consider me."

"I trust Molly's judgment. Come by and let me show you around." He dug a business card out of his wallet. "We've got a nice little campus. I'm very proud of what we've done." His smile made it hard not to like the man. "Our business department needs a teacher too if you're interested."

"I've never taught before, Mr. Clark."

"You should give it a try. Our students could use a dose of reality. They get a little starry-eyed."

"We've all been guilty of that at least once. I'll think about it, Mr. Clark, and give you a call." She'd never thought about having a college as a client. It might be interesting to see the place.

"Good, you do that." He nodded. "Now I'd better find my wife before she runs off and leaves me." He disappeared into the crowd.

Devon sat in the Bronco as Mike drove out of the hospital parking lot. She'd met him there so they could make it to his party on time. A three car pile-up had flooded the emergency room with multiple trauma victims so he hadn't been able to go home as planned. He was telling her about his long, tense day. She was having a hard time paying attention, but not because the subject was gruesome. It was his quick kiss when he walked over to her that had thrown her for a loop. She hadn't expected it. He didn't seem to notice her surprise or lackluster response.

The prospect of being alone with him in his house made her edgy. It was hard to hold her hands still and folding them didn't help. Mike had never given her any reason to worry, but her guard was up just the same. After so many negative experiences with men, distrust was an automatic reflex. It was a not a wound she talked about, but it was one she understood intimately. Especially now, it filled her with a sense of loss and sadness.

He drove up to a white frame house shaded by a cluster of gnarled post oak and stopped. The window air conditioner dripped as they walked up the concrete slab front porch to the door. The neat but sparsely decorated main room was living room, dining room and kitchen.

"Make yourself at home. Just take me a few minutes to change. There's pop and beer in the refrigerator if you want a drink." He disappeared behind a door.

Devon roamed around taking stock of the little things that told her something about him. He had a few magazines and a paperback on an end table. The secondhand brown tweed recliner and hunter-green couch had lived-in lumps and bumps. The television with a VCR sitting on top rested on a spindlelegged table painted white. It was a nomad's house. Nothing matched. The only personal things were several framed photos scattered around. She tried to guess who was who, looking for a family resemblance in a large group. She smiled recognizing Mike as the boy proudly holding up a fish. There was a photo of him in a military uniform too. He was younger and quite handsome.

She was holding a framed photo she had just picked up when he came into the room again. He was barefoot, wearing khaki slacks and finishing buttoning a plaid short sleeved shirt. She glanced at the picture of a smiling, older woman with an infant in her arms. Mike had her eyes and smile. "This your Mom?"

"Yeah, just got that. That's my sister Sandy's latest addition to the clan." He walked up to stand beside her. "They named him Jason."

She noticed his aftershave and took a deep breath. He smelled like a man should. She took a step away from him to set the photograph down on the coffee table. "You look a lot like her."

"That's what everybody says. Oh, damn, I forgot about the guacamole." He shook his head and frowned.

She straightened up. "Guacamole?"

"I was supposed to bring dip and chips but forgot all about it." He scanned the living room looking for something. "I must have left the recipe one of the nurses gave me at the hospital. Do you know how to make it?" He glanced at her.

"Sure, if you have all the ingredients."

He walked past her toward the small niche of a kitchen and she followed. "Bonnie gave me a list. I picked the stuff up at the grocery store yesterday." He opened the refrigerator. "Let's see, I've got avocados, lemons, tomatoes, and onions." He began to hand them out to her. "Do you use anything else?"

"Just salt. I'll need a bowl, knife, fork and a cutting board. How about an apron?" She didn't want to get any avocado on her blouse.

He slid open the bottom drawer and took out a folded cloth. "All I have is this BBQ apron somebody gave me at the Christmas party. Here." He grabbed a bowl from a cabinet and set it on the counter. "I tried making this stuff once but it didn't taste like much." He pulled open a drawer. The silverware clinked.

After she explained the steps in the process, they stood slicing and dicing side by side, both of them blinking from the sting of the onions. She laughed as he struggled to hang on to a slippery, peeled avocado.

"I've had fish put up less fight than this." He finally speared it with a fork. Once the chopping phase was finished, he rinsed his hands and became a spectator.

She squeezed some lemon juice into the bowl. "Now that we've mashed the avocado, we mix in the diced tomatoes and onions." She stirred. "The real art to it is getting just the right amount of lemon and salt." She scooped up a little of the thick mixture in a clean spoon, tasted a small amount. It was just about right. She held the rest up for him. He leaned forward and sampled the half spoonful. She dropped the spoon in the sink and turned to watch him savor the mixture. "That seems salty enough and yet tangy, don't you think?"

She watched his mouth. He licked his lips and nodded before he swallowed. He was very close. It was one of those breathless moments, when she could feel her heart beating and knew exactly what was about to happen. He leaned down and kissed her. When her lips touched his, she closed her eyes to shut out the outside world, lost in the warm sensation. He put his arms around her, drawing her closer.

Her body wanted to melt into him but the thinking part of her knew she wasn't ready. She pulled away from him. "I've got guacamole on my hands, Mike." With her hands held in the air, she slipped out of his arms and turned to face the sink. She pushed the faucet lever up with her elbow to rinse her hands.

"I don't care." He whispered as his hands slipped around her waist. Chills scattered, racing across her skin. He wrapped his arms around her ribs, pulling her closer, until she was pressed against him. The hair on the back of her neck stood up as his lips touched her ear.

She couldn't move. Her body was cold and rigid. "Stop."

He moved his head. She couldn't feel his breath on her neck.

"What's wrong?"

She couldn't answer. Words wouldn't come out. He stepped back.

Warm water from the faucet ran down her fingers to the palms of her hands. Slowly the feeling came back and she shut the water off in the sink. "I can't do this." She turned to walk away.

"Wait." He was in the way and touched her arm.

"Don't." She pulled her arm away. "I'm sorry if I gave you the wrong idea." She kept her back to him.

"I've upset you but I don't know how." He moved to her left and leaned against the counter to look at her face.

She turned her head away from him. She didn't want to remember the touch of his lips whispering in her ear or the arms surrounding her. She shivered. "I can't explain." Tears welled up.

"Did I scare you? I'd like to understand."

She stared at the sink, at the avocado skins and dark seeds and squeezed lemon. He deserved an answer. She took a deep breath before starting. "He grabbed me from behind and wrapped his arms around me." Her voice wavered. "I could barely breathe." When she raised her head, he looked stricken. His brows were furrowed over eyes focused on her face and his lips parted, at a loss for words. "He said 'we were going to have a little fun,' that I'd like it." When tears rolled down her cheeks, she leaned against the edge of the counter. Her shoulders rose and fell with each deliberate breath pushing the memories away.

He gently placed his fingers on her hand. "I'm sorry."

"Me too." She straightened up and pulled a paper towel off the roll. "I hate to cry." She sniffed and dabbed at her hot face.

"I didn't mean to stir up bad memories."

"You didn't know." She glanced at him briefly before looking back down. There were black smudges on the moist paper in her hand. Her mascara must be smeared all over.

"No, Devon."

She raised her head. With a half-hearted smile on his face, he looked uncomfortable standing there.

"You've been through a lot. I should have known better than to get carried away." He crossed his arms.

"I'm a big girl, Mike." She looked him straight in the eye. "I like you. You know that." She took a deep breath and started folding the paper towel in her hands. "I just wasn't prepared for you to come up behind me."

"You can trust me, Devon." He uncrossed his arms. "The last thing I want to do is scare you or make you cry."

"I know." She sniffed. "I must look awful."

He smiled. "Just a few smudges to fix."

She shook her head. "Oh doctor, you are a kind, kind man. We better clean up this mess in the sink before we leave."

"I can handle that." He grabbed one of the empty plastic bags on the counter and opened it with a snap of the wrist. "Let me get this slippery stuff cleaned up. You did the hard part." He glanced at her. "Thanks for helping, Devon."

"Thank you for understanding." She tried to smile. "Do you have some plastic wrap to cover the bowl?"

"Sure, it's in the second drawer."

The drive to the party passed with small talk. After a few wrong turns, they finally found the place. When they drove up to the rambling one story house, the party was in full swing, judging by the number of cars in the driveway and lining the road.

The prospect of engaging in pleasant but inane conversations with people she didn't know reminded her of the endless cocktail parties she'd once endured. This promised to be more lighthearted and entertaining if the music and laughter they could hear from the road were any indication. She needed to laugh. They gathered up their contribution to the feast and headed for the front door.

Mike was welcomed with a shout as they walked in and were directed to the back of the house. The glass doors opened onto a well-lit patio. The food was set up on several tables near the kitchen. They put out the guacamole and chips they'd brought with the help of a couple of young women, whom Mike introduced as nurses from the emergency room. Someone's rendition of *San Antonio Stroll* blared out of the speakers drowning out all hope of carrying on a normal conversation.

Mike grabbed her hand and leaned down so she could hear him. "How about a dance?"

Several couples were putting on a marvelous show with their fancy footwork. She hated to admit she'd never danced to Cotton-eyed Joe or any other line dance. It seemed down right unTexan. In fact, it had been years since she'd danced anything and she hadn't exactly been Ginger Rogers then. "Mike, I'm so rusty I'll squeak."

"So am I. Come on." He led her to the spot where the others were dancing. He surprised her when he gave an authentic Texas 'ah-ha' and hooked an arm around her waist to pull her into his arms. They spun around with more energy than precision, occasionally bumping into other couples, through two songs before stopping to get something to eat. They nibbled on guacamole and bean dip with taco chips and ate spicy taco salad casserole.

Mike introduced her to the different knots of people talking. More than once she felt as if she were invisible because her participation in the conversations was minimal. Not that anyone was being rude or that she was purposely being distant. She just didn't know what they were talking about most of the time. The topics, diseases or injuries were all labeled with Latin names and involved detailed remedies and procedures. They weren't discussing people, just ailments as if they existed independently. Maybe they had to reduce it all to organs, fluids and vital signs to deal with so much misery every day.

Several doctors asked Mike if he'd heard about the fellowship in Seattle. She remembered him mention it in passing, but never in detail. His whole demeanor changed when the subject came up. His smile was broader and his voice had an enthusiasm she hadn't heard before. He expected to know something soon, he told them. He was a different man during these conversations, a man in love with his work.

When the music started up again, an attractive, fast-talking young woman grabbed Mike's arm pulling him toward the dance area. He shot Devon a quick look and she waved him on. "I'm going to get something to drink."

She was waiting by the makeshift bar when a woman walked up and smiled. "Hi. My name's Barbara. I work in the emergency room. You came with Mike, right?"

"Yes, I'm Devon. This is quite a party." Devon noticed Barbara's wedding ring when the woman lifted her glass. "Seems a lot of couples work together at the hospital. Is your husband a doctor?"

"No, thank goodness. It's hard enough to get away from work without taking it home with you." The nurse smiled at her and motioned toward the dancers with her drink. "Dr. Owen is quite a catch. Every single nurse in the hospital finds a way to walk through the ER when he's around. But he seems to be more interested in you."

There was a teasing quality in the woman's voice that Devon wasn't crazy about. "Really? I hadn't noticed."

The nurse laughed, then something caught her eye. "Uh-oh. My husband just gave me the signal. He hates these hospital parties. I'd better see what's got him stirred up. Good to meet you." The woman hurried off across the patio.

Devon watched Mike dancing. She did like him, had even come to trust him. He'd become a good friend. She would miss him if he left before she did. She realized it was probably more a matter of when than if. There wasn't a lot to keep a stranger here. Heck, there wasn't a lot to keep her here except family. And the fact that she had nothing to go to yet.

When the music stopped again, Mike walked back to her. "I'm beginning to remember which foot is my left and that I'm suppose to lead. Want to take another spin around the patio and see how many couples we can bump into?"

She smiled. "Sure."

But this time, the music was slow, the Spanish lyrics soft. He put his arms around her and held her close. Her cheek touched his as they danced and she closed her eyes. She couldn't ignore the feel of his body or how it made her warm. Maybe she could fall in love again, when she was ready.

They didn't stay much longer. Mike had to work the next morning and she was tired. They made their way through the parked cars jamming the road. It was pitch black when they turned onto the paved two lane road.

"Hope you weren't too bored with all the shop talk tonight, Devon. I got a little wrapped up in the surgery Dr. Philips was describing."

"There were moments when I wished I'd brought along a medical dictionary. However, the parts I did understand were nauseating enough to make me glad I wasn't eating guacamole at the time. I decided ignorance is bliss with your friends."

"How about some fresh air?" Mike laughed and rolled down his window. "That's one thing I like about Texas. It's warm and not raining all the time like Seattle. Your mother would like you to stay around here, wouldn't she?"

"Sure, she's lonesome without Dad. I wouldn't mind staying relatively close. One of these days, she'll sell the ranch. It would make it easier to talk her into moving if Jamie and I settle down in Texas."

"Thinking about some place like San Antonio or Dallas then?"

"I don't know yet." She hated sounding so disorganized out loud and her frustration added some unintended bite to her answer.

"Irritating to be treading water in a pool of uncertainty, isn't it?" He glanced over. "I know how it feels. I should have heard from the university by now. I'm giving them a call tomorrow so I'll know, one way or the other." His voice trailed off.

They sat in the darkness with only the hum of the engine and the flicker of the white lines in the headlights to remind her they were moving. "I gathered from your conversation you really want this fellowship. What's so special about it?"

He took his eyes off the road just long enough to glance her way. "Are you kidding? It's one of the best training programs in the country. Revolutionize the ER some day. Any doctor worth a damn would jump at the chance." The excitement in his voice told her as much as the words that rushed out of his mouth. "I mean, who doesn't want to be the best? That's the name of the game. The best hospitals are searching for doctors with that kind of training. Plus, just the chance to do research will be fantastic."

"You'd be doing research too?"

"Lots of it during the program, as well as attending seminars and working in the hospital, of course. It will be four to six years of intense work."

He suddenly reminded her of Alan. "Doesn't sound like you'll have much free time."

"I'll have days off."

"To study." She threw the comment away out the window. He was a good man with enough ambition to blot out the rest of the world. She turned her head back to watch him drive. "What if you don't get in?"

"Then I'll find a job in Seattle and reapply next year."

He was going to move with or without the fellowship. She didn't ask him any more questions. The answers all led to Seattle.

They pulled up to her car. It was parked underneath one of the bright lights in the hospital lot. He walked around and opened her door.

He put his arms around her and kissed her as she got out. She couldn't enjoy it. He gave her a gentle squeeze. "I have to work the next couple of days but let's do something after that, just the two of us."

"It's going to be pretty dull around here when you go." She couldn't say she'd miss him out loud. "When will you have to leave, September?"

"No. Classes start the first week of July."

She pulled away from him feeling like she been doused with ice water. "That's only a few weeks away."

"That's why I want to go out while we can."

"But . . .." She took a couple of steps back and stared at him. He'd been so sweet all night as if she meant something to him, but he hadn't bothered to mention, even once, that he was within weeks of packing his bags. Suddenly she felt stupid.

"I thought you knew." His raised brow hinted that he was puzzled.

That set her off. "What's going on, Mike?"

He looked confused. "What do you mean?"

She could have strangled him. "What do you want from me?" For the first time in their short friendship, he didn't have anything clever to say. Too furious to say another word, she whirled around and searched through her purse for her car keys.

"Why are you mad?"

She turned around ready to tear into him. "Do you have any real feelings for me or can you just turn them on and off like a faucet to have someone to cuddle up with?" Alan had been an expert. She should have seen it coming.

He shook his head and stared at her like she was nuts. "Of course, I really like you, damn it!" He crossed his arms at first looking as mad as she felt. Next thing she knew he was gesturing with both hands. "Look, you have to understand. This training is something really special. I've worked for a long time to have a chance at it. It's not one of those things you think about twice."

She knew a lot about coming in second. "I don't expect you to think twice. That wasn't the point." She tried to calm down enough to reconnect with her brain while fishing for her keys. She glanced around the parking lot hoping they weren't making a spectacle when she noticed the hospital behind them. It was the foundation of their short relationship. She'd been injured and he'd picked up the pieces.

"I'm sorry if I didn't tell you." His apology was barked out more than spoken. He didn't look angry anymore, just solemn as he poked his hands into his pockets.

She set her purse on the roof of her car. "You don't have to apologize." She crossed her arms before she leaned against her car and looked at him. "I shouldn't have yelled at you." It was hard to say what she felt but she was sorting it out. "I've been trying to pull myself together ever since I got home. And you've been really great to me." She squeezed the keys in her hand. "I know we're just friends but it hurt my feelings that you didn't say something before now about leaving so soon."

He walked the few steps separating them. "I think we could be more than friends."

With unblinking sincerity, he looked as if he meant it, but it didn't change the realities staring her in the face. "No, Mike, it would never work. You've got a long, tough road ahead of you in Seattle. I've got a son to raise and family here. I don't want what you want."

"Maybe you do."

"No. I'm sorry, but I don't." It hurt to say it, but she knew it was true. She picked up her purse and unlocked the car door. "I have to get home."

"Devon." He held the door open. "There are telephones lines and planes that go all the way to Seattle."

She tossed her purse across to the passenger seat before she looked at him. "It's not the same. You know that." She touched his cheek with her hand. "I will miss you."

His eyes took on a sadness that matched the way she felt inside. "And I'll miss you."

She turned away and sat down. He was still holding the door. She looked up. "Let me know if you got the fellowship."

He nodded. "I'll call you tomorrow."

"Good. I'll keep my fingers crossed for you." He returned her smile and shut the door.

J oe had run out of patience and time. His business was going sour. Not a soul had been down this dead-end road in days. He took a long drag on his cigarette as he leaned against the fender, watching the older woman's car disappear from sight. The ranch hand would be at the cattle auction all day. The kid was playing in the front yard.

He dropped his smoke and crushed it under his boot. Time to move. He walked to the cab and opened the door, glancing briefly at the wooden shipping crate in the bed of his truck. She'd insisted he bring it. The cold that came from some place deep down smoldered in the very center of him. He could hear his mother's bitter command and see her eyes cut into him. 'I want them buried deep in the bowels of the earth, Joe, in an unmarked grave. That ways prayers can't reach as the Devil snatches them.' He spit on the crumbling pavement. Crazy old woman didn't appreciate how big a hole it would take to bury a four-foot by three-foot box or how hard the ground was here. He climbed in his truck and sat down. Hell, Ma wasn't all there these days. He'd take care of things like he always did. She didn't have to know everything.

He could kill the Taylor woman with a single bullet from the road. Be fast and simple but he wouldn't. He would deliver his mother's message before the woman drew her last breath. He owed his brother that much. Joe looked back toward the house. The boy was riding his bike down the long driveway.

"Well, look at that." He focused the glasses on the boy turning onto the paved road. He checked the front door, still closed. Joe started the engine and drove off.

He slowed down as he approached the driveway. He couldn't see anyone standing by the front windows. The next ranch house was a half-mile away over the rise. The kid steered the small blue bike along a little worn path at the edge of the road. Joe moved in on his target at a crawl. He put the transmission in neutral and revved the motor a couple of times. It produced the desired effect. With a startled jerk, the boy glanced over his shoulder weaving a bit, almost losing his balance. Joe shifted into drive and headed straight for the bike. The kid tumbled into the ditch.

Joe slammed the vehicle in park. He jumped out of the truck and looked for any witnesses as he ran around it. "You okay, kid?"

The little boy scowled at him and rubbed his arm as he stood up. "You made me fall." He bent over to pick up his bike.

Joe grabbed the boy's baseball cap off the road, scooped him up in the crook of his arm and kicked the bike the rest of the way into the ditch.

"Hey, put me down." The kid started to kick and squirm trying to get out of his grasp. "Let go!"

Joe tightened his arm around the boy's stomach and covered his mouth with his hand. "Hold still or I'll beat the crap out of you!" He carried his wiggling captive to the open door, dropped him on the seat and held him down with one arm while he got in and drove off. He checked his rear view mirror. Nothing. With the son as bait, she would come crawling to him. Save him from having to worry about somebody spotting him at the house.

Devon was sitting in the den at her father's desk. She had the house to herself. Jamie was at Tommy's playing so she could get some work done on her list of job opportunities and decide which was worth sending a résumé. Some of them were long shots, but they were in Texas. The local junior college needed marketing help, maybe there were others out there. It had been a relief to tell Janet Blake she wasn't going back to the West Coast. Time to start fresh again. Leave the unhappy memories behind.

The disc jockey's voice came back on as the music died. "It's ten in the A.M. Gonna be hot today, like two habeñeros in love. Ooh, dawgies." The DJ whooped as if he was doing a promo for a TV western. Devon chuckled knowing the clown was sitting in an air-conditioned booth somewhere in the middle of Austin.

The phone rang. She was still smiling when she answered. "Hello."

"I've got somethin' of yours." The deep, raspy male voice made the simple words sound ugly.

She started to hang up but stopped, hearing Jamie's voice in the background. When he cried out a panicked 'Mama', she jumped to her feet and shouted into the phone, "Jamie!" There was no answer. Her fingers tightened around the phone in her hand. She was afraid to breathe, straining to decipher the muffled sounds coming through the receiver.

"Shut up, you squallin' brat." The angry command sickened her.

She heard a frightened whimper in the background. "Please don't hurt him." It came out as a frantic shout. She held one hand over her mouth to stop a sob. Calm down, calm down, listen, think. She took a deep breath trying to do that.

"Got your attention?"

"Yes." Her mouth was too dry to swallow. "What do you want."

"We got some talkin' to do." He sounded sure of himself. "I'm gonna lock your boy up in a crate until we're done with our business. Gonna get mighty hot in there after the sun has cooked it a while."

He stopped talking. She closed her eyes, listening for any sound, but heard only the beating of her own heart. Unable to bear the silence a minute longer, she shouted into the receiver. "Tell me. What do you want?"

"You remember the spot where you killed my brother, Johnny?"

She didn't answer, couldn't. Her mind was reeling. Those cruel, blue eyes were cutting into her and Mrs. Colton's threat, 'an eye for an eye', echoed like a screeching curse. She was locked in place, holding the phone to her ear, waiting.

"Be there. If I see the cops or anybody comin' except you, your boy will be dead in a heart beat." He emphasized those last words with chilling ease. "You've got thirty minutes."

"Wait." The sound of the dial tone crushed any chance of striking a bargain. She stood with the phone in her shaking hand. She should call

Buck for help. It might be Jamie's only chance. She couldn't trust anything the man on the phone had said. She dialed the sheriff's office. The phone rang three times before a man finally answered. "I have an emergency. This is Devon . . .." The office noise in the background disappeared. The line was dead. She threw the receiver down on the desk and closed her eyes squeezing them tight to fend off the tears she couldn't afford to shed. *God, please don't let him hurt my baby, that's all I ask. I was the one.*

Thirty minutes. She opened her eyes and looked at her watch. The seconds ticked away. No time to search for help. If the man on the phone was anything like his brother . . . that thought made her shudder. He was probably big like Johnny. She had to find a way to even the odds, have a fighting chance. The guns.

She opened the second drawer of the desk, scooped up the ring of keys and ran. She flung open the closet door in her mother's bedroom. Quickly finding the brass key, she unlocked the cabinet, grabbed a box of shells and the smaller revolver and ran down the hall. Her car would never make it on that old road. She sprinted to Pop's truck. Whatever the man had planned, she would deal with it. There was no choice. She slammed the door, twisted the key and heard the engine roar as she pushed down on the gas pedal.

Devon drove over the rise and stopped. A sudden flurry of shakes seized her making it hard to hold onto the steering wheel or keep a steady pressure on the accelerator. The heat blurred the scattered gray-green mesquite into wavy clumps. The ridges on either side ran parallel for some distance before the larger one on the left roamed north. The road curved between the ridges. Slabs of limestone, bright white in the sun, lay crumbled like broken bones on her right. They had been in the background when she'd fought with Colton. Nausea settled over her like a thick cloud, an unbidden response that was a part of the memory. She shifted into park, needing to hold still, and swallowed trying to rid herself of the sickening lump in her throat.

She looked at the revolver her father had given her. *Don't point it at something unless you intend to shoot it,* he'd told her. She grabbed the box of shells lying on the seat beside her and shook out six bullets. The brass glistened in her sweaty palm. She picked up the gun, pushed the release and flipped open the cylinder. Her fingers trembled as she filled each chamber. She snapped the cylinder in place and laid the gun across her lap.

Her hands in tight fists clutched the steering wheel as she bounced along the weathered road. Sweat rolled down the side of her face. A steely calm took over. Thoughts taking command of the jitters. She would try to explain she hadn't meant to kill his brother if he would listen, or beg for Jamie's release if that's what it took. With a flex of her jaw she decided. She would shoot him if she had to.

There was something up ahead to the right, just off the road. Maybe it was the box the man had mentioned. She accelerated. The heat would be suffocating in it. Thinking about Jamie, frightened and suffering, was a weight she couldn't bear, not now, and she tried to blot out the images of him. As she sped closer, she could see what looked like a wooden crate nestled in a narrow draw, fringed with scrub brush. Her skin prickled as if every nerve ending wanted to touch what lay ahead.

A spray of fine particles dusted her face as a loud pop broke the silence. She flinched and swerved to the left. A spider web of cracks surrounded a hole just below the rear view mirror. Bits of glass scattered across the seat glittered in the sunlight. He was shooting at her. A hole punched in the back of the seat was inches from her shoulder. There were two more sharp cracks of a rifle followed by loud bangs. The steering wheel took on a life of its own and pulled hard to the right. He'd blown out the tires. She yanked it back to the left and pushed down on the accelerator, trying to get as close to the crate as she could, but the truck slowed to a crawl, useless. Devon killed the engine and opened her door. She should make a run for it but there was no cover, no place to hide. She sat on the floor under the steering wheel letting the engine serve as a shield, trying to think while waiting for more bullets to rain down on her.

There were no more gunshots. The quiet was unnerving. She snatched the gun laying on the seat and held it in both hands, wishing she could take comfort in its presence. It was useless at a distance. She was shivering. Colton wasn't going to give her a chance to talk. She pictured Jamie, confined and terrified, hearing the shots, wondering what was hap-pening. Tears burned her eyes. She buried her face in her arms. There was no time to cry. She raised her head and summoned the courage to move. Getting to Jamie was all that mattered.

Holding onto the open door to support her shaking legs, she eased out of her hiding place and peeked over the hood. It wasn't too far to the crate, maybe thirty or forty yards across open ground. At least it was made out of wood. There would be cracks between the boards to let air in. That made it easier for her to breathe.

She shoved the barrel of the revolver through her belt and pulled out her shirt to hide it. Staying low, she crept forward and peered around the front bumper scanning the rocky slope for the gunman. He was up there, somewhere. Maybe she could get him out in the open. She cupped her hands around her mouth and yelled.

"You said we had things to talk about. I'm here. Where are you?"

There was no reply. She saw a flash of something slip between several boulders. There was no time to hesitate if he was walking down to finish her off. She started to run, praying he was as poor a shot as every bad guy in the movies.

Shots kicked up puffs of sand around her, stinging her bare arms. A burning sensation sliced through her thigh and she faltered, caught in the tangle of her own feet. She fell, landing with a hard thud that knocked the wind out of her. She raised her head looking for him while gasping to get her breath back.

The shooting stopped as suddenly as it had started. The glint of metal reflected off something on a flat boulder. "Waiting to see if I can get up?" She was panting, stirring up dust with each breath. "You are one mean son of a bitch."

She pushed herself up to her hands and knees. Her leg was bleeding but she was able to limp on it. She yelled at the crate as she hobbled toward it. "Jamie, are you all right?" There was no answer. Her mouth was so dry it was hard to talk. She called him again, louder this time. Still no response. He was gagged. She wouldn't consider any other explanation.

"He can't hear you."

She flinched in surprise and almost tripped at the sound of his voice. A man appeared walking out of a patch of mesquite and cedar brush that bordered the edge of the slope.

She swayed trying to keep her balance. "What have you done to him?" She didn't want him to hear her anguish but the words betrayed her.

His face was in the shadow cast by his broadbrimmed hat. He moved a few steps closer standing between her and the crate. He tossed a red baseball cap, Jamie's, at her feet. "I wanted you to know how it feels." He sounded as cold and lifeless as the mirrored lenses hiding his eyes.

"How what feels?" Her heart was picking up speed dreading the answer.

He pulled a revolver out of his holster. It was a large, powerful one, at least a .357, like her father's. "Use your head, woman. How it feels to lose a son, like my mother did when you killed my brother."

When he pointed the gun toward the box, the horror of what he was going to do came slamming down on top of her. "No, don't please." She screamed, tried to run.

The gunshot echoed off the ridge as the wood splintered on one end. She stumbled and fell. The searing ache was too big. A wail burst out of her, a torrent of pain. She wrapped her arms around her head to block out the sun and rocked in misery.

He pushed her over with his boot. "How does it feel to lose a son?" He was leaning over her, yelling.

He'd taken off his sunglasses. The look of contempt in his steel-blue eyes matched the ugly sneer on his face. She became hatred, hard and cold, as she glared at him. The jab in her ribs as she rolled over reminded her of the weapon she carried. It gave her strength and a numb indifference to anything that might happen afterward.

When she screamed at him, a fury of sounds instead of words that were rage and nothing more, he turned away from her. She pulled out her revolver holding it in both hands to control the trembling. Pulling back the hammer, she pointed it at the back of his head and fired.

His head snapped to one side as his hand covered his ear. He spun around and ran to kick the pistol out of her hand just as she started to pull the trigger again. It went off but the barrel was pointed away from him. She got up on one knee and tried to grab it but he got there first.

He picked it up with his left hand. His ear was bloody. "You need more than a pea shooter to get rid of me." He raised his revolver and riddled the box with holes. The blasts covered her screams.

She pushed herself up and stood on wobbly legs. Tears blurred her sight. She rubbed her hand over her eyes to see him clearly. Words were the only weapon she had left and they shot out of her. "You sick bastard. You aren't a man anymore than your brother was. Your crazy mother raised two cowards."

He put his revolver in the holster on his side. He raised his head slowly. The corner of his upper lip twitched. "Your boy ain't hurtin' anymore." His voice was an angry rasp. "But you hurt real bad, don't you?"

"No, you son of a bitch." She yelled at him wanting to rob him of that satisfaction if she could. "I'll see you in hell first."

He raised her pistol and fired. It felt like he'd hit her in the chest with his fist. She was knocked off balance and tumbled to the ground. A crushing ache filled her and she gasped for air. He towered over her holding the barrel to her forehead. She closed her eyes ready for the peace of death. Grief tasted like blood and she choked.

"I'm not going to make it easy. I want you to die slow like my brother. I'll give you your gun back. Didn't do you much good, did it?" He laughed.

She watched him empty the cylinder, wipe off the handle and throw it down before walking away. The sun was hot and so bright it burned her eyes. She turned her head and stared at the splintered wood of the crate.

Her chest was a yawning crater emptied of her heart. As she inched closer, pulling and pushing her body across the ground on her stomach sorrow wound round and round, ever tighter. Between her gasps, she whispered his name. Finally, her hand touched a rough board leaving a faint red smear as it slid down. There was no answer, no chance to say she was sorry or good-bye, or that she loved him one last time. The coarse sand scratched her cheek. She felt a breeze touch her hair, heard her mother's voice. Her eyelids fluttered, fighting to stay open. Shapes melted into a growing darkness filled with silence.

The chills racing across her skin woke her. She shivered, wished for a blanket. What had she been dreaming? She raised her heavy eyelids and caught a fuzzy glimpse of gray light before they slipped down. Moonlight, she thought. She needed to do something. The idea slipped by unopened.

An insistent buzzing told her to wake up. Something was wrong. She opened her eyes and blinked at the small dim light above her. Her throat burned. When she tried to swallow, she couldn't. Her heart jolted in her chest. She gasped for a breath, feeling the thing clogging her mouth and seeing a blue tube curving from her lips. She bit down. It didn't budge. Air filled her lungs. Relief. She turned her head toward the mechanical puffing sound, searching for the source across the white sheets. A box beside the bed beeped and lights flashed on it. A silver post next to the box rose, dangling a bag of clear liquid. On the other side of the post, a faint pool of light touched another bed, its occupant turned away from her.

With concentrated effort, she wiggled the fingers of her right hand. She was so thirsty. Her arm ached as she bent her elbow and touched her mouth. Her lips were dry and rough. She tugged at the tubing but her fingers were too weak to pull it out and her hand fell down to rest on her chest.

A woman's face appeared above her. Devon could see her dark eyes blink behind gold wire glasses. "Try to relax. The ventilator has to stay in to help you breathe." The woman dressed in white turned away.

Frustration was a fist in her prison of silence until a slender thread of warmth crept up her arm, expanding as it went higher. She couldn't keep her eyes open.

A star burst of splintered light flashed with the brilliance of the sun behind it. She was running, afraid, panting hard and fast, searching. Stinging bits of sand chased her. Blasts of sound like sharp claps of thunder hurt her ears. She shouted for Jamie, fighting tears, begging him to answer. A burning jolt knocked her off her feet. She was falling, helpless. Her body jerked in a painful spasm. Devon opened her eyes to see a white ceiling. A phone was ringing.

Bright sunshine flooded into the large room through a window on the opposite wall. There were other beds nearby, all with blinking machines beside them. Several men in green were huddled by a door talking. A nurse was standing by a white counter with a telephone in her hand. Devon touched her side and felt the ache. The nightmare was not a dream.

The image of the bullet-riddled crate seared in her memory filled her head and burned her eyes. Her body curled, shriveled. She'd lost him, her precious son. Tears filled her closed eyes. No more morning hugs or toothless smiles or goodnight kisses. She covered her face with her arms. There was no escape, no way to blot out the memory of his cry for help on the phone. She'd failed. Jamie had paid the terrible price. His small body torn by the bullets slicing through the wooden box. The savagery of the man twisted like a knife deep in her heart. She screamed, wanting to tear the sky and shake the world apart. The ventilator stopped the sound. When the mechanical push of air started filling her lungs she fought it, pushed against it, hating it. Surrounded by a rising chorus of beeps, she lashed out at the blue tubing. But soon, hands were forcing her down. They were stronger. The stern faces looking down at her demanded she hold still. She stared at them while they tied her hands to the rails of the bed. Too exhausted to fight . . . left in a numb emptiness.

Devon felt someone touch her hand and opened her eyes. Her mother was standing beside the bed.

"Hi, honey." She touched Devon's cheek. "You feeling better now?" There was a sad droop around her eyes and her tightly drawn lips fought to hold a smile. She was mourning too.

"They said you were upset earlier." Ellie glanced over her shoulder.

Her leg throbbed. A minor misery. It didn't matter, nothing did. Tears rolled down her cheeks.

Her mother's voice shook. "Don't cry, honey, don't cry." Ellie leaned over the bed and wiped at the tears. "Does it hurt? The doctor said you're going to be okay. All that matters is the two of you are safe."

Mom had said the two of you. It was like a bolt of lightning. She raised her head off the pillow, tried to sit up and make some kind of noise. She had to be sure she'd heard those words.

Ellie held her shoulders, forced her down. "Take it easy, honey, lay down. Are trying to ask me something?"

Devon nodded her head. Every muscle tense.

"About what? Jamie?"

Devon nodded again, harder this time.

"Don't worry about him. He's playing downstairs, right now."

Those words were a gift. She fell back onto the pillow, limp. The man had lied. Jamie was alive. A new round of tears, happy ones, started rolling down her cheeks. She rejoiced when her lungs filled with air. By some miracle, she had survived.

"Did you think he was hurt?" Her mother raised her eyebrows.

When she nodded, Ellie leaned over and hugged her. Her voice was whisper soft. "Oh, honey. Everything's going to be all right. All you have to worry about is getting well." After a few moments, Ellie straightened up. "You've got me bawling like a baby." She searched her purse for a tissue and wiped her eyes. She pulled another out and dried Devon's face too.

Mike walked up to the bed. He smiled when he saw her. "Hi. Great to see those blue eyes open." Devon noticed the dark circles under his eyes. "Dr. Jackson is on his way up to check on you."

Devon pointed to her mouth.

Mike nodded. "You're doing so well, I wouldn't be surprised if he takes you off the ventilator." He looked behind him. "Here he comes now."

"Good, then she can talk." Ellie turned as a man in blue scrubs stopped at the foot of the bed.

"Dr. Jackson, this is Mrs. Taylor, Devon's mother."

"Nice to meet you, ma'am. Sorry I didn't get to talk to you last night."

"I'm sure you were busy, Doctor. My main concern is how my daughter is doing." Ellie moved so the doctor could stand at the side of the bed. A nurse took a position across from him on the other side. She put down a tray with an assortment of packets and things on a bedside table.

"Good afternoon, Devon, I'm Dr. Jackson, I don't imagine you remember me." He was a middle-aged man with very curly reddish brown hair. "I was just reviewing your chart and everything looks good. Are the pain medications keeping you comfortable?" Devon nodded. "Since your lung is performing well, I don't see any reason to keep you on the ventilator. I know it's uncomfortable. We'll keep the chest tube in a bit longer." He put his hands on the side of the mattress and leaned on them. "The procedure to remove the tubing going down your throat is simple. You need to blow out as I pull. It'll just take a second but it will trigger the gag reflex as it slips out."

The nurse picked up a plastic kidney-shaped basin. She put it on Devon's lap and smiled. "Just in case you need it."

"Ready?" The doctor took hold of the tube.

Devon couldn't ask any questions, so she did the only thing she could, she nodded. She wanted to be able to talk.

"On the count of three then. One, two, three."

He was right. She gagged and her stomach retched as the tubing slipped out of her throat. She coughed and choked, fighting the urge to vomit. Her throat burned.

"It may a take a while to be able to talk. Try to relax. The nurse has some ice chips to whet your whistle."

The woman fished out a piece of ice from a cup with a spoon and offered it to her. Deliciously cold, it disappeared too quickly. She would have loved to have a mouth full of ice, to let it melt and trickle down her raw throat.

Mike was at the foot of the bed. He smiled. "Tastes great, doesn't it."

The nurse put the cup down. Devon wanted to ask for more but a hoarse noise was all that came out.

"Let me give you a quick rundown of your injuries, Devon. A bullet punctured the lower left lobe of your lung. So like a balloon it collapsed and you couldn't breath normally. It's called a pneumothorax when that happens. We insert a chest tube through the ribs and put you on a ventilator to restore normal respiratory function again. Surgery isn't necessary because the lung will quickly repair itself."

Devon took a breath. It hurt a little but she could feel the air rushing in and her chest expanding.

"There weren't any broken bones. So after making sure you were ventilated, we dealt with the other small-caliber bullet wounds. There were a number of superficial ones. The two deeper ones traveled through muscle tissue. The damage was minimal since the bullet fragments missed major arteries and nerves."

He was talking so fast it was hard to understand. Maybe it was the pain killers.

"We irrigated the wounds to clean out any debris. I want to take a look at the one in your arm." He removed the bandage on her sore upper arm. The gauze was bloody. He dropped it in the plastic tray on her lap. "The bullet went through the bicep here and exited here." He pointed to the two spots. "Good, it's stopped seeping. The entry and exit wounds will heal on their own but you will need to keep them clean and dry. The arm will be stiff and painful for a while."

He didn't have to tell her that.

He opened a small packet of gauze the nurse handed him, covered the holes, and wrapped a bandage around her arm to keep it in place. "In a few days, you won't have to cover it. Now, I want to check your leg." Dr. Jackson lifted the sheet.

She'd been unprepared the sight. Blue and black melted together with a topping of an orange yellow wash painted on her thigh for good measure. Devon's thoughts, brought on by a wave of revulsion, were too fleeting, too childish to utter out loud. Her knee was swollen. Her ankle had disappeared. Only the toes that fanned out like pudgy fruit on a cactus made it look anything like a foot. The nurse had her leg propped up with pillows. It didn't look like it belonged to her or anything human. It was a monstrosity.

He lifted her leg to remove the bandage around her thigh. A sharp pain flashed up her body. Devon grimaced, trying to contain the groan.

With two fingers, Dr. Jackson pressed down on the area above her knee. It was tender. "This bullet sliced through several muscles. We had to do a little repair work and close up the exit wound. That's why you have the stitches. You were lucky the bullet didn't travel deeper and sever the femoral artery. You may have a little numbness but it will probably disappear as the wound heals and swelling goes down." He wrapped a fresh bandage loosely around her thigh and pulled the sheet over it again. "Everything looks all right. You're running a slight fever. Don't think it's anything to worry about. There's an antibiotic in the IV to limit the chance of infection."

"Why is her ankle so swollen and bruised?" Ellie was frowning.

Dr. Jackson straightened up and looked at her mother. "Part of the answer is gravity, ma'am. It pulled the blood down as she moved. The torn muscles in her thigh coordinate lifting and straightening the leg. Trying to walk or run over rough ground with the damaged thigh, some of the ligaments of the knee and ankle were wrenched, over extended. Keeping her leg elevated will help the swelling go down." He looked at Devon and smiled for the first time. "You'll need some physical therapy to get full range of motion back, but there won't be any permanent disability."

She started to talk but had to resort to a whisper to get a sound out. "When can I go home?"

"I want to make sure your lung is functioning normally. And I want that temperature down for at least twenty-four hours before I release you. So I'd say, you should be able to leave by the weekend if all goes well." The doctor glanced at his watch. "I'll be back this evening to check on you. I'll decide then if we can take the chest tube out."

"Thank you, Doctor."

"You're welcome." Dr. Jackson turned and walked away. The nurse gathered up the basin and old bandaging and left.

She looked at Mike and her mother. "What day is it?" Her voice was a hoarse rasp.

"Tuesday. Here, have some more ice. It'll help your throat." Mike fed her as if she were a baby. "They are going to transfer you to a room downstairs in a little while."

She held her mother's hand. "How's Jamie?"

"Like I told you, honey, he is fine."

"What happened to him?" Her voice gave out.

"He says, a man grabbed him when he was riding his bike. After they called you, from a pay phone, they drove around a while, then the man told him to get out of his truck." The quick shake of her head and the rising pitch of her voice made it clear Ellie was upset. "He just drove off and left him out in the middle of nowhere. A woman driving to town saw him and stopped. Took him straight to the police."

Devon was too wrung out to feel much more than relief at this point.

"The hospital rules won't let him come up here because he's too young, Devon. But they promised me he can visit once you're transferred."

She let her head sink into the pillow, too tired to hold it up. "Good."

Her mother kissed her cheek. "You rest now. We'll visit later. I love you." She patted her hand before turning to walk away.

Mike was still standing beside the bed with a cup in his hand. He helped her get a sip of water. She glanced up at him. "Am I really all right?"

"Yes. They found you in time."

"Who?"

"I'm not sure, but I know the sheriff's office called the chopper to bring you in." He glanced at his watch. "I'm on duty now so I have to get downstairs. I'll check back in a little while." He smiled and turned away.

She closed her eyes.

She left the other place, whatever they called it. The drugs made her a little dizzy and created moments of nausea as the orderly rolled her around. She was wheeled out of the elevator. The long hallway of open doors had a tall window at the very end to let in the bright sun of the world outside. It reminded her of the hot sun baking the ground as she waited to die. She shivered under the light cotton blanket.

Transferred to her new bed in the empty room, she heard the rattle of food trays rolling down the corridor. She knew it was food. It smelled awful. She wasn't hungry. Her throat ached for something cool and wet. She was exhausted. The medicine blunted everything in order to ease the steady ache that gnawed at her. She just wanted to forget.

She'd been asleep. For how long she didn't know. They'd given her something for the nausea. She'd eaten some crackers.

Mike walked into her room pulling a chair over to the side of her bed. "There's a young man on his way up to see you." He picked up the bed control. "I'll raise your head a little."

Devon glanced toward the door anxious to see with her own eyes that her son was all right. Ellie appeared in the doorway with Jamie by her side. He was wearing jeans and a tee shirt. He looked perfect. Her chin began to tremble.

His face lit up when he saw her. "Mama!"

Seeing how easily he moved as he raced toward the bed, her eyes filled with tears. "Jamie." She reached for him, hungry to hold him again. He used the chair to climb onto the bed and fell into her arms.

She hugged him, discomfort ignored, drinking in the sweet smell of him, noticing how soft his hair was on her cheek. She kissed the side of his face. "Oh, Jamie, I love you." She squeezed him tighter as tears streamed down her face.

"Don't cry, Mama." Jamie buried his face in her shoulder. "I love you too." He pressed his wet face against the side of her neck.

"I'm okay, honey." Her voice wavered. She closed her eyes and forced herself to take slow, steady breaths. "Let me look at you." He pushed himself away and rocked back on his knees. She brushed her hand across her cheek to wipe away the tears. "You okay?"

"Uh-huh. Can you come home to Granny's with us tonight?"

"Not tonight but soon."

She glanced at her mother, noticing the dark circles under her eyes. Ellie grabbed a tissue from the box beside her and dabbed at her nose.

Jamie frowned, pointing at the IV in her arm. "You can't come because of that?"

"Yes." That made for a simple explanation.

"What does it do?"

Mike stepped closer to the side of the bed. "There is medicine in the plastic bag, Jamie." He pointed as he went through his explanation. "It goes down that tube and into your mother's arm a little at a time."

He tilted his head. "Can't she have a pill?"

"Sometimes people need stronger medicine than a pill."

He looked at her with a worried frown across his brow. "Does it hurt?"

"No." She sighed and leaned her head back.

Ellie picked her purse up off the foot of the bed. "Think it's time to get off the bed now, Jamie. We need to take it easy with your mother so she can get well."

"Do I have to?"

Devon nodded, unable to talk. She was choking on emotion.

"She needs a rest to get her strength back." Ellie helped him off the bed to the chair but let him stand on it. "Would you like us to bring you something from home when we come back, Devon?"

"I can bring you something too, Mama." Jamie grabbed her hand.

He looked so hopeful she had to think of something. "A Dr. Pepper with lots of ice for my sore throat." Her voice croaked.

He nodded his head. "You sound like a bullfrog, Mama."

She smiled and spoke in a gravelly whisper. "I feel like one."

"I'll bring your toothbrush and a few toiletries too, Devon." Ellie gave her hand a pat. "See you later." Her mother touched Jamie's shoulder. "We'd better get a move on, Jamie."

"Give me a kiss." Devon leaned over a bit and Jamie stretched to meet her halfway so she could reach his cheek. "Be sweet."

"Bye, Mama." He climbed down and turned his head to watch her as they walked away. He stopped at the door and waved.

Mike was still standing by the bed. "I'm going to get out of here too." He kissed her on the forehead and smiled. "Get some rest." He moved the chair away from the bed and headed out the door.

Devon closed her eyes. She heard someone walk in and peeked just long enough to see a nurse inject something into her IV.

Devon wasn't asleep. She was simply miserable. The throbbing from her leg had crept past the last of the medication, waking her. Her mouth was dry and her stomach was queasy. She kept her eyes closed, not wanting to face the world. Everything took too much effort. Right now, she wanted to be blissfully whacked into a stupor. She wondered how much of this never-ending day had passed. She opened her eyes. The stripes of sunlight from the partially closed blinds that had decorated the white ceiling tiles above her bed were gone but she could see daylight.

The automatic blood pressure machine clicked on. She tensed up waiting for the tight squeeze of the cuff she had come to dread. She had asked the young nurse if they could set the damn thing below the crush level but she didn't get any sympathy. 'It's not any tighter than a hand operated sphygmomanometer,' the nurse had assured her, as if being able to say the name of the contraption proved she knew everything there was to know about them. Devon folded her fingers into her palms as the increasing pressure squeezed. She wished she could wrap the nurse's chubby arm in this gadget to see if the girl felt the same after it clamped on with such vengeance.

Devon saw the Reverend Billy Clyde Stanford, Bible in hand, walk by her darkened room. She hoped he wasn't trying to find her. He reappeared at her doorway. A little moan escaped her lips as she quickly closed her eyes. Unfortunately, at that precise moment, Georgia, the one RN on the floor, walked in and flipped on the lights to check her IV. She apologized for waking her.

The reverend took that as his signal from God, granting him permission to bother her, and entered. "Good evening, sister." He was wearing the same blue suit he'd worn for his first sermon. Bristling with confidence, the young man's smile and rosy cheeks were on fire for God. "I heard about your tangle with the Devil and God's wonderful deliverance from the jaws of death."

Devon looked up at Georgia, wishing she could ask her to kick him out. The nurse raised her eyebrows in sympathy and stole a quick glance at the knucklehead, but didn't say anything.

"I thought I might be of some service as God's disciple. I hope you are feeling well."

Georgia deserted her. Devon would tell him the unvarnished truth. "I hurt all over and want to sleep."

His smile drooped. "Perhaps we should pray and ask our Father to ease your discomfort." Without further comment, he closed his eyes and raised his hand heavenward. "Dear Lord, this evening we ask for Your blessings on this dear lady. Give her strength Lord, to deal with the injuries so cruelly inflicted upon her. Bless the Taylor household and help them follow in Your righteous path. Amen." He opened his eyes, smiling, as if congratulating himself for soothing the afflicted. As he looked down at her, he cocked his head to one side and frowned. "Is something wrong?"

She toyed with the idea of telling him she thought he was a pompous ass but that took more energy than she had. "Why are you here?"

His mouth hung open as he blinked in surprise. "It is part of my duty to visit members of my church while they are suffering and comfort them in their times of trial."

He thought she was a duty. She'd pop that bubble. "I'm not a member of your church."

"But your mother . . . we all need help with the burdens God has given us to carry."

The idea behind his words stung and the beat of her heart picked up speed. "God selected this 'burden' for me?" Her body tensed as she stared at him. "What happened to 'God is love'?"

"He cannot protect us from the sin in this world because we are free to choose it and yet He forgives us over and over. Surely you agree that is the highest, purest love of all." He wasn't smiling anymore.

"So God let me run into the Coltons?" Her jaw tightened in anger as she glared at him. "And terrorizing my seven-year-old son was okay?" Her fingernails dug into the light blanket bunched at her waist.

Billy Clyde held out the black Bible in his right hand and looked at it. "Well, no." He was stammering. "I am certainly not able to understand God's plan. I am simply His servant." She could see him swallow. "I am confident God has a reason for all things."

She looked away, trying to calm the bright flare of contempt inside her. "There's bound to be someone in this hospital who needs your brand of comfort, but it isn't me. Good-bye, Mr. Stanford." She closed her eyes and turned away from him.

"I understand the past few days have been difficult." There was a rising hint of uncertainty in his sputtering piety. "I will pray for you and your family, Ms. Taylor."

She heard his heavy footsteps as he walked out of her room. Her breathing slowly settled down. Her empty stomach was grumbling and her muscles ached. She wished she could sleep.

"What in the world did you say to the preacher?" Devon opened her eyes. Ellie stood beside the bed. Her cheeks were flushed.

Devon glanced toward the window. It was still daylight. "I told him to go spout gospel somewhere else." She let anger color her explanation. "The imbecile made all the excuses for God I could take."

"Devon! What an ugly thing to say. He was just trying to help." Her mother frowned and shook her head.

She stared at the foot of the bed. But she couldn't stop herself from raising her voice anymore than control the trembling of her hands. "He said God gave me this burden to carry. Is that pile of crap supposed to help?" She shut up, seeing her mother's tight-lipped expression.

"God has a purpose for you just as He has for all of us. He helped you survive. I believe that all the way to my toes. I imagine the Reverend's words just didn't come out right, Devon."

"I'm not so sure. He is so sanctimonious he must glow in the dark. He's nothing like Reverend Thomas."

"It's not fair to compare them. Pastor Thomas was more experienced. He didn't expect too much from mere mortals."

"Well, I don't want to see Billy Clyde ever again, period."

"All right, I've got the picture." Ellie's voice rose to quiet her.

A dull ache throbbed in her head and drained all the fight out of her. She leaned back and tried to relax. "Look, I'm not feeling well enough to carry on a theological argument."

"I've got to find Jamie. Mike was going to help him with a little surprise. I'll be back in a few minutes."

Devon pulled the sheet over her shoulder and closed her eyes but thoughts kept boiling away. She was thoroughly mad at the little pink-faced minister and God. The trite litany of Sunday school and sermons couldn't help her deal with the savagery of the Coltons. She needed something with teeth in it.

Jamie was all smiles when he walked in. The surprise was a popsicle. It provided a sweet and soothing ending to one hell of a day.

The night shift nurse woke her before daylight, hanging up her last IV bag with antibiotics. She was one step closer to leaving. It was the only good thing about the restless night.

Bright and early for the rest of the world, Sheriff Buck Blanton stood at her door with a bouquet of flowers and a big grin that seemed out of place here. "There you are." He sauntered in and put the vase of flowers down on her bedside table. "Thought these flowers might spruce up the room a little."

"They're beautiful." Her voice still sounded hoarse. Devon pushed the button on the controls to raise her head and shifted her hips on the mattress to get comfortable.

"How you doin'?" He took off his hat and held it.

"I'm feeling better." Which was true with a fresh dose of painkillers in her, but otherwise a bald-faced lie. "Mike said you saved my life calling for the helicopter to pick me up. Thank you, Buck."

"The medics did the life saving but I'm glad I was there to help. I was on my way out to warn you I'd heard Joe Colton was around. Hank was the main reason we found you so quickly. He saw you drive out the back road like the devil was after you so we put two and two together."

Feeling weak with surprise, she leaned back, letting the pillow support her head. "Hank was at the ranch?"

"Yep, didn't go to the sale. Stayed to work on a pump." Buck put one hand on the raised side rail on the bed. "If you're up to it, Devon, I'd like to ask you a couple of questions. I'm tryin' to get a handle on just what happened."

She'd avoided remembering. The drugs had helped muddle things. "What do you want to know?"

He sat down on the chair beside the bed. "I've talked to Jamie. Apparently, a man drove up to him in a white pickup truck and grabbed him when he was riding his bike on the road. Wasn't too far from the house. Did you see any of that?"

"No, I didn't." She wondered what would have happened if she had. She shook off the thought. "I was in the house when I got a phone call. The man identified himself as Colton's brother. He had Jamie. I heard him in the background."

"So he told you to meet him at that spot on Comanche Wash?"

"He said he'd put Jamie in a crate and I had to come out there to get him. He gave me thirty minutes." She looked down at her hands. "I called your office but the phone went dead."

"Someone tore down the telephone line to your place. There must have been at least two of them."

"I only saw one man. He was tall, had dark hair and a mustache. He had those light blue Colton eyes though."

"Sounds like the same man Jamie described. So you drove out there but didn't actually see Jamie, just the crate?"

She nodded. "He shot out the tires before I could drive up to it, so I tried to run."

Buck's jaw tightened. "Son of a bitch used you for target practice."

She looked at the bare wall, the color of sand. "He said he wanted me to know how it felt to lose a son." Her voice shook, the words barely audible. She closed her eyes to regain control.

When she opened them, Buck was staring at her. His brow furrowed. "That's why the crate was full of holes. You thought Jamie was in there."

She nodded, blinking away tears.

He took her hand. "I'm sorry I wasn't there to help you." His frown deepened. "Wish I'd gotten my hands on that son of a bitch."

No one had mentioned Joe. The life drained out of her. "He got away."

He shook his head, his mouth a grim, straight line. "State patrol caught up with him in Oklahoma yesterday. He tried to outrun them. Ended up wrapped around a telephone pole. Died instantly."

A thought chilled her. "Are there any more brothers?"

Buck patted her hand. "Already checked. No more brothers or kissin' cousins." He put both hands on the side rail of the bed. "The Oklahoma law had been on to Joe's drug operation for some time. They're holding Mrs. Colton. She had bags of twenty dollar bills stashed in her house."

She covered her arms with the sheet. "Did she send Joe after me?"

"I asked them to question her. May go up there if they find out anything. Don't you worry, I'll get to the bottom of this mess." He glanced at his watch. "I'd better go. You take care of yourself." After he gave her a quick peck on the cheek, he walked out.

She was left with the unasked question. Who helped Joe Colton? Buck didn't say it, but she knew that's what was troubling him.

Two huge bouquets from Aunt Rose and Aunt Margaret were delivered to her room. They added some more color to the bleak place. When the phone rang, she stretched to reach it.

"Devon, is that you?" There was some hesitation in the question but she recognized Patsy's voice.

"Yes, it's me."

"You sound awful. Mama just called me and said someone shot you. How are you?"

"The doctor says I'm going to be fine." It was easy to say things like that on the phone.

"And Jamie's all right?"

"Yes."

She could hear Patsy breathing. "What did that monster do to you?"

"I was shot in the chest and leg. It collapsed my lung but I'm breathing fine now."

"How long will you have to be in the hospital?"

"Another couple of days."

"Well, that's good." Patsy sighed into the phone. "Listen, if there is anything I can do, just ask. We'd be happy to have Jamie come for a visit while you're recuperating."

"Thanks, Patsy, but I think Mom and I can handle things. I'd miss him." She couldn't say she was afraid to let him leave. There were many things to hide. Many fears that lingered in the back of her mind. She was alone with them.

The lunch carts clattered down the hall. She hoped she'd get something better than the orange juice and gruel they'd called breakfast. Confined to her bed with little privacy, she was generally helpless, waiting for bedpans or a chance to wash her face and brush her teeth. The horrible minutes before she was shot replayed over and over bringing tears she didn't want to shed. The monotony of the room, like the drip of the IV, gave her little else to think about.

A man stopped in the doorway of her room. He was tall and lean except for a slight paunch around his belt. He wore jeans and a white, long sleeved cowboy shirt. An uneasiness, cool and fleeting like goose bumps, made her shiver. She eyed the nurses' call button lying on the sheet next to her hand.

"Hello, Ms. Taylor, I'm Dr. Green. May I come in?" He smiled and walked partway in with a lanky awkwardness that made him look harmless.

"Hello." She raised the head of the bed as he stopped beside it.

His brown hair, thinning on top, was pulled back behind his ears into a narrow ponytail. "I'm the clinical psychologist on staff here. Your mother asked me to talk with Jamie."

Dread took up all the space in her chest and it was hard to squeeze out the words that raced to her lips. "Is something wrong?"

He shook his head and held up one hand to stop her. "No, I didn't mean to scare you. He seems to be doing fine." He smiled. "Kids have a lot of spring in them."

She breathed easier but could not relax. The shrink was still here, there was more.

He sat down on the chair. "As I said, I've talked to him and your mother. I understand this is his second traumatic experience in less than six months."

"Yes."

"We've only had one short conversation so it's hard to evaluate him. He wants to talk about it but naturally it scares him. Having a trained counselor work with him will make it easier. Children tend to blame themselves when bad things happen."

She sat up without the support of the mattress, as confused as she was worried. "Why would he do that?"

"Consider this." Dr. Green held out his open hands, fingers touching, to form a sphere. "A young child's universe is very small. His immediate family fulfills all his physical needs. He cries, he falls, they come running. So in his mind, he is at the center of his world, things happen because of him. If something goes wrong, it's his fault." He lowered his hands and smiled. "Makes sense from his perspective."

"Yes, but he's old enough to understand that's not true, isn't he?" There was that fearful clutch around her heart again, that he might be injured in some invisible way.

"Once their world starts to expand with school and other activities, a child gradually begins to see the bigger picture. At seven, I imagine Jamie is at that stage. Trauma often results in a step backward. After all he's been through, I would expect him to need some help over the next few months." He was studying her face. "How are you handling all this?"

She wondered if he could see the confusion in her eyes. She glanced out the window before looking back at him. "I'll be fine once I can get around on my own."

"Good." His pager started beeping. He looked down at it and shut it off. "I'm sorry, but I have to answer this. I wanted to let you know I've talked with him. I'll stop back later to answer any questions you have."

"What can I do to help him?" The question burned inside her.

"Let him know you love him. A good hug is better than any medicine I could prescribe."

After he left, she leaned back and closed her eyes. She had all the energy of a limp rag. She could love Jamie. At the moment, that was all she could manage.

It was wonderful to be free of the IV's and other gadgets, measuring and beeping. Devon finished off her first meal of real food, if hospital food could ever be called that. Since her throat was still sore from the tube, lunch consisted of soup, applesauce, bread and a tough, fruity mass of green gelatin. She gently rubbed her forearm, which had been bruised by the needles. Outside the window, a crow was sitting on the edge of the roof that angled away from her room. When she heard heavy footsteps stop in the hall, she turned to see who it was.

"You feeling up to a quick visit from an old friend?" Frank, straw hat in hand, was standing in the doorway. His familiar face gave her a rush of much needed energy.

"Hi, come in." Her hoarse voice was an octave too low. She brushed the hair away from her face with her hand. She must look awful.

He walked in, glancing at all the flowers around the room. "I just heard about you last night. I brought Dad over for a checkup this morning, so I hoped it'd be okay if I stopped by." He was looking her over.

Thankfully, the sheet was covering up her leg. "I'm glad you did."

"Sounds like you could use a drink." He walked over and put down his hat on the bedside table. "Whatever cola is in here is still cold." He held the plastic cup so the straw touched her lips. The cool soda had lost most of its fizz but felt good going down.

"If it's any consolation, I've been in your shoes a couple of times." He set the cup down. "The last time, I was rodeoin' in Denver. Bucked off a horse named Dyn-o-mite. Broke my leg and then the dang bronc kicked me and broke two ribs. Hurt like hell. I hated that horse, wished I could've given him a smack with a two-by-four right between the eyes."

She was laughing when a flash of white caught her eye. Mike walked in. He was wearing blue scrubs and the mandatory starched, white coat of 'doctorhood'. "I see you have company."

Frank smiled, nodded his head in Mike's direction and held out his hand across the bed. "Howdy, I'm Frank Jessup."

Mike was looking Frank over as if he were a germ on a slide but he shook his hand. "Mike Owen. You must be a friend of Devon's?"

Frank winked at her before answering. "We go back a long way. You the doctor taking care of her?"

"No, Dr. Jackson is her attending physician. I work in emergency. Just keeping tabs on her for personal reasons." After a brief smile, he looked down at her. "Feeling better with some food in your stomach?"

"Yes, it helps with the pain pills." The energy she'd had seconds ago was fading.

Mike leaned down to look in her eyes. "You look tired."

"I'm fine." She was enjoying having someone to talk to.

"Don't want to wear you out." Frank touched her arm.

"You haven't." She smiled up at Frank.

"She's had a couple of tough days."

Frank picked up his hat. "Dad's probably waiting for me downstairs, Devon. I'll stop by the ranch one of these days and see how you're doing."

When Frank raised his head, his smile broadened as he looked at Mike. "Nice to meet you, Doctor."

Mike nodded. "Same here."

She shook her head. They were behaving like boys wanting to take her to a prom. And she couldn't even dance. "Thanks for stopping by, Frank."

"You take it easy." He settled his hat on his head and turned to leave but snapped his fingers and stopped in his tracks. "I almost forgot. Annie drew a picture to cheer you up. I'd have been in a heap of trouble if I didn't give it to you." He took a rolled up piece of paper out of his shirt pocket. "Want me to leave it here on the table?"

"No, let me see it." He handed it to her. She unrolled the drawing paper and saw a bright yellow sun and a large pink, smiling flower. The cockeyed 'A' and bumpy 'n's' across the bottom of the page brought a smile to her lips. She looked up at Frank. "Tell Annie I think it's beautiful."

A pleased grin spread across Frank's face and brought his dimple out again. "I will. Get well, Shorty. I'll buy you an ice-cream cone once you're out."

"It's a deal." She watched him saunter out of the room.

"So, he's got kids?" Mike was still watching the door.

"Uh-huh, two girls. Annie is four." She stretched her arm to put the drawing on the table. "His wife died when Annie was a baby."

He turned around and looked at her. "What does he do?"

She wondered why he cared. "He's a rancher, trains roping horses."

He crossed his arms. "They all have the same kind of walk, a little bowlegged."

"He's not bowlegged. He's just got a little hitch in his get-along." She smiled and glanced toward the door.

Jamie and her mother had left after watching her try to eat her tasteless evening meal. She had just closed her eyes when she noticed the squeaking. She concentrated on it as it got closer, trying to imagine what creature had perfected such an irritating sound. Suddenly it stopped. She opened her eyes and turned her head toward the wide door that was only closed when the nurse gave her a wet washcloth and fresh gown. To her surprise, Loretta was standing just inside the doorway, grinning sheepishly.

"I bet I woke you up. Damn new shoes." They both glanced down at her white leather sandals. When she walked in on tiptoe, Devon chuckled. Her friend could have made the Grinch laugh.

Loretta was holding a beautiful bouquet of yellow roses. She looked around for a place to set them down. "Hell, you've got more flowers in here than the florist. Maybe I should take these to the funeral home and see if there's some poor old soul without any friends who needs them." Loretta was grinning from ear to ear. She was all fixed up in a matching blouse and gathered skirt, and was even wearing lipstick.

"You look nice, Retta. Did you get all dressed up just to stop by and give me a hard time?" Devon smiled even though her attempt at a smart remark was lame. Putting on a happy face and stiff upper lip for everybody who walked in was getting harder but she didn't have to try for Loretta. "The flowers are beautiful. Thank you."

"Oh, they smell even better than they look." Loretta lowered the vase and held the blooms close to Devon's nose. "Figured some of these might cover up the god-awful stuff this place cooks up to make the patients miserable enough to want to leave."

Devon closed her eyes and took an appreciative sniff. The thick as velvet fragrance had a touch of dew and pungent juice from the stem blended together. It softened the aching pull of muscle across her chest with the pleasure of first spring days when flowers are delicate and sweet like a baby's skin after a bath. She opened her eyes and smiled at her friend.

"They're yellow too, notice? Like that sun out there, which I can tell you, was blazin' hot today." Putting down the vase on the long tray table beside Devon's bed, Loretta pulled the front of her blouse away from her chest to fan herself. "Stickin' to myself something fierce. Tammy Jo would have come with me but her bunch has got some kind of crud, the ebola or somethin'."

She stopped as she studied the mound of leg confining Devon to the bed. Leaning over while looking cautiously at the doorway, she whispered. "Can you get up or have they got you so you can't even pee in private?"

Leave it to Loretta to get right down to the nitty-gritty. Devon started to laugh and winced from the pain in her side.

"You all right, Devon?" A furrow wrinkled Loretta's brow.

"Yes, it just hurts to laugh right now."

"I talked to your mama the other evening to see how you were doing." Loretta found a spot to sit on the bed beside her. "Honey, I'm sure sorry you've had such a bad time of it. You've had all hell break loose since you've come home." She leaned down carefully to hug Devon. "You just hang in there. Got nowhere to go but up."

"Uh-huh." Devon was afraid it was a very long way up.

She could tell Loretta was fighting tears by the tight, uneven sound of her voice. It was more than she could bear. Devon fought to hold in the breath that wavered on the brink of tears. They held each other without a word. Feeling under control at last, she forced a cheerful tone and patted her friend on the shoulder. "Hey, I'm doing fine."

Loretta sat up and blinked away the tears filling her eyes. "Damn right you are." Her words rushed out in relief. She looked Devon in the eye, accepting her bluff without a challenge. "You were always the toughest damn little cuss I knew in elementary school." Loretta pulled out a tissue with a sniffle and dabbed at her nose. "That's why I like you so much." She laughed, not her usual, rousing laugh but a sweet and gentle one.

At this point, Devon latched onto all the teasing Loretta could dish out. It helped stop the tears. "And you were the tallest, skinniest thing with brown freckles I'd ever seen."

"I know, me and the baby giraffes in the zoo."

They shared another hearty laugh and even though the effort made her chest ache, it took Devon far from the hospital and back to those quiet summer evenings by the river.

"Well, I know I shouldn't stay too long. Guess you'll be getting out of here pretty soon, huh?" Loretta stood up.

"Tomorrow, I think." Devon's desire to leave the hospital was dampened by the throbbing in her leg.

"Good. Listen, when you get home, let me know if I can help. Be glad to keep Jamie for you and let him play with Billy." She walked to the foot of the bed.

"I will. Thanks for coming, Loretta."

Devon looked out the hospital window at the bright sunshine. Her mother and Jamie would be showing up soon to take her home. As much as she wanted to leave, she wasn't sure she was ready. Since last night, the nurse had helped her transfer from bed to a wheelchair, to go to the restroom, and back again into bed. Her limbs had trembled uncontrollably from the exertion. It had been exhausting and unexpectedly frightening. Devon was tired and weak and afraid.

She looked down at the sheet pulled up to her waist and took a kind of mangled inventory. Her leg was a dead weight that showered her with sparks of pain when she moved it. The knee and ankle were too swollen to bend. On her arms, there were cuts still tender to the touch where bullets had skimmed across the skin. The deeper wound in her right arm, where the bullet had gone straight through the muscle, was sore and swollen. One more thing to make it harder to move herself around.

"Good morning. How's my favorite patient?" Mike walked in with yellow and pink papers in his hand.

"Fine." She wished saying it would make it so. She hated complaining. All it did was make the other person try to say something comforting and there weren't any words that could do that.

He held up the papers before putting them down on the table. "Dr. Jackson has signed the release order. And I've got you scheduled to go by physical therapy before you leave. Your mother and I thought it would be easier to get that started while you're here."

Just the word 'physical' brought to mind sweaty people jumping around and bending in places that already ached on her. "What will they do?" She wasn't sure she really wanted to know after days of being poked and prodded.

"A number of things." He crossed his arms, all business. "They'll assess your mobility, set up a therapy schedule and teach you how to use crutches. Ever used them?"

"No." Crutches meant standing. She hated gravity now. It made the back of her knee throb and her foot ache as if it would explode. Her body tensed at the thought of falling: the sharp pull of already sore muscles, the pain of hitting the ground and the disheartening struggle to get up. She was too weak to move herself around, she wanted to scream. But she didn't. It would sound childish.

Mike looked uneasy as a frown flashed across his face. "Devon, I need to tell you something."

She took a shallow breath and waited for the bad news.

"The timing is lousy." He leaned forward and wrapped his fingers around the top bar of the lowered bed rail. "I got the fellowship in Seattle. The letter was sent to the wrong address." He smiled, but it was stiff with uncomfortable corners, not a real smile at all.

"Congratulations." She managed a smile, touched his hand with her fingertips. He relaxed his grip on the railing.

He turned his hand over to grasp hers. "I wish I had more time to help you through this, Devon."

"Hey, don't worry about me. I'm going to be fine."

"I know you will." He glanced toward the door. "I have to leave next week to get up there before classes start."

"Oh, that fast?" She suddenly realized she wasn't the one that was going to be hurt by Mike's quick departure. Poor Jamie, he'd gotten so attached to Mike. "Have you told Jamie?"

His jaw tightened. "No, I haven't had a good opportunity."

She lay back with the weight of a new problem. Jamie had been through so much. Now he was losing someone very special to him. "I'll tell him."

"I'm really going to miss him."

She looked at Mike's melancholy smile. Maybe he had some idea of how hard this was going to be for Jamie. "And he's going to miss you."

"I process out of the hospital in a couple of days. I'll come over when I get a chance."

"That would be nice if you can, but I know you'll be busy." She slipped into the safety of the mundane. "You have a lot to do, packing and making arrangements in Seattle."

He shook his head. "Not really. The furniture stays in the place. Everything I own will fit in my truck." He sat on the edge of the bed by her feet. "I have a friend checking out a couple of apartments for me."

"Well then, you're all set." Hearing Jamie's voice in the hallway, she put on a smile.

Mike stood up as her rambunctious son came bounding in, literally bouncing with energy. His noisy exuberance was unsettling like a sudden clap of thunder. She leaned back to rest, realizing how exhausting this moving around was going to be. Ellie, carrying a small bag in one hand, rushed in quickly on Jamie's heels fussing at him for running in the hospital and disturbing sick people.

Undeterred by his grandmother's scowling, Jamie pulled a chair over to the bed with a screech. Mike moved, allowing him to push it against the bed rail. Once he was standing on the chair and at eye level, he beamed at her. "Ready to go home, Mom?"

"Yes, I am."

"I've got your clothes, Devon." Ellie put the little carry-on down at the foot of the bed and opened it. "The nurse suggested these baggy things will be easier to put on while your leg is sore." She held up a large pair of blue exercise pants before laying them down.

Mike picked up the papers he'd left on the bedside table and handed them to her mother. "I've got her all signed out, Ellie. She just has that appointment in physical therapy next door before she goes home. I'll tell the nurse you'll need an orderly in a few minutes."

"Okay. Now you two skedaddle and give us some privacy so Devon can get dressed."

Feeling like a paroled convict longing for a breath of fresh air, she had one more hoop to go through before she was free. A husky black orderly helped her transfer to a wheelchair. Her mother and Jamie loaded up her things to take to the car. They'd meet her after therapy.

The physical therapy unit was in a separate building. The discomfort caused by the sharp jar of the wheels rolling over the seams of the sidewalk was almost worth the feel of the breeze and sun touching her arms and face. The hot air was full of smells she couldn't identify but had missed just the same.

The automatic doors whooshed as the wheelchair rolled up to the door. The carpeted corridor had wooden rails on each side. They pulled up to a circular counter with two women answering phones and shuffling papers around. The orderly grabbed a clipboard and handed it to her. "You're supposed to sign in to let them know you're here for an appointment. Good luck, ma'am." He walked away and she signed her name.

Her leg ached like an unpleasant hum that gets worse the longer it lasts. A young woman in slacks walked up.

"My name is Joanne, Ms. Taylor." She calmly hinted at a smile. "I'll be helping you through your therapy sessions. Today, we'll do an evaluation and a little stretching." While Joanne looked her over with clinical detachment she performed her own inspection. Late twentyish, trim and stiff-backed like a Marine. Her straight, brown hair was cut short, a golden bead in each pierced ear, and just a touch of makeup.

Joanne moved behind her and started pushing her down a hallway pocked with small rooms. "Do you have any questions before we start?"

The muscles across the back of her shoulders and along her neck were tight and ached. "Yes. When is it going to stop hurting?" That was what she really wanted to know.

"That's one of those questions that has no definite answer." She pushed Devon into a room with an examination table and assorted, oddly shaped gadgets scattered around on shelves and hanging from pegs on the wall. "The muscles are swollen and the nerves are irritated. It's going to be painful for a while but I think you'll find it manageable soon."

Joanne's vague and inadequate answer to her question rumbled around in her head. The lower lid of her right eye began to twitch. One more thing to add to her long list of physical frustrations. "What does manageable mean?"

"It means, it will get better a little at a time." Seeing a flash in Joanne's eyes, Devon decided she didn't like answering questions. This woman was all business. "Soft tissue starts healing quickly by making scar tissue. My job is to help you get back to using your leg normally again as soon as possible."

Looking at Joanne's tanned, strong arms as she positioned the wheelchair next to the table and set the brakes, Devon didn't think Joanne had ever needed help.

"We have to provide some movement to keep the tissues pliable. Do you need help or can you get up here on your own?"

Devon's sore arms shook as she pushed herself up to stand in an effort to hold on to the little bit of pride she had left. She clung to the edge of the gray vinyl like a baby learning to walk. Tears filled her eyes and her chin trembled realizing she couldn't make it. It was humiliating. Thankfully, Joanne couldn't see her face.

"Let me give you a hand." Joanne grabbed her around the middle and lifted her to get her hips on the padded table. Devon lay back, every muscle trembling as the therapist raised her legs.

Joanne appeared above her. "We are going to stick to basics today." Joanne measured the range of motion or rather the lack of it. Devon couldn't lift her leg, bend her knee or rotate her ankle to make a circle with her toes. Her leg trembled in spastic waves with the smallest effort. Her arms and chest ached as she strained to move. Finally it was over.

"Go home and rest, Devon. We'll hold off on the crutches until next time to give your arms a couple more days to heal." She handed her a piece of paper before rolling her down the hall. "I've written down the stretches you should try to do everyday. Just do the best you can with them."

Devon had underestimated the power of pain to make her afraid to move. She had underestimated how demoralizing it was to feel helpless. Ellie and Jamie were waiting for her in the chairs by the reception desk. They smiled at her but she couldn't smile back. She was rolled out of the building feeling betrayed by her body. She didn't answer her mother when she asked how therapy had gone as they rode home in the Cadillac. Propped up with pillows, she leaned against the locked door while her legs were stretched out straight across the back seat. A sharp-edged burn ate into her thigh. Her body was in revolt and her brain was ready to surrender.

She stared out the side window until a movement caught her eye. Jamie was sitting in the front seat with Ellie. His brow was furrowed as he cast a dark glance her way. It echoed her own disappointment but it wounded her more deeply. She closed her eyes to hide the tears.

Ellie honked the horn when they drove up the driveway toward the house. Hank came running to the car when they stopped and helped her out of the back seat. She didn't cry out when it hurt because he was smiling and doing the best he could. He rolled her in the wheelchair across the walk to the front door proud of his handiwork. He'd fixed a plywood ramp to help get her inside. They'd tried to anticipate and prepare for her every need. They pointed out things in the house they'd done. The doorway to the bathroom was too narrow to roll through. Hank removed the door. Her mother bustled around moving furniture and adding extra tables beside her bed. Dinner was eaten at a table skewed to allow for the wheelchair and her jutting straight leg. She wasn't hungry. The household was in turmoil because of her and all she could say was thank you, over and over again.

Her first day at home was a test of endurance. She was determined to cut back on the pain medication hating the dull, thick tongued way her brain worked when she took it. It was a big mistake. She didn't want to leave her bed unless she had to. Every trip to the bathroom was a major outlay of energy and a painful challenge to endure. She was shaky and weak which left her little choice but to stay put until necessity dictated otherwise.

Aunt Jessie came for a visit Sunday afternoon. That would have been a pleasure except for the fact she'd gotten a ride from Louise and Gerald so they were ushered into her inner sanctum too. Jessie gave her a hug and kiss on the cheek.

"Girl, you have worried me to death. It's mighty good to see you with my own eyes."

Louise chimed in. "Yes, honey, its wonderful to see you." But she kept her distance. Maybe her least favorite aunt could see the anger in her eyes. If she did, Devon didn't care. Uncle Gerry nodded his head, solemn as a judge but didn't utter a sound. They only stayed a short time, which was just as well.

The dark night that followed was one long nightmare. Johnny Colton's arms came out of the shadows and shoved her down to the hard ground. His weight made it hard to breathe as his rough hands slid up her rib cage. 'Don't fight me.' The words felt hot in her ear as she struggled free. His angry roar shook the air and closed around her. 'I'm not through with you.' She turned to run but Joe stood in front of her. He held a revolver in his hand. The long, silver barrel gleamed in the glaring sun. Blast after blast crashed like thunder between Jamie's screams. Devon woke with a sudden jolt, cold sweat clinging to her skin. Sitting in the darkness, she was sure they had both come back from the dead.

The hall light came on. Ellie stood at the door. "Devon, are you all right? I thought I heard you scream."

"Did I?"

Mom sat down on the bed looking at her face in the dim light. "You look awful." She touched her arm. "And you feel cold. Like for me to sit with you a while?"

"Would you mind?"

"Not at all. Can I get you a drink of water?"

"No, Mom."

"Lay back down then. I'll stay right here."

The next morning, she was in bed staring at a magazine, unable to concentrate on the empty-headed articles, when her mother walked in with a load of folded clothes in her arms.

"Had these things washed days ago but never took the time to put them away." Devon felt useless as she watched Ellie open drawers, deposit an item and close them.

"Mike called a while ago. He wanted to come by for a visit. I told him I had to take Jamie to the dentist tomorrow. He offered to stay with you while we're gone. Give me time to get some other things done too."

"That's fine." She put down the magazine trying to remember what day it was. "Maybe he's coming to say goodbye."

Ellie paused amid laundry sorting. "What do you mean?"

"He's leaving for Seattle soon."

Ellie turned to look at her. Mike hadn't mentioned it judging by the shocked expression on her face.

Wrinkling her brow, Mom opened her mouth but hesitated. "He never said a word to me. Are you sure, Devon?"

"After the hospital party he told me he'd applied for a fellowship. The morning I left the hospital, he told me he'd been selected." She was angry with him for not telling her mother, at least.

Ellie shook her head. "I thought he liked it around here."

"It's a fellowship for special training in a big medical center for the brightest and best." She looked out the window at the empty tire swing. "There's nothing to keep him here, Mom." She said it like a quick snip of the scissors. That was the way she thought of him now. Detached.

"There's more to life than a wad of money and people patting you on the back, unless I've been out in the sticks too long." Her mother pressed her lips together the way she always did when she was unhappy about something. She bent over to pick up a pair of socks she'd dropped on the floor.

"But Dr. Mike is teaching me baseball. I'm his pal!" Jamie stood in the bedroom doorway. The hurt in his voice was palpable.

Mike should have been the one to look at Jamie's disappointed face, damn it. "Come here, Jamie." She held out her arm. He stepped just inside the door, but no closer. She looked him in the eye. "He did teach you. You play just as well as the other kids." He bowed his head and his shoulders drooped.

She was stuck with the job of making excuses. "Mike is going to work in a big hospital in Seattle, Jamie. You know grownups have to move sometimes for a good job and leave friends behind, just like we did."

He raised his head. He was frowning, tears in his eyes. "But we didn't like that job, Mama." He spun around and ran out of the room.

"Shit." She pounded the mattress with her fist. Furious with Mike and frustrated she couldn't chase after Jamie, she slumped over on her side and hammered her fist into the pillow. "I should have made him tell Jamie." Every part of her hurt worse than it had five minutes ago.

"Calm down." Ellie stood at the bedroom door. "Being seven years old isn't any easier than being sixty sometimes. I'm disappointed too." She sounded tired. "I'll let him stew for a while before I talk to him. He'll be all right."

There was no way she could calm down. She was too angry about everything. Her mother turned to leave. "Shut the door." Mom did. Once she was alone, she turned on the radio by the bed cranking up the volume until it was just noise choking out everything else. There was no place to set aside thankfulness and scream at the injustices done but in the solitude of this room. Here she poured out her rage.

Ellie stood in the hallway outside the bedroom door, listening to the storm of sound and wondering if it could be good for Devon. She put her hand on the doorknob but hesitated. The troubling feeling of not knowing what to do weighed her down and she felt old and tired.

"Why is she mad at us?" Jamie was scowling at her. He stood just a few feet away in the doorway to his room on the opposite side of the hall.

Ellie walked over to him. "She's not mad at us, honey." She noticed everyone of his books was on the floor rather than the bookshelf and his toys had been dumped out of their plastic containers in a pile into the middle of the floor. "Jamie, what happened in here?"

He turned away from her. "Nothing." He plopped himself down on the bed, rolled over on his stomach, and let one arm dangle off the edge to fiddle with the pile of toy debris he'd left on the floor.

"Looks like you're the one who's mad." She sat down on his bed with a sigh. "Been tough around here, hasn't it?" She leaned back to lie down on the bed, glad to finally get off her feet, and stared at the ceiling. This day felt as if it were two days long already.

"If you want to know what I think, I think your mama is just plain cranky. She's got to be awfully tired of feeling bad. That the way you're feeling too?"

He didn't say anything. She turned her head to see what Jamie was doing. He was flying a little airplane on a very bumpy ride. She rolled over on her side and put her hand on his back. "Your mama loves you more than anything in this world, Jamie. I love you too." He dropped the airplane. She rubbed her hand across his shoulders, back and forth several times hoping to soothe him. "When she's feeling so bad it's hard for her to let you know it, but she does."

He rolled over to face her, his eyes open wide, full of the sadness of an abandoned waif. "Are you sure, Granny?"

"How about a hug for your tired old granny?" He scooted over and nestled against her.

She brushed her cheek across his and gave him a squeeze. "Do you know how much she loves you?" She could feel him shake his head. "Why she'd climb the highest mountain, up and down, and swim the great blue ocean, twice."

"That's a lot." He raised his head so he could see her face.

"Yes, it's true. It's hard, I know, but we've got to let get her strength back before she can be your full-time mama again." She relaxed her arm letting him gradually roll onto his back. "By the way that reminds me, have you checked on Calico's kittens today?"

"No." He was watching her. His eyes didn't look so sad.

"Me either. We should make sure they're all right." She patted him on the chest. "Tell you what, I'll give you a hand by picking up your books while you put your toys back where they belong. Then we'll see about those little rascals."

"Okay."

It wasn't a happy okay but she'd take what she could get at the moment. She sat up. He crawled off the bed and started picking up his toys. He was a sweet child. If only none of this had happened to either of them. She sighed and stood up. She only had so much energy.

Late that afternoon when Jamie was outside with Hank and the pot roast was cooking, Ellie decided to talk to Devon. The music had stopped and it had been quiet for a while. She knocked lightly before peeking in, trying not to wake her daughter if she were napping.

Devon's eyes were open watching her as she opened the door wider. "Did you have a chance to take a nap?"

"Yes."

"Good." She walked to the side of the bed. "I hope you feel better."

"Some." Devon was staring at the covers on the bed.

Her daughter's short answers did little to help her judge if she should mention Jamie. She didn't have a lot of time to pussyfoot around. "I've got a pot roast cooking. Would you like to eat in the kitchen or maybe we could bring our dinner in here with you tonight."

"I'm not hungry."

"You have to eat something and so does Jamie." She didn't like to see Devon's downcast eyes. "Honey, he's upset and needs you. I'm a poor substitute. You don't feel good, I know that, but for a little while tonight you need to talk to him."

Devon glanced up at her with watery eyes. "I'm not doing a very good job, am I?"

The pain she saw in her daughter's face and heard in her trembling voice brought tears to Ellie's eyes. She sat down on the bed. "You're doing the best you can, Devon, I know that. None of this is easy."

After dinner, Devon sat at the table watching as Ellie cleared the dishes. It had been a quiet meal. She'd had nothing to say. It was as if a part of her had died and seeing Jamie just made it worse.

"Jamie, why don't you help your mother back to the bedroom while I clean up the kitchen. Those wheels bumped into the table by the couch when we rolled in here. Maybe you can clear the way for your mama."

He had been silent, watching her from his chair. He stood up and guided her along in the wheelchair as she turned the wheels. When they stopped beside her bed, he looked down at his feet.

"Mama, I'm sorry."

"You're sorry?" She looked away from him feeling the choking squeeze of her throat as tears filled her eyes. The heartache she felt became a cry of sorrow. Her hand covering her mouth couldn't stop it or hide the sound that brought Jamie's arms wrapping around her. Tears rolled down her cheeks and she hugged him tight. Thankful he was safe and whole. Knowing she'd had no part in that. Wishing she could forgive herself.

It felt like an eternity since she could do anything by herself. Devon closed her eyes already exhausted even though the day had just begun. Getting fed and dressed was a chore. She didn't think she could stand one more day. Her puffy foot, propped up on the pillows, mocked her into thinking she'd never be able to walk on it. After Ellie and Jamie had left, Mike appeared at her bedroom door with a smile. He walked in with a grace she noticed and resented.

"Time to get you moving." His smile slowly faded to a determined straight line as he squared his shoulders.

She needed him to be the good doctor and console her to quiet the frustration that churned inside her. Instead he walked away. It felt like a cold shove. She rolled onto her side as best she could with her leg elevated, hiding her face with her arm while secretly watching him walk to the window.

"I'm too frazzled for torture this morning."

He stood by the window opening the shade, letting in the harsh glare of another endless, summer day. The black button eyes on her old teddy bear gleamed in the sunlight. She rolled over on her back hoping to silence the ache of her leg. At least he could have asked her if she wanted the damn light streaming in.

"You have to get those injured muscles moving or . . .."

"Or what?" The words snapped out of her. He turned his head to look at her. Now she had his attention. "Do you have any idea how it feels to be treated like a two year old?"

His eyebrows shot up and his lips parted but he didn't say anything. Maybe he would get off the doctoring and just listen. All her resentment began to rush out in a flurry of words.

"I can't perform on command like a trained monkey." She gathered a handful of covers with her fingers hoping he'd understand.

"Devon, it's important to do the therapy, even if it hurts."

'If it hurts'. That first tiny word sizzled and popped, like water on a hot skillet. The restraint she'd struggled to maintain evaporated. "If? That's right I forgot, it doesn't hurt you a bit. Must be great to give orders you don't have to take."

He frowned. When he started to smile, she knew another pep talk was brewing, he'd spouted them every time he'd come near her in the hospital. She refused to look at him.

"Devon, I know it hurts."

"Like hell you do." She clamped her teeth together and glared at him. "Not unless you've been shot full of holes like I have. And you haven't, have you?"

His face reddened as he stood there. "That's not the point and you know it, Devon. You have to stretch those . . .."

"I don't have to do anything. Leave me the hell alone. You've probably got some packing to do, don't you?"

Mike glared at her. "I'm trying to help, dammit."

"I sure as hell didn't ask for it. Go play doctor somewhere else."

"Now you're acting like a two year old." His face was turning red.

"And you're being a cocky, know-it-all son of a bitch! Get out of here and close the door."

"If you want to stay cooped up in here and feel sorry for yourself, that's up to you." He did an about-face and in three long strides was out of the room, slamming the door behind him.

Devon looked around the empty room, glad to be rid of him. The sunlight poured in through the window. God, she wanted to get up and yank that damn shade down. She covered her head with a pillow instead.

S he had one arm wrapped around her old teddy bear when she heard a knock on the bedroom door. He was back. "Go peddle your help to someone else, Mike." She tossed the stuffed animal off the bed at the sound of several more muffled knocks but didn't bother to look as the door hinge squeaked.

"Ms. Taylor, may I come in?"

Not recognizing the voice, she let out an aggravated huff and lifted her head. The psychologist from the hospital stood in the half-opened doorway.

"I'm Dr. Green from the hospital, remember?"

The shrink, sure, why not. Mike had sent for reinforcements. She was boiling hot again. "Is the whole damn hospital going to traipse through here?"

"I thought your mother told you I was going to stop by." He opened the door a bit more but didn't walk in.

She sat up, wishing him away. "I'm in no mood to talk in case you haven't noticed."

"Actually, I was on my way home. Thought I'd stop in and touch base with you about Jamie, since it's hard for you to get around."

She caught her breath, hearing Jamie's name. It changed everything. "Come in, come in." She waved her hand to hurry him along.

He grabbed the chair beside the chest of drawers and pulled it over. His knees bumped into the mattress when he sat down. "Sorry. Think I'd be use to these long legs by now." He smiled. "I just needed to talk to you for a minute. I've met with your son twice, as you know. I think we will work together just fine. The abduction has stirred up some fears, but nothing I didn't expect. We can work through those." He leveled a look at her that she couldn't turn away from. "There's one thing you need to understand about this process. To help him, I need to know how you're doing. The reason I say that is, right now he's worried about you."

It was overwhelming to feel so loaded down, to have Jamie depending on her when she couldn't take care of herself. "I can't tell you how I'm doing."

"Why not?"

He was playing Freud, but the fight in her was gone. "Because I don't know." She said the words softly, admitting surrender, before turning her head away from him, not caring what he thought. She stared at the shaft of light streaming through her window, feeling cut off from the fresh air outside, from the rest of life.

"I don't know any of the details of what happened to you. I'm sure it was frightening."

She was tired of the probing without asking. "Some things are worse than fear." She tightened the muscles of her stomach like armor with the onslaught of memories that placed the blame squarely on her shoulders.

"It's almost funny." Mad at herself, she looked him in the eye. "He shot me in the chest with my own gun. A textbook case of stupidity, thinking I could protect Jamie from that bastard." She shook her head and looked out the window at the swing hanging motionless from the tree branch. "He tossed Jamie's hat at me. Said my son was in the crate." She could see the wooden box and the gun. "Then he pulled out his revolver and started shooting at it." She choked. "I couldn't stop him."

She covered her face with her hands to hide her grief. Her chest heaved but she was past the point where crying brought any relief. There wasn't a sound in the room, nothing from the man sitting beside her. When she opened her eyes, Dr. Green was looking at her. There was something different in his expression, something softer, sympathetic. She wiped away the tears that slipped down her cheeks and dried her hands on the sheet.

"He could have died because of me. Every time I look at him, that's what haunts me." A deep sigh rushed out of her like a final breath.

He touched the top of her hand. "It's okay."

She moved her hand away. Hair fell across her eyes as she shook her head. "No. I'm supposed to protect him."

"You did the best you could, Devon, as much as anyone could." He put the box of tissues on the bed. She pulled out several and dried her face.

She raised her head looking for some hint of duplicity in his face, but saw only his calm expression. "I hate lying here. I'm sick of crying and tired of hurting. I scream and cuss to get the mad out of me, but it doesn't help, nothing does." She used both hands to brush the hair away from her face. "Everything's all jumbled up in my head."

"You're just starting to recover. Those emotions are a natural reaction to what's happened to you. They can be confusing and powerful."

She rested her head on the headboard. "They're stronger than I am."

"Then maybe you need help fighting back." He smiled when she glanced over at him.

She felt better hearing him say that. "Maybe I do."

"I am tired." She inched down between the sheets.

Her father's face began to fade and break apart like fog. A soft knock made her open her eyelids.

"Sorry if I woke you up." Mike was peeking around the door cautiously.

She drew in a long breath.

He edged into the room. "It's late but I thought I'd heat up some soup. Would you like some?"

She glanced at the bedside clock. It was after two. "I'm surprised you want to feed me." She couldn't look him in the eye. She should apologize but the words wouldn't come out.

He stepped closer to the bed. "I like you too much to let you starve. Besides it wouldn't be very good for my reputation if I let a patient shrivel up and blow away."

He smiled when she looked at him. It was amazing he was able to joke. She wasn't proud of herself for screaming at him but anger had roared out of her like an uncontrollable beast.

"Devon, you were right. I can't imagine how tough it is for you. I was talking to Hank outside. I realized I've been angry that you got hurt too. I'm sorry I lost my temper."

She blinked to head off the tears building up and stared at the foot of the bed. "I'm sorry for screaming at you." She broke a short, uncomfortable silence. "This has been a little like riding a roller coaster wearing a blindfold." She looked up at him wondering if he understood how lost she felt. "I'm not as tough as I thought."

"I shouldn't have pushed you so hard. You need some time, that's all." He was standing beside the bed now with both hands stuck in his pockets. She could hear him jingling coins absentmindedly as he stood there, not saying a word. "Well, I'm not accomplishing much just standing here. I'll go warm up that soup."

She laid her head on the pillow and looked at the ceiling. He didn't understand she was talking about more than her physical injuries. That was his focus, fixing things that were visible on an x-ray. It was just as well. She was the only one who knew what was broken and the only one who would know when it was healed.

"Come on. You've been inside all week. Time you got some fresh air." Ellie stood with her hands on her hips looking like she wasn't about to take 'no' for an answer. "I woke up this morning with an itch to paint and I want some company."

Devon grumbled a bit before she sat up in bed. Her leg was still painful to move but her arms were stronger and not as sore, making life easier. There were different ways to do things. If you put your mind to it. If you were willing and desperate enough. In truth, she was bored. Anything had to be better than sitting in the house all day, even if it hurt. She transferred to the wheelchair and rolled through the house following her mother out to the deck.

It was a glorious morning. The bright sunshine, clear blue sky and warm breeze promised a well-cooked afternoon ahead. It lifted her spirits. Her mother's easel was set up. Her watercolors rested on a table beside it.

There was blank paper and several charcoal pencils on the low patio table beside the glider.

"I've got everything you need within reach. Now feast your eyes on this gorgeous sight and put it on the paper. I'll give you some color when you're ready for it."

"Mom, you know I'm no good at this."

Ellie shot a quick disapproving look in her direction. "Well, try. You may just find out it's fun." Her mother turned away studying the pasture spread out before them and ignored her.

Devon looked in the same general direction. Four longhorns were lounging under the wide branches of a large white oak as if they didn't want to socialize with the mixed breeds scattered across the field. She could see Hank's truck in the distance. It was parked near a patch of small trees. Jamie was beside Hank. He was running trying to keep up with the cowboy's long-legged stroll. Maggie was trotting along beside them, her black and white coat in sharp contrast to the pale, dry grass.

"I didn't know Jamie was out with Hank. What are they doing?" She looked over at her mother. The basic outlines of the rolling pasture and trees were sketched on her paper.

"Don't know. He takes Jamie out with him to do a lot of things. They both seem to enjoy it." Her mother's hands were moving in quick short strokes adding in the shape of the truck and the two figures.

She envied her mother's gift for capturing the meat and potatoes of life, simple joys that should be burned into memory but are all too often forgotten. She looked back toward the pasture and saw a small steer stand up and trot off. Jamie, waving his arms in the air, was running with Maggie behind the loping animal while Hank stood watching them. Her son was happy. She could see it all the way from here. It warmed her heart and gave her hope.

"You're not putting anything on that piece of paper." Ellie had stopped sketching. "What do you see when you look out there?"

"Jamie enjoying a beautiful day." Her gaze drifted up and she stared at the bluff, knowing what lay beyond it. "And some other not so pleasant things." She glanced at the blank paper on her lap.

"Good memories will crowd out the bad."

Devon looked at her mother. What an amazing woman she was, always positive and reassuring. Even in the worst of times, she never gave up. Ellie'd taken care of Jamie, consoled him when he needed it and nursed her through two catastrophes without complaint. How lucky she was to have such a woman on her side.

"I'm sorry I've been such a pain to live with, Mom."

"You haven't been." Her mother smiled.

Devon knew she'd been awful. She needed to admit it, to make amends and try to change. "Yes, I have. I'm sorry."

Mom leaned down and touched her face. "There is nothing to be sorry for, honey. You're doing the best you can."

The oversized cotton knit pants, cut up the seam to midthigh along the outside edge and pinned together, hid the fading bruises, the scars and swollen parts except for her toes. They stuck out of the elastic bandage wrapped around her ankle and foot. Her mother thought her knee wasn't quite as swollen now. Devon wondered if it was just wishful thinking. She dreaded seeing Joanne again. Her insides were churning as a young man rolled her down the hall toward certain agony. He'd walked up to her so chipper she'd decided she hated him. She was wheeled into a large room, very much like a gymnasium except for the windows all along one wall. Patients filled almost every chair and mat.

"We're pretty busy today, Ms. Taylor. I'll park you right here until they're ready for you." He walked away and stopped to talk to Joanne, who was working with someone sitting on a contraption exercising his knee. She looked toward Devon with a nod.

Not far away from her, a young man lying on one of the gray exercise mats winced as a burly therapist pushed his knee toward his chest. She could feel his pain mirrored in the ache of her own leg and turned away. Her own fear of what lay ahead fluttered inside her like a trapped bird. Shifting her attention to a row of tables along the wall to her right, she watched the more benign treatments going on. A woman in a pink duster was talking to an older man. He was making a fist, then opening his fingers.

"You're new, aren't you?" Devon turned to look at the smiling woman sitting in a chair not far from her. The tanned, curlyheaded blonde was wrapped in warm, peach tones that accentuated her big blue eyes.

"Yes, I guess I am." Devon was caught off guard a bit and the nasty thought that she wasn't up to talking to 'Little Bo Peep' popped into her head. End of conversation. She was too jittery to make small talk.

"How did you hurt your leg?" The question came out sweet as syrup.

"Trampled by elephants." The brassy answer flashed out recklessly.

A hearty laugh percolated out of Miss Peep. "Oh, I love that one. Hope I can remember it. I'm sorry if I was being too snoopy. It helps pass the time."

Devon looked at the good-natured woman, wishing she hadn't been so snippy. Her right arm was bandaged from elbow to fingertips.

"My name is Jennifer Williams, but my friends just call me, Jen." Her drawl was definitely from the Old South, maybe the Carolinas.

"Mine's Devon. I'm not usually such a smart mouth. Afraid I'm not at my best right now." She motioned toward her leg held straight out in front of her like a battering ram by the extension on her wheelchair.

A big, generous smile blossomed across Jen's face. "Well, you're in the right place. This is the inner sanctum for the less than perfect. They do good work here, you'll see. You'll be back on your feet and cleaning house in no time."

"Great." Although she wrinkled her brow in a halfhearted scowl, she did look forward to doing simple, everyday things, even housework.

Another therapist, with a head full of fuzzy brown curls, walked over to her new colleague with a jolly bounce. Her name tag declared she was Bobbi with an *i* and no *e*. "I'm ready for you Mrs. Williams. Got the heat on simmer." She laughed and held out her hand.

Jen chuckled and turned with a cheerful grin toward Devon. "Good to meet you, Devon. Maybe I'll see you next time."

Devon dipped her head in a perfunctory nod. She was surprised to see her new acquaintance struggle to stand, taking the therapist's hand to steady herself. After a slow, angular hobble over to the line of tables, Jen awkwardly crumpled into a chair. She'd had no idea the woman was crippled. A wash of regret soaked through Devon, shrinking her smart-ass bravado. There wasn't a hole deep enough for her to crawl in.

She studied the faces of the other patients scattered around the room. With their pursed lips, furrowed brows, and tight jaws they concentrated on their work, tasks the outside world would have considered child's play. None of them looked angry. They were too busy. Jen was chatting amiably with her therapist while going through some kind of routine with her arm. Only an occasional grimace gave away her discomfort. That woman wasn't a cripple.

Joanne walked up to her. "Hi, ready to go?" Joanne didn't wait for her response but rolled her over to the mats.

When they stopped, Joanne came around to set the brakes on the chair and helped her shift out of the wheelchair to the raised mat. "Hey, you're using that arm a lot better. Not as sore now, I'll bet."

Devon looked up at her. "Guess I've been a wimp about this whole thing."

Joanne squatted down. "Don't be so rough on yourself, Devon." Her voice was just above a whisper. "You have a painful injury, especially the first few weeks when it's swollen and tender. It isn't easy for anybody in here, including you." She smiled and stood up. "I'll get some warm towels to relax those muscles." She walked briskly to a little room in the back.

Devon unpinned the pant leg and looked down at her thigh. She hated the way it looked. The once smooth skin of her thigh was depressed where the bullet went through and came out. The new scars were red. Little scabs crusted over the dots where the stitches had been. Her knee and ankle didn't seem a bit smaller to her. She took a furtive glance at the patients around her. In the midst of wrecked bodies and the variety of long, ugly slashes across exposed skin, there was no room for wounded pride. It was a luxury no one in here could afford. The shallowness of her self-pity was hard to admit, but it was inescapable in this company.

Once the warm pads were wrapped around her thigh, she leaned back to rest. The heat soaked down to the bone. It felt wonderful. She closed her eyes vowing to be as tough and determined as everyone else in the room appeared to be.

It wasn't long before Joanne returned. "I think your ankle and knee aren't as swollen. You've been keeping it elevated obviously." She smiled and peeled off the toweling. "Okay. Just small stretches at first, Devon."

The slow, painful process of moving . . . up, down, and side to side began.

Dr. Green, clad in jeans and a crisply pressed short sleeved shirt, held the door open for her. She didn't really know what to expect as she rolled through. Maybe she didn't need him at all. She was feeling a little better. They had worked out an agreement over the phone to keep costs down. A quick five sessions, with part of the bill chalked up to a conference discussing Jamie's progress.

There was a bank of oak bookshelves on one wall, a desk, and several upholstered chairs clustered around a coffee table and a grass green rug. He moved a chair to clear a path for her. Two big picture windows looked out on the parking lot. They were tinted a blue gray to keep the interior from boiling on a hot summer afternoon like this. But it was too cool in the room as far as Devon was concerned. She wasn't sure if it was nerves or the air conditioning that made the chill bumps on her arms.

"I'm glad you could come in."

"I won't snap at you today. I'm too tired to raise a ruckus." She rolled up beside one of the chairs, facing the window.

"I'm not worried." Dr. Green laughed and sat down in a big brown leather chair. "I see you've got a brace on."

"Yes." She glanced at the ankle splint. "Joanne said it would help."

"So how did physical therapy go?"

"Okay, I guess, but tiring. Had me stand up and put some weight on my leg using crutches. I'm too shaky on them to feel comfortable but I'm supposed to start using them instead of the wheelchair." She touched the silver rails on the wheels with her hands. "Have you ever been in that big therapy room?" She looked up at him.

"No, I haven't."

"It's hard to take. Seeing people so messed up."

"It made you uncomfortable?"

"It's not fair." She glanced at him before lowering her head to stare at her folded hands. "I have no right to feel sorry for myself."

"Why not?"

"Because most of them have lost something they'll never get back." Her throat was dry.

"And you haven't?"

"I'm in one piece. I'll be able to get around on my own eventually." She looked up. He'd moved. One long leg was crossed over the other, his boot resting on the other knee.

"True, your body is healing. How about the rest of you?"

She shifted in the wheelchair not wanting to answer. "May I have a drink of water?"

"Certainly." He got up and walked over to a side table. There was a pitcher and a stack of paper cups. He filled a cup from the pitcher, brought it to her and placed it in her hand. "There you are." The brown leather chair creaked as he sat down.

"Thanks." She took several sips before setting the cup down. Her thigh throbbed from the therapy session. She rubbed it with her hand. "The preacher thought I should be grateful God didn't let that bastard kill us both." She shook her head picturing the pudgy, young reverend spouting nonsense that had done everything but comfort.

"You don't feel grateful." His eyes focused on hers when she looked at him.

"Damn right." She snapped the words out and crushed the angry words blaming God between her teeth, before they escaped. The room was hot, stuffy. She drank the rest of her water tasting a familiar bitterness, one festering since TJ's funeral. It was cold as buried stone and tight as a knot. "God should have kept Jamie out of it." She lowered her head to keep from saying more.

"And what happened to you, doesn't matter?"

Her fingernails bit into the palms of her hands. She raised her head. "Yes, it matters. I hope the cowardly son of a bitch is burning in hell, right beside his brother."

The sound of her voice was a disappointment, weak, quaking instead of a screaming outrage heard for miles. She took a deep breath, feeling the sore spot in her back where the bullet was lodged. It was a reminder that she'd survived them both and it calmed the inner storm for the moment. "I need to make sense of all . . . this." She opened her hands and raised them above her lap while glancing down at her legs.

"What will help you do that?"

"Find a reason for the misery."

"And what happens if you don't find one?"

She looked up at those steady hazel eyes. "I don't know." She leaned back in the wheelchair her hands dangling from the end of the armrests. She was emptied out and lost in a place she didn't like.

Ellie checked the potatoes. They were done. The ham was baked and green beans cooked. Her farewell dinner for Mike was just about ready. She still thought it was a shame he was leaving. Even though Devon insisted they were just good friends, she couldn't help feeling their relationship could have been more than that with a little more time. And poor Jamie was upset. He was outside somewhere sulking. She saw Mike's Bronco turn into the driveway.

"He's here, Devon." She called out to let her know. Devon couldn't see the front yard from the den.

When Mike walked into the kitchen, he looked worn out. The whites of his eyes were bloodshot as if he hadn't had much sleep.

"Sorry I'm late, Ellie."

"I'm glad you were, I'm a little slow getting supper ready. Devon's in the den resting on the couch."

"She's not in bed?"

Ellie walked over to him and whispered. "She's back in the world of the living."

"Good." He smiled.

"Yes, it is. Go talk to her while I'm finishing up."

He nodded and walked into the den.

Devon straightened up hearing Mike's voice in the kitchen and practiced a smile. She was sitting with her legs stretched out on the couch. She'd decided to use crutches tonight and sit at the table in a regular chair.

Mike walked in and smiled. "Hey, glad to see you're getting up and around." He sat down on the easy chair next to her, bending forward, his elbows resting on his knees. "You look good."

"I'm feeling better. Are you all packed and ready to go?"

"Yeah. Took me longer than I thought to clear out of my place."

"It always takes longer than you think. You look tired."

"I am." He let out an exhausted sigh and rubbed his hands over his eyes. "I'm going to drive to Abilene tonight and stay with a friend stationed at Dyess. Put me a little farther down the road."

Ellie stood at the door to the kitchen with a dishtowel in her hand. "Sorry to interrupt, but I'm in the middle of mashing the potatoes. Would you mind going out to find Jamie, Mike? Supper will be ready shortly."

"Sure, Ellie." He stood up.

After he had left the room, she looked at her mother wondering why she hadn't called Jamie to come in.

Ellie was a mind reader. "I thought I'd give them a chance to talk alone." Without further comment, she returned to the kitchen. Devon was stuck in the house. All she could do was hope they did talk and that it would help Jamie.

Jamie came running around the house to the front yard and hopped on the tire swing. Ellie watched through the kitchen window. Mike walked up and stood beside the trunk in the shade. He was talking.

Jamie was swinging and not even looking at Mike. Mike crossed his arms and said something else. Jamie frowned, leaned back and pumped with his body to swing higher.

Mike grabbed the tire and stopped it. He hung on to it and turned it so Jamie would have to look at him. His expression was grim. He said something. Her grandson shifted his weight with a jerk, but Mike hung on.

Mike said something else before he gave the tire a spin. Jamie looked straight up as the twisted rope slowly unwound spinning him around and around.

It must be exasperating for him, Ellie though, as Mike turned away from the house and leaned against the tree trunk. Children looked at things with their hearts, not their heads. That's what made it so hard for adults to reason with them. He'd hurt Jamie's feelings and Mike needed to know it. Jamie started rocking the tire until he was swinging high enough to touch a branch with his foot

Mike straightened up and said something. Jamie let one foot touch the ground, his shoe scuffing the patch of dirt underneath the swing until it stopped. He hopped off the tire, never looking up at Mike even once, as they walked past the kitchen window. She had a feeling it was going to be a quiet dinner.

Devon sat at one end of the dinner table. It wasn't her usual place but it was easier with her leg propped up on the other chair. Her foot throbbed if she sat with it on the floor for long. Her mother had cooked a big supper as if it were a festive occasion. The fellowship was a wonderful opportunity for Mike, and to get through the meal they had to focus on the positives. But Jamie's unhappiness made such subterfuge hard to maintain. He nibbled in silence, rarely looking up from his plate.

"So Mike, how long does it take to drive all the way to Seattle? More potatoes?" Mom held up the bowl.

He raised his hand to fend off the dish. "No thanks, Ellie. It takes a couple of long days to get up there. Probably spend a night with my mother before I head into Seattle."

"She'll be glad you'll be living closer to home." Ellie smiled at him.

"Yes, I think so. She's been having trouble with her blood pressure lately so I'll be able to keep closer tabs on her condition." He looked down at his plate and poked at a green bean with his fork. "As I mentioned to Devon earlier, I hope you can all come up to Seattle for a visit sometime and let us show you around. I'd love to take Jamie fishing or camping in the mountains."

Devon watched him. Any chance for a lasting relationship between them had been flawed from the start. They were going their separate ways. She knew it and so did he. She'd seen it happen too many times. New friendships torpedoed by distance. They dissolved like sugar until a name in an address book was all that remained.

"My husband went through there on his way to Korea years ago. Said the mountains were beautiful." Her mother surveyed the table. "Well, how about some coffee and dessert?"

"As much as I'd like to stay, Ellie, I really need to go to make it to Abilene tonight." He stood and gathered his plate and utensils.

Her mother popped up out of her chair. "Don't worry about the table, Mike. You've a long trip ahead of you."

"It tasted great, Ellie. I'm going to miss your cooking." He walked around the table and carried his dishes to the sink anyway.

"Glad you could have dinner with us. Least I could do after all your help at the hospital, Mike." Ellie waited by the sink and gave him a quick hug when he turned around. "We'll miss you. Take care of yourself."

"I'm going to miss you too."

Devon's face was warm. That sinking feeling that came with farewells had settled over her. She was terrible at good-byes, never able to say what she wanted. All week she'd been volatile and unpredictable, like homemade fireworks on the Fourth of July but she was running out of dynamite. She didn't want to dissolve into tears, to make him think she was crying for him and make it harder, because that wouldn't be true. She had too many things to cry about to narrow it down. Determined to control herself, she pushed away from the table to face him with a smile. The pillow under her foot on the other chair tumbled off.

Mike picked it up and squatted down to put it back under her leg. "Don't get up. We'll say goodbye right here, okay?" She nodded. His smile was different, not smooth and steady. A nervous little twitch at the corners of it made her think these last face-to-face words weren't easy for him either. "I'll call you when I get home." He stretched over her injured leg to kiss her cheek.

She sniffed as she took a breath and smiled as best she could. "Thank you. For everything." The words were barely audible but they came out. "Be careful."

"I will." He touched her hand briefly before standing up.

He turned to Jamie, who was still sitting in his chair. He leaned forward and put his hand on her son's shoulder. "You're going to be a fine baseball player, Jamie. Hope you can come up and visit sometime."

"I don't want you to go." Jamie cried the words, his face screwed up like misery itself. The chair scraped across the floor as he jumped to his feet and tearfully wrapped his arms around Mike's waist.

Devon covered her mouth and glanced up at Mike, her vision blurred by her own tears. His Adam's apple bobbed and his lips tightened. He leaned down and patted Jamie on the back.

"Walk out to the car with me, Jamie. I've got something for you." Mike turned toward the door, keeping one arm around Jamie's shoulders. He glanced back at her with an expression drained of pleasure, before he left. She felt sorry for both of them. Jamie couldn't hide his disappointment or his love. Mike would know he'd hurt him and have to leave.

She wasn't steady enough with crutches to go outside yet. She exchanged a look with her mother. Her mother trailed behind them.

She dried her eyes with her napkin and turned her chair away from the table to face the door. She'd allowed Jamie to get too attached to Mike. A mistake he was paying for in tears. But Mike had to share in the blame. He should have known better. He missed not having a son and had used Jamie to fill that void.

She heard an engine start and watched the door. Jamie rushed in crying and holding something in the crook of his arm. He crashed into her, wrapping his arms around her neck. The aches she felt couldn't match the pain in his sobs. Her mother started clearing the table without comment.

Devon held him against her, doubting that anything she could say right now would help. As the bout of tears eased, he leaned his head against her shoulder letting her console him with hugs and kisses. He rubbed his hand across his drippy nose reaching for Mike's gift wedged between them.

"It's a first base mitt, Mama." He turned the well-used baseball glove over to examine it. His fingers ran along the stitching. "He said his daddy gave it to him, a long time ago." His hand was lost in the large mitt as he slipped it on and punched the leather pocket with his balled up fist. "It's all broke in, better than a new one. He said it was special, just like me."

She combed the hair away from his tear-stained face. "You are special, honey." Maybe having the glove would make it easier for him to be left behind. His heart would mend. She realized he'd said good-bye many times and would many more. He needed to make happy memories and she would keep a watchful eye to keep his heart from being broken.

O ver the next two weeks, Devon's recovery was steady. She could put most of her weight on her foot, making it easier to use crutches and even a cane at times. She could bend her knee, which was a triumph of its own. Loretta brought her son, Billie, over to play with Jamie when she visited Devon. Dr. Green said he was doing very well and it seemed that as she grew stronger so did he.

For the first time, they'd left her alone for a large part of the day, even though Hank was working somewhere on the ranch. Devon managed to take care of herself as well as struggle through her exercises. It felt like an accomplishment even if someone healthy would think it laughable. Awakened from a short nap by the sound of the kitchen door slamming, she was sitting up when Jamie came running into her bedroom. She patted the bed beside her. "Come here and tell me what you did today."

He jumped up on the bed grinning from ear to ear and wrapped her in an enthusiastic hug.

"Well, you must have had fun. How was Tommy?"

"They have puppies now, Mom, bunches of them." His blue eyes were wide with excitement.

Devon was glad to see him so cheerful. "What's the name of Tommy's bird dog again."

"Duchess." Jamie sat back on his heels on the bed. "Their eyes aren't open yet. Could I open my eyes when I was born?"

"Yes, you looked right at me and smiled." She laughed. "What did you do besides play with the puppies?"

"We played pirates in Tommy's pool after the puppies got tired."

"Did you hang up your wet swimsuit?"

"Yep, Granny made me. Want to see my pictures?" He ran out of the room before she could answer. When he came bounding back in he had rolled up papers in his hands.

He spread out his crayon artwork on the bed. There were horses, cattle, dogs and trees scattered through most of them. One looked different from the others. The colors were darker. Two figures faced each other. One was some kind of animal, dark and foreboding. The other was smiling, dressed all in blue with a red cape, holding a yellow sword in his hand. There was a large black rectangle in the corner of the paper.

"This is interesting." Devon pointed to the sword picture and could feel the change in Jamie. He wasn't bouncing up and down on his knees anymore and he was quiet. His expression was solemn and hard to read. She wondered if she should ask him about this one. She swallowed and worked up her courage. She pointed to the black square. "What's this? A house?"

Jamie jabbed at the picture with a finger. "No, it's a box. Max is going to put the bad guy in there and lock him up."

"Oh, I see." She worked to sound calm. She put her arm around him. She kissed the side of his face and kept her lips on his warm skin. "Jamie, it's okay to talk about what happened to us."

"I don't like that day." He turned to see her face. "He hurt you real bad. I hate him." He was frowning, his bottom lip jutting out.

"I know. But he can't hurt anybody now." She touched his cheek. "Do you want to tell me about it?"

"No." He was uncertain of her. She could see it in his eyes.

She knew what he needed to hear. "I love you, very much. You don't have to worry about me, Jamie. I'm going to be okay." She resisted the urge to hug him and looked down. She took one of his hands and held it in hers. "When you're ready, you can tell me about it, even the bad stuff."

Devon switched off the lamp on her bedside table and stretched out, pulling the sheet over her. It was just after ten. With her eyes closed the only noise she heard was the mechanical hum of the air conditioner. She drifted toward sleep. When something warm touched her arm, she opened her eyes with a start. In the dim light coming through her open door, she recognized Jamie's silhouette standing beside the bed.

"Mama, can I sleep with you?"

"What's the matter, honey?" She put her hand out to find his arm.

"Please, Mama." He sounded fretful and upset.

"Okay, come on." She threw the sheet back and moved over to make room for him. As soon as she covered him, he nestled close to her body. She slid her arm under his shoulders and pulled him closer, his head resting in the hollow between her neck and shoulder. He smelled of little boy, sweet with a hint of ground in dirt. She touched her lips to his forehead. The hair around his face was damp. "Were you having a bad dream?"

He didn't answer her, but simply nodded his head.

"Well, you're safe in here with me." She put her other arm around him in a satisfying embrace, relaxed her arms and yawned. With a slight move of her neck to adjust her pillow, she closed her eyes listening to the soft rush of air that crested like waves then broke free as they exhaled.

He wiggled, working his arms through the covers until they wrapped around her neck. "We don't have to worry anymore do we, Mama?"

"What do you mean, Jamie?" His unexpected question caught her unprepared. She began to pat him gently on the back as she had done a thousand times during his short life.

"We don't have to worry about the bad guys."

"That's right, honey." He was restless. The rustle of the sheets and his uneven breathing told her there would be more. She waited, taking shallow breaths, listening for whatever came next, hoping she would say the right thing.

"And you aren't mad at me, are you?" His voice sounded uncertain. The words came out in hesitant pieces.

Confusion mixed with guilt. "Why would I be mad at you, Jamie?"

"That man said I was helping him and he hurt you." His words ended in a sob.

"Oh, Jamie, no." She tightened her arms around him. "Honey, you didn't do anything to help him." He was trying not to cry. She could feel the fitful rise and fall of his chest.

"He had a big box of snakes, Mama. He said, if I didn't sit still he'd let them bite me."

"Jamie, I'm glad you were smart and kept still. That was the very best thing you could have done." Even in the darkness, it was hard to listen and not see sparks of red. She pushed a growing anger aside and brushed her son's hair away from his hot face to comfort him.

"Are you sure?" The question was full of doubt.

"Yes." She kissed him on the cheek.

"Good." He patted her neck with one hand.

After a few minutes of silence, the sound of his breathing became slow and steady. She moved her arm out from under him and made sure he was covered.

Staring into the black that clung to the ceiling, Devon wished she could go to sleep. "Damn you, Joe Colton."

Jamie rolled over and his arm flopped across her chest. She put her hand over his and turned her head to see what time it was. Eleven o'clock. She closed her eyes but it was useless.

The Coltons enjoyed inflicting pain. Someone must have mistreated them. She couldn't believe a person would behave like that otherwise. Which brought her to Mrs. Colton. Remembering the old woman's cold, unforgiving eyes it was hard to believe she hadn't at least known what Joe had planned. But it turned her stomach to think a mother, even a crazy, vengeful one, would hurt a young child like Jamie.

She touched his warm, small hand. He was still her baby in so many ways. Joe had taken great pleasure in taunting her, using her son like a weapon but he hadn't hurt him. Why? He must have decided Jamie didn't have anything to do with his brother's death. Making her think he was dead was all Joe needed to get revenge.

She wasn't sure what she was supposed to feel lying here in the dark. The man had shot her in the chest without so much as a blink of remorse. And yet, when he'd held the gun to her head, he hadn't pulled the trigger. It was a huge risk, to leave her breathing and able to identify him. Maybe he'd been willing to risk it just to extend her suffering, like he'd said. And he'd figured he could outrun the law. Criminals never expected to get caught. She'd heard Buck say that many times.

The next morning, Devon limped across the hard, uneven ground using her cane to keep her balance. She was headed for her thinking place at the back corner of the corral fence behind the barn. She complained out loud, from frustration not pain for a change, when she almost stumbled. Watching every step slowed her down. There was no reason to hurry. Mom had taken Jamie to Vacation Bible School in town. It was a week long diversion for him during the long summer days. He needed to get away, to put the bad behind him. So did she. Thoughts of Joe Colton had plagued her all night.

She walked along the corral fence until she reached the corner. Shaded by the old, live oak tree, she leaned against the rough wood of the middle board to rest. A warm breeze rustled the leaves overhead. She hung her cane on the fence and noticed she had an audience.

"How am I supposed to do this day in and day out?" Three young heifers stood in the pasture watching her. They seemed to be listening as they munched on grass. She took a deep breath and exhaled, giving life to an uncertain sigh. "I keep waiting to feel . . . normal. Maybe I never will." She looked up at the wide branches of a tree, much older than she was, to escape the despair in the word 'never'. A short, disapproving bellow made her look over at her four-legged companions. Two sets of brown bovine eyes were still focused on her. But one white head shook.

"You're right." She clapped her hands together to chase away the blues. "I am alive and almost kicking."

"Hello?"

She jumped until she realized it was Hank's voice. "Hank?"

He appeared at the corner of the barn. "Hi, I thought I heard somebody talkin'." He was walking toward her. "You okay?"

"I was out getting a little exercise." She laughed, suddenly a little self-conscious. "Talking to the cows while I rest a minute."

He stopped beside her. "They're good listeners." He grinned. "Don't gossip either."

"They must be the only ones in the county that don't. I thought you were gone."

"Oh, I was. Had to come back. Forgot my glasses." He patted the black frames partially sticking out of his shirt pocket. "Can't read the fine print without them anymore." He waved his hand toward her cane hanging on the fence. "You all right out here alone? Kind of rough ground with that bum ankle."

"The therapist said I needed to practice walking on different surfaces. Get back to the real world. So here I am." She slapped her hand on her thigh where her jeans covered a scar.

Hank nodded. "Well, if you don't need help, I guess I'll go on."

"Can I ask you something?" She blurted it out.

"Sure thing. What do you need?"

"No, it's not a thing, it's . . . an answer. . . to a question that keeps bothering me."

"Oh." He rubbed his chin. "Can't promise you I got one that'll fit."

"Why do you think Joe Colton let Jamie go?"

Hank shook his head and stared at the pasture in front of him. "No tellin'." His jaw muscles tensed. "Only drunks and cowards hurt children."

She focused on the far-off ridge. "I've been trying to figure out how a man like Colton thinks. He put a gun to my head, but didn't pull the trigger." She glanced at Hank. He'd crossed his arms. There was a hard, unreadable expression on his face. "He took a big risk leaving me alive."

Hank turned his head and studied her face. "Cold-blooded killin' takes a man without a soul. Maybe lookin' at you up close reminded him that he had one."

She wondered if that was it. "It's hard to know how to feel, if I hate him."

Hank looked down at his feet. "I reckon it would be." He was quiet for a minute before raising his head. "Hate never seems to do anybody much good, Devon." He turned and looked at her. "It eats away at folks."

A prime example came to mind, Alan and his mother. It was a waste of energy to hate a dead man. She pushed off the fence board and stood on her feet.

"I don't want that to happen."

He crossed his arms again. "Then don't let it."

"Right." She smiled, maybe it was that easy, just a choice.

Hank nodded and glanced at his wristwatch. "I've got to move on. Sure you don't want some help back to the house?"

She grabbed her cane. "No, I'll be fine. Thanks, Hank."

Devon sat on the chair facing Dr. Green. It was hard to hold still. He was drinking coffee. She hadn't wanted any. Her brain couldn't handle any more caffeine.

"Jamie showed me his drawings when he got home the other day. I'm worried about the one he wouldn't talk about."

"Max slaying the dragon of all bad things?" He smiled. "That's how he describes him to me. Sometimes the dragon takes more human form."

She nodded, surprised he knew what she was referring to without asking.

"He wouldn't say much except he was going to lock him up."

The doctor leaned back in his chair. "A pretty reasonable thing to do with bad people in our culture. What troubles you about it?"

"He was upset, angry just showing it to me." She clasped her hands together. "I'm worried that the Coltons frightened him so badly he'll never be just a happy kid again."

"He was frightened, but he is learning how to deal with it."

She rubbed her fingers back and forth across the nubby fabric on the arm of her chair. "He woke up from a nightmare that night. He asked if I was mad at him, as if it was his fault Joe Colton shot me."

He raised his hands to form the sphere with his fingers again. "It goes back to that child's way of looking at the world, I mentioned before. He is starting to understand the world doesn't work that way." He smiled and let one hand close around the other. "Maybe he wanted to check and make sure you didn't believe it." He settled back in the soft brown leather.

"I told him I didn't." She stared at the blur of green on the floor while thinking through that night and what Jamie had said, before looking up at the doctor. "Why has he waited until now to tell me about the kidnapping?"

He studied her face. "Jamie was protecting you."

She sat up, feeling some vague alarm. "From what?"

"His fear."

"Oh, God." She sank back in her chair. She put her elbow on the arm of the chair, resting her head on her hand.

"You're hiding your fear from him, aren't you?"

She looked up. "I've told him not to worry, that I'd keep him safe. What a lie."

"No. He needed to be reassured."

She sat up, shaking her head. "But I can't protect him, not from men like the Coltons." She stood up and pointed an accusing finger to the world outside the office windows. "I shudder to think how many more are out there, just like them. It's almost paralyzing."

Dr. Green stood, walked to the window and looked out. "I'd be willing to bet there have been outlaws as long as humans have roamed the earth." He turned his head and glanced at her. "We protect the people we love as best we can, as you did."

She crossed her arms. "That's easier said than done."

"You're not alone in that assessment." He looked at her eyes, a hint of · a smile on his calm face. "However, none of us has a choice but to try."

It took her a minute to identify the blue and white truck pulling up. She wondered what in the world Frank Jessup was doing here in the middle of the day. It didn't matter. She was sprawled out in the sand like a fool. Hopefully, he hadn't seen her less than graceful attempt to keep her balance before she fell with a bone-jarring thud on her rump.

He ran over. "You all right?" He bent over and put his hand on her shoulder.

Devon looked up at him and blew away the hair covering her eye, with a quick puff. His brow was wrinkled in concern. "Yes, dammit, only my pride is bruised."

He straightened up and grinned. "I didn't know you still liked to play in the dirt." That's what he'd called getting bucked off a horse during their junior rodeo days.

"Very funny."

He surveyed the area around the house. "You out here by yourself?"

"I don't need a baby sitter." She arched her right eyebrow daring him to make another smart comment. "I wanted to get some fresh air." She sat up and slapped at the dust on her jeans. "Lost my balance on this uneven ground."

"Need help gettin' up?" He leaned over and held out a hand.

She stared at it with her lips clamped together wavering between 'yes' and a mule-headed 'no'.

"Guess that's a 'no'." Frank sat down right beside her. "It wouldn't kill you to let me help."

Devon fixed her eyes on his, tilting her head slightly. "You don't have to take it personally, either." She glanced at her foot. Her ankle was hurting after the fall. "I'll get up on my own."

"Gettin' hot out here. Think it's going to take long?" He winked at her when she looked at him.

"What are you doing here, Frank? Out joy riding?" Devon got up on her good knee. He sat there watching her. It made her feel like a klutz. She pushed herself up with her good leg doing most of the work and using the cane to keep her balance.

"I was seein' a man about a horse."

She frowned suspecting he was pulling her leg.

He grinned. "Really. The Howard's are selling a colt so I was in the neighborhood." He stood up and dusted himself off. "Thought I'd see how you were doin' and maybe talk you into a glass of ice water." That irresistible twinkle in his eyes reminded her of all the times they'd tried to outdo each other.

"You could whet your whistle in the trough over there, but I imagine the ice we put in every morning to satisfy rodeo cowboys has melted by now." She tried to keep a straight face but she lost the battle as Frank rubbed one hand across his chin and looked toward the corral as if he was considering a drink from the big metal tub.

"Well, I was really hoping for something with ice."

She laughed. "Come on inside." She watched the ground in front of her as she walked beside him toward the house.

He held the kitchen door open for her. Once inside, she hung the cane on the counter and washed her hands in the sink. "How about some iced tea?"

"Sounds great." He stood beside her. "You hurt your ankle in the fall? You're favoring it. Maybe you should sit down."

"No, it's all right, just a little swollen and stiff still. I only use the cane and the ankle brace outside where the ground is rough." She opened a cabinet and reached for a couple of glasses. "Could you get the ice , Frank?"

He took the ice out of the freezer and brought it over. "I heard your doctor friend left town last month."

She raised her head in surprise. "Yes. He moved to Seattle to go back for some more medical training."

"That okay with you?" He was watching her closely as if he expected her to explode.

It was none of his business. She dropped several ice cubes into each glass with noisy clunks, wondering what kind of gossip was floating around. She faced him. "We were just friends, Frank." She didn't so much as blink. He nodded but he had a halfhearted, I'm getting my leg pulled kind of look that irritated her.

She poured the tea from the pitcher while he returned the ice cube tray to the freezer. He carried their filled glasses to the table and waited to pull a chair out for her before sitting down himself.

He hung his hat on the knob on back of the chair beside him. "How's Jamie doing?"

She was glad he'd changed the subject. "Okay, he's in Vacation Bible School this week." She sprinkled a bit of sugar in her glass and stirred, watching the ice float in circles. "How are the girls?"

"Fine. Took them up to Ft. Worth to spend a week with their mother's folks." He took a sip and stared at his glass for a moment after he set it down. "They need to see the girls every so often, especially Annie. She changes every day. She looks a lot like Tracey." His voice was softer.

She wanted to ask about his wife but looked out the window instead. It was probably hard to talk about. Missing someone who loved you would be twice as hard.

"Jamie ever go visit his dad?" He glanced her way.

"No, Alan isn't that kind of father." She slid her fingertips across the surface of her cool glass.

"That's a shame." He shook his head.

"Yes, it is, but that's the way he wants it." She looked him in the eye making it clear.

Frank took a drink and shifted in his seat. "What are you going to do once you're all healed, go west again?"

"No, I'm not going back to California. I'm going to find a job in Texas. Somewhere close enough to give Mom a hand, when she needs it."

"Hard to run a place this big alone." He was watching something outside through the large window. She didn't see anything unusual. She wondered if it was family or something else that had brought him back here.

"May I ask you something, Frank?"

"Sure." He swirled the tea in his glass before he raised his glass and drank. There was a wet circle on the table.

"Why did you decide to come back here and settle down?"

"I got tired of being bucked off a horse or a bull, for one thing." He grinned. "I liked the crowds clapping in the stands and I made money at it, but it was tough." He leaned back in his chair and straightened out his legs. "Always wanted to raise horses. When I found out the Smith's place was for sale, at a price I could afford, I bought it. The girls like it out there and so do I."

He glanced at the clock on the wall. "I'd better go. Have a lot to do before supper." He drained his glass in a big gulp. "Thanks for the tea." He pushed his chair away from the table and stood. She did too.

He reached for his hat. "I was thinkin', maybe, we could go out to dinner some time." He looked down, slid the fingers of one hand across the brim of his hat before glancing up. "I miss having someone to talk to, other than the girls, I mean." The lonesomeness in his voice ran straight through the words and strummed a familiar chord in her heart.

She smiled. "Hot dogs and macaroni and cheese for dinner gets old after awhile."

"Sure does, even if you add tacos to the menu." He grinned as he settled his hat on his head just right. "I'll give you a call some time."

"Once I'm getting around a little better that would be nice, Frank."

He looked straight at her without so much as a blink. "Glad to see you're doing okay." He walked to the kitchen door and opened it before glancing back. "I'll find my way out. Stay inside where it's cool. 'Bye."

She watched him through the kitchen window as he walked to his truck, with that little hitch in his get-along. He was a good-hearted, dependable, and honest man, like so many other men she'd known. The world was a better place because of them.

Devon heard the knock on the front door while she was in the den reading the business section from Sunday's newspaper. The fleeting thought, that it couldn't be anybody they knew, occurred to her. A sudden uneasiness stopped her from getting up off the couch. She began to tremble, hearing the heavy rap again. How she wished her mother were inside and not out with Hank and Jamie. With contempt for her own cowardice, she convinced herself that someone up to no good wouldn't worry about knocking. She stood up. Her legs were wobbly. She grabbed her cane and squeezed the handle as she steadied herself. Jamie's baseball bat leaned against the wall. She stopped long enough to move it closer to the entryway.

She walked, more timidly than she cared to admit, to the hall where she could see the front porch and driveway through the window. She didn't recognize the dusty, blue dodge sedan baking in the bright sun. A stocky man in dark trousers and a white dress shirt stood by the door. He was looking out toward the road so all she could see was his back. When he turned, she recognized him. Relief was mix with irritation. The young preacher was all ready in trouble as far as she was concerned and he hadn't said a word yet.

She opened the door letting in a blast of dry, oven-hot air. She hoped her expression was relatively benign. "Reverend Stanton, what a surprise. I'm afraid my mother isn't here right now."

She remembered all too well how his ministerial hokum had affected her in the hospital. She was in no mood to repeat that scene. She stood squarely in the middle of the doorway, cane held in a wider than normal angle away from her body, to discourage any thought he might have of coming in.

Billy Clyde had perspiration beading above his mouth and across his forehead. His smile faded as he looked at her. "Ah, actually ma'am, I came to see you." He swallowed nervously and squared his shoulders as if he were facing Daniel's lions.

That amused her. Her hands relaxed on the soft grip of the cane. "You came to see me? Why?" She tilted her head a little as she watched him squirm.

"Well, I must confess I've come to apologize." Once the words started, they tumbled out of him. "After my visit with you in the hospital, I realized that I had failed to be of any comfort."

That was an understatement and it pleased her with a childishly mischievous tickle that he'd noticed. He looked down and scuffed his dusty, black shoes in the fine layer of sandy grit on the porch.

"I have prayed for guidance since that day, truly I have. Asking God for the wisdom of a shepherd to understand the needs of my flock. I'm afraid I'm ill-prepared to deal with such difficult trials as yours and those of others in the congregation." His voice trailed off. When he raised his head his expression was as forlorn as a child's.

In spite of her efforts to ignore it, her throat tightened in response to the suffering on Billy Clyde's pink face. He started rambling. Apparently, he wasn't going to be satisfied until he had sufficiently flailed away at his transgressions in full. She'd had enough therapy to know it would probably do him good to get it off his chest.

She could hear the air conditioner straining to counteract the heat pouring into the house through the open door. "Would you like a glass of iced tea?" She couldn't believe the words were coming out of her own mouth.

He looked as surprised as she felt. "It is mighty hot out here. You sure it wouldn't be too much trouble, ma'am?" He motioned toward the cane with one hand.

"Oh, I think I can manage it, Mr. Stanton." She stepped away from the door and turned to wait for him. He took a hesitant step inside and closed the door. She headed for the kitchen with the preacher in tow.

Imagining the look on her mother's face when she described this visit, produced a smile that no one could see, but she could feel.

"Have you read, *The Bridge of San Luis Rey*, Dr. Green?" She glanced in his direction.

He rubbed his chin as if he was searching through his memory. "Right off hand, it's not ringing any bells."

"My English teacher in high school had me read it after my brother died. I was remembering it last night."

"What's it about?" He leaned back in his chair, lacing his hands behind his head.

"It takes place in Chile or Peru, somewhere in the Andes." She imagined the books along the shelves in the office were the rugged peaks of high mountains. "Five people are killed when a rope bridge over a deep ravine suddenly breaks. The villagers are upset. How could God let innocent people die? So a priest does some research. He's sure he'll find the victims' sins to justify their deaths in this literal fall from God's grace." She glanced toward the doctor, listening to her. "It seems we always to want to blame someone."

"Did the story help you deal with your brother's death?"

"No, all I could see was the senseless tragedy in it. I have a little different perspective now."

"How?" He rested his chin in the palm of his hand as he leaned on his elbow pressed into the soft arm of his chair. He looked at her with that steady gaze waiting for her to fill in the blanks.

"Well, for one thing, I can identify with someone grappling with the whims of fate and not coming up with any easy answers." She tried to laugh but there was no pleasure in it. "The point wasn't that they died unfairly but that all the priest found was the good they'd left behind."

As she glanced out the window, a nervous flutter stirred her heart. "I know something now." The fat clouds were clumping together. Maybe it would rain. She turned toward him. "I didn't deserve to be hurt. It wasn't a punishment. I didn't cause it to happen. It may sound simple-minded, but I feel better."

"It's not simple. It's an important step in healing." He leaned forward and smiled. "Now you can decide how you're going to live."

She walked into the bathroom. "Ready for me to shampoo your hair?"

Jamie looked up at her from the bathtub, a flotilla of toys covering the surface of the water. "Mom, remember when I asked you about second grade and you said you didn't know and I was supposed to ask you later?"

"Yes, I remember." She picked up the shampoo from the counter.

"Do you know yet?"

She closed the door to the bathroom. "I'm trying to work that out. It may take awhile to find a job." She got down on her knees beside the tub.

He was piloting a plastic boat around a dinosaur floating on its side. "What kind of job do you want?"

She wished she could just order one up like a pizza. "I'd like one where I could see you off to school every morning and be back when you got home." He smiled at her. "Unfortunately, most businesses don't keep those kinds of hours."

He tilted his head to the side. "Does Granny have a job?"

"Yes. She runs the ranch and sells cattle."

He frowned. "Uncle Hank does that."

She laughed. "He works for Granny, Jamie. He does the things around the place she can't do. When he needs help, Granny hires some other men to give him a hand."

"Maybe you can help her, too and that can be your job." The look of hope in his eyes and excitement in his voice made it clear he thought he'd found the perfect solution.

"It takes a lot of money to run a ranch, Jamie. She couldn't afford to pay me, too." She took the cap off the shampoo bottle. "You like living here with Granny, don't you?"

"Yep. It's fun to ride around with Hank and Maggie and take care of the cows. And when Tommy comes over, Granny doesn't care if we make noise."

In the midst of the simple utility of a bathroom, it was easier to keep focused on the bottom line. "There is a lot more space to have fun in. But I have to earn money to pay for the things we need. We need to take care of ourselves."

He was scooping up water in his hands. "You can have the money in my piggy bank." He peeked up at her.

She leaned closer. "Thanks for being so generous, Jamie, but that's your money reserved just for you."

"How much does it take?"

She filled the plastic cup with bath water. "I guess that all depends on what we decide we need, what's important."

"I think Granny is important, don't you, Mom?" The earnest tone of his voice was matched by the expression on his face as his brows raised with hope. "She was real lonesome before we came. She told me when you were sick."

That put a lump in her throat. He was doing a great job of getting right to the heart of the matter. Clearly, he'd come to depend on her mother in the last couple of months. She tipped his chin up. "I don't want to leave her alone either, Jamie." She poured the water over his head.

As Dr. Green had said, it was up to her to decide how she was going to live. After coming so close to losing everything, her priorities were simple. The people she loved came first, a salary or a job title a distant second. "If I could find a decent job somewhere around here, we wouldn't be rich but we could get by."

Jamie wiped off his face with his hands. "Do we have to be rich like my daddy?"

She sat back on her heels, surprised he knew anything about Alan's money. His frown made her think he didn't like whatever he'd heard. "Where did you hear that?"

"I heard Granny talking to Mabel."

She should have guessed. Aggravation rumbled around inside her. Her mother seemed to forget how good children were at overhearing things. However, imagining how his other grandmother would have bristled at his comment, she smiled at the irony of it all. "No, Jamie, we don't have to be rich."

"Good, 'cause I like it here." He nodded his head as if that was all there was to it.

"I know." She poured a little shampoo out into her palm. Right now, staying felt like the right thing to do, for all of them. There were opportunities, even though they were meager ones. She could make ends meet.

"I'll make you a deal, Jamie." She spoke with a deliberate firmness to hold his attention. "If, and that may be a very big if, I can find a job to cover our expenses, we'll stay until next summer."

"Yahoo! Oh, boy. We can stay!"

She shushed him. "Wait a minute." She leaned down. The smile left his face. He focused his blue eyes on hers. "I don't have a job yet and I haven't talked to Granny, either. Promise me you won't say a word until I talk to her."

He nodded and pretended to turn a key to lock his mouth.

She smiled. "Okay, it better stay that way. Now close your eyes." She spread the shampoo through his hair and scrubbed. She was glad he was happy, but wondered about her own sanity. Her chances for a decent job were better in Austin or San Antonio, even though a couple of the queries she'd sent out had been dead ends. It would be hard eking out a living around here, but she'd try.

Devon carried a load of warm clothes in her arms and dropped them on the couch. Jamie was in bed. She noticed the stack of envelopes on the desk beside her mother. "Finished with the bills?"

Her mother was putting a file away in the bottom drawer. "Yes. If the price of beef will stay up, I think we'll do all right this year."

She grabbed a tee shirt and began folding. "Mom, I've been thinking. I hate to make Jamie change schools again. He's had enough to deal with this year. I've decided to look for a job around here."

Her mother's face brightened with a smile. "Be good for him to stay in one place and put down some roots."

She picked up a pair of white socks. There was a hole in one toe. She stared at it, not sure how to say what she was thinking. "I know we've disrupted your life ever since we got here, Mom. I noticed a little house for rent on the way to town. I'm going to check it out. I figured you might like to have some peace and quiet."

"I had six months of it after your father died. I don't care for living in an empty house. With two spare bedrooms here, I'm not about to let you live in some shack." Ellie shook her head, rounded up her pen and checkbook and deposited them in the middle drawer. "You paid the doctor bills and those put you back a penny, I know. And Jamie's not any trouble. He's got enough room around here to make all the noise he wants."

"Then while we're living with you, I want to pay for our share of the expenses, Mom. And I'll help you around the place. It isn't fair for you otherwise."

Her mother was going to argue with her. Ellie opened her mouth to say something, but closed it without saying a word. She stood up and pushed her chair under the desk. "Okay, if it will make you feel better."

"It will, Mom." Devon snapped a pair of Jamie's jeans in the air to straighten the legs. Her mother walked over to the easy chair beside the couch and started gathering up the newspaper and magazines spread across the coffee table.

"I talked to Mr. Clark, Molly's friend, at Travis Junior College. He's still searching for someone to help with the new marketing plan. It's a short project and I doubt that it will pay much but it would bring in some cash while I look around. I made an appointment on Wednesday morning to discuss the details."

Ellie stopped moving and smiled. "That sounds promising. There may be more opportunities around here than you think."

"Maybe." It was going to be a struggle, Devon knew that. "Right now, I'm just glad to have it settled."

"Me too. I hated to think of the two of you leaving."

She piled the assorted stacks of clothes on top of one another and picked them up to carry them back to the bedrooms. "Well, you may change your mind. Little boys can be handful, Mom."

"So can daughters." Mom chuckled.

Ellie and Devon decided to go shopping in Braddock the next day for a change. Jamie needed some new clothes for school. If Devon wanted to work and be a participant in life beyond the confines of home and Blanco Springs again, this trip would be a first step. She was strong physically but still uneasy.

Devon had insisted on driving her car. Being chauffeured around made her feel helpless. They ate lunch at the Little Rooster and splurged on dessert to celebrate. The air-conditioned mall was a pleasure after the sweltering heat outside. There were back-to-school banners in every window display. She was glad she'd made a decision about the coming school year. It was a relief to have part of the future mapped out. After doing some window shopping, they headed for Penney's.

Ellie was trying on shoes. With Jamie in tow, Devon headed for the boys' clothes. He was growing like a weed. He needed a new pair of jeans, shorts, socks, underwear and a few tee shirts. Sorting through a pile of jeans looking for Jamie's size, she realized he wasn't standing beside her anymore. She quickly scanned the racks and mounds of clothes on tables. She spotted him a couple of rows away, partially hidden by a rack of tee shirts. A man she didn't recognize, standing beside a tall display panel, was leaning over talking to him. She stiffened and dropped the clothes hanging over her arm. Her heart was racing as she hurried toward her son, brushing clothes aside in the narrow aisle. She breathed a bit easier seeing a blonde woman with a toddler squatting beside Jamie.

The blonde was smiling and stood up as she approached. "Hi, you must be Jamie's mama." She was pretty and young, all of twenty, maybe. "I'm Lila, and this is my husband, Billy, and," she lifted the pink-cheeked child to hold her in her arms, "this little angel is Katie."

The woman's name, so familiar, buzzed around in her brain until it registered. This was the woman who had found Jamie on the road. A flood of relief escaped with her sigh. She could have hugged the young woman, except the toddler in her arms was between them and eyeing Devon with suspicion.

"Lila, it's wonderful to meet you. I am so grateful you found Jamie and helped him."

"I knew something was wrong when I spotted him out there. Wouldn't have been able to sleep that night if I hadn't stopped." She looked down at Jamie and smiled. "He was a real brave boy."

Jamie was tickling the toddler's bare feet. The little girl giggled and kicked at him. Devon focused on the adults. The young man was more than smiling, he was beaming. Lila leaned over and put little Katie down on the floor. She couldn't see Lila's face so she talked to Billy.

"I know my mother talked to you. We tried to call you later so I could say thank you, but there was no answer."

Lila glanced up. "Oh, we went up to see my folks in Oklahoma City for a couple of weeks."

Devon looked down at her. "Well, I really would like to show my appreciation somehow."

"Ma'am," the young man interrupted her, "your 'thank you' is plenty. Knowing he's all right and back home is all the reward we need." Lila stood up, holding the baby. He touched his daughter's hair with great tenderness. "We know how we'd feel if Katie got lost."

What a sweet and proud young man he was. Devon wanted to hug all of them but resisted the urge. She didn't want to embarrass Billy or start the baby crying.

"Thank you with all my heart." She touched Lila's arm, she had to, to make it real. Tears crept into her eyes. She wasn't ashamed of them. Katie reached out to her. Devon laughed and took her hand. "I think you should come to dinner." She said it to the baby.

Lila nudged Billy with her elbow. They exchanged a glance. "Well, ma'am, I guess we could come, especially if it's fried chicken." Billy smiled. "Katie loves chicken."

"Then that's what we'll have." Devon was pleased. "How about next Sunday?"

Billy looked at his young wife and she nodded. "That would be fine with us, ma'am."

Devon stood, feeling too antsy to sit still, and took a couple of steps toward the window to look at the parked cars outside. She'd thought she would be feeling more together by her last visit.

"I don't have the nerve to drive more than a mile in any direction by myself." She shook her head and paced back and forth. She stopped. "I worry about Jamie when he's with me and when he's not." She glanced toward Dr. Green, patiently listening to her. "I catch myself hovering around him like some neurotic worrywart." She turned her head toward the window and combed the fingers on one hand through her hair.

"Give yourself time. You're doing fine."

She dropped her arm to her side and walked back to her chair. "I'm going around in circles. I have to get out there, petrified or not, and see how it goes."

"But that scares you."

"Yes, but I guess no one's ever died from being scared." She tried out a halfhearted smile. She sat down, looking at him while the idea that had been churning around inside her for two days started to slosh like a single towel in a washing machine. "I was thinking it might help to go back to where it happened."

"How would that help?" There was no approval or disapproval on his face, just the usual interest without commitment, while he listened.

She glanced down suddenly feeling foolish. "Sounds like the show-down in a spaghetti western, doesn't it?" She looked up. "I keep thinking, if I can go out there, I can handle anyplace."

He didn't say anything for a moment, just rubbed his chin with one hand. "Then try it." He leaned forward. "Just remember, you don't have to do it all at once. Small steps still get you where you're going. My mother used to say that, not Freud by the way, but it's true."

Seeing his smile gave her courage. She needed it. She glanced around the room, the bookcase with its imaginary mountain ranges of books on each shelf, and his oak desk that never had more than a phone and a book or two on it.

"I can come back to see you if I manage to trip myself up?"

égai

"You bet."

She stood up knowing she was leaving behind some of the heartaches. "Thank you for helping us with this terrible mess."

He was beside her. "You're welcome. Give me a call in a week or so and let me know how you're doing."

"I will." She held out her hand and he took it.

His handshake was strong but gentle. Then she was on her own.

I t was cowardice, not injuries nor opportunity, holding her back. Nobody was home to talk her out of it. Standing on the deck with the ranch stretching out in front of her, Devon had imagined danger hiding behind each patch of brush during the past weeks of recuperation. She didn't want to feel like a prisoner any longer, but she would until she could go back out there and face whatever was waiting for her. Her eyes settled on Lookout Point and she thought of her father. He'd be asking her what she was waiting for.

She slid the door to the den open and closed it with a thud behind her. After scribbling a quick note for her mother, she grabbed the keys. She started to breathe faster as she limped to the pickup. There was a spare tire in the truck bed. She checked before she got in. Listening to the engine crank, she almost wished it wouldn't turn over, but it did. Hank was driving in when she passed the barn.

He stopped his vehicle as she pulled up beside him. "Mornin', Devon. Where you going?"

She hesitated, not wanting to tell him what she intended to do in case she failed. "I'm going for a drive."

He paused for a moment before saying anything. "Be gone long?"

"Depends on how far I decide to go." She tightened her grip on the steering wheel.

He lifted his hat and wiped off his forehead with his sleeve before putting the hat back on. "Goin' to be a hot one today. I put a jug of fresh water behind the seat yesterday. I'm on channel twelve on the CB. You know how to work the radio in that truck?"

"Yes." She leaned over, turned it on. "I'm on twelve too."

"Well, guess I'd better git." He smiled and slowly drove off.

She glanced in her rear view mirror. Hank parked his truck by the shed. There was nothing in front of her but solitude, and nothing to stop her but second thoughts. She put her foot on the accelerator and headed across the pasture.

She was fine until she saw the cattle guard. The truck slowed to a roll as her foot retreated to the sandy floor mat. She stopped just short of it as if it were the boundary to her own private version of hell. Her heart was thumping in her chest. The truck engine hummed waiting for her to make up her mind. She glanced out her window at the twisted oak posts and barbed wire boundary of the ranch. Hiding behind four walls or wire fences wasn't a life.

"Come on. You've made it this far." She opened and closed her fingers around the steering wheel before latching onto it with a vengeance. She ignored the jitters making her a little sick to her stomach and gave the engine some gas. The hollow metal ring of the pipes as the tires rolled over the cattle guard sang out to the open country.

There was no breeze blowing through the window. She was driving too slowly to create one. Poking along, she kept a sharp eye out for the deep holes that had been her undoing the first time. Sweat dripped down the side of her face. The hot air was closing in around her.

She rolled down the last hill to the flat stretching out before her and stopped. Her body trembled. This was an ordinary spot to everyone but her. The sun beat down so roasting hot that she could see shimmering waves of heat curl the air in front of her.

The courage she'd marshaled to drive out here had evaporated, leaving her mouth so dry she couldn't swallow. The urge to run overpowered her initial instinct to cower in a tight ball under the steering wheel. She opened the door. A chill, the clammy kind that pulls a plug somewhere and instantly drains the energy out of every muscle, rushed down her body, causing her legs to crumple as her feet touched the ground. She grabbed the door to keep from falling and dropped to sit on the floor of the cab. Her feet were firmly planted on earth, while the rest of her, doubled over, waited for her head to stop spinning.

She stared at her feet trying to forget where she was and focus on the tiny pieces of pale rock mixed among the grains of sand and bits of broken twig until they became a blur. Mumbling a litany of reassurances, she felt the panic ease. No one was here waiting for her. That part of the nightmare was over. The longer she sat, the less she trembled and the more clear-headed she felt. There wasn't a sound except for an occasional puff of wind stirring the sand around the wheels. Even the bugs thought it was too hot to fly. A movement caught her eye. An ant started to climb over her boot on its way to somewhere, undeterred by the extra mountain of leather he had to cross over.

Searching behind the seat with her hand, she found the plastic water jug. Pulling it out and unscrewing the lid, she took a gulp, several of them. She stood up finally and glanced around. The gray-green mesquite, the scratchy bundles of scrub cedar, and parched clumps of grass were hanging onto the spare soil for dear life. All of it was too damn stubborn to give up. It was as silent as a graveyard. Her enemies were gone, phantoms now.

A breeze ruffled her hair. She looked up at the screech of a hawk. Clouds were drifting in, their shadows moved like black ghosts across the hills. She took a step and then another, away from the shelter of the truck. She listened. The wind whispered an ancient chant of hunters long ago, both red and white, while the lacy leaves of the mesquite danced and the sand scampered like a mischievous child across the hard, dry earth.

By the time Devon drove up to the house, Ellie was back from town. When she walked into the kitchen, her mother looked at her with eyes searching for explanations.

"I'm okay, Mom." She dropped the keys on the counter.

"You had me worried."

She gazed out the window by the dinner table. "I wanted to see it again, that's all."

"I could have gone with you."

She turned to her mother and could smile finally. "I needed to go alone, Mom. To prove I could."

Her mother's worried frown faded away. "Did it help?"

"Yes. I'll give you a hand with dinner after I wash up."

"You don't have to. I'm just frying some chicken."

"I want to." She walked toward the den heading for the bathroom.

Jamie left for his second day of school with an enthusiastic wave to her from the school bus window. After tending to the early morning chores and picking up her son's clothes and toys scattered around the house, Devon sat at the desk in the den reviewing the files the college administration office had given her as background information. She heard the door open and close in the kitchen. Her mother was talking to her painting buddy, Mabel Thomas.

When Devon carried her mug into the kitchen, Ellie was getting down two cups and saucers as fresh coffee dripped into the glass pot. Mabel was looping the strap of her colorful purse over the back of a chair.

"Hi, Devon. You look bright-eyed and bushy-tailed this mornin'." Mabel, with her dangling earrings swinging, gave her a quick hug. "Going to have a cup with us?"

She loved the kitchen in the morning. It was bright, and full of the smell of coffee. "If there's enough to go around." Her mother was filling their cups. "I've got to get back to work in a minute."

"That's right. Ellie said you're doing a project for the college."

Devon poured coffee in her mug and sat down at the table. "I'm looking at their market focus to see if there's a way to attract more students."

"Tell them to add some art classes." Mabel had a quick mind and a tongue to match and never shied away from stating her opinion on any subject. "Your mama tell you about our trip to Big D?"

Ellie interrupted. "I told you the other day I'd have to think about it."

Mabel set her cup down on the saucer a little harder than necessary. "What's there to think about? The art show is featuring watercolors this year. I know you want to see Nell's exhibit. Earlene said that new mall has some great little shops too. I need a new dress and so do you. I've got your wardrobe memorized."

"I'd like to go, but I can't be gone that long, Mabel. Ask Bea or Alice to go with you." Her mother took a sip from her cup.

"I don't want to go with them. We've always gone together." Mabel glanced in Devon's direction with an expectant lift of her brow. "I can't imagine why spending a grand total of four or five days in Dallas would be so impossible, can you Devon?"

"No, I can't." She turned and looked at her mother. "You didn't mention the art show was coming up. Why don't you go, Mom?"

"I've got too much to do." Ellie got up and walked to the cupboard.

Devon glanced at Mabel and she shrugged. "I can keep an eye on things, Mom, that was part of our deal. You won't be selling the cattle for a couple more weeks."

"You've got your own work to do now, Devon. I'm not going to make you do mine." Her mother carried a plate of cookies back to the table and sat down after delivering a look that said 'don't ask me why'.

"You deserve some time off. Jamie and I can handle the chores."

"I don't want to go into it, right now." Without another word, Ellie picked up a cookie and took a bite. There was an awkward silence.

"Well, this coffee is talking up a storm." Mabel stood up. "I'm going to the powder room while y'all discuss it."

Once Mabel left, Ellie leaned toward Devon. "I've thought about it and I'm not going to leave you here by yourself that long."

She was surprised to be the reason her mother was staying home. She lowered her voice, arguing back. "Mom, I don't need a babysitter."

With that steady, probing look, which had ruined many a fib when she was growing up, Ellie concentrated on her eyes. "Can you handle being here alone at night?"

Devon crumbled inside a little, knowing that before she wouldn't have been asked. Lying in bed, hearing every creak and rattle in a house plunged into the pitch black of a country night would test her. Her mother must have noticed the light on in her room in the middle of the night. But she had to deal with it. In this real, cruel world her mother's presence was little more than a security blanket anyway. She drew in a fresh breath to pull herself together.

"Mom, you can't hold my hand forever. I'll handle it."

Ellie hadn't replied when Mabel breezed in and clapped her hands. "Well, what's the verdict? Are we going or do we have to trot this horse around some more, Ellie?"

Devon stood up with her coffee mug in hand. "It's fine with me."

Mom looked first in her direction and then at Mabel. "I guess Devon can hold down the fort for a few days. I do need a new dress."

Devon exhaled and smiled at the vote of confidence. "Well, I've got a lot of reading to do while you two plan your trip."

As she left the kitchen, she heard her mother ask. "What time would we need to leave, Mabel?"

"Bright and early, Thursday. I figure if I drive we can get there by lunch time."

Devon chuckled. Mabel had a lead foot and a knack for fun. Mom would come home with a grin and a new dress or two.

When Mabel drove up honking her horn two days later, Ellie was packed and ready. As they fiddled around putting the suitcases in the trunk, they reminded her of kids going off to camp. Devon gave her mother a hug and stood outside until the car drove through the gate and turned onto the road. For the first time in months, she was on her own again and so was Ellie. And that felt good. She hoped the feeling would last through the night ahead of her.

Devon leaned down and gave Jamie a goodnight kiss.

"Mom, it feels funny tonight without Granny here."

"Missing her already? She just left this morning."

"I know." He narrowed his eyes, looking at her as if she had a wart on her nose. "Are you feeling brave, Mama?"

"What?" She laughed at the strange question.

"I heard Granny tell Uncle Hank you might be scared of the dark."

She straightened up and put her hands on her hips. "Jamie, it is not polite to listen to other people's conversations. Understand?"

"Yes, ma'am. Want to know what Hank said?"

"Oh, Jamie!" She put her hand on her head in exasperation, not sure she wanted to know. She crossed her arms and looked at him. His eyes were bright and alert. "Alright, tell me. You're going to blurt it out anyway."

The words rushed out of him. "He said that he was afraid of the dark sometimes too."

With a relief she tried not to show, she smiled. "Well, good. Now go to sleep."

"Aren't you surprised?" He sounded perplexed.

"Hank always surprises me." Which was the truth. "We're going swimming tomorrow in Jenk's Pool with Billy, remember, so get some sleep." She switched off his bedside lamp, flipped on the nightlight, and turned to leave.

"Did you find my goggles?"

She looked over her shoulder. "Yes, they were under your bed. Sleep tight. We'll have pancakes for breakfast."

"Oh, boy." He grinned. "Can we make crazy ones?" She nodded. He yawned, curled up and closed his eyes.

She left his room and walked down the hall. Now that he was in bed, the silence magnified every sound: the click of the mantle clock as she passed, the padding of her bare feet on the cool, stone floor, the whine of the air conditioner. From the sliding glass door, the broad pasture spreading out behind the house was a cavernous black, the animals and trees swallowed by the night. The moon, reduced to an occasional muted glow, was lost in the clouds.

She rattled each window and checked every door with paranoid thoroughness as she roamed the house. "Goin' to run all night, goin' to run all day," she sang to herself to fill up the quiet, looking around, especially behind her as she walked. "Bet my money . . . on a bobtailed nag, somebody . . . bet . . . on the bay." Why she was singing that particular song she couldn't say except the tune came out of the blue and it sounded like a happy song even if she was whispering it.

From the dark living room window, she searched the shadows of the pecan trees in front of the house for any movement and followed the driveway rolling toward the road until it faded from sight. The light over the kitchen sink was on. The pole light outside lit up the well-worn ground around the barn and shed, the rough wood doors closed. Nothing out of place that she could see.

"Nine o'clock and all is well." She whispered her findings to no one while wandering back to the den with its single table lamp burning, hoping to find something else to think about. Something other than the jittery, skin-crawling feeling of being alone, or rather the only adult, the less than capable protector of her son, sitting in a house a half mile from the nearest people and too many miles from the nearest policeman.

She picked up the phone on the desk. The dial tone buzzed reassuringly. She put it back on its cradle. She caught a glimpse of herself in the hallway mirror. With her hands on her hips, she quietly let the woman staring back have it.

"Devon, this is pathetic. There is nothing out there that is going to come in here and you know it." She ran her fingers through her hair, pulling it away from her face and took a deep breath. "Great. Now you're talking to yourself."

Flipping on the overhead light, she walked back to the couch and turned on the television. With remote in hand, she rummaged through the channels. Cop show, no. Click. Some drama with a teary-eyed child. Not tonight. Click. A *Hee-Haw* rerun. Five minutes of pickin' and grinnin'. Click. News. Hot tomorrow. That wasn't news. Tornado watch near Dallas. "Up next—local woman found stabbed." Click, click. The light from the television screen disappeared. She'd wasted twenty-five minutes. Might as well go to bed.

After completing one last round of checking the doors and peering out the windows, she brushed her teeth and put on a nightgown. Lying in bed, she stared at the ceiling and listened to the house creak. After getting up a time or two to satisfy herself that the sounds were nothing out of the ordinary, she settled down again feeling every lump in the mattress. If, and it was just an if, someone were roaming around outside it would take a while for the law to get out here. She thought about the guns locked up in Pop's closet. They could help or be a problem. Still a shotgun pointed in the right direction even at a distance could be a convincing argument to back off. She might get some sleep if she got it out and put it in her closet, unloaded of course, where she could get to it.

The keys jingled in her hand as she opened the closet door and turned on the light. As she turned the key in the lock, she felt queasy. She hated being afraid. The gun cabinet door squeaked when she opened it. The rifles and shotguns stood upright, waiting. She lifted the lighter twenty gauge, double-barreled shotgun out of its niche and picked out four shells from the open box. She laid the shells on top of the metal cabinet and locked it. The gun was heavy. She carried it with the barrel pointing at the floor. The four shells were clutched in her hand. She pushed the light switch off and walked back to her room. She glanced as she passed Jamie's bedroom door. He was sleeping peacefully.

She put the shells in the drawer of her bedside table and sat down on the mattress. Sliding the lever on the top to one side, the action broke open, the barrels flipped down to reveal the empty side-by-side chambers. She laid it down and got under the covers feeling cold suddenly. Resting her back against the headboard, she looked at it, remembering what it could do. The metal shot would explode out the barrel and blossom out to shred anything in its path. It was powerful enough to knock a man off his feet and cut him in half. She didn't want to use it, ever. But fear had put it here beside her and she couldn't put it back.

When she woke up the next morning, it was still laying there. She locked it in the gun safe. Maybe she wouldn't need it to sleep tonight.

The cloudless sky was a brilliant blue as Devon drove over the hills and down the winding road beside the river, with trees along its banks. It was hot, in the high nineties. The river was more like a shallow stream this time of year. She was behind Loretta's suburban, its back windows filled with bags of potato chips, ice chests, water gear and bouncing kids. Jamie had wanted to ride with Billie but she'd kept him with her. They turned off the main road onto the dusty, caliche road until they reached the Jenkins place and drove across their pasture to the flat sandy area under the trees. There were several cars and trucks parked in the shade and she could see people splashing in the water. She recognized one truck. It was Frank's blue and white Chevy. She smiled, glad he'd put aside work for a few hours to bring the girls and have some fun too.

She parked beside the suburban. Jamie was out the door before she'd turned the engine off. "Jamie, wait a minute." But she was too late, he was roughhousing with Billy and some other boys crowding around Clayton and Loretta.

She walked around her car to remind him. "Jamie, don't go in the water until I've had a chance to show you where it's deep." He could swim but without the painted boundaries of a man-made pool he might get into trouble. The white rock bottom of the clear spring could be deceptive in judging the depth of the water.

"We'll show him." Loretta's older son, Travis, stood by the two younger boys.

She looked at Travis's face before glancing down at Jamie's and those anxious eyes that said every second he waited was an eternity. "Okay."Jamie smiled and trotted off with the others. She followed them a few steps, but hung back at the edge of the trees as they splashed into the water.

It was just like she'd remembered. The rock wall behind the water was still the color of a palomino's mane. The three terraced pools, filled with blue spring water that bubbled up from the fractured limestone below, were nestled together, sparkling like a string of jewels in the sun. Hollywood couldn't have designed a more beautiful spot.

Travis was pointing out the shallow areas to Jamie when someone jumped off the slab ledge and doubled up to cannonball into the deepest pool on the far right. The sound, when he hit the surface, became a thundering boom magnified by the rocks. Her son stood in silent awe, just like every other young one playing in the shallow water, to watch the gush of water rise in the air.

"Travis will keep an eye on him for a few minutes, Devon." Loretta had stopped beside her, holding a plastic laundry basket full of towels.

"Need some help?"

"No, we can get it." Clayton, Loretta's good-natured, six foot six hunk of burning love, walked by carrying a big ice chest.

"Thanks for inviting us, Loretta." She glanced toward the water. Jamie was romping through the shallows laughing with a group of boys his size.

"Hey, you're always invited to our unofficial class reunion and baptism service." Loretta smiled and carried her load to a picnic table among the scattered grove of lawn chairs.

Devon gathered up her bag of towels and dry clothes as well as the snacks she'd brought in the car. She swung the cooler full of juice and pop, noticing how easy it was. Maybe she was stronger than before, or maybe she just felt that way because it had been so long since she'd done ordinary things with ease. She walked toward the picnic table, checking on Jamie with quick glances while watching her step on the uneven ground. It had become a habit to look down every so often. She said hello to the men and women sitting in the shade as she walked up. She recognized Pete and Jimmy Lee even though they were both losing their hair. Loretta refreshed her memory with the names of the rest. It had been fifteen years since she'd seen many of them, but they had shared a childhood and she was eager to remember. The years had been harder on some than on others. The two heavy smokers were already coughing. A couple of the wives, wearing too much makeup, looked her over critically. Even though her leg was no longer swollen or bruised, Devon was glad she had cutoffs and a tee shirt over her swimsuit. The clothes hid the scars.

"Well, I think I'll go for a swim and cool off." Loretta was already heading for the water. Since she didn't have a lot to say to any of them, none of adults sitting in the shade seemed to mind if she left.

Devon walked to the water's edge, slipped off her sandals and wiggled her toes. The loose sand scattered over the rocks was very warm. She shed her tee shirt tossing it onto a flat boulder nearby. The sun warmed her shoulders as she straightened a strap on her bathing suit. It was silly maybe but she was shy about letting anyone see the scars on her thigh. They weren't particularly ugly, anymore than the ones on her arm. In time when they weren't so pink, they'd be less noticeable. But they were a mark that something had happened to her, and that something made her different. She glanced back toward the women sitting in the shade. Knowing what had happened to her probably scared them. She wouldn't let that stop her from having fun, not today. She slipped off her cutoffs, tossed them over to her shirt and stepped into the cool water.

Jamie was standing waist-deep in the water with Billie, splashing and yelling. She recognized Beth in the group of shrieking girls being chased through the water by several long-legged boys. After telling Jamie where she was headed, she skirted the higher shallow pool to avoid the thrashing kids and ventured out to the calm, deeper water of the lower section.

She stretched out to glide across the surface with a relaxed breaststroke. She floated past Annie dog-paddling her little arms off toward Frank as he encouraged her to kick harder. Being in the water was a new kind of freedom. The men and older boys diving off their perch into the deepest blue, pool caused barely a ripple as she swam toward the solitude of the farthest edge. Balance, friction, falling didn't exist in this luscious coolness. Her muscles flexed and relaxed through every smooth stroke. With each pull of her arms and kick of her legs, she felt whole again.

Loretta was floating on her back, her toes sticking up above the water. "Nice way to spend a hot Saturday afternoon, isn't it?"

"Hmm-mm." Devon grabbed hold of a narrow rock ledge just above the water. She absent-mindedly kicked her feet back and forth. "It's hard to believe this place is still so clean and beautiful and empty."

"Part of the charm of being a hick is having places like this." Loretta winked at her. There was a little extra sparkle in her eye.

"You're a regular chamber of commerce, Loretta." She nodded her head toward the shore. "I hate to spoil our surroundings but what's going on with Jasper's wife? She was sizing me up like I was the wicked witch of the west."

"Ignore her. She's got a terminal case of city girl bitch-itis." A loud boom made them both look toward the divers. "Uh-oh, looks like the grown boys are tuning up for the mine is bigger than yours contest. You'd think the men could resist the urge to show how big a splash they can make. Uh-oh, here comes my honey. We might want to consider moving unless you want my Moby Dick washing us out to sea."

"I should have known the peace and quiet was too good to last." She joined Loretta in a slow retreat around the outer edge of the pool while keeping a watchful eye on Jamie roughhousing amongst a tangle of other kids. When it was shallow enough to stand up they were close to Frank and Annie.

"Hi, Devon. Glad to see you're free of the stick." Frank smiled while Annie made a churning beeline for her.

After she paddled up, Devon held her around the waist to let her rest and cough up the water she'd swallowed. Naturally, she was wearing a pink bathing suit.

"Did you see me swim? Daddy teached me." Her eyes sparkled like the sun shining on the water surrounding them.

"Yes, I did. You're very good, just like a fish." The child was irresistible and warmed that special spot in her heart reserved for dainty little girls. She spun around, whirling the child through the water. Annie tossed her head back and giggled at the sky.

She waited a minute after she stopped spinning to let her get her bearings. "Ready to swim back to your dad now?" Annie nodded her wet head so Devon turned her around and let her go. Her reward was a face full of water from the first kick. She laughed and shook off the drops clinging to her face and hair.

Loretta waved at someone. "Hey, Becky Mackenzie showed up after all. Come on, Devon."

"See you and your mermaid later, Frank." Devon turned and waded over to Becky with Loretta.

They found a broad ledge along one edge of the shallow pool where they could sit in the water to stay cool and talk. While the younger children applauded each ka-boom and mammoth splash produced by the older ones, the women pointed out which child belonged to what family and talked about their children shamelessly, as if they were the most important things in their lives. Because they were. It felt so good, all she could do was smile.

Once the showing off in the deep pool was over, most of the adults abandoned the sun for refreshments in the shade. Devon stopped to see if Jamie needed more sunscreen. He was in a huddle on shore with Billie and one of Becky's boys.

"Mom, can I jump off the rock? Billie and Clint can." He was pointing to the wide slab that jutted out over the diving pool.

They were all the same age and close to the same size. "Do you all promise to keep an eye out for each other? And make certain you don't jump on top of one another?" The three faces looking up at her all nodded in response. "Tell you what, I'll stand on the edge and watch you all the first time."

They accepted her condition without comment and she lagged behind as they headed for the rock outcropping. A huddle of scrawny girls stood in middle of the little trail, blocking their path.

"Hey." Billie stomped over to the giggling bunch. "We're going to dive off now. This rock is for the boys."

A girl standing next to Beth scowled at him. "Says who?"

Jamie and Clint, in unison, backed Billie up. "Yeah, girls can't dive here."

Devon could see Travis and a couple of older boys heading for the group. They were laughing and pointing. TJ used to do that. The girls saw them too.

"Here comes, Stephen. Oh, I'm going to die. Let's go."

Beth frowned at the swooning, curlyheaded girl. "I'm not leaving, Jeannie. We can dive off that rock just like the boys." Frank had raised a daughter with spunk.

"They're laughing at us." A little blonde shielded the side of her face with her hand.

Beth put her hands on her hips with a huff. "Don't go soft in the head. They're laughing at the little kids, Donna Mae." She glanced with scorn at the three younger boys clumped together.

The drama going on riled Devon even though it was a trivial thing. Being female was already hard enough. And these little characters, especially hers, weren't going to get away with such gender nonsense. She marched past all of them and climbed the narrow path between the rock outcropping to the top of the ledge.

"Gentlemen, this rock is here for anyone who'd like to jump off." She looked down at the pint-sized men who had started the whole thing and the slightly older ones who had joined them. If life was a game, it was time to play fair. The little ones had their mouths open. The older boys were smiling and nudging each other.

She turned and addressed the gangly, ponytailed girls staring up at her and smiled. "Ladies, I think you were first in line."

The girls tittered among themselves and scrambled up the path. They didn't waste any time. They jumped off together, screamed on the way down, and came up giggling.

It was only six feet or so from the rock to the water's surface but the clear water of the deep, blue pool made the distance look more like twenty feet. When Billie, Clint and Jamie stood beside her and nervously eyed the water, she wondered if they were going to jump at all. Machismo took time to muster at seven.

She wanted to laugh at the fix they'd gotten themselves into, but didn't dare. They could take the plunge or walk back down the trail, but she wasn't going to stand up here all day. The rock was cooking her feet.

"Let me go first, okay fellas?" Maybe it would help if they could see the ripples on the surface.

Jamie's eyes widened. "You're going to dive, Mom?"

"No, I'm going to jump in feet first. Big difference. I'll float around a minute out of the way to watch your splashes, if you want."

She looked down to make sure the girls were gone and no one else was below her. She heard a shrill whistle that rose at the end. She couldn't see him but knew it was Frank egging her on. With that, she stepped back for a running start and flew off, feeling a bit like a kid again herself.

"We had fun swimming today, huh, Mom?

"Yes we did." She pulled the sheet over him.

"Did you say Granny will be back Monday or Tuesday?"

She leaned over to give him a kiss. "Tuesday. She's driving back from the art show with Mabel after lunch."

"Do you think she's having fun?"

"I hope so. Good night, honey. Sweet dreams." She started to leave.

"Can we have pancakes again tomorrow morning?"

She stopped and turned. "No, Jamie. Two straight days of sugar is enough, besides you used up the last of the syrup, remember?"

"Oh, yeah. Do you like Annie's dad?"

"Sure. We've know each other since we were kids." She looked at him. He had a strange look on his face. "What?"

"I think he likes you too. He was looking at you funny."

"He looks at everybody funny." He was matchmaking again. She chuckled and turned to leave.

"Mom? I'm not sleepy. Can I look at my space book for awhile?"

"Read away, Rocket Man."

He sat up and made his blastoff sound, launching his hand up and over to grab the book off the bedside table.

She shook her head. "Good night."

Devon stood on the deck watching the day fade away. Everything seemed to be idly dreaming along with her on this warm summer night. The faint chorus of frogs and crickets were singing up a storm. Just the tops of the clouds puffing up to the north, still blushed a pale pink. The rest of the sky was clear, washed by the last strokes of soft, watercolor blues. Somewhere in the distance, a coyote howled. A childhood memory of a peaceful evening so much like this one came to mind.

"That old coyote is crying, Daddy."

"He's just hollering, short stuff. Telling his kin he's doing okay." She had let out a puppy-sized yelp of her own and made him laugh.

"See, it's good for the soul to let the world know you're here and doin' the best you can. That's what the cowboy told the coyotes before they knew how to howl."

"A cowboy, Daddy?"

"Darn tootin', honey, a Texas cowboy."

She could still see his broad smile even though she was standing on the deck without him now. Nestled in the immense quiet, she took a deep breath tasting the promise of rain in the breeze. She leaned back holding onto the railing and watched the tiny pinpoints sparkle in the deep blue sky. A brassy full moon was slowly rising, floating along the horizon on its trip to join the stars. She heard the sound of the glass door sliding open and turned her head. Jamie was standing there in his pajamas.

He whispered. "Mama."

"Mm-hmm." It seemed sacrilegious to disturb the peace with words.

He stepped closer. "I can't go to sleep."

"Come here." She held out her arm. "The moon's like a giant flash-light." She let him stand in front of her, put her arms over his shoulders and clasped her hands together on his chest to hold him close.

He put one hand over hers. "If we had a really high ladder, we could touch it, I bet."

"Who knows, someday you may ride in a rocket and go up there." She leaned down and kissed his soft hair.

A high-pitched howl broke the silence. The sound was coming from some place beyond the barn.

"That coyote's not far away."

"Why does he do that?"

"He's telling the world he's doing fine. Sounded like a young one." She smiled. "That old cowboy must still be teaching them how to howl at the moon."

Jamie cocked his head and looked up at her. "What cowboy?"

"You've never heard of one of the most famous cowboys in Texas?"

Jamie shook his head. "What's his name?"

"Darn Tootin." She chuckled when she said it out loud.

"That's a funny name." Jamie laughed.

The sound warmed her from the inside out, just like her memories and she laughed for the pleasure of it. It had been a wonderful day and there was no reason to keep in the joy of it.

"Can't the little coyotes learn to howl from their mama or daddy?"

"Oh, I think they do most of time, but sometimes he lends a hand. It's a story my dad told me a long time ago. I'm not sure if I remember how it goes."

"Try to remember, Mom."

It didn't matter if he understood it was all a joke. That would come soon enough. But she hoped the coyote could hear their laughter as she started the tall tale. Maybe Pop could hear it, too.